Orphaned Warrior

Book Five of the Dragon Spawn Chronicles

By Dawn Ross

© 2024

“A kid needs at least one person who never gives up on them, no matter what.”

– Amos Burton (The Expanse)

Orphaned Warrior

Book Five of the Dragon Spawn Chronicles

by Dawn Ross

Copyright 2024 Dawn Ross

This book is licensed for your personal enjoyment only. If you enjoy it and want others to enjoy it, please consider purchasing another copy to share and/or leave a review on Amazon, Goodreads, or other sites that promote books. Except for a brief quotation in a review, you may not reprint or publish any part of this book without prior written consent from the author.

Cover
Cyborg art by Jon Stubbington. Spaceship purchased from freestyledesingworks through 123rf.com under their standard license agreement. The starry background is a public domain image from NASA. Images combined by germancreative on fiverr.com.

Special Thanks

I'd like to extend a special thanks to all the beta readers and editors who helped me make this novel shine. And additional thanks to my final editor, Grace Bridges, who has been instrumental in helping me with content and line edits as well as with pointing out opportunities for story improvement.

Reviews for StarFire Dragons

"A thoughtful novel that owes a debt to
Star Trek but works on its own terms."
—Kirkus Reviews

"A subtle space opera that explores the ethical
conundrums of intergalactic relations with main
characters who are worth rooting for."
—Becca Saffier, *Reedsy Discovery*

"Fans of epic sci-fi that look for realistic characters and complex
yet believable settings will find *Starfire Dragons*
a powerful introductory story that promises more, yet
nicely concludes its immediate dilemmas."
—D. Donovan, Senior Reviewer, *Midwest Book Review*

Orphaned Warrior

Book Five of the Dragon Spawn Chronicles

by Dawn Ross

1
Disembark

The third-rate space liner jerked as the docking clamps grappled it into place. A male voice broke from the speaker, giving them strict instructions to stay in their seats until the green indicator light came on. The cramped passengers ignored him and removed their safety harnesses and grabbed their possessions.

Jori remained seated. He'd long since gone nose-blind to the fetid odor of spoiled sweat festering in his chair's tattered cushioning. This concave seat was designed for an average-sized adult, providing too much room to adequately protect children like himself. At least he was tall enough to fit into the adjustable head-brace.

Although ready to get off this crowded junkheap, his nerves twitched at the uncertainty awaiting him. Another space station, a different guardian, and one more trip before he could finally settle. But what did settling mean? He still didn't know what to expect. Would he get a new family? Stay in a group home? Or did the Prontaean Cooperative have something more sinister in mind for him?

It was enough to make him want to run away. If only he had somewhere else to go.

This line of thinking only heightened his agitation so he distracted himself by studying the diversity of passengers. A man so lanky, his head looked oversized rose slowly. He probably wasn't used to the Avalon space station's gravitational setting. The short, stocky woman sitting across from him appeared to have the opposite reaction when her gravity-built muscles caused her to jump out of her seat.

A family of four in shabby clothes bickered. They had black hair like his, though theirs were dirty and unkept. Jori still had the fleshiness of youth in his cheeks, his face was more angular than their chubby, rounded ones. The boy, who was only a year or two older than Jori, kept flicking his little sister's ear, making her whine. His parents did nothing, even as the behavior escalated.

The rascal elbowed his sister hard enough to make her fall. She cried out and he cackled obnoxiously. Jori clenched his fists, wishing he could punch the bully in the face and show him what it felt like to be mistreated. He settled for scowling at the boy instead and received a derogatory gesture in return. The father ordered him to not be rude, but that only made the boy turn the same gesture onto him.

Jori's chest tightened. If he'd ever acted like that, his father would've knocked him across the deck. This was why he was here, though—safe from that violent chima and practically an orphan since he'd been taken so far from home that his parents might as well be dead.

A pang pinched his insides as he looked back on the day a commander from the Prontaean Cooperative had rescued him from his abusive father. It'd meant separating him from his mother too, but that couldn't be helped. Father had exiled her beyond his reach.

He touched his chest, feeling the necklace hidden beneath his clothes. It'd been a gift to his mother long ago and he found it after she'd been spirited away. He kept it as a keepsake, but in truth, it symbolized his loneliness.

His new life with the Cooperative was supposed to be better. *Ha!* So far, he'd only exchanged one unpleasant situation for another. Since he was a promising warrior from an enemy race, the Prontaean Cooperative Council had ordered he be sent to a faraway planet, cutting him off from the commander who wanted to adopt him. And thanks to the information kept in his file, his travels had included a series of temporary guardians who treated him like a criminal. *Chimas*.

Jori glanced at his current guardian, who blocked his way by commanding the aisle seat. Lockhart's severe presence and no-nonsense demeanor indicated he was a soldier, not a caretaker. Even when sleeping, he seemed vigilant.

He had a formidable lifeforce coupled with a surly attitude that ensured none of these dubious passengers gave him any trouble. Jori shot him a glower. The only one this man didn't intimidate was him. He'd been around soldiers for all eleven years of his life.

While many were loudmouthed bullies who'd sooner put a knife in you than smile—warriors far more vicious than Lockhart—others, like Sensei Jeruko, were good men who fought for the right reasons.

His stomach cinched at the thought of his mentor. Sensei Jeruko was dead, as was Jori's older brother—two more people gone from his life forever.

A squeal of machinery sent Jori's teeth rattling. It stopped almost as soon as it started, followed by an equalization of pressure that made his ears pop. The green light blinked on, accompanied by a discordant signal that warbled like a half-dead bird.

Still, his guardian remained seated. Jori waited in silence, keeping his complaints to himself. It wasn't like he had anywhere to go. After a far-flung journey of different guardians trading him off at a series of space stations, he dreaded the prospect of meeting yet another one.

"Let's go," Lockhart said when the cabin was nearly empty.

Without a word, Jori unbuckled the threadbare harness. Lockhart pulled his black duffle bag the size of that bully's sister from the overhead compartment. Jori grabbed his own meager pack from the open area under his seat.

Lockhart made him walk in front as they exited. Jori moved with a haste that kept the man from stepping on his heels but slow enough to not appear like a convict attempting to escape.

They disembarked the space liner and onto the metal gangplank. Lockhart's boots clomped with confidence and the implicit message that he had the power to break heads. Jori stepped softer so as not to draw attention to himself in this unfamiliar territory.

Like Lockhart, he assessed his surroundings. Eight station guards, four to either side of them, regarded the passengers with hard eyes. They all held RR-5 phaser rifles with a firmness that showed their capabilities. But they weren't the most dangerous people in the docking bay.

A trio of scraggly men stood apart, but Jori got the feeling they were together. He'd seen them on the liner whispering, just a pair at a time. His ability to sense emotions picked up on their knavish and malevolent natures.

At some unseen signal, their mood tightened into the intense focus of predators. Still spread out, they closed in with a casual air on a man with a cybernetic arm. Jori tensed as the taller thug with mangy brown hair approached from the left while the one with round, bright-blue eyes came from the right. The third man with a long face stuck his hand in his pocket and slipped in from behind. Jori almost said something, but Lockhart's emotions ticked up.

"Shit," he muttered, grabbing Jori's shoulder. "Stay here."

The cybernetic man flinched when the brown-haired man stepped beside him and flashed a carnivorous smile. The blue-eyed man also neared and Jori sensed the prey's increased alarm.

Lockhart stormed forward, his footsteps loud enough to create a resonant echo. "Hey! Something going on here?"

The brown-haired man put up his hands. "No trouble here."

The guards snapped to alertness. Two hastened over. The cybernetic man edged away. The thug with the long face shadowed him. Jori's heart skipped at how Lockhart and the guards only fixated on the other two men.

"Chusho," he cursed under his breath. He left his spot and weaved his way around the other travelers.

The long-faced man neared within a few strides of the unsuspecting cyborg. Jori picked up his pace. The man pulled something from his pocket. A knife. Jori broke into a sprint as the man lunged toward his prey.

"Watch out!" Jori called.

The cyborg turned. The blade flashed and the man jumped backward in time to avoid the jab. Jori dove in from the side and tackled the thug's knees. They both fell, but Jori's was more controlled as he rolled out of knife-range.

Like a dummy, his focus was entirely on the long-faced man. Someone grabbed his shirt and hauled him back.

Lockhart growled. "What the hell are you doing?"

"He has a knife!"

Two guards rushed in and disarmed the thug.

Lockhart jerked him around, towering over him with an accusatory glare. "So you jump in the middle of it, you idiot? You could've been killed."

Jori yanked out of his hold. "What do you care?"

"It's my job to look after you. You act out, I *lose* my job."

Tears formed in Jori's eyes unbidden as he fumed. Of course this was about his job.

His anger wasn't just at Lockhart. Despite the loneliness of being taken away from all the people he'd ever cared about, he wanted a fresh start. As the son of the notorious Dragon Emperor and a skilled warrior in his own right, nearly everyone judged him. This was supposed to be his chance to become someone else. He didn't have to be a warrior anymore. He could be anything.

But here he was, getting into a fight—doing exactly what he'd hoped to never have to do again.

The brown-haired man hopped onto a luggage cart. "MEGAs are among us! Look at that man!" He pointed at the wide-eyed cyborg. "He's a thief! Taking our jobs, stealing food from our mouths, destroying the lives of good, honest, hardworking folks!"

Jori blinked at how vehemently this thug believed in his own righteousness. The MEGA Injunction limited the activities of enhanced individuals for a reason. Thanks to a certain MEGA who'd snuck his way into a position as an admiral's aide, prejudice against augmented persons had been rekindled. The hatred fueled by fear intensified when they discovered that MEGA-Man, a powerful cybernetic being, was in control.

A crowd gathered around the thug, many of them vigorously voicing their agreement. Four guards stepped in and ordered him down. The man complied but continued to yell insults and agitate the onlookers.

Lockhart grabbed a hold of Jori again, his arm this time. "Let's get out of here before you create more trouble."

Jori bit his tongue and let the man lead him away. They passed the cybernetic man who dipped his head in thanks. Jori's stomach knotted. This man had a diminished lifeforce. That meant he also had brain implants. And *that* meant he was like the other cyborg he'd encountered—the admiral's aide, Gottfried, who'd killed a bunch of people just to push augmentations as an evolutionary ideal.

Lockhart kept vigilant as they entered the main station. Jori did the same, glancing from side to side, looking for potential threats, hideouts, and escape routes. The throng of people surprised him. Not even the Depnaugh space station outside of Cooperative territory had this much wretchedness. From those who wore raggedy clothes and hung their heads, to gangs dressed in mismatched warrior garb and carried themselves like cutthroats, the place reeked of distress.

Aren't Prontaean Cooperative territories supposed to be more civilized? He wanted to ask, but Lockhart never bothered with more than a few cutting words. Jori had adopted his closed-mouth behavior. Not that it was difficult. He had no reason to speak to anyone nowadays anyway.

The only person in the Cooperative he'd ever connected with was hundreds of light years away. He missed the commander, but the man was better off without him. His mother didn't need him in her life either.

Jori wiped a tear from his eye and pushed his fear and loneliness aside. The prospect of a new life loomed ahead. His only choice was to be swept along at the Cooperative's whim and hope for the best.

2
Aromatherapy

Like a summertime water lily, Zaina Noman's emotions blossomed at the wonderment of Avalon's shops. Being from a planetary metropolis, she thought she'd seen it all. But her city didn't have such interesting products designed for life in space.

Nearly every shop on this station sold space-friendly goods, from fancy enviro-suits to dispensers that kept food and water from floating around in microgravity. She even found a harness-like contraption used to strap you to a toilet. The clerk had insinuated it was just as good for bedroom activities. Not that she had known what it was when she picked it up. Nor did she need such a thing. Her life was too busy for a partner. Besides, both the ship she'd traveled on and this space station had artificial gravity.

She could've come here to meet her new charge on a less expensive ship—one without gravity or other amenities she'd taken for granted. Thankfully, a colleague had warned her about how crowded those could be.

Her doctor had told her the emotions of others affected her. She didn't know how to separate her feelings and so tended to carry their weight on her shoulders. Too many burdens and she'd crumble.

That likelihood had increased ever since she'd experienced an assault some months back. All it'd take was one person raising their voice and her chest would constrict.

Against her better judgment, she forged ahead and made the trip. She had a job to do and didn't trust anyone else to do it right.

She wondered about the young person she'd be meeting soon. He'd had traumatic experiences as well. Hopefully it provided a commonality to help them connect but the things in his file put her on edge if she dwelled on them too long.

Thankfully, the shops distracted her. The sophistication of the wares in this district meant fewer people and most minded their own business. It suited her perfectly.

A floral fragrance tantalized her nose. She followed it to a shop with a wonderful display of elegant products that made all her worries melt away.

Various flameless candles patterned with stylish motifs lined the shelves. Fancy perfume bottles and exquisitely designed aromatherapy diffusers decorated the tables. She smiled at the shopkeeper, which prompted the woman to approach.

"What can I help you with?" The short, grey-haired woman's eyes twinkled with warmth.

Zaina had no intention of buying anything. The trip here had taken up most of her budget. But maybe a little something—a small memento—wouldn't hurt.

She carefully picked up a bulbous diffuser and cupped it in her palm. Its curved, narrow neck reminded her of a swan. The milky white glass infused with colored streaks appealed to her fondness for fun brightness. "This is absolutely lovely. Does it have programming features?"

"Certainly." The woman touched the back of the device where a few small buttons were located. "Set the voice activations here. Program the timer so you can have it automatically turn on and off. It also has three settings—low to high—and it can play music."

"Really? Is it pre-set music or can I choose my own?"

"Both."

Zaina noted the price marked on the bottom and almost put it down. It was so beautiful, though. And her old one was on the fritz. However, she allowed her reluctance to show. "I like this, but I'm not sure. Do you also sell the oils?"

"Of course." The woman swept her hand toward a giant shelf along the rear wall. "What are you looking for? We have relaxing mixtures, scents to help you sleep, ones to give you energy—"

Zaina huffed out a laugh. "I need all those. Anxiety, sleeplessness, fatigue, depression. You name it—I have it."

The woman patted her arm. "The galaxy can be an overwhelming place. Most of us have these issues to some degree or another." She plucked a bottle from the middle of over a hundred scents. "May I suggest this one? It contains real sandalwood with a hint of lavender and rose. Plus a lovely extract from the arnielis plant that grows only on an island on the planet Falmouth." The woman went on about its fantastic healing properties and how the inhabitants were one of the happiest societies in the galaxy.

Zaina stepped back. "Sounds expensive."

"It *is* a bit pricy, I'm afraid. But if you purchase the diffuser, I'll give you a discount."

That sounded good until the woman gave her the price. Her pulse quickened. She fluttered her hand, trying to cool the heat flushing over her face.

"I'll tell you what," the woman said. "I'll throw in a couple of sample scents." She picked up a thumb-sized jar, popped open the lid, and waved it under Zaina's nose.

The muskiness held a hint of jasmine and made Zaina sigh. She inhaled, long and deep, savoring it. "Oh, that's lovely. And powerful. How long will that bottle last?"

"Over five hundred hours."

Zaina reconsidered. Surely she could afford this one indulgence. Besides, anything contributing to her health was an investment.

"You have a deal," she said.

"Wonderful. I'll go package it for you." The woman's smile broadened before she hastened to the back.

Zaina checked the time on her wristlet. Her guest should arrive soon. Her anxiety kicked up, churning faster as she completed her purchase and left the shop.

She never knew what to expect when encountering new people. Reports never gave the full picture. She couldn't count the number of times meeting someone in person had shattered her preconceived notions. It would likely be the same now. Fortunately, this would lead to the best part of her job. Her work was tough, but the rewards were immeasurable.

As she traversed the Avalon space station, the stress on her nerves doubled. The crowd thickened and the people here changed. Their clothes were more worn and they didn't seem as healthy, which indicated they came from the poorer sections of society. Many here wore a frown, including the shopkeepers. Others were more despondent. The downright angry expression of one man sent her heart thudding as the memory of her assault flashed behind her eyes.

She rubbed her arms, determined not to let her past trauma interfere with her job. Helping people kept her going and gave her life meaning.

And her new charge needed her at her best.

3
Advocate

Jori gritted his teeth, refusing to react to Lockhart's grip. *What the hell is he so upset about?* Yes, he'd disobeyed, but only to keep someone from getting hurt.

Cyborgs, especially ones with a weak or nonexistent lifeforce, unsettled him, but that didn't mean they deserved harm. The brown-haired man had made a reasonable argument, yet the stench of his aura named him the real villain. His level of hate reminded Jori of all those who had harmed *him*. It shouldn't matter whether the victim was a cyborg or the son of a tyrant, anyone who hurt someone out of anger and hate was the evildoer.

"Next time I tell you to stay put, you stay put," Lockhart said.

Jori glowered in reply. It wouldn't do any good to argue with this chima. He locked eyes with him instead, refusing to shy away.

Lockhart's emotions heated with each passing second, but he relented with a growl. "Let's find your new guardian so I can go home."

Jori bit back a retort. The man was a jerk, but not like those three in the bay. He complied as Lockhart ushered him down the wide but crowded hallway, glad to soon be rid of him.

They stuck close to a wall portraying a conglomeration of chaotic color. Graffiti covered nearly every spare centimeter on the lower half and sometimes reached to the ceiling. Intricate art melded with crude. Symbols and letters from various cultures abounded, almost nothing written in the universal language.

The assault on the eyes was bad enough. The smell was worse. Sour mixed with pungent and pungent mingled with acrid. It was no wonder. Red-robed Hamilins smoked some sort of brown stub. A sharp perfume wafted off the Maesterdons who wore fancy blue suits with white lace frills. And from the ragtag band slouched against the opposite wall came the foul scent of unwashed bodies.

Jori searched the swarm of humanity, wondering which one would be his next guardian. People from all walks of life abounded. Affluent couples avoided the ruffians hunting for easy prey. A group of four garishly dressed men and women wearing white face paint laughed with genuine cheer. Travelers with tattered clothes, warriors clad in either crisp or bedraggled armor, and the well-to-do with their fine threads—so many exotic differences.

None paid him any mind. A mixture of concern and curiosity budded while Lockhart's impatience seethed. Maybe his new guardian fled their responsibility. He scanned again. This time, recognition sparked among the throng. He used his ability to search for the source. He still didn't see them, but his senses told him it was a woman. Her pleasant lifeforce radiated from the crowd like a lone flower growing in the muck.

His hope expanded until he finally saw her. Her big, bright-brown eyes caught his and she smiled. Jori almost staggered. Could this really be her? She was so unlike his previous guardians.

As he neared, her smile widened. Jori attempted to return the gesture, but the shock of her open sincerity froze his facial muscles.

She faced Lockhart with the same pleasantness and put out her hand. "Hello. I'm Zaina. Zaina Noman. I believe you're looking for me."

Lockhart ignored her hand. His glower deepened as he looked her up and down, likely noting the same thing Jori had. Her plain maroon blouse and nondescript black pants contained no form of armor nor anything else to mark her as military. "You're his next escort?"

"I'm his advocate." Her emotions faltered as she withdrew her hand, but she held her head high. She was tall, but not too tall, and thin, but not too thin. Her hair was dark brown, almost black like Jori's. The tan of her skin was similar too. And she had a short chin that didn't jut with the same boldness as her tone.

"They didn't send a soldier?"

"No."

"You saw his file, right? This kid has killed people."

"In self-defense," Jori said, both annoyed and desperate. He didn't want this kind woman to think he was a monster.

"I'm well aware of what's in his file. But this is supposed to be a fresh start. A new beginning." She glanced at him and smiled once again. The genuineness of it made Jori's cheeks warm.

Lockhart scoffed. "Whatever. My job here is done."

He handed her his tablet, and she signed off. After Lockhart left, the woman's shoulders sagged with relief. This was the opposite of every other handoff he'd encountered. If not for the authenticity of her emotions and her amicable lifeforce, he would've assumed this was some sort of trick.

Despite how she faced him with a friendly sparkle in her eyes, he automatically fell into a military at-ease stance.

"Let's try this again." She put out her hand once more. "Hello. My name is Zaina Noman. I'm your new advocate."

Her base mood was a little frazzled, but her aura reassured him. "Jori." He let his bearing relax and took her hand, surprised at its gentleness. "Advocate? Everyone else has been calling themselves my escort or guardian." *Or guard.*

Her eyes tilted with sympathy. "I'm sorry you've had such a rough time. Technically, I'm your guardian but it's not my favorite term. I have a fancier administrative title, but I like advocate better. Don't you?"

He did but... "Does this mean you're taking me the rest of the way to Marvdacht?"

"Yes. I have an office there, so I'll also be your advocate in your new home."

"Home? I thought I was going to some sort of..." He was about to say *child-prison* but opted for something more neutral. "... Childcare place."

"Yes. The C.F.C., or Children First Center. But I like *home* better. Don't you?" Her eyes twinkled at the second use of the phrase.

Jori blinked. *Home* did sound better, but he couldn't imagine it having the same meaning. "Yes, ma'am."

"Call me Zaina, or Miss Zaina, if you prefer. But please, not Miss Noman. It's too formal—makes me feel like your boss rather than your friend." She touched his shoulder. "Would you like something to eat? Anything you want. You name it. They have a variety of restaurants on this station. I even saw an Angolan café."

Jori hesitated, unsure how to respond. None of his other guardians had asked him this. It wasn't like they hadn't fed him. They bought him food when *they* were hungry, never bothering to find out what he wanted. His stomach roiled at the thought of his last meal with Lockhart. The man had purchased a plate of pseudo-meat drowned in a sticky, sweet goo. Jori's first bite made him gag. When he scraped off the sauce, Lockhart got pissed, called him ungrateful, and took it away.

He hadn't eaten since, so nodded. Zaina's smile spread, turning her cheeks pink. She led the way but allowed him to be beside her rather than in front or behind. He walked in a daze. This seemed unreal. She was too nice.

Her voice carried a genuine interest when she asked him what he liked. He had no answer, having eaten mostly fabricated food designed more for nutrition than taste. After working out whether he preferred plain or savory—*plain*—sweet or spicy—*neither*—she decided on a place and led him farther into the station.

A cheer rang out from down the hall, snapping Jori to the moment. His focused senses detected a disgruntled crowd. Zaina stopped short as the hubbub turned into jeers. Her constant underlying anxiety ticked up a notch, but she clenched her jaw and kept going.

As they came around the curvature of the corridor, the crowd appeared in their line-of-sight. Their attention fell on a middle-aged man with pure white hair standing on a platform. When his wide mouth opened, it took up half his face. His voice rang out, but Jori only caught pieces of it until they neared.

"—working for eighteen years at my shop. A MEGA moved onto the station, making the same repairs, and I no longer make what I need to support myself, let alone my family. They've destroyed my livelihood!" He paced, taking only two steps before turning around with a stomp. His pale skin reddened and his eyes burned. "We must have stronger laws. It's not enough to ban MEGAs from governing or policing agencies. We should ban all enhancements!"

Jori swallowed. MEGA—Mechanically Enhanced, Genetically Altered. He was neither, but he'd inherited several exceptional abilities that caused people to distrust him. The Cooperative authorities had ordered invasive tests. If he wasn't careful, this angry mob might make the same assumption. Perhaps take their hate further like those men in the bay.

The hostile speech made Zaina nervous as well, but probably not for the same reason. She ushered him past, keeping her eyes straight ahead. When they cleared the area and no longer distinguished the man's words, Zaina deflated with a puff.

"How has your trip been so far?" she asked, likely to distract herself from her own anxiousness.

Everyone treated him like a criminal, but she didn't need to know that. "It's been alright."

"See any interesting sights or do anything fun?"

"No."

She asked him other things. Since he had nothing positive to contribute, he answered in clipped tones. That didn't deter her as she politely prodded him with more questions. By the time they got settled at the restaurant and halfway through their meal, Jori felt more at ease. The food helped. He didn't usually pay attention to what he ate beyond nutrition, but the soy cubes and vegetables over rice had just enough seasoning to add flavor without being overpowering.

"Our next transport isn't for several days, but there are plenty of activities available here," she said. "What would you like to do?"

He desperately wanted to lash out all his frustrations on a holo-fighting program but didn't want to frighten her. Besides, the warrior's life was behind him.

"I've seen a few VR-Ex centers," she said. "Have you ever been to one of those?"

Jori saddened. In what seemed like a lifetime ago, he and his brother had attended a virtual reality experience center on the Depnaugh space station. It'd been carefree without their domineering father around to criticize their frivolity. And now his brother was dead.

He shoved the memory aside and answered. "Once. It was interesting but didn't feel real."

"Really? I found the details amazing. The one I visited even added odors. The smell of the virtual garden was so realistic, I wanted to live there." She laughed.

Jori sensed her stress abate and was glad. "The one I went to did as well, but it had no life to it."

She cocked her head. "I think I know what you mean. You're sentio-animi, so you can sense emotions, right?"

"Not just emotions, but life," he replied, trying to be more forthcoming. "Even plants emit something. So walking in a forest and not sensing anything was disconcerting."

"Ah. I get it. That's interesting. I never knew that about flora. What do they feel like?"

Jori glanced up in thought. No one had ever asked him that, so he'd never had to explain it. It was a simple fact of his life. "There's a constant hum. When it's just plants, it's comforting. They don't carry emotions, but there's a peaceful quality to them. People are another matter."

She huffed. "That, I get. I'm not a sentio, but I have a strong intuition of sorts. It's almost like reading emotions, though I don't always recognize when they belong to someone else."

Jori's ease swelled. She wasn't exactly like him, but perhaps close enough for her to understand him.

"I get vibes from people," she continued. "If they're negative, they affect me. Do you have trouble with that too?"

"Occasionally. I've learned to block most of it."

"Really? How do you do that?"

Jori had to stop and think again. He'd been doing it for so long that it was automatic. "Meditation. Exercise. Sometimes I don't realize I'm taking stuff in, and I have to take the time to recognize it and force it out."

Her eyes widened in wonderment. "You must teach me that."

"Sure."

Her smile spread and the admiration emanating from her triggered a heat in Jori's cheeks. "Why aren't you afraid I'll make trouble? All the others were."

She pulled back. "Do you plan on making trouble?"

Jori frowned. "No."

She flicked her hand. "Then there's no reason for me to treat you like you will."

"What about the stuff in my file?" Like the *prone to violence* warning, his level nine martial ability, his skills in weaponry, and about the lives he'd taken.

She leaned in and spoke solemnly. "In my experience, those reports are only from one perspective. I like to reserve judgment until I get the other side of the story."

Jori's chest tightened. Dread of having to relive his past paired with shock that someone wanted to know his viewpoint.

She touched his hand. "You can tell me when you're ready. Or not. It's up to you. Either way, you don't need to fear my judgment."

Jori cleared his throat and looked down at his plate, trying to hide the tears building in his eyes. She saw anyway and patted his arm.

He must make sure he never let this woman down.

4
Bot Shop

The lodgings on this floor of the space station were questionably clean, as evidenced by an acrid odor that seemed to come from nowhere and everywhere. But at least the pale blue bedding had a fresh scent. And, unlike the rooms on the lower floors, this place had a private bathroom and a kitchenette. A large painting of an unnamed ocean added a touch of hominess, as did the rose-red armchair in the corner.

Zaina Noman sipped her tea, enjoying the cozy quietude away from the negative undercurrent fermenting through the more populated areas of the station. It frightened her that MEGAs had infiltrated governments all over the galaxy, but she also sympathized with the augmented community. Few could find jobs, which led them to homelessness and crime.

This MEGA upheaval added another worry—especially with her new charge. Jori's records showed that the MEGA Inspections Office had tested him. Everything came up negative, but they'd placed a permanent note in his file about his special abilities. A sentio-animi who also had a high proficiency in mathematics, language, and science, plus amazing muscle memory, high endurance, and an above-average ability to recover from injuries—things extremists might put him in the MEGA category for.

She shuddered as her imagination exploded with a series of scenarios where anti-MEGA activists discovered the extent of his skills and attacked. Based on her own recent experience with violence, she wouldn't be able to protect him.

An irrational thought about him having the ability to defend himself crossed her mind. Notes in his file mentioned martial arts and a proficient use of weapons—not *a weapon*, but *weapons*, plural. "*Not to be underestimated*," it said.

Goosebumps prickled her arms. She might've taken on a charge beyond her skill.

She chewed her lip and studied him as he read something on the tablet she'd given him. His dark narrow eyes and boyish face showed no hint of his violent abilities. Nor did they show any emotion. He was polite and seemed appreciative but kept to himself. Granted, they'd only met two days ago, and were in what her field called the *honeymoon phase* where children tended to be withdrawn.

What would he be like once that phase ended? The records spoke of a brutal past, and children who'd been through that sort of trauma usually had trouble managing their emotions. Was that what had happened when he'd taken a life? The file provided no details.

Doubts about her qualifications festered. Getting attacked by a parent who'd just had his parental rights terminated didn't help. His bellowing voice, fiery eyes, and thunderous fists had turned her from an advocate of the innocent to a victim herself. Even now, the thought of any kind of violence made her insides constrict to where she felt she might implode.

It was too late to back out. Failure to handle any aspect of this case would have debilitating consequences for this poor child.

She massaged her brow, though it was her heart that ached. Jori carried himself too much like a soldier. And despite how hard he tried to hide it, she detected his loneliness. Father, parental rights terminated. Mother, location unknown. Brother, presumed dead.

She took another sip of her tea and vowed to do everything in her power to help him. After all, she had a magical touch—at least that's what people had said. She had a unique ability to talk with children, help them calm down, and ask the right questions that enabled them to think through their difficulties.

Someone long ago had helped her during her own tumultuous childhood—abandoned by her mother and left with an alcoholic father. Now it was her turn to pay it forward. With him, she'd start with steering him away from anything related to soldiery and help him find a peaceful hobby.

Jori rose once again. The space in their quarters was just enough for him to stretch. He lifted his arms, inhaled, then exhaled. She was familiar with the routine by now. After the stretches, he'd do something aerobic.

He was undoubtedly restless and bored—not a great combination for a troubled child. Who was she to keep him cooped up because of *her* anxiety and fears? God knew she tended to overthink situations. Maybe things had settled down.

She set aside her own tablet. "What do you say we do a little shopping today? Just to browse and get out of this tiny room?"

He snapped into a soldier's stance with his hands clasped behind his back. "Yes, s—m—I mean, alright."

She winced. Even after she'd assured him that he didn't need to call her sir or ma'am, the soldier in him couldn't help it. She'd never dealt with someone so disciplined before and so had no idea how to encourage a new habit. He must've sensed her emotions because when she put her hand on his shoulder, he lowered his head.

"It's alright," she said.

His throat bobbed as though it wasn't.

*****

Jori fell into the assurance of Zaina's eyes. She was amazing. Her lifeforce was much like Commander Hapker's—optimistic and understanding. She was genuinely kind like him, perhaps even more so. She carried a lot of anxiety, though. And sometimes her restless sleep had woken him. Yet she began each day with an infectious optimism.

"We'll stick to the nicer parts of the station," she said. "Maybe head to the garden afterward."

He perked up. The garden had lots of trees and shrubs, a grassy area with pebbled trails crisscrossing through. It even had animals living there—things he didn't get to see often having lived on a spaceship his whole life. "Alright."

They headed out, paying to use the conveyor rather than walking. She'd been more intent on avoiding people ever since he'd pointed out two thugs following them the other day. The situation had increased his vigilance while making her so nervous that she looked ready to vomit.

They exited the car at a clean and quiet section of shops. An Angolan café lay across the hall. The spicy scent wafting from it made his nose itch. Zaina had bought him a spicy snack from there yesterday, wanting him to experience different flavors. When he coughed it out, she'd laughed—good-naturedly, of course.

This time, they bypassed it and headed in a direction they hadn't gone yet. Like Zaina, Jori observed the various shops with casual interest. Assorted appliances suited for microgravity, clothing and shoes for all kinds of activities and conditions, toys, home décor, tools, dinnerware, beauty salons. The station had it all.

He tried to make sense of why people would want most of this frivolous junk. What was the use of vases or pink shoes, anyway? Back home, he only had what he needed—his uniforms, uniform accessories, a few hand-held weapons, and five pieces of dishware. If he lived on his own, some of these appliances would be necessary, but not the fancy ones. He'd also need tools, but not much else. Even if he wasn't a warrior anymore, he couldn't ever imagine wanting such useless comforts.

They stopped at a clothing store displaying examples of the wares made by a fabricor. She touched the kiosk and it blinked to life. "I have a small budget for clothes. Do you want to take a look?"

"No, thank you," Jori replied. After wearing a uniform for most of his existence, picking out things to wear had been a frustrating experience. When he needed new clothes, he'd stick with the same simple pullover shirts and two-pocketed pants. Dark colors only. Lighter colors made him feel conspicuous.

"Alright." Zaina touched the screen, turning it off.

They moved on. The next shop captured his attention. Refurbished bots for just about every purpose imaginable—except military. No artillery or combat bots here. That tall engineering bot with its multiple arms was interesting, though. As was the shorter rectangular mechanic bot.

"Do you want to check it out?" Zaina asked.

Jori almost said no until he saw the shopkeeper sitting on the floor with his legs crossed and an old cylindrical maintenance bot in front of him. The man had warm, dark skin and facial features that reminded him of an older and leaner version of Lieutenant

Gresher—someone who had been kind rather than judgmental of his heritage. This shopkeeper's chin was more pointed and there was nothing soldier-like about his physique.

Jori approached with cautious eagerness as the man studied the diagnostic computer on his lap. He had no delusions about being able to help, but the prospect of solving a programming problem drew him in.

The man, too engrossed in his work, finally noticed him and blinked. Then a smile spread across his face. "What can I help you with, young man?"

The kindness emanating from him encouraged Jori to give a small smile in return. "I'm just curious. I haven't seen an H-2000 bot in a while."

"You're familiar with them?"

"Quite. Their functions are limited, but what they do, they do well."

The man grinned with pleasure. "Indeed. They're not made anymore, but I think every ship should have one."

Ziana leaned in, emitting a passing interest. "What does an H-2000 do?"

The man looked at Jori. "You go ahead and explain."

Jori automatically fell into the at-ease military stance, then groaned inwardly. He was no longer a warrior. No need to act like one. He relaxed and cleared his throat. "It's a maintenance bot. The H stands for Hephaestus, a craftsman god from ancient mythology. This isn't a craft bot, but in its day, it was good at troubleshooting and fixing things in creative ways. Although technology has changed a bit since it came out, it has adapted well."

"Very good," the man replied.

Jori's cheeks flushed. "So what's wrong with this one?"

"The AI generated a script that was supposed to help it with a task, and it somehow affected another section of code. I'm trying to determine whether I should revert to a prior version or try to fix it."

The man pointed at the readout. Jori flinched at his mechanical hand.

The man's face fell. "Sorry. Machine accident. I would've preferred to have my hand regrown, but couldn't afford it."

Jori's stomach knotted. The regrowth procedure was why he was here with Zaina rather than adopted by Commander J.D. Hapker. Hapker had received a terrible injury to his arm in the fight against Gottfried and his MEGA-soldiers. When he had to be taken to a medical ship, the Cooperative used it as an opportunity to send Jori elsewhere.

"It's alright," Zaina said. "I think it just surprised him is all. We have nothing against anyone with augmentations."

Jori dipped his head, though a part of him disagreed, especially when it came to Gottfried. The man never should've been allowed to become the aide to an admiral, but he'd hidden his ability and used his position to perpetuate his skewed beliefs about MEGA superiority. His murderous actions had put the Cooperative on high alert and set a panic throughout the galaxy.

The shopkeeper wiggled his fingers. "Not augmented. Just replaced. I admit a part of me would've loved to get a bionic hand or one that'd reshape itself into tools, but this was all I could afford. My name is Nadeem, by the way."

Jori shook off his surprise and pushed back his shame. He of all people should know better than to make assumptions.

Nadeem showed Jori the script and described what it had done. Jori pulled up a stool and sat beside him. Zaina joined them. He sensed she didn't understand most of what they discussed, but genuine interest radiated from her.

A rising anger infiltrated Jori's senses, but he remained rapt as Nadeem explained. As the emotions rose, his attention divided.

Nadeem paused to type. Jori's focus shifted outward and his heart leapt. He rose with a swiftness that toppled his stool. "Something is happening."

Zaina's eyes popped. "What? What is it?"

Pockets of disturbances from all over the space station peppered his senses. One comprising about ten people advanced closer. "Anger, and lots of it."

Nadeem cocked his head and eyed Jori. Before he could explain, a bellow resounded from just outside the shop. "Here's another one!"

A muscular man with a face and arms as hairy as a bear stormed into the room and pointed a giant finger. "You!"

Nadeem jumped to his feet and leapt back. “Me? I didn’t do anything.”

“You’re a MEGA! You’re one of those freaks!”

Nadeem waved his hands. “No. This is just a prosthetic. No enhanced features.”

Jori’s chest hitched. “He’s telling the truth!”

The enraged bear of a man didn’t listen. He pushed through Jori and Zaina and stomped over to Nadeem.

Zaina yelped and fell on her backside. Jori rushed to help her as Nadeem backed away with his hands up. Zaina’s face contorted in pure terror. Jori grasped her arm, urging her to get up, but her feet didn’t seem to hold her weight.

More people entered. Their rage clashed against Zaina’s fright, crippling Jori’s ability to think. A hefty woman swung a sizeable wrench and smashed a bot. The clang of metal resounded through the shop and snapped Jori into battle-focus.

“Get up, Zaina,” he said. “We have to get out of here.”

Her head sprang up and down like the pistons of a motor. She rose but her legs wobbled.

“A girl is now dead because of you people!” another woman screamed.

A bald man with a red beard and carrying a metal pipe struck a nearby bot. Zaina collapsed and clapped her arms over her ears. A high-pitched yell tore through her throat. Jori perceived her paralyzing fear and shielded her.

No one came for her, though. The bear-man cornered Nadeem. His fist slammed down. The shopkeeper cried out and covered his head against a barrage of punches.

Jori glanced around for something—anything—he could use as a weapon to stop these maniacs. A detached robotic arm across the room looked promising, but he wouldn’t leave Zaina. What if they mistook her for a MEGA?

Nadeem fell. Bear-man kept hitting him, landing one in the man’s kidney and making him squawk. Two more people joined in, one punching and one kicking, while others smashed up his shop.

Jori clenched his fists, wavering between helping the shopkeeper and staying to protect Zaina. He tugged at her arm.

"We have to do something." His heart raced, each rapid beat threatening to jump out of his chest. "Come on! Please!"

"I-I can't." She tucked her head between her knees.

Damn it! Nadeem's pain pierced his senses. He wanted to stop those chimas but couldn't risk abandoning her. "Zaina, please. Get up. Run. Hide. Something! I have to help Nadeem before they kill him."

Zaina remained. Her panic was almost as strong as Nadeem's suffering. He'd seen this behavior before, mostly from slaves or shokukin workers. The level of irrationality in this state had always baffled him. Moreso now when he wrestled between his desire to shake her or leave her.

The hefty woman stormed over. Jori's frustration fled and he threw his arms around Zaina. "Don't hurt her. She's a good person."

The woman's glower deepened. "What are you two doing in here? You with him?" She thumbed behind her.

"No. We're just here checking out the shop."

She jabbed her finger at him. "If you're lying, boy, there'll be a reckoning. We're sick of MEGAs."

Jori's throat grated as though he'd swallowed sand. The woman moved on, swiping several bot parts from a table as she went by.

"If you know what's good for you, you'll close shop and find some hole to live in, you fucker." The bear-man spit on Nadeem, who was in the same fetal position as Zaina, but hugging the floor rather than the wall.

The attackers left to hunt for their next victim. Jori waited until they were several meters away before checking on Nadeem. He knelt beside the man and touched his arm. "They're gone."

Nadeem choked out a sob. Saliva filled Jori's mouth and he swallowed it down. He used both his sixth sense and his eyes to assess the man's injuries. His pain was intense, but Jori didn't detect the pain of death lurking.

Those chimas! Obviously, MEGAs weren't the only bad guys.

*****

Zaina Noman shook as though smothered by the freezing snow of an avalanche. How could people act like this? Nadeem had seemed so nice, yet they beat him all the same.

Her breath came out in ragged bursts as she tightened her arms around her head and lay curled on the floor. Going into space was supposed to be an adventure. Instead, it was a living nightmare.

The violence ceased and the yells lessened as the attackers moved on. She wanted to get up, but her entire body locked in place. Not even the prospect of running away from this madness allowed her to move.

"They're gone." Jori's voice came from faraway. It took her a moment to realize he had left to help Nadeem. Parts of their conversation registered through her panic. Nadeem sounded good for a man who'd just taken a beating. He even had the wherewithal to activate his comm and call for a medic. Jori found a first aid kit and aided the man further, all while talking calmly.

Bless that boy.

His fortitude and empathy gave her a mental nudge. Her whimpers turned into weeping as shame smothered her fear. She was supposed to be protecting him and here he was taking care of her and Nadeem *by himself*. What kind of advocate was she?

The worst one possible. Jori deserved better.

Dear God. Please help me!

5
Degenerates

A smokey haze drifted through the tavern. Degenerate men and women hung out in groups, some smoking rolled tobacco and others sucking it from a bong. They sat at dented and scratched metal tables and on worn and stained chairs. The low lighting almost hid the insects scavenging on the dirty floor.

Major Abelard Blakesley gulped down the last of the astringent vodka and curled his lips. At least it was better than the whores here. Not that he'd expected much from a place called Sailor's Wharf. No self-respecting merchant would call themselves a sailor, or a space station a wharf.

A gaunt woman with hot pink hair and gaudy makeup approached him with a half-toothless smile. Her sour body odor nearly made him gag. He put up his palm and glowered. She took the hint and moved on.

What a shithole. Why his commanding officer liked sleazy women was beyond him. That wasn't true. He knew. Places like this didn't care about their merchandise, so patrons could use the wares however they chose.

Blakesley preferred much classier establishments—ones where the women looked good, smelled good, felt good, and were genuinely eager to please. But Vance had told him to wait here, so he waited.

He went back to watching the newscast from the big screen hanging on a wall across from him. It was the same story telecasted through multiple channels—sixteen-year-old girl murdered by a purported MEGA. They showed the worst possible photo of the assailant—a bedraggled young man not much older than her and with a mechanical leg that was more likely just a prosthetic. They'd all sensationalized the reports, disregarding the lack of details on how the victim was killed or why. It might've been an accident, or even self-defense against a MEGA-hater, but of course the news would never say that.

A man with a full beard and a missing front tooth walked by. He glanced at Blakesley and flicked his hand at the screen. "Can you believe this shit? Those fucking MEGAs have just declared war."

Blakesley smiled without humor. *You have no idea.*

A door on the upper balcony opened. The old-fashioned hinges creaked. Blakesley slumped with relief as Vance exited and headed down the dilapidated stairway.

Vance was a super-soldier, designed and augmented to be the best. He had a broad and muscular frame that made Blakesley look like a reed. They differed in another major way as well. Blakesley raked his hand through his curly, light-golden-brown hair. Many a woman had told him how much they loved it. His beard, too. Vance had no hair—not even on his dimpled chin. If not for his light brown eyes flecked with gold, his head would've resembled a block of granite.

Although Blakesley didn't look the least bit intimidating—it'd be harder to attract women if he looked like a stone-faced behemoth—he was also a super-soldier. He could best every man in this tavern, both physically and intellectually. Unlike Vance, he didn't need to use brain implants either. The only cybernetic tech he had was a communication chip embedded in his ear. Of course, he never let his natural abilities outshine Vance's. No point in provoking a beast who toed the line of sanity.

Vance grabbed a few napkins from the counter and wiped his hands.

Revulsion budded in Blakesley's mouth as the cloth soaked up slick and congealed blood. Chunks of hair came up with it. Blakesley wondered whether Vance had left the whore alive, but only for a moment. It wasn't his business.

"Time just ran out," Vance said. "Let's get back to the ship."

"What about the boy?"

"It's too risky to fight through the station to get him."

"Fight?"

"The situation here has turned volatile."

Ah. The news story probably had everyone in a tizzy. Let them rant. The galaxy would soon have a lot more to worry about than the death of one stupid teenager. Yet Blakesley hesitated. It didn't seem wise to leave the boy behind. Retrieving him was an important part of their mission. Failure would hamper his ambition, but he dared not argue.

"I know where he'll be. Someone's on the way to fetch him," Vance said, exercising both his ability to read thoughts and see the future. He tossed the napkins into a nearby recycler and grabbed more. After loosening the vambrace of his uniform, he pulled back the sleeve underneath, revealing more blood.

Blakesley waited with mock patience as Vance cleaned the minicomputer implanted on his forearm, using the folded tip of the napkin to trace the buttons and display. For someone who liked to draw blood, he sure could be fastidious.

"What the fuck is that?" a whore yelled, pointing at Vance's arm. "You a MEGA?"

Vance gave her a flat smile. "You best move on, sweetheart."

She backed up from the dangerous glint in Vance's eyes. Blakesley shifted his feet and hoped this was the end of it. But as soon as she was far enough away, she cried out, "He's a MEGA! He's one of them!"

A dozen heads turned their way, but most had the wisdom to stay put. One did not.

A man with a mane of unruly blond hair and shoulders almost as wide as Vance's rose with a menacing purpose. "Your kind don't belong here. You best leave now."

Vance kept his smile and casually finished cleaning the blood. "I'll leave when I'm good and ready."

The blond man scowled. He glanced around, looking for help, and found none. A flash of nervousness crossed through his features, but the fool thrust out his chest and approached with a jabbing finger.

Here we go. Though thinner, Blakesley could take out this man with one strike. Multi-level blackbelt against a thug—it'd be as easy as clipping his fingernails. But Vance had a fresh taste of blood and undoubtedly wanted more.

Vance squared up and met him with a flat smile. The fool was oblivious to the threat. When he jabbed his finger again, Vance grabbed it and twisted. The audible snap was almost as loud as the man's cry. Vance smashed his fist into the man's temple and silenced him. Then he wrapped his arm around his neck and jerked. The crackle of grating vertebrae made Blakesley's stomach heave.

Vance let go. The blond-haired victim's head folded at an odd angle as his body collapsed. Normally, Blakesley would've grumbled at this unnecessary display of dominance. But since part of their mission was to inflame the MEGA-haters, he looked on with a cool detachment.

"Anyone else got a problem?" Vance asked as though inviting them all out to breakfast.

No one dared answer. Blakesley eyed his commanding officer, waiting for his next move. The man could be unpredictable—especially when it came to violence. Sometimes he'd kill in a snap and be done. And sometimes he'd go into a rage and kill everyone within reach.

"Get back to the ship," Vance said to Blakesley without taking his eyes off those in the tavern. "Alert the crew. Tell them we're leaving."

Blakesley released his breath. It seemed the mood was for the former—unless security came. If that happened, Vance would take them out with bloodthirsty glee.

Fucking psychopath.

6
Tunnel Rats

Jori squeezed Zaina's hand the way he'd sometimes done for his mother. He wished he could take her fears away, but he also wished she were stronger—more like Commander Hapker. He coaxed her into a sitting position but her head remained tucked between her knees. Not knowing what else to do, he did what the commander had always done for him and rested his hand on her shoulder.

"I'm so sorry," she kept repeating.

Jori forgot all about his frustration. Her earlier fear was as strong as the guilt she felt now. He wondered what horrible experience she'd had that'd caused her breakdown, but this wasn't the time to ask.

Nadeem pushed himself onto his elbow and winced. An anguished hiss followed, but he seemed determined.

"Stay down!" Jori rose but remained with Zaina. "Wait for the medics."

Nadeem flopped on his back and pulled his arm over his eyes. The flatness of his emotions indicated he'd reverted to a numb state that Jori knew all too well. The worst was over. Crying wouldn't help. In his experience, the best thing to do was gather your wits and move on. If only Zaina had Nadeem's will.

Men and women in light blue garb rushed in with a med bot and a gurney. Considering the chaos of the station, their swiftness surprised him. Perhaps they'd been nearby helping someone else. Or maybe the rioters had retained enough humanity to let them by. Either way, he was grateful.

"Over there," he said, pointing to Nadeem.

They hurried over with their scanners and checked his wounds with the same emotions as battle-focused soldiers. The words *concussion, contusion, traumatic iritis*, and *nasal fracture* came up. Jori's worry diminished, but not his guilt. Calling the authorities the moment this had all started should've been his first instinct. Thanks to his father's expectations that he figure out how to get out of trouble on his own, it hadn't occurred to him.

With everything assessed, the medics put Nadeem on the gurney and headed out. One medic veered over. "Are you alright, ma'am?"

Zaina didn't respond.

"She's not hurt," Jori said. "She's just scared."

The man dipped his head. "You two need to lie low until security comes. It's crazy out there."

Jori swallowed. The hate expanding through the station pressed inside his skull. He and Zaina weren't MEGAs, but experience suggested the outrage could spread beyond MEGAs.

The last medic left, leaving him and Zaina alone in a ravaged shop. Screws and gears were strewn about. A service bot with a battered torso rested on its side. One of its arms sprawled out, connected only by a single wire. A mangled metal sheet that'd once encased another bot lay next to it. A hydraulic motor had skidded underneath a table. It'd be a miracle if Nadeem got everything working again.

Zaina lifted her head. Her brows drew together as she scanned the room. "They're gone?"

Jori sighed. "For now. But they might return, so we need to go somewhere safe."

She eased to her feet, keeping her shoulders hunched. Jori pressed against her hip, offering support. She pulled at her blouse and smoothed her pants with a trembling hand. He took her other hand, squeezing her ice-cold fingers to get her blood flowing again.

A sense of comfort emanated from her, but her other emotions were still too turbulent. He considered the one person in his life who'd always faced storms with a remarkable calm. "*Breathe*," Sensei Jeruko would say. "*Gaining control starts with your breath*."

"Take some deep breaths," Jori said.

She sniffed and rubbed her nose, then nodded. Her first intake of air rattled. She took several more and Jori joined her until they evened out.

She gripped his hand in return. "Is this why you're so calm? Meditation?"

"Yes. I also did a body scan."

"Body scan?"

"I focus on each part of my body and imagine them relaxing."

She wiped her nose again, then searched through her bag until she found something to clean it with. "I've tried meditation. It never seems to work for me. Maybe I'll try a body scan next time."

"Meditation worked this time," he said.

Her mouth quirked, almost into a smile. "You're right. I'm sorry. Here you are looking after me when I should be looking after you. Are you alright?" She appraised him with brows curved in concern.

"I'm fine," he replied, glad her harder emotions had yielded enough to let her compassion through. "We should go."

Her head bobbed wearily. "Okay. Thank you. I'll do better, I promise."

He led her out with cautious steps. The electrified burnt odor of phaser fire wafted by, indicating the rioters must've gotten a hold of weapons. But the corridors were empty, save for a few terrified onlookers.

The security gates of some shops were down. He paused. Nadeem's store probably had one too. It was an option, but he preferred they get back to their quarters. Anyone looking for trouble in the lodging section of the station had to beat both the level-security access and the door lock.

Crashing and yelling resounded from around both curved ends of the corridor. Jori detected the accompanying hostility and instinctively looked for a weapon. He wished they were further away. The conveyor was so close, but he doubted Zaina would make it.

Sure enough, her panic heightened, making her halt. "We can't go that way."

Another clatter followed by a string of curses elicited Jori's agreement as well as his irritation. If he were by himself, he'd press on, certain that his smallness would help him slip by.

They headed back only to discover the fighting there had also neared. Yells and screams mixed with the smacks and thuds of hand-to-hand combat. The plasma scent grew stronger too.

Zaina's throat bobbed. "What do we do?"

Her rising trepidation triggered his own. He inhaled deeply and forced his mind to work. "We hide until it blows over."

She lowered her head in assent. Jori led her back to Nadeem's shop, hoping the rioters would leave it alone since they'd already torn it apart.

Zaina resisted. "Here?"

Jori tugged her hand. "It'll be alright. Nadeem has to sleep sometime, which means he must have a security gate. We can lock ourselves inside."

She eyed the ravaged shop and panted.

"Breathe." Jori inhaled, making a show of filling his chest. She copied him. "Hold." He held it in for a count of eight, then did it again. Although his concentration wavered when he remembered the times he'd sat in meditation with Sensei Jeruko, he felt better.

Her anxiety remained, but it lessened enough to give her the strength to ease forward. "Th-that's a good idea. We'll lock ourselves in."

Phaser blasts struck the other side of the hall as the mayhem echoed closer. The rioters hadn't yet appeared from around the curve of the hallway, but the nearness of their rage still barraged Jori's senses. He yanked Zaina's hand and darted inside the shop. She followed, albeit clumsily, but he directed her to a corner concealed by a tall machine.

He returned to the storefront, searching for a way to shut it. Where the hell was the closing mechanism? No keypads, biometric scanners, not even a switch. *Chusho*. This must be one of those remote activated devices. Nadeem likely had access to it from a tablet or something. He was gone now, and Jori had no time to search for it.

Two men and a woman zipped by with their heads swiveling to find new victims. One saw him and snarled. Jori braced himself for a fight, but the man discounted him and kept going.

He dashed back to Zaina as more people stormed through the corridor. Crashes and bangs echoed with destruction. Zaina huddled against the machine and huffed. Tears streamed down her face, but he sensed her attempting to get a hold of herself. However, the terror wafting off her was almost as strong as the raging from the crowd. Fortunately, the amount of adrenaline coursing through Jori's body muted his own emotions.

A woman screamed. "I'm not a MEGA! Please stop!"

Jori detected a touch of her fear and anguish but didn't feel her pain, indicating she was likely one of those MEGAs with brain modifications. His impulse was to run and help her, but again he stayed with Zaina, hoping his calm composure would rub off on her.

Vexation welled up when the woman cried out once more. *Damn it!* If those people killed her, he'd never forgive himself. The intense focus of a military force entered his senses. He poked his head out from behind the cover. A dozen soldiers in heavy armor marched down the corridor blasting their phaser rifles. Lifeforces dimmed but didn't disappear. Jori suspected the rioters had merely been stunned. The blue shimmers coming off the energy shields of the troops indicated the return fire was deadlier, but they had protection.

Zaina's cries redirected his attention. He wrapped his arm around her shoulder. "It will be alright. Soldiers are here."

It was almost a lie. Despite the help, they were caught in the middle of full-fledged warfare. If a rioter ran in here, he and Zaina would be in danger again.

His battle-focus tightened, allowing him to analyze the situation. Several throwable objects were littered about, but what they needed was an impenetrable hiding spot or an escape route.

A nearby upper vent caught his eye. He could easily reach it by climbing onto the shelf beneath. The opening seemed wide enough for him and Zaina to get into, but he wasn't sure whether the shaft narrowed or where it led. He was familiar with the layout of most spaceships, including their ventilation systems, but not of space stations.

Anywhere is better than here. But would Zaina follow?

He gripped her shoulders. "Zaina. Look at me." She didn't respond. Jori shook her. "Please! I need you."

She snapped up and he detected a surge of her will.

Jori held her eyes. "We have to get out of here, which means you need to move."

She wagged her head. "No. No. You can't go out there."

"Not out there," Jori said. "I have an idea." She remained unresponsive. His heartbeat ticked faster. If trouble came, he'd have no choice but to fight. Despite his skills, it'd likely be a losing one. He jostled her. "Listen! I have a plan. It's perfect. It'll put us out of harm's way, but you *must* move."

She met his eyes once more.

Jori pressed down his panic. "You can do this. Please trust me. Can you do that?"

She nodded and choked back a sob. "I'm sorry. Yes. I'm pulling it together."

Jori's shoulders sagged. "Alright," he said, and pointed to a rear corner of the shop. "The first thing we need to do is go over there."

She tensed.

"Breathe," Jori commanded, partly out of frustration. "It's a short distance and I don't sense anyone close enough to see us. Remember my ability?" She didn't answer. "Trust it. Trust *me*."

She huffed as though preparing herself for an arduous task, then straightened. Jori tugged her over to the far wall, grabbing one of Nadeem's tools along the way. "Hold on while I remove the cover from the vent."

Her eyes followed the shelf up, and a touch of optimism broke through her fear.

He ushered her into a nook and climbed. The metal frame wobbled, so he shifted his weight to keep it steady. The yelling outside hadn't subsided, but he reached the top with no one noticing.

Removing the vent screws was easy, though time seemed to drag. He left one in, allowing the cover to hang. This would allow him to pull it back into place later. The inside reminded him of an instance where he'd crawled through a maintenance tunnel to escape super-soldiers determined to kill him. It was nearly the same size and had the same short but wide rectangular shape that was just big enough for him—and an adult like Zaina—to navigate. One difference, those tubes didn't have an electric barrier.

He eyed the shimmering energy shield without worry. Disabling it would alert security, but they wouldn't bother with intruders at a time like this. He grabbed random bot parts from the shelf. Shoving them inside caused the barrier to short out. To ensure it didn't reboot, he pried off the control box cover. He evaluated its electronic guts and found the right place to disrupt the electric flow. A jab of the insulated screwdriver sent out a spark and disabled it.

He leapt down and grasped Zaina's hand. "Let's get inside."

She nodded. Jori held the shelving while she climbed. With a little effort, she wormed her way in, headfirst. He followed but scooted in backward. Even though he'd left the cover hanging, getting it back in place was trickier. Angling the screw and screwdriver required that he poke his short fingers through the small squares of the grating.

His hand shook and his joints ached. His chest tightened, and he forced it to relax. They were safe inside now. Those rioters were too fired up to go through the trouble of searching out-of-the-way vents.

He got an opposing corner screw in place and puffed. Leaving the other screws behind, he contorted his body and clumsily turned around in the tight space. "Alright. We're good," he said, his voice echoing. "Move forward, but slowly."

Jori crawled on his hands and knees while her tallness forced her to squirm on her belly. The noise from outside echoed at first, but eventually tapered off. A focused determination peeked through Zaina's intense emotions. She no longer panted in fear, but from exertion. Jori huffed too, although he had an easier time of it. Now that they were away from danger, his battle-focus waned, leaving him with an ache that penetrated his bones.

Zaina stopped at a vertical chute. "Now what?"

"Move over," he said.

She did. It wasn't much room, but his small size allowed him to squeeze by.

He peered down. Unlike maintenance tunnels, it had no ladder. The tube was narrow enough that they could brace themselves, but one slip might result in a deadly fall.

Since the darkness didn't allow him to see how far down it went, he banged the side of the chute and hoped the echo would tell him. It didn't. Focusing his senses, he reassessed the situation behind him. The rage waged on. The pain of several deaths poked through but were too distant to overwhelm him.

Another sensation whispered, but this time from below. He pinpointed the faint lifeforce and confirmed it came from somewhere down the shaft. Someone else must've entered the vents. Since they held no anger, he suspected they'd come here to avoid the chaos as well.

"Hello?" Jori's cautious voice amplified as it reverberated against the metal walls, making him wince.

A panicked sensation responded.

"It's alright," Jori said. "We're trying to hide, too."

"Who's with ya?" a man asked tentatively.

"Me and my guardian. She's terrified. I'm worried about her. We need to get somewhere safe."

"You a MEGA or a MEGA-hater?" The man kept his tone neutral, which gave Jori no clue which side he was on.

"Neither. We don't have any augmentations. Nor do we hate anyone. We just want to get away."

"That's good. That's good. Alright. Come on down. I can block the shaft so that if ya' fall, you won't go far."

Jori glanced at Zaina, seeing only shadows. Her emotions signified her willingness to try. He went in first, bracing himself by reaching out with both hands and feet on either side.

Zaina twisted to get into position. Her feet kicked and scraped the metal wall. When positioned, she stretched out her legs to follow his example. When her foot braced the other side, it skidded with a metallic screech. "It's too slippery!"

"Take off your shoes," Jori said before her emotions spiraled again.

"Okay." She took in a shaky breath. "Okay. I've got this." The echoing shuffle of her removing them sounded eerily like the scuttle of rats. She tried once more. This time, her feet held as she followed Jori down.

The man's lifeforce didn't strengthen as Jori crept closer. The muted sensation was reminiscent of other cyborgs he'd met. He swallowed down his unease. *Not all MEGAs are bad.* Besides, this one emitted enough for Jori to determine he harbored no malice.

He reached the man's arms. The air flow around him indicated another horizontal shaft, so he wriggled in. Zaina followed, the tighter fit making them grunt until they each had their own space.

"My name's Rodrigo, by the way. Rigo for short. Sometimes they call me Mouse 'cause—well, I don't know. Or sometimes…" He cleared his throat. "Sorry. I rattle on when I'm nervous."

"My name is Zaina Noman," she replied, her fear reduced to wariness.

Jori hesitated. Despite having kept his given name, an irrational fear lived in the back of his mind. He shook it away. The universe was too big of a place for his father to find out he was alive. Still, he decided not to answer.

Fortunately, Rigo didn't push it. "Hey, uh… Before we move on, I need to tell you something," the man said. "I'm a MEGA. Got me a fancy mechanical eye and a nifty hand with all kinds o' gadgets on it."

Jori's suspicion heightened. His memory flashed back to Gottfried and how hard he had tried to befriend him.

"We're alright with that," Zaina said. "I've got nothing against anyone unless they give me a reason."

Jori appreciated the strength of her voice. Her emotions still threatened to degrade, but at least she was trying. He hoped it wouldn't mean she'd be too ready to trust this stranger. But they had no choice at this point.

"Good. Good." Rodrigo bobbed his head. "We should get going. I know how to get to the docking bay from here."

"The docking bay?" Zaina asked.

"Yeah. We gotta leave this station. There's a ship that'll take us."

Jori tensed. Something was off.

Zaina hesitated too, but probably for a different reason. "Leave? Shouldn't we just wait until security gets everything calmed down?"

"Security's overwhelmed. Those thugs have already breached their headquarters and are taking control. Nowhere in this station is safe. Not for me, anyway. You might be alright, but I wouldn't want to stay someplace where blood-thirsty folk are in charge."

Chusho. "He's right," Jori said, sensing the intensifying rage throughout the station. "Those people are beyond reason. They're bound to hurt anyone." Staying inside here would only be safe for so long. All it would take was one MEGA getting caught trying to escape through a vent and they'd all be flushed out and presumed guilty.

Zaina's breath quickened.

"Breathe," Jori reminded her.

She did, long and deep. The strength of her panic lessened. "Alright. We'll go with you."

Rigo led the way. "It's crazy out there, ya know? I got chased by three guys. They almost caught me, too, but I'm like a mouse, ya know? I can get to lots of places other people can't. Squeezed under a hatch that hadn't finished closing and threw stuff at 'em when they tried to get under too. They eventually gave up and I found the vent. It was hell opening it, ya know? I had to—"

"This ship you're taking us to," Jori interrupted. "What kind is it?"

"Oh, it's a good ship. You'll see. You don't need to worry. It's run by good people. Good people."

"Are they MEGAs too?"

"Some, but not all. We're a free ship. Belong to no one. The Cooperative's rules don't apply, so you all will be completely safe from these haters. They saved my friend, Jake, ya know. Treated him right."

The man prattled on. Jori gritted his teeth. Running into Rigo had seemed fortunate, but he couldn't shake this feeling that it wasn't a coincidence. Gottfried had acted like an ally because he intended to take Jori to his MEGA leader, who'd use him to further his cause. What if Rodrigo wanted the same thing?

Jori shook off his unease. It must be his imagination. It was unlikely that anyone knew who or where he was. And running into someone who *did* know him and who happened to meet him in the vents of a giant space station seemed far-fetched.

The Cooperative Council had provided him with a new identity, changing both his family name and history. Not even Commander Hapker could track him down.

7
Looters and Haters

The end of the shaft neared. Light from beyond illuminated the inside vent with an eerie luminance, creating stagnant shadows. The more Jori and the others progressed, the grimier it appeared. Rust, dirt, and mold clung to the alloy walls like insatiable parasites. Jori stuck his elbow in something dry yet sticky. Further on, little black pellets dotted near the edges.

Rats—the bane of every ship and harbor since mankind had first braved the endless seas. Or in this case, infinite space.

"We're here!" Rodrigo fiddled with the security control box. After the barrier sputtered out, he crawled to the grate. Jori squeezed in beside him and peeked through, relieved to find the floor was only a few dozen centimeters down. Getting out of this cramped space would be easy. Avoiding trouble would not.

Although the bay was vast, too many people swarmed about, and most were looters. A gang of toughs surrounded one cart of baggage, glowering around what was clearly their pilfered property. Pockets of others ransacked everything from luggage to toolboxes, working in either small groups or larger ones. Clothes, shoes, broken novelties, even food was strewn about, contributing to the chaotic maze they'd have to wade through.

The trio of pillagers nearby were his immediate concern. They emptied the contents from a heap of abandoned travel bags with a crazed madness that resembled battle lust. It was difficult to tell whether they were MEGA-haters, thugs, or just ordinary people caught up in the freedom of being able to do whatever they wanted.

He suspected the latter as a woman whooped and pulled a tablet from a suitcase. She tucked it into her pants and resumed rummaging with childish glee.

Zaina and peered over Jori's shoulder. "Which docking hatch leads to your friend's ship?" she asked Rigo.

"Dock B11. Third one down."

Jori strained to see it, then swallowed the lump in his throat. "Is there a closer vent?"

"Yeah, but only if you want to drop several meters."

Jori's neck prickled at how he knew that. Calling himself a mouse hinted at his penchant for exploring small spaces, but for what purpose? To find *him*? *Impossible. You're overthinking it.* There's no way Rodrigo could've known to look for him in the vents.

"So what do we do?" Zaina asked, her anxiety kicking up a notch and prompting him to stick with the plan.

"We wait," Jori said before Rodrigo answered. He hadn't intended to interrupt, but his lack of trust prompted a desire to control some aspect of this scheme. "The people here are about finished. As soon as they move on, we make a run for that hiding spot." He pointed to an empty luggage cart. Its bed was too short to hide behind, but the driver's cab was perfect.

"What about Rodrigo?" Zaina asked. "What if they notice his cybernetics?"

At first, Jori suspected she worried about getting caught with a MEGA. But her tilted brows suggested she might be more concerned about him.

"Don't worry," Rigo replied. "Mouse, remember? No one pays any attention to a mouse."

His optimism tweaked Jori's nerves. Following this fool was a bad idea. He and Zaina should back up and hope the rioters wouldn't find them. As he pulled away to do that very thing, a magnitude of rage clashing with unrelenting pain and terror exploded through his senses. The sensation derived from elsewhere on the station, but it represented the dangers erupting everywhere. And since some MEGAs had dimmed or nonexistent lifeforces, the sources of combined fright likely came from regular people. *Damn it*. Just as he'd suspected.

While the looters picked through the travel bags, Rigo undid the vent screws. The grating was wider here, allowing his larger fingers to work with quiet ease.

Rodrigo finished up the final screw as the nearby looters tossed the last suitcase aside. The woman snatched up an emptied bag and stuffed her loot into it. The burly man did the same and they sauntered off with the lean grey-haired man flaunting the smugness of a job well-done.

Rigo removed the grate. Jori stopped him before he exited. "Let me go first."

"What? No way," Zaina said. "It's too dangerous."

"I'm a child," Jori replied. "I doubt anyone will give me a second glance." He considered adding about his sensing ability but didn't want Rodrigo to know anything else about him.

He did another quick assessment with his senses, then crawled out and motioned for the others. "Walk like you belong here. Being sneaky may draw unwanted attention. And Rodrigo…" The man's head bobbed. "Keep between us. Hold this hand over your eye and put your cybernetic one in your pocket. Act like you're injured."

They walked casually. Jori kept his fear under control and held his head high. Zaina and Rodrigo hung theirs down, making him feel like he was in charge. In a way, he was. He took the lead, glancing about to gauge potential hiding places, the number of people about, and which ones posed the biggest threats.

They reached the cart but found too many individuals in their line of sight. Another location nearby seemed promising, but they had to pass a quartet of looters to get there.

"Chusho," he mumbled. He turned to his companions. "We have to keep moving, but it's risky. I think these people will ignore us, but…"

"We gotta try," Zaina replied as her eyes darted about. "Rigo, you up for it?"

Rodrigo bobbed his head.

Jori filled his lungs. "Alright, let's go. And remember, act casual."

They made it past the looters. Jori almost expelled his breath, but a man with a wide girth stepped in front of them. "Hey! Where do you think you're going?"

Zaina's anxiety shot like a rocket, and she froze. Rigo did as well. Though his emotions were more muted, Jori felt his rising distress. The mouse had been confident enough in the vents, but out here where being a MEGA might mean death was another matter.

Jori took the lead, intentionally this time. He faced the man with a loosened posture so he didn't fall into his military stance. "We're just trying to stay out of the way."

"You MEGAs?" The man thrust his chest out.

Jori almost stepped back but refused to be intimidated. "We're visitors here, like you. And we want to find someplace safe. The rioters are attacking everyone, not just MEGAs."

The man's eyes narrowed as he inspected them. He stopped on Rodrigo. "What's wrong with your eye?"

"Th-they threw something at me. It hurts."

"Yeah? Let me see." The man leaned toward him.

Without thinking, Jori maneuvered between them. "What for?"

"I'm trying to stop the bleeding," Rodrigo said. "If I let go, I could bleed out."

The man's skepticism remained as me moved on to Zaina. "What's your problem?"

Zaina's mouth opened, but she didn't speak.

Jori's heart skipped a beat. "She's terrified. Some people run when they're scared. Some fight. And some, like her, freeze."

"Look, we don't want any trouble," Rigo said. "We just wanna get somewhere safe."

The man considered it. His hesitation made Jori's neck ache from the tightness.

A woman who'd been foraging through a pile of discarded stuff straightened and pointed at Rigo. "Hey! Haven't I seen you before?"

Rodrigo wagged his head. "I-I don't know. It's a big station, but it's possible, ya know? Maybe—"

"I *have* seen you. I'm sure of it." She put her hands on her hips and squinted. "You're one of them, aren't you? That's why you're covering your eye."

Rigo backed up. "N-no. I'm just hurt is all."

She jabbed her finger. "You're a MEGA!"

Chusho! Jori gritted his teeth against the promise of violence.

Red rage took over the man's face. He lunged for Rodrigo. Jori moved in his way only to get shoved aside. Anticipating the move, he swept out his leg and tripped him. The resounding smack of the man crashing to the floor was followed by a snarl and curse.

"It's a MEGA!" The woman pointed at the now running Rodrigo. "Get him! Get him!"

"Run!" Jori snatched Zaina's arm and tugged. She took a halting step.

The wide-mouthed woman advanced, her anger twisting her features. "Hey! Are you one too?"

Jori yanked harder. Zaina staggered but didn't move fast enough to avoid the woman barreling in. Jori wheeled into her way, slapping her arm aside as she reached for Zaina. She raised her palm as though to slap him. He punched her in the gut, causing her to double over with a grunt.

Zaina screamed as the hefty man got to his feet and charged. Fortunately, it compelled her to break into a run. The enraged woman pounced for Jori. He dodged her and darted after Zaina, passing the man. People gawked as he and his two friends jetted onward, but even with the woman screaming about MEGA traitors enticed them away from their looting.

Rodrigo stopped at a gate and stabbed the comm button. "It's me—Mouse! I need in. Quick!"

Zaina reached Rigo's side and clutched his arm, panting like a rabbit that'd just escaped the jaws of a blackbeast. The hefty man charged with teeth bared. Jori pivoted and plowed into him. The man tried to push him off, but Jori's momentum made the move awkward. The two of them tumbled. Jori rolled aside. He grabbed something from an open suitcase and flung it. The shoe smacked the man in the face, making him bellow.

"Leave us alone!" Jori tossed a heavy bottle. The man shielded his head, but Jori hadn't aimed for that. The item plunged into the man's gut hard enough to evoke a grunt.

A hiss of equalizing pressure superseded the whine of the B11 dock hatch. Jori kept the man at bay with the contents of the suitcase until he was sure Rodrigo and Zaina were inside. He scrambled for something heavier than clothes as the man lunged for him. His fingers grasped something solid at the last moment. He flung it, then raced for the hatch and dove through. Landing on his hands and knees with a crack, he scuttled in. Rodrigo smacked the close button. The hatch lowered but not fast enough. The man belly-flopped halfway in. He snatched Jori's lower leg and pulled with the strength of a bear. Jori kicked with his other foot, smashing into the man's nose.

The man released him with a yowl and let go. "You'll get yours, you freaks!" He hollered as he backed out before the hatch closed on him.

The resounding click of the lock signaled their final separation from the hostilities. Jori rose, his breaths heaving. Rodrigo wrung his hands. Zaina braced herself against the wall and threw up.

When she finished, she wiped her hand across her mouth. Her eyes fell on Jori and her guardedness struck him like a punch in the gut. *Oh no.* He clutched a vain hope their situation had caused her emotions, but he suspected his violence had unsettled her.

His eyes stung as he glanced away from her judgment.

Rodrigo swept out his hand. "Here we go. The *Sublime Liberty*."

A new angst fell over Jori as he eyed the passageway. It was like any other tube that connected a ship to a station. The tunnel was made from a thick but flexible material reinforced with titanium segments that would close off in an emergency. If he were to view it from outside, he'd see a worm-like structure.

Only a few centimeters separated him from the void of space, but that wasn't what bothered him. Rigo was a cyborg. Were his shipmates too? Once again, he remembered how Gottfried had tried so hard to first sway then force Jori to side with MEGAs, and hoped it wouldn't be the same here.

He filled his lungs and straightened his shoulders. There was no turning back, even if he wanted to, so he might as well go forward. It helped that the ship's name promised succor.

While Rigo pressed the call button beside the door, Jori studied his features. Rodrigo was a youngish man, probably in his early twenties. He had short reddish-brown hair, no facial hair, and a square jaw. His non-enhanced eye had a narrowness like Jori's but more elongated and his lid heavier. Though lean, the slump of his shoulders almost resembled the mouse he'd claimed to be.

"Go ahead," a deep male voice responded through the comm.

"Hey, uh. I got Jori and a woman named Zaina here. Let us in."

Jori's blood seemed to turn to ice. *How did he know my name?*

8
Cyber Soldiers

Zaina Noman's stomach whirled like a blender chopping ice. She hunched and held her gut while attempting to blink the spots from her eyes. They were safe now, but a myriad of unpleasant images spun in her head. The most horrifying was the rage on that man's face as he'd tried to harm them. Her next thoughts swirled around imaginary fears as she and the others marched through the skywalk connecting them to an unfamiliar ship.

Recalling what Jori had done made her uneasy as well. She didn't mean to be wary of him. It wasn't like he'd been violent without provocation. Heck, he'd just saved her. But she kept seeing the cold determination on his face. The look reminded her of a big black cat she'd seen during a virtual nature experience. The intensity of its eyes as it stalked then attacked its prey matched the boy's in every way but the color. At least Jori hadn't been fierce like the man back home who'd assaulted her.

She jumped as the opposite hatch hissed open and the clomp of boots resounded through the walkway. A half dozen heavily armored soldiers entered, all carrying rifles and wearing helmets that hid their faces.

Rodrigo patted her arm. "It's alright. Those are my friends."

Her mouth fell open. Rigo's meek demeanor had made her think his ship was a civilian one, but these men screamed elite commandos.

"Don't worry," Rodrigo added. "We have more of our people out there, so they're going to help 'em."

She clutched her chest and leaned against the wall. The soldiers passed, radiating menace with their heavy strides and purposeful bearings.

Rigo nudged her shoulder. "We should get going."

Yes. Get moving. She wanted to but couldn't tear her eyes away from the soldiers' backs.

The lead one pressed the door panel. As the hatch to the station slid up, Zaina faltered from a wave of dizziness. Her vision compressed until all she saw were the people in the bay. The eyes of the big man who'd attacked them grew. He twisted his torso and looked ready to run. An energy blast struck his back. His limbs splayed like an octopus before crashing on the hard floor.

The man was dead. They'd killed him. Zaina didn't know how she knew his life had been extinguished, but she did. That man might've done away with her, but she couldn't quell her horror.

She retched, though nothing came out. Someone grabbed her arm and tugged. This time, her feet moved.

*****

Curses of pain and anger spewed from the docking bay as the soldiers opened fire. The big man lay dead. Another body sprawled nearby. The pain of death stabbed through Jori's head. It rivaled the foreboding writhing in his gut, making it difficult to rein in his emotions.

The lack of lifeforces from those soldiers meant they were augmented even more so than Rigo. Not a hint of emotion emanated from them as they indiscriminately murdered people. He was on a ship of MEGAs—MEGAs who knew his name. It was Gottfried all over again.

"Let's go," Rigo said, tugging on his arm.

Jori yanked out of his hold, intent on getting out of here. Rodrigo released him but kept going with Zaina. Jori halted and worked the dryness from his mouth. He couldn't abandon her, but he probably couldn't convince her to go with him either. He had a sinking feeling the soldiers wouldn't let him leave anyway. Besides, where would he go? The space station wasn't any safer. The discordance detected by his ability told him several battles waged throughout the station. People were dying everywhere.

Chusho. He decided to stay with Zaina and jogged after her. It was a vain hope, but maybe they'd be safe with these MEGAs.

He passed through the threshold onto the *Sublime Liberty* and halted. A new panic clutched his throat as he met another squad of soldiers. Only one had a lifeforce and it was too weak for him to get a reading.

Zaina's emotions flared as two massive soldiers held her between them. Rigo wrung his hands and smiled tentatively. Jori's knees buckled at the triumph he emitted. The tiny hope that he'd only imagined Rigo saying his name snuffed out like a flame in a vacuum.

"It'll be alright," Rodrigo said. "We won't hurt you. But my boss wants us to put you in the brig for a while… Only until we sort this out." He cast a sideways glance at Zaina.

Jori's fear flipped into anger. "It's not a coincidence that we ran into you, is it? You came for us on purpose."

Rigo bobbed his head. "Yes. Yes. But only because you're important."

Chusho. Somehow MEGA-Man's operatives had kept track of him. As impossible as it seemed, Rodrigo had even known to find in the vents.

"Important?" Zaina asked, swaying as though about to faint. "Important how?" She glanced at Jori, her wariness spiking once again.

Jori didn't answer. If she was afraid of him now, she'd be more terrified to learn he was the son of the Dragon Emperor.

"You're both important," Rodrigo said. Jori doubted this was true, but Rigo believed his own words. "Now, please, come with me. I promise you'll be treated well. These are my friends, ya know. Good people. Good people."

Jori sensed his honesty but still didn't believe it. His temper burned, but he obeyed. The time for getting out of this mess would present itself.

Zaina nodded, but then she shook her head and Jori felt her growing distrust. "This isn't right. We're supposed to be on the station. We have a transport coming up and we need to be on it. I'm his advocate. I need to—"

"No!" Rigo wrung his hands. "It's not safe there. You'll get hurt. Or worse… Killed."

Jori eyed him, doubting the cause of his panic. He regarded the soldiers surrounding them and deflated. "It's too late," he said to Zaina. "There's no going back."

"But we must!" Zaina cried, struggling with vain against her captors.

Rodrigo grinned. "It's okay. You'll be safe here. I promise."

Zaina looked to Jori. "Can you tell whether he's telling the truth?"

Jori hesitated. Rigo wasn't lying, but only because he believed they were truly safe. Explaining this to Zaina wouldn't help the situation, so he simply answered her question. "Yes."

The soldiers escorted them through a hall painted in pure white. A metallic smell mingled with antiseptic, magnifying the cleanliness of this place. Not even the Cooperative ships he'd been on had been this immaculate.

Occasional windows revealed workrooms or labs that were just as pristine. They seemed ordinary enough until he passed one that looked like a hospital room. A bald woman lay in a bed. Her skin was nearly as white as the surrounding walls. Tubes and wires radiated from her head and chest.

Jori almost choked from the chill that spread over him.

Zaina cried out. "W-what are they doing to her?"

"She's alright," Rigo said. "That's Quintina. She's been having trouble with her CPU, so they had to do surgery."

Zaina gasped. "Oh my God."

Jori shared her sentiment, though no god had any part in this. This was humanity's doing.

The soldiers ushered them along without speaking or even bothering to look at them. Like machines, they had a purpose, and they acted with no thought or concern. Jori couldn't see their faces, but he imagined them all as stone-faced as Gottfried's super-soldiers.

His heart drummed so hard, he was sure it'd burst from his chest. He was a prisoner once again, but this time with no real allies. Before all this, he had Commander Hapker to protect him. Zaina was his advocate now. He couldn't have asked for a better one, but not in this situation. Her emotions had too much control over her—and she probably hated him.

They took a conveyor. When the car halted, the soldiers pressed around him, forcing him out. Jori eyed the gloomy corridor. The walls here might have once been white. The lower half was now soiled brown or dirty grey where the paint had peeled off. A wet, rotting odor permeated the air and turned his stomach.

The plasti-glass cell doors were so smeared with grime, he could barely see through them. Inside was worse. The floor was empty but filthy. Brown and black blotches coated nearly every surface except the yellowed mattress of the bed. He grimaced. Not even the brig on his father's ship was this disgusting.

Zaina covered her mouth. Jori thought she'd throw up again, but she bent over and sobbed instead.

"It's just temporary," Rigo said as he patted her shoulder.

She wouldn't go inside, so the soldiers picked her up and put her in as though moving a piece of furniture. Jori fought a wave of dizziness and reluctantly followed.

The plasti-glass door squealed shut. The lock clanked in place with finality. Zaina's despair heightened Jori's own but he didn't cry. He stood there, unmoving, without a single thought running through his head. After all, there was no point. His fate was as well-sealed as the door of his cage.

9
Prisoners

Despair pervaded every centimeter of the prison. It shifted through the air and clung to the walls like a festering infection. Shadows melded with the lighted glow into a seamless dredge.

Jori sat on the rickety bed beside Zaina and patted her shoulder. It surprised him she had any tears left. He wanted to cry too but forced the useless emotions aside.

This wasn't the first time he'd found himself in a cell. After Commander Hapker had rescued him from his father, the Prontaean Cooperative authorities raised a fuss. More than the political ramifications of taking the Dragon Emperor's son were at stake. Jori's turbulent history with a Cooperative expedition vessel compelled them to put him in the brig of a military ship.

Jori's spirit had fallen to an all-time low, a little like how Zaina was now but less anxious and more ready to give up. If not for the commander, he might've.

His sinuses burned at the memory of Hapker's warm hazel eyes. The man was a solider but unlike any soldier he'd ever met. Rather than be filled with hate and full of a burning desire to fight, Hapker treated everyone with an amenable respect and only fought as a last resort. As a child raised in a warrior society, this was a novelty. The commander provided a perspective Jori had never experienced before, and one that felt right.

If only Hapker were here now. He'd know just what to do and what to say to instill optimism, something both he and Zaina desperately needed.

An approaching lifeforce diverted his attention. It didn't seem hostile, but he kept his hope at bay anyway. "I'll be over here for when someone comes," he told Zaina as he pointed at the door and rose.

She grasped his hand and met his eyes. "I'm sorry."

He dipped his head, not knowing what else to say, and peered through the cell door. A man in a royal blue uniform arrived with two seemingly lifeless armored soldiers. This time, they wore no helmets—and were as stone-faced as he'd imagined.

The man in the sharp uniform bore a leaner frame. His curly light brown hair and matching beard seemed too scruffy for a soldier. It didn't help that his eyes appeared half closed as though he was tired. But his lifeforce emitted alertness tainted with self-importance and ambition.

The plasti-glass door opened with a high-pitched grind. Jori automatically fell into his military stance with his hands clasped behind him and his shoulders pulled back. The man smiled down at him. Disdain flashed through his emotions so quickly, Jori wondered whether it'd been there at all.

"Greetings. I'm Major Abelard Blakesley. And you must be Jori—Jori Tran now, as I understand it."

A wave of dizziness almost made Jori's knees give out. Tran was the new surname given to him by the Cooperative authorities when they'd agreed to make him a citizen. That this man knew it meant some of MEGA-Man's operatives were still hidden within the Cooperative ranks—and they definitely wanted him for something, just like Gottfried had. This whole thing had been an elaborate trap, and, like a fool, he'd been caught.

He clenched his teeth, letting anger overcome his fear. A biting remark lurked just behind his lips, but he kept it there. Sensei Jeruko had taught him better than to make idle threats. It was better to wait, observe, and evaluate, then leap from the tall grass like a blackbeast out for blood.

Blakesley's eyes fell on Zaina and his smile softened. "And who is this?"

"Z-Zaina Noman," she replied. "I'm his caregiver."

"Ah. Caregiver. I see." Blakesley exuded a pleasantness that grew when he regarded her. "Lovely to meet you."

Zaina stood, her eyes wide with desperation. "Let us out of here. Please. Let us go. We've done nothing wrong. All I wanted to do was get him away from the violence." She placed her hand on Jori's shoulder, causing his knees to nearly buckle under the weight of her attempt to provide him comfort. He savored the sensation, relieved that she'd still be there for him despite her crippling emotions.

Blakesley dipped his head. "You're safe here. As far as getting out of this cell, I'm sure that will happen soon enough. But it's not my decision."

Jori frowned. "Whose is it?"

"His name is Vance. He's our captain but doesn't like to be called that. You must always call him Vance, and he'll be along shortly."

"Why are we locked up?" Jori asked. "You can't possibly be worried we'll make trouble."

"No. Certainly not." Blakesley emitted a condescension that didn't show on his face. "But we can't allow you freedom on our ship until we impart the rules and complete a security check. How do I know you're not more than you seem?"

His knowing smile made the back of Jori's neck prickle. "We're no threat to you."

A flicker of doubt flittered through Blakesley's emotions, but he dipped his head. "I'm inclined to agree and will pass my opinion along to Vance." He bowed once more, then activated the closing mechanism.

Jori advanced. "Wait! I have questions. Where are—" The prison door shut.

"In due time," Blakesley replied, then left.

Jori huffed. The promise of being let out after a security check didn't ease his mind any more than the man himself. Blakesley was a soldier—possibly a MEGA soldier up to no good considering the galactic political upheaval. Even though he'd spoken the truth at every turn, Jori knew he was caught in a web of trouble.

"I don't understand why we're in this place." Zaina glanced about the cell, her brow curling in anguish. "It's horrible. Why would Rodrigo bring us here?"

Jori grasped her hand, hoping to keep her from spiraling back down into terror. She flinched instead, then cleared her throat and clasped her hands in front of her.

Guilt crept up in Jori's middle, though he didn't understand what to be ashamed of. "Don't worry," he said, pretending she hadn't jerked away from him like he was some sort of disease. "Blakesley was telling the truth."

Her shoulders fell. "Thank goodness." Her eyes tilted as she smiled at him. It was forced, but he also got the sense her attempt was genuine. "Thanks for helping us," she added, a hint of fear lurking behind her words.

"But…" Her brows furrowed, so he pressed on. "You're scared of me now."

Her breath wavered as she inhaled. "Not scared. I-I'm just surprised at how easily you handled it. You seemed so…" She shook her head and massaged her temple.

Jori dropped his chin to his chest and tried not to fiddle his fingers. "The place I'm from, it was dangerous. If I hadn't learned to defend myself, I'd be dead." Hell, he *should* be dead. He'd escaped many threats to his life but only the goodwill of Commander Hapker and his captain enabled him to survive his father's wrath.

She reached out, probably to offer a consoling touch, but dropped her arm at the last moment. "I understand, but hopefully that savagery is behind us."

Jori glanced away. Did she intend to imply *he* was savage too? "I didn't mean to scare you."

"I know. And I didn't mean to…" She filled her lungs and exhaled slowly. "The things in your file. I didn't want to believe them."

"I don't hurt people," Jori replied hurriedly. "Whatever my file says I did, I did in defense. Same with those in the docking bay. I was afraid of what they'd do to us—to you."

She wiped her eye with a knuckle. "I understand. I've just never seen—"

"I won't do it again," Jori interjected. "I don't want to be a warrior anymore. Believe me. I only want to—"

The main door to the brig opened. Jori only sensed Blakesley, but another came with him. This one also wore a royal blue uniform, but his was enhanced with black armor trimmed with silver. No insignia indicated his rank, but Jori didn't doubt this was the man in charge—Blakesley had called him Vance.

Vance was as big as a senshi warrior and carried himself with the same dangerous purpose. His head was shaved the same way as some senshi, but he looked nothing like Jori's people. His face was a little fleshier than the sharp-boned warriors back home, and bore a broad flat nose and a dimpled chin.

The man planted himself before the plasti-glass prison door with his hands behind him in a solid military stance. His eyes drilled into Jori like a hungry blackbeast, and he wore the kind of smile a spider might give a fly.

Jori barely detected his lifeforce and shivered at how void of compassion it was. He swallowed down his anxiety and jutted his chin. "What do you want with me?"

No one answered. Vance remained as unmoving as a statue while Major Blakesley turned away, emitting irritation. The major tapped the panel by the door and a subtle hum denoted the activation of a sound barrier. His lips moved as he spoke to Vance, but Jori didn't hear a word. Neither the emotions nor the features of the two men conveyed what their conversation entailed.

Jori held Vance's persistent stare despite how it made his skin crawl. After countless agonizing seconds, he questioned his resolve. The man was likely a cyborg and could probably do this for hours.

Jori gritted his teeth. He must not show fear. His father always said emotion was a weakness. In this case, it was true.

More time crept by. Jori's legs ached and his heart raced. Still, the man didn't waver.

Jori could stand it no longer. He glanced away with a growl. "Chima," he muttered, hoping to display enough defiance to make up for quitting the staring game.

He returned to Zaina with an unsettling feeling weighing him down. When the men left, Jori blew out the breath he'd been holding.

Zaina covered her mouth and choked out another sob. Jori broke from his own fear and put his arm over her shoulder. He wanted to tell her it would be alright but couldn't bring himself to lie.

10
Space Debris

Major Abelard Blakesley shifted his weight. The bridge of the *Black Thresher*, aka *Sublime Liberty*, made him yearn for the openness of an arena. A tight circle of workstations lined the entire room. The crew had only a little maneuverability, but it didn't matter. Half were so cybernetic, they no longer acknowledged discomfort. The only person who had space sat in the oversized captain's chair in the middle area. And unfortunately, this man was the only one who mattered.

Blakesley side-eyed Vance and hoped he hid his loathing well enough that the man couldn't sense it. He'd barely kept any of his emotions in check today. Bringing that boy on board had triggered resentment. Now he was compelled to partake in a massacre.

He watched the largest of the front viewscreens with a bitterness rising in his throat. A close-up image of the Avalon space station took up the entire scene. Its double gravity wheels were only a half kilometer in diameter, but large enough to house over a thousand shops and residential spaces. The main rotating drum in the middle was about the same width while the height of its fanning solar panels extended further. The station rotated around a red dwarf star, its panels always facing it and glowing a darker red. When viewed from the side, they resembled bloody daggers.

A digitized dashed yellow line spread from the bottom screen to the station. The line struck. Vance's stiff features remained the same, but an ugly glint sparked his eyes. Blakesley soured as he waited for the light waves to travel back to their sensors. A brief explosion from the uppermost ring sent debris hurling in all directions. The fire snuffed out almost as soon as it had started, leaving only glowing embers clinging to the last bit of oxygen.

Blakesley squirmed in his seat.

"You should be enjoying this," Vance said from the raised chair beside him. "The space station harbors our oppressors."

"MEGAs too." *And numerous other innocent people.*

"We gave them a warning. It's not our fault they didn't listen."

Still seems like a waste. MEGAs had disabled the station's shields. Some returned to the *Black Thresher* in time, but others stayed to ensure the defenses remained down. They knew their fate and accepted it. Of course, some were so computer-like, they no longer *had* a sense of self-preservation.

Apparently, MEGA-Man had planned this attack. Arrive in like a civilian ship with the innocuous name of *Sublime Liberty*, then switch the transponders to the *Black Thresher*—an unknown MEGA ship—and strike. Come to find out, even the news story that triggered the MEGA-haters had been staged. Blakesley marveled at MEGA-Man's ability to pull strings and wished he'd helped orchestrate it. He might've gone about it a little differently by not sacrificing as many people. But with Vance being the favorite, Blakesley was often confined to the sidelines.

The soft tremor of another weapon-fire ran through the *Black Thresher*. The corresponding dashed line appeared on the display. A different section of the space station blew apart. Although Blakesley had no friends there, Vance's coldness to killing thousands of people sent a shiver down to his toes. The man took life without thought or remorse, which made him more dangerous than anyone else here.

Vance fired several more times before ordering the ship to depart. The retreat was unnecessary since the riots on the station kept everyone too busy to launch an effective counterattack. But a series of other unpleasant tasks called them away.

Blakesley swallowed down his distaste and set the coordinates for their next mission. Although this one would also be bloody, he looked forward to it. A chance at direct revenge with no innocent bystanders was more his style. He was a soldier, not a demented, blood-lusting beast.

*****

Jori's dream exploded into a nightmare. One moment he was racing through the forest, the next, leaves burst into flames and screams blared among the trees. The pain of death seared into his soul like an exploding star.

The image disappeared as his mind woke, but the residual sensation of hundreds of voices shouting in anguish remained. He wrapped his arms around his head, hoping to stop the clamor, and moaned. Just as it lessened, a new burst shot through his skull.

People were dying. They were far away, but their numbers amplified their terror. He wasn't certain what had happened, but he had a guess. The space station they'd been on was now space junk.

Who'd done it and why? Did the battle get so bad that the station guards resorted to blowing protestors up? Or had the protestors found a stash of explosives and took it upon themselves to destroy the MEGAs? Or worse, the ship he was on had attacked.

Regardless, this MEGA dispute had erupted into a war. Everyone was in danger now. Not just him and Zaina, but people all over the known galaxy would respond with violence. He was in more trouble now than ever.

11
Rules

The pain of death had long since vanished, but the memory of the massacre ate at Jori's insides. Thanks to his father's warmongering, he'd experienced this type of pain many times before. The difference was he no longer had anyone to help him deal with it.

He touched the necklace under his shirt. If Mother were here, she'd stroke his hair while he rested his head in her lap. Sensei Jeruko would offer to lead a meditation session. Or Commander Hapker would say the right comforting words of wisdom.

Oh, and his brother—he'd tell Jori to suck it up. The thought almost made him laugh. His brother's attitude had always been harder. He still had a good heart, though—or at least he used to. He was dead now, as was Sense Jeruko.

Jori exhaled in a whisper like a soft keening. He forced himself out of bed. The fogginess in his head and the ache in his body groaned in protest. Although he wanted to surrender to more sleep, lying around wouldn't help him out of this situation.

Zaina was awake as well yet remained curled up under the meager blanket. Her numb emotions weren't a good thing.

When he'd been in that state, Commander Hapker had helped by taking him to the gymnasium. That wasn't possible now.

"Would you like to join me for a little tai chi?" he asked.

"I just want to lie here," she replied in a weak voice.

Her despondency weighed heavily on his own, but he pushed through. "I know it's hard but getting up and stretching will help." She didn't respond. Hapker had made a similar statement, which Jori also ignored. It wasn't until the commander offered it as a joint activity that he finally got up. Maybe it'd work with Zaina, too. "I can teach you and we can do it together."

As hoped, that last part made her stir. She filled her lungs, inspiring motivation, and rose. The stress of the situation etched her features. Her shoulders slumped, her eyes drooped and the skin under them sagged. The wrinkles in her clothes complemented the dishevelment of her hair.

She sat there, unmoving and looking down at the floor. Jori approached and touched the top of her hand. She snapped upright as though surprised to see him there.

"Will you join me?" he asked.

She managed a smile and stood. Jori relaxed at how she no longer seemed afraid of him. He explained the proper breathing method and showed her the beginning moves. She followed along halfheartedly at first, but her mood lifted as they progressed. His did as well, though the worry about their situation lurked in the back of his mind.

Two familiar sensations neared, breaking his concentration and triggering his apprehension. "Hey," he said to Zaina. "Major Blakesley and Rodrigo are coming."

Her emotions jumped with eagerness. "You think they're gonna let us out?"

He shrugged. She waited at the plasti-glass door and fixed her gaze on the brig entrance. When the men appeared, she broke into a grin. Rodrigo returned it. His posture slumped, but this seemed to be his natural pose. He also wrung his hands, though Jori didn't sense any nervousness.

Blakesley carried himself with the same military mien as before. After opening the cell door, he planted himself before them and clasped his hands behind his back. It matched Jori's stance, although his held more impatience than discipline.

Zaina pressed her palms in prayer. "Oh, thank God. Rigo. Where are we? Why are we here?"

"It's okay. It's okay. These are my friends. They just want to make sure you're good peoples, ya know? I told them you were, but they have their rules. They gotta—"

Blakesley cleared his throat. "We've checked out your records and agree you are welcome guests. I'll take you to better accommodations as soon as we get a bio scan and cover some ground rules."

"Bio scan?" Zaina asked.

Blakesley dipped his head and smiled. It seemed genuine for her, but he exuded a sourness when he looked at Jori. "We have sensitive areas where you're not permitted, and our biometric authentications systems will ensure you can't go there."

All ships had restricted certain areas, but the way Blakesley said it made Jori wonder what they were hiding. "What kind of vessel is this?"

"It's a multi-purpose ship. We have scientists here as well as a military force."

"Who do you work for?" Jori asked, though he suspected the answer.

Blakesley's lip curled, but he turned it into a smile and jutted his chin. "I am the major of a MEGA unit and I serve justice."

A sourness rose in Jori's throat. He'd heard something similar from Gottfried about how serving justice meant getting equality for cyborgs, even at the cost of innocent people. "Did *you* attack that space station?"

Both Blakesley's and Zaina's eyes widened, although hers were more shocked at the news. Blakesley seemed more surprised that Jori knew. He worked his jaw as though contemplating an answer. "You will need to ask Vance about that."

The saliva in Jori's mouth dried up. The reply was as good as saying yes.

Blakesley waved for them to follow him. "Rule number one, you may only visit places we've given you access to. I'll send you a list. Don't worry if you make a mistake. A failed bio-scan will alert you. If you sneak or force yourself into a restricted area, there will be swift and painful consequences."

Zaina's throat bobbed, though that last part seemed directed at Jori.

"Two. You'll follow Vance's orders. Never question them. He doesn't like it. His punishments are far worse than anything I'd do."

Jori clenched his ice-cold hands.

Zaina swayed. her hand flew to her chest. "Oh my."

Blakesley halted. His brows twisted. "No need to worry, miss," he said with no reassurance in his voice. "Just follow the rules and you'll be fine."

She didn't seem convinced but nodded.

Blakesley took her arm in his and smiled. "It'll be alright. I promise."

Jori hid his surprise at his tenderness. His emotions weren't quite compassion, but close enough that she emitted relief and let him lead her along.

They left the brig and came upon a security office manned by a hefty woman with a myriad of cybernetic parts. From eye to lower jaw and neck to her bionic arm, metal plates, rods, and wires connected and interwove through her, giving her a more sinister look than her aura suggested. That she still had a lifeforce amazed him. But perhaps most of her augmentations had been to the body rather than the brain.

She eyed them as they passed. Her emotions flickered in interest when she regarded Blakesley. Then jealousy for Zaina. And for Jori, an unexpected curiosity and respect. Jori wanted to rub away the discomfort crawling up his arms but kept a formal demeanor.

"The third rule," Blakesley continued, "is you'll say no disparaging words against MEGAs. You helped this man." He flicked his hand at Rodrigo, who bobbed his head eagerly. "So we'll help you."

"And what will you do with us?" Jori asked in a challenging tone. "We have someplace we're supposed to be."

"You will stay on this ship until we complete our mission."

Jori detected a lie, and it made his heart race. If Vance had the same plans for him as Gottfried, then he was in serious trouble. "And what mission is that?" he demanded, trying to keep up the pretense of being brave.

"That is not your business."

Chusho. Since they'd already attacked a space station, he suspected their next assignment involved more killing. He'd hoped being a part of the Cooperative meant living a more peaceful life, but violent people found him no matter where he went.

They moved closer to the right wall of the corridor as a yellow cleaning bot whirred by. A sweet yet tangy scent followed it, reminding him of a juicy orange fruit he'd had on Hapker's ship. Taller than Jori, the bot resembled other cleaning bots he'd seen except it washed both the walls and the floors. No wonder this place gleamed with sterility.

Zaina wrung her hands. "C-can I contact my boss? Tell him we'll be delayed?"

"That is up to Vance."

Jori didn't like the sound of that. "When can we talk to him? To Vance?"

Blakesley shrugged. "If he wants to talk, he'll send for you."

Jori gritted his teeth but also swallowed down his dread.

Damn it. Being trapped on a ship full of MEGAs seemed much worse than when he'd been detained on a Cooperative battleship. At least the Cooperative had to act in accordance with their guiding principles. He doubted the people here had those scruples.

The weight of his predicament settled into his bones.

12
We're the Same

A feeble glow of pallid light revealed a space as gloomy as Jori's mood. He slouched on the padded metal chair in their new quarters. The room was small, barely big enough for their beds, the tiny kitchen area, and the bathroom with a curtain for a door. The desolate brown walls were as mundane as the flat grey tiles of the floor. Even his chair was a dull neutral color. Not a single piece of décor added any brightness. It was as utilitarian as his bedroom on his father's ship, yet somehow more depressing.

Whatever Vance intended, it didn't seem immediately nefarious, though Jori worried. Had he killed a bunch of people on the station in defense or offense? And what was this other mission Blakesley had mentioned?

He wished Hapker was here. At least the commander would discuss their situation. All Zaina wanted to do was rest. He glanced over at her as she slumped over the table with her head cradled in the crook of her arm. She wasn't asleep, but she might as well have been. Not even resignation emanated from her.

The door comm buzzed. Zaina startled from her repose, causing a squeak to the metal table as it strained against the bolts that fixed it to the floor.

Jori eased from his seat. A trickle of boredom came from outside their room. "It's alright. I don't sense any hostility."

He activated the door. It swished open to reveal several things at once—emerald green eyes, jet-black hair, pointed chin, and a blindingly white lab coat. Though the man's features were jarring, his lifeforce was dull.

"Hello. You must be Jori."

"Yes." Jori didn't bother saying more, staying neutral until he got his bearings.

"I'm Doctor Humphrey. I'm here to escort you. Vance wishes to speak to you."

Zaina rose from her own chair and bumped the table, causing her tea to jiggle and splash.

The doctor waved her down. "Just the boy."

Her sudden irritation energized her. "Most certainly not. I'm his guardian and I will accompany him."

The doctor cleared his throat. "That's not a good idea, ma'am. Vance gave an order. I cannot disobey."

Uneasiness wafted from the man, making Jori's spine tingle. This was the second time someone had alluded to Vance's hardline nature.

"It's alright," Jori said to Zaina.

"It most certainly is not alright," she replied in a heated tone. "I don't care if he's the captain. I'm not leaving you."

Doctor Humphrey hissed as his demeanor snapped from calm to angry. "If you know what's good for you, you'll refer to him as *Vance*, ma'am."

Jori's heart pattered. He turned to Zaina with an imploring look. "Please. I should go alone. We don't know what Vance is like—"

"Which is why I should go with you." She planted her hands on her hips.

Jori spoke calmly, hoping she'd hear the caution in his tone. "It won't help. We've been warned about how he expects his orders to be followed, so I think we should listen."

"I can't let you go alone. What if he tries to hurt you?"

"Begging your pardon, ma'am," the doctor said, "but if Vance wants to hurt him, he will. There's nothing you can do to stop it."

A sizzle ran down Jori's spine. "Zaina, please. He's right. Don't worry. I doubt he would've given us our own quarters if he intended to harm us."

She shook her head. "It doesn't feel right."

Jori agreed. "We don't have a choice. We're at his mercy. I've been in enough situations like this to know what I can fight and what I can't."

Her eyes turned down with pity. "Oh my, child. I'm so sorry you had to go through things like that. You shouldn't have to again."

Jori shrugged it off. Although he hated the uncertainty and the creepiness surrounding this new state of affairs, his experience told him to keep a level head, analyze the situation, and proceed with caution. "I'll be alright."

Her eyes watered, but she blinked the tears away and sighed.

With a little more coaxing, she finally agreed. He followed Doctor Humphrey, studying the curved hallway, its intersections, the placements of the toolboxes and first aid kits, and anything else that told him what kind of ship he was on. Sensei Jeruko had made him memorize the layout of every large spaceship in the known galaxy, but this one wasn't familiar.

Its ceiling was taller than in most other ships. The halls curved but angularly, as though he walked around a hectogon. Oddly, one corridor had an inclined hallway and turned at a forty-five degree angle. Even the gravitational pull here felt different.

The conveyor was stranger still. Except for the floor, the car was oval rather than rectangular. And again, it was taller than expected. After he got inside and they traveled to their destination, it seemed to run differently as well. The ride was smoother and quieter, and he didn't detect the turns.

MEGAs must have their own ships now. The thought prickled his spine.

They exited the conveyor to a wider, brighter corridor. A clean, crisp aroma permeated the air. The colorful pattern of the carpeted floor hurt his eyes. The bright yellow walls too. Most useless were the tables along the inner curve that were decorated with statues, vases, and other artistic décor. The opulence reminded him of the palaces of the more arrogant lords back home. Either this Vance guy was important or just thought highly of himself.

When they reached a broad ornamental door that looked more like the entrance to a throne room, his anxiety increased. Someone this egotistical would not be easy to deal with.

Before Doctor Humphrey pressed the comm button, the door swished open. Jori startled, then collected himself with the jut of his chin.

Vance loomed over him with a smile that seemed to gloat. "There you are. I've been waiting."

"S-sorry, S-sir." Humphrey said. "I came as fast as I could,"

Vance ignored him and stared at Jori with an inexplicable interest. "Come in. Have a seat."

He moved aside and let Jori pass, not once taking his eyes off him. Jori controlled his breathing, trying to ease the fluttering of his stomach. He entered a room that was more lavish than the hallway and almost threw up. The feeling likely came from his nervousness, but he had to give some credit to the plush furniture, lush ivory carpet, giant decorative urns, ornate lamps, and the gaudy tapestries depicting detailed scenes.

He took the chair that seemed the least ostentatious. At first, he thought it was faux leather, but the soft yet grainy texture plus the hint of musk wafting from it suggested it'd been made from a real animal. This was indeed a luxury considering the furnishings of most ships tended to be fabricated from easily recycled material.

Vance grasped another padded armchair and slid it over before him. With the ease of a satiated lion, he sat and leaned forward with his elbows on his knees. His gold-flecked brown eyes bored like a laser drill. Jori stifled the urge to squirm and held his own gaze.

"Don't be nervous," Vance finally said.

Jori flinched inwardly. He'd been holding a flat expression and blocking his emotions, so the man must've guessed.

A gloating smile spread across Vance's face. "My sentio ability is much stronger than yours."

Jori suppressed a shiver and concentrated harder on his mental wall. The staring contest went on for another few minutes until he could stand it no longer. "Why do you keep looking at me like that?"

"We're the same, you and I."

Jori swallowed the saliva that sprang into his mouth.

"Yeah," Vance continued with that same mocking smile. "I know what you are. You can't hide it from me."

Terror sizzled in Jori's veins. Vance knew he was the Dragon Emperor's last surviving heir. Then again, maybe he didn't and was only trying to get him to confess. Jori dared not divulge anything. Like Sensei Jeruko always said, "*It's best to keep your skills to yourself. That way, you have the advantage of surprise.*"

"Can my guardian make a call?"

"No one's calling anybody," Vance replied, still not moving his eyes.

"She's supposed to take me to Marvdacht. If she doesn't, people might come looking for us."

"*Marvdacht.*" His lips curled and Jori sensed something from him. It was deep, almost imperceptible, but there like a volcano ready to explode. "You don't want to go to that place."

He didn't, but he didn't want to be here either. "I trust her—my guardian. Her name is Zaina. Perhaps Marvdacht is unpleasant, but she's not. She needs to call her boss."

Vance smacked the arm of his chair and lurched forward, causing Jori to press into the back of his own chair. "No one's calling anybody!"

Adrenaline shot through Jori's veins. His mental wall slipped.

Vance eased away, the hateful glower still present. Jori swayed under a wave of dizziness. An oppressive heat fell over him, making it difficult to take in air. He forced himself to sit upright.

When the quivering in his chin subsided, he wet his mouth and asked, "What will you do with us?"

Like a switch, Vance's fury cut off and he was back to his hard, flat look. "Nothing… If you behave."

Sweat trickled down the side of Jori's face. He swept it away like he was angry, but it was an act. Despite having dealt with violent people his entire life, this man terrified him. Was it some kind of power or did the outburst simply remind him of his father?

"Will we ever be allowed to leave?" Jori asked.

"We'll see."

Jori swallowed down the hard lump that had formed in his throat. "So what do you want now? Why am I here in your quarters?"

Vance's smug smile returned. "We're the same, you and I."

13
Anxiety Attack

Zaina Noman's heart strained as though ensnared by a tangle of thorns. She paced up and down the hall. The major had said they could leave their room, but she imagined a bunch of hard-faced soldiers appearing to force her back inside. Honestly, that didn't bother her as much as Jori being gone. Her stomach jittered so much that she suspected it would lurch to her throat at any moment. She wrung her hands and bit her lip, hoping the pain would distract her.

This wasn't right. She shouldn't have let the boy go alone. Who knew what Vance would do to him? He could be hurting Jori and here she was doing nothing. Some advocate she was.

I must get to him before it's too late. Her fear of violence paled compared to her worry about Jori. She ignored the whispering that said the excruciating terror would prevail once she met danger head-on. For now, her mind was made up.

She headed down the empty hall with near purposeful strides. The thin carpet muffled her hasty steps. Doors lined the way, telling her this was a residential area, yet she hadn't seen a single soul. Encouraging but eerie.

The cool air caused her to shake—or was that from her nervousness? She reached the conveyor, pressed the button, and waited for the car. A minute passed, and still no car. A prickling sensation formed in her fingertips and spread to her hands. She wrung them, but nothing changed.

Her heart palpitated. *Not this again.* An anxiety attack was the last thing she needed right now. She attempted to regulate her breathing the way her doctor had advised but couldn't concentrate.

The car finally arrived. The double doors slid open with annoying slowness. She pushed inside and pressed her hand to the bio-sensor. It beeped its approval. She pulled away, hugging the side wall. A wave of heat swept through her. If she didn't get her anxiety under control soon, she'd faint. She opened her mouth to tell the computer where to go, only she had no idea where Jori was. Surely the captain had an office somewhere.

"Captain's office," she managed to say. The interface buzzed in a grating tone, signifying her command was invalid. *That's right. He likes to be called by name.* "Vance's office."

It beeped again. Her head spun with both anguish and dizziness. With the car door remaining open, a whoosh of air entered and chilled her. Her breaths quickened. She heaved but nothing came up. Her mouth was dry. She placed one hand on her chest and the other against the wall and panted.

Even knowing the cause of these symptoms, she couldn't help but think the worst. What if it wasn't an anxiety attack after all? What if it was a heart attack? Who would help Jori if she died? What about all the children she watched over? Sareena was only covering for her temporarily. She was too old to carry out her position for long. Who'd take over then? And would they know how to soothe Guita after a nightmare or manage Elias when he had a meltdown? Oh, and poor Adela. She was such a sweet girl. If anyone said something harsh, she'd wilt.

The tingling sensation moved to the back of her neck and her face. She slumped in the corner of the car and put her head between her knees. *This is stupid.* She was too young for a heart attack. All she had to do was force herself to breathe normally. She could do this. She *had* to do this.

"Oh my! What happened?" someone outside the car yelled.

She was too disoriented to register who. Their footsteps echoed as they entered the car. An arm wrapped around her shoulder.

"Are you alright?"

She raised her head. Major Blakesley knelt beside her with wide eyes. She tried to nod but was too weak.

"Infirmary!" he called out.

For a moment, she wondered who the heck he was talking to. Then the doors closed and the car moved. Relief fell over her and she found it easier to breathe.

"My dear, please tell me what's wrong," Blakesley said with his brow wrinkled with worry.

She appreciated his genuineness, and it eased her somewhat. "I wasn't allowed…" The stress continued to affect her. She filled her lungs and tried again. "I couldn't go with Jori to see your boss."

"Ah. Yes. Well, Vance doesn't consider the wishes of others when he gives his orders. I assure you that Jori will be alright, though."

"I'm supposed to accompany him." Her voice came out in a whine. "It's not just my job, it's the law."

"Hmm. Another thing Vance doesn't think about." He patted her hand. "Don't worry. Your charge is in safe hands."

She rubbed her brow. She believed *him*, but not this Vance guy.

The doors opened. Blakesley put his arm under her shoulder and hauled her up. "Help!" he called out. "Someone help her!" He half carried her as her weakened legs refused to work.

Two medics arrived and picked her up. The androgynous one turned, revealing a metal plate with ports on the side of its head, nearly making her choke. *My God! Why would anyone do that to themselves?*

Her breath hitched in rapid succession. New tears fell.

Blakesley made a noise that almost sounded like an irritated groan, but the way he rushed back to her side and grasped her hand told her she'd been mistaken.

"My dear lady!" he said with unfeigned concern. "Everything will be alright. I promise."

They hauled her onto a bed and the androgynous cyborg placed an oxygen mask over her nose. She gulped in the sweet air as more tears streamed down the sides of her face.

The cyborg ran a scanning device down her. "Classic anxiety attack," he said in a monotone voice. "Current treatment sufficient." Like a robot, he set down the scanner, turned at a strict one hundred eighty degrees, and walked away.

Blakesley grasped her hand. "Thank goodness. A beautiful lady such as yourself shouldn't have to suffer."

Without meaning to, she chuckled.

"What's so funny?" he asked in mock offense. "I'm serious."

She lifted the mask long enough to speak. "You're quite the charmer."

An amused grin spread across his face. "Guilty. I'm serious about how lovely you are, though."

She wagged her head, suppressing a bashful giggle. His flattery settled her, but she knew better than to take him seriously. Nothing spelled disingenuous as much as overplayed flirtation.

An older woman arrived and smiled down at her. Chin-length red hair sprinkled with grey framed close-set eyes lying deep in their sockets. "Hello, there. I'm Doctor Claessen. How are you feeling?"

"I'm doing better, thank you."

The doctor tapped the mask. "Keep this on for a few minutes more and you can leave. And remember, next time you get stressed out, just breathe. It's the best remedy."

Zaina almost rolled her eyes. All doctors gave the same instructions, but they had no idea how daunting it was to do when stress hijacked both the brain and body.

"I understand," the woman said as though she'd read her mind. "It's tough. But try, alright? As much excitement as you've given us today, I'd prefer you didn't have to come back for another treatment."

"Thank you," Zaina replied.

"Do you take anxiety medication?" Doctor Claessen asked.

Zaina shook her head. "I don't like the side effects."

"I understand. Try valerian or chamomile tea instead."

As if I haven't already. She nodded anyway.

The doctor left. Blakesley squeezed her hand. "Perhaps next time you're overwhelmed, you can call me. I'll get you a comm. I'll also make sure you have access to the medical wing, just in case."

She gripped his hand in return. Between the kindness of Blakesley and Doctor Claessen, her fear for Jori lessened. If people like this served Vance, maybe that man wasn't as bad as she'd been led to believe.

"Can you…" She removed the mask altogether and hesitated. She hated taking advantage of someone's generosity, but the situation demanded it. "Can you do me another a favor?"

"Name it," he said earnestly.

"*Please* allow me to contact my boss. He must be worried."

Blakesley's eyes turned down. "I spoke to Vance… His answer is no."

The anxiety she'd almost put down shot back to the forefront. She tried to pull away only to have him tighten his grip.

"Not yet," he said like a plea. "We're on a mission and can't risk anyone sending out a communication. Just wait a little while."

"But I thought we weren't prisoners."

"You're not." He loosened his hold and sighed. "I'll tell you what. You give me the address, and I'll find a way to reach him."

She blinked in surprise and her anxiety abated somewhat. "Yes. Please do." Her composure returned. "Tell him Jori is alright as well."

"Of course." He flashed a sour smile, then his eyes tilted quizzically. "I noticed you didn't ask me to contact your family."

"I don't have one."

"No family? No one?"

"Just me and the children."

He pulled back. "Children?"

She almost laughed at the quickness of his withdrawal. "I work with children like Jori with no families. They're not actually mine, per se. But they're my responsibility and I love them."

Blakesley glanced upward as though relieved. "Ah. I see. You are a generous woman to dedicate yourself to the young and vulnerable."

If she hadn't been recovering from an internal assault, she would've giggled. He really was a charmer.

14
The Stensons

Free from intense scrutiny, the tension in Jori's body unraveled, leaving a dwindling prickling sensation in its wake. Pausing to reorient himself, he closed his eyes and filled his lungs. He'd finally been allowed to leave Vance's unsettling presence, but the weirdness of his visit remained.

"Hurry," Doctor Humphrey said.

Jori shook himself and moved. His legs wobbled a bit, but he had them under control by the time they reached the conveyor.

"Infirmary," the doctor ordered the computer.

"Infirmary? Why are we going there?"

"Vance's orders."

A fresh surge of adrenaline buzzed through Jori's veins.

"Why?" Jori asked.

"We don't question. We just do."

Jori pressed his lips together and tried not to worry. His mind jumped to those times when the MEGA Inspectors had run tests on him to see if he was a MEGA. They'd come up with nothing, but perhaps the people here had other methods.

Those tests hadn't been horrible. Some had caused discomfort, but not having a choice and being treated like a specimen had rattled him more. And now it was happening again. The uncertainty crawling through him almost made him want to go back and face his father's wrath. At least with him, he knew what to expect.

"Let's go," the doctor said.

Jori blinked, having just realized the conveyor opened. He followed the doctor with heavy strides. When they reached the wide, doorless entrance, he froze. This was no ordinary medical facility. The beds were the same, but the diagnostic equipment resembled something a mechanic would use—clunky with articulated arms ending in various implements, including screwdrivers and wrenches. Rather than IV tubes and electrodes, wires and cords extended from another machine. His fears reignited. What if Vance wanted to turn him into a cyborg?

A tall man nearby studied a screen. His skin was almost the same color of bronze as the plate on the back of his head. A wire connected to it and plugged into an electron microscope. The image on the monitor appeared to be living tissue, but Jori didn't have enough knowledge about biology to tell what it was.

"Jori!" a woman's voice rang out and halted the bile that had crept up his throat.

He snapped his attention to the person sitting up on the bed to the left. Relief that he'd only been brought here for her sake prompted a grin that spread across his face. As he rushed to her side, her predicament occurred to him. "What happened? Why are you here?"

Major Blakesley's mouth twisted, but he moved aside and let Jori take his place.

"I'm fine," Zaina replied with a weak smile. "It was just an anxiety attack. I was worried about you. I kept imagining the worst and hating that I couldn't do a darned thing to stop it."

"It's alright," Jori said hurriedly. "He didn't hurt me."

"What did he want?"

Jori's mouth went dry. He wasn't sure how to answer. He wouldn't lie, but if he told the truth, she might have another attack.

Fortunately, Blakesley answered for him. "Just some routine questions, my dear."

Jori didn't contradict him, so her shoulders relaxed in acceptance.

After Blakesley bid them goodbye, Zaina grasped Jori's hand. "I'm so sorry this keeps happening. I wanted so badly to come meet you that I ignored my shortcomings."

The shame she exuded prompted his forgiveness. "It's alright. You didn't know this would happen."

"That may be true, but I was well aware of my health issues."

"What health issues?"

She waved her hand down her body. "This cursed anxiety that's been keeping me from properly taking care of you. My doctor warned me I needed more time to recover, but..." Her features sagged. “I believed I could handle it. I’m so sorry I was wrong.”

Tears welled in her eyes, causing Jori’s sinuses to burn. He tightened his hold on her hand, wishing he knew what to say to make her feel better. “Recover from what?” he said instead.

Her throat bobbed. “I—”

A red-haired doctor arrived, cutting their conversation short. She wore the same white lab coat that many others here did. Like everything about this place that screamed of sterility, she smelled of antiseptic. She didn’t have any cybernetic parts that Jori could see, but her emotions were muted. He detected just enough of her lifeforce to tell she wanted to help, but no empathy lay behind it.

“You’re free to go,” she said to Zaina, then turned to Jori. “If you would stick around for a few moments, I’ll retrieve Doctor Stenson.”

Jori stepped back. “I don’t need to see a doctor.”

“Vance’s orders, I’m afraid. Not to worry. I believe this is just a physical.”

Jori scowled. “That won’t be necessary. Zaina and I will return to our quarters.”

“I advise you to wait,” the woman said with a smile that belied the coldness of her tone.

Her eyebrow lifted, but that didn’t halt him as quickly as the two nearby cyborgs who stopped their work and pivoted to face him. Zaina’s eyes darted about. Jori was more subtle as he took stock of the situation. He could rush out of the infirmary, but would Zaina follow or freeze? And what good would running do, anyway? Vance would force him to return.

Zaina clutched Jori’s arm and cocked her head. Jori gave her a slight nod and answered her unspoken question. “Alright. I’ll wait.”

“And I’ll wait with you,” Zaina said.

She scooted off the bed. Jori detected her wooziness and hugged her side. She huffed and steadied herself. “I’m okay.”

“Ah! There you are,” a male voice called.

A stout man with skinny legs strode over to them. His short dark hair was in a bit of a disarray. Raggedy hair complemented his bushy brows. A smile spread across his square, clean-shaven jaw. His hazel eyes twinkled with a friendliness that matched his lifeforce. "Greetings." He put out his hand for Zaina. She took it hesitantly. "I'm Doctor Stenson… But call me Stephen. My wife Celine is Doctor Stenson too, so it's easier to keep us straight if you use our first names."

He pointed his thumb at the woman approaching from behind. She was small compared to him—short and thin. Her auburn hair was pulled back in a tight ponytail, the style accentuating her long, narrow nose that looked like a perfect triangle when viewed from the side. Like her husband, her lifeforce was strong. It was also odd.

"My name is Zaina and this is Jori," Zaina said warily.

Stephen shook Jori's hand next. "I'm so glad to meet you, young man. I hear you're quite special."

Jori yanked his hand away. Doctor Stenson startled, then cleared his throat. "Sorry. I didn't mean anything by it. I intended it as a compliment."

Jori narrowed his eyes. "But you know about me?"

The man put his hands in the hip pockets of his lab coat. "You're a sentio-animi and you're highly intelligent. I've also heard about some fantastic fighting abilities. Yet you're not a MEGA."

"How do you know all that?" Zaina asked, indignant.

Jori's mouth dried. Thanks to Gottfried, every MEGA probably knew by now. *Chusho*. He *hadn't* been brought here by accident.

Doctor Stenson bounced on his toes. "I'm not a MEGA either, by the way," he said, ignoring Zaina. "Neither is my wife. But that hasn't kept people from making assumptions."

Jori hardened his features, hoping he looked as unimpressed as he felt. "What do you want?"

The doctor didn't seem to notice his challenging tone and answered cheerfully. "I'm supposed to take a blood sample. Don't worry. It won't hurt. Just a quick prick and you're all done."

"What do you need my blood for?"

"I was told to analyze your DNA."

Jori frowned. "You already know I'm not a MEGA, so why?"

Doctor Stenson's face fell. "Vance wants me to verify. And…" He looked down at his feet.

"And what?" Jori demanded.

He sighed. "And isolate your abilities."

Jori stepped back and clenched his fists. "What for?"

The doctor's countenance wavered between anxious lip-chewing and sorrowful brow-shifting. "I'm afraid we do a lot of genetic harvesting here."

Zaina darkened. "You can't do that without permission from a parent or guardian and I absolutely forbid you."

Doctor Stenson glanced down again. "We have no choice. When Vance wants something, he gets it."

The man's fear spiked and enhanced Jori's own, sending a prickle like ice through his veins. This was in line with what Gottfried had wanted him for too.

"I don't care what he wants." Zaina plopped her fists on her hips. "He's not getting it."

Jori appreciated her protectiveness even though she'd probably cower if the doctor was more forceful—or if Vance was here. The urge to stand firm with her gripped him like a vice, but something Sensei Jeruko used to say gave him pause. *"Take your time to assess the situation. Look for opportunities and plan. Fighting when you're not in immediate danger will only complicate your objective."*

He put his hand on Zaina's arm. "The doctor is right."

She shook her head and turned away. "Oh no. Not this again. I'm not letting you out of sight so they can poke and prod you. I have a job to do, and damn it, these people need to respect it."

Doctor Stenson raised his palms. "Oh, you can stay. He didn't say you couldn't be here."

She halted. Her lips pressed together. "This shouldn't be happening at all. If this Vance guy had any regard for the law at all, he'd get permission first."

"He's a MEGA," Jori grumbled. "Chances are, he's already flouted the law."

The doctor's brows tilted in sympathy. "That's correct. Vance does what he wants and doesn't care how it affects others. Take my wife and I, for example. He wants our talent and so we're stuck here. We've been here five years now, and I've learned the hard way that he won't be denied."

The doctor glanced at his wife and exuded sorrow. She didn't seem to register his attention. Her eyes flicked as though reading something and her sensations indicated she was deep in thought, but she had no accompanying emotions. Jori knew a simpleton like this from back home. The man was a pure genius in engineering, but not so good at other things. From the way Stephen looked at her, he assumed she used to be different once.

Zaina didn't seem to notice this exchange. She clutched her stomach. "Y-you've been a prisoner for five years?"

The doctor replied only with a sad frown.

"What will we do?" Zaina asked. "We can't stay here."

Jori deflated. A heaviness shrouded his mood. "Maybe he'll let you leave." *Just you, though. I'll have to fight to get away.*

15
Jealousy and Remorse

Lost in a fleet of fantasies, Major Abelard Blakesley leaned back in his office chair with his hands clasped behind his head. Zaina danced in his mind's eye, her curves almost as enticing as her coy smile. He wasn't in love or anything so mundane. Just infatuated. Zaina was all human, and she had a classy way about her that made him ache. She'd be a wonderful alternative to Phoebe who had to activate her emotion chip for him.

He released a longing sigh. The opportunity to woo a woman rather than pay for one got his blood racing to where he no longer noticed the chill of his small little office.

The ding from his monitor brought him out of his reverie. Despite the annoyance at the interruption, he dived into the report. His gut soured as he scrolled down the screen. Item after item painted a picture almost too perfect to believe, boosting his vexation. Did this kid have any flaws?

He growled at the photo of the boy and turned away, fuming. The shelf beside him encased several medals. Karate, judo, sojutsu, kajukenbo, you name it, he'd probably studied it or something similar, and won corresponding martial competitions. In his younger years, he'd traveled the galaxy to take part in formal events. His winnings extended beyond awards. All the money, fame, and women had bestowed a sublime happiness.

And it all had come crashing down when someone discovered his parents had been genetically altered. This invalidated all his accomplishments, leaving him friendless, penniless, and disgraced. In the eyes of all his friends, he'd become worse than a piece of rubbish.

Jori thought he had it bad. *Ha!* That spoiled little imp could've had anything he wanted if he hadn't squandered it just to save the life of his enemy. What an idiot. His misery was his own fault.

Blakesley bit the inside of his cheek, drawing blood. He admitted that a part of him was jealous of the boy's skills, but his dislike ran deeper. MEGA-Man had singled Jori out for greatness, and rather than be grateful, all the imp did was bemoan his fate.

To be fair, Blakesley had done the same but only for a time. The more he denied what he was, the harder his situation became. It wasn't until he had to take up residence in a rundown part of a city where MEGAs were more common that his life finally turned around.

This old shopkeeper with a cybernetic eye had given him a job. The man liked to talk. He'd rattle on about many things, but one topic gave Blakesley the first spark of hope since his family's betrayal. "*Mankind is destined for more*," the man would say. "*All we have to do is strive for our own evolution*." Blakesley remembered his bitterness as the shopkeeper ranted about governments keeping them from reaching their full potential.

One day a regular customer invited him to become part of a secret organization set on undermining the status quo. After a few years of service, he got promoted to Vance's second-in-command.

He hated Vance with a passion but would endure anything to regain his supremacy. MEGA-Man needed him for his DNA and Blakesley took pride in the super-soldiers it'd helped create.

Helped was the operative word. MEGA-Man considered Vance the optimal source.

Blakesley chafed at being second best, especially since Vance only entrusted him with administrative tasks. With this boy here now, his importance might diminish further and MEGA-Man would see him as dispensable.

He returned to his computer screen and scrolled back to the top. No mechanical enhancements or genetic alterations found, it stated. This was probably true. A report from his superiors declared most of Jori's ancestors from before the MEGA Injunction had been genetically augmented. Over the generations, the known genetic markers had transformed into unique sequences. Thanks to the injunction's grandfather clause, the boy didn't qualify as a MEGA. *Lucky little imp.*

Sentio-animi perception. Stamina. Above average intelligence. Fast healing ability. Exceptional reflexes and agility. All this confirmed the Cooperative's findings, which included class four marksmanship and level nine martial combat. The damn kid was only eleven years old! No wonder MEGA-Man wanted him on his side.

Blakesley slammed his fist onto his desk. *It's so unfair!*

He sat back again and ran his fingers through his beard. He'd have to diminish this boy's importance somehow—show Vance that he wasn't as great as everyone thought. An idea occurred to him, but did he dare? If Vance found out, he'd receive more than a simple reprimand. The man didn't tolerate deception.

He returned to Doctor Stenson's report. Although it was risky, he couldn't let that boy supplant him.

It took some time to locate the parts he needed. The doctor had highlighted several promising genetic codes. He commented on what they meant and why they supported previous reports on the boy's abilities.

Blakesley pinpointed the qualities that competed with his own. He reworded, downplayed, or deleted just enough to make it seem the boy fell short of his own skills, but not so much as to be suspicious. Of course, he altered the DNA sequences as well. Programming wasn't his strongest suit, but he was adequate.

When it was done, Jori appeared no better than any other super-soldier. He still had importance as the Dragon Emperor's son, but only as a puppet.

Blakesley lauded his own cleverness and grinned.

*****

Chilly air clung to the skin and seeped into the bones. The frigidity of the room didn't abate despite the command to the thermostat. Zaina Noman rubbed her nose and tightened her blanket around her shoulders. She considered reporting the issue to maintenance, but perhaps she'd wait until she saw Blakesley. He'd be arriving later to give her a tour of the ship. Besides, being cold was the least of her worries.

She frowned at Jori who sat at the small table and picked at his food. He'd always been withdrawn, but it seemed worse now. Now might be a good time to explain why she'd been having difficulties.

Sitting up made her head spin. She closed her eyes, waiting for it to pass, then drew in deeply. "Hey," she said, opening her eyes. When he glanced up, she pressed on. "I owe you an explanation."

Though his expression remained flat, she recognized it as dejection. Her words wouldn't lift his spirits, but maybe they'd help him understand.

She folded her hands in her lap. "A few months ago, I was assaulted."

His eyes widened, then he glowered. "Someone hurt you?"

"Yes. Badly. I would've been scarred for life had I not received regenerative treatment. I've always suffered from anxiety, and it got so much worse afterward. Every time someone looks at me with even the least bit of hostility, my chest tightens. I jump at loud noises. If they yell, my body locks up."

"Why would anyone hurt you?" he asked, his brows tilting the other way in apparent sympathy.

"Well, not all the children I work with are parentless. Many of those children have been removed from their homes because their parents are… Well, let's just say they have no business being parents. We'd rescued this one girl from a man who was highly abusive. He found out where she was located and bullied his way into our facility. I tried to calm him down, but everything I said only made him worse. Next thing I knew, I was on the floor getting…"

She took in a shaky breath as the rampant horror of it replayed in her mind. His unintelligible curses, the rage in his bloodshot eyes, the blood on his fists as he pounded on her. Then there were the sickening cracks as her bones gave way. *Oh God.*

"I'm sorry," he said.

His tone carried such compassion that she broke through the surface of her drowning emotions. Realizing she was trembling, she forced herself to return to the moment. Jori remained seated but he glanced back down at his plate, hunching over as though preoccupied.

Watching him as he rested his cheek on his fist and poked a piece of fab-meat made her rise. She ignored the ache in her body and ambled over. "Hey," she said as she eased into the chair across from him. "Did something happen with Vance?"

Jori stopped stirring. His eyes flicked to her but returned to the food, telling her she'd guessed correctly.

She reached out to him. "Please tell me. Did he hurt you?" The shake of his head was almost imperceptible. "Did he *threaten* to hurt you?"

The muscles in his neck and jaw went taut. "If I tell you, you might have another anxiety attack."

Well, crap. "I knew I shouldn't have let you go alone."

"You wouldn't have been able to help me. Not with your…" He waved with his fork.

Her shame returned, buffeting her like a blast of arctic wind. "With my paralyzing fear." She leaned in, almost in prayer. "Oh, Jori. I'm so sorry. I realize I keep saying that, but I mean it… With all my heart." She wagged her head. "All this time, you've been taking care of me instead of the other way around. I completely understand why you're so upset with me."

Jori straightened. "I'm not upset with you."

The force of his words surprised her. "Well, you should be. I've done nothing but fail you at every turn."

He turned away, trying to hide his watery eyes. It broke her heart and caused her own sadness to spill out. What the hell was wrong with her? She had to get herself together. That this was beyond her experience didn't matter. This boy needed her.

She grasped his hand. "I'll do better. I promise."

Tears spilled down his cheeks. "Vance," he choked out. "You can't go against him." He hardened his eyes to stress his words. "He *will* hurt you, maybe even kill you. And if he does that, I'll have no one."

Her chin trembled. She wanted to say she would help him regardless, but her fear locked up her voice.

Damn me. I can't even help myself.

16
A New Path

The stark white halls stretched onward like an arctic wasteland. Only the occasional cleaning or maintenance bot broke up the monotony. Jori stifled a yawn, wishing he'd stayed in his room rather than joined Zaina on a tour led by Major Blakesley. Every hall was the same. Every space was much like the next. Even the cafeteria, which resembled the same boring sterility as the sitting areas. Perhaps a ship full of half-humans didn't care about aesthetics.

He trailed Zaina and the major, paying only a little attention to their conversation. Zaina seemed enraptured by the man as she hooked her arm into his. It made sense, considering how much Blakesley fawned over her. Jori appreciated how her spirits had lifted but chafed at being ignored. At least Blakesley's regard was genuine. Why did his emotions have to sour every time he looked at Jori? What had he done to deserve this disdain? The emotion felt like jealousy, but what for? He was an orphan. No family. No friends. Just a prisoner of some maniac who kept repeating that stupid phrase about them being the same.

"Ah. Here we are," Blakesley said. "My favorite place."

Jori's disquiet fled as he beheld the vast gymnasium. It had everything for weight training, aerobics, gymnastics, and sports. As Blakesley led them around, Jori's heart swelled at the sight of the combat area. Blakesley stopped before a crewmember who fought against a holo-man on a machine that looked more sophisticated than the one back home. Every such virtual sparring device he'd seen used haptics. But this one created a more realistic image and appeared to provide better contact feedback.

He yearned to go check it out but a glance at Zaina changed his mind. If she saw how violent he could be, she might be afraid of him again.

"You're quite the martial artist yourself, aren't you, Jori?" Blakesley asked. His tone made it seem he was genuinely interested, but a sense of resentment lurked behind his smile.

"I'm no longer a warrior," Jori replied hurriedly. His conscience twinged at the near lie. It was true since he'd never become a Dragon Warrior. But the desire to release all his tension by fighting a holo-program gripped him like an unquenchable thirst.

Zaina beamed down at him. "He's on a different path now."

Jori's cheeks burned but he couldn't quell his longing. It wasn't like he'd hurt anyone on a holo-machine. His interest lay only in the thrill of the challenge. But no. She was right. He should be on a *different path*.

Rodrigo approached wearing a wide smile along with a sleeveless workout suit that also bared his gangly legs. "Hey, friends."

"Rigo!" Zaina said in a drawn-out cheerful tone. "Good to see you again. Are you working out here?"

Rodrigo wrung his hands and bobbed his head. "Yes. Yes. Just got done running. I wanna play tenisi but it takes two players."

"Tenisi?" Zaina asked.

"Yeah. You use this racquet thing to hit a ball back and forth over a net."

Jori perked up. It sounded a little like a game he and the commander used to play. "I'll play with you."

"Yeah?" Rigo's smile seemed both glad and surprised.

"That's a great idea," said Zaina.

Blakesley agreed and suggested he and Zaina do an activity together as well. Jori suspected he chose something from the other side of the gym on purpose but it irked him more than it worried him. Blakesley hadn't directed his jealousy toward her, nor did he hold any malice. And Zaina was happy. Besides, perhaps her befriending the major would help them somehow. She could get more information from him while Jori worked on Rodrigo.

The major ordered them clothes through the main fabricor. Jori and Zaina returned to their quarters while Blakesley went to his.

As they waited for the bot to deliver their outfits, Zaina touched his shoulder. "I hope I didn't overstep."

Jori cocked his head.

She sat on the edge of her bed and folded her hands. "About being on a new path."

Jori glanced away from the earnestness reflected in her eyes.

"I'm not judging you for having military training," she continued. "But you have the opportunity to discover another way to live. A whole new future lies before you. With your intellect, you can go into the sciences, be a chemist, geologist, or even a physicist. Or perhaps engineering is more to your taste. And don't discount the arts."

A new path. It's what he wanted, wasn't it? A new start? Logic told him this was for the best, but he couldn't help but feel like he'd be abandoning a part of himself. It had to be done, though. And she'd touched on two things that already interested him. Computer science was another. "I enjoy programming."

She smiled. "See? There you go. That's an excellent field of study."

Her genuine satisfaction clashed with his misgiving, but he returned her smile. After the bot arrived and they changed into their workout clothes, they headed back to the gym and went their separate ways.

Rodrigo bounced on his toes in childish glee. He gave a brief overview on how to play, then the game began.

Jori beat him in the first match… And the second. After the third, boredom set in. He might've enjoyed himself more if he'd been playing against Commander Hapker.

His mood dipped as he reminisced about the times they'd played wall ball together. The first time, when they'd considered one another the enemy, had been an intense contest—almost like a battle.

As they learned to trust each other, the competition became friendlier. Jori remembered the lopsided grin the commander wore once when he'd won a match. Jori had teased him about taking pride in being able to beat a mere boy. Hapker had laughed in response, then told Jori to call him J.D.

Jori's heart had swelled at the honor bestowed upon him. Yet he'd never felt comfortable saying Hapker's informal name. Using his surname demonstrated his respect and returned the honor.

Rigo put on a determined face, but he seemed incapable of sending the ball back. The man had no coordination. Even when he got in range, he still missed.

Jori directed the ball in Rigo's path, hoping for an easy return. Rigo swung. The ball struck the corner of his racquet and flew wildly out of bounds.

Rodrigo bent over and panted. "I can't seem to hit the ball today."

Jori bit his tongue and wondered whether the man had ever managed to hit it. "Maybe we should take a break."

"Yeah. A break." Rigo straightened as much as his hunched back allowed and ambled over to Jori's side. "Ya know, if I had more cybernetics, I bet I'd be good at this. I should get one of those chips that augment muscle memory."

Jori frowned. "You don't need a chip. You just need more practice."

"Naw. A chip would be better. I can be of more help to MEGA-Man."

The eager grin on Rodrigo's face curled Jori's stomach. So did verifying who sponsored this crew. He hadn't broken a sweat during the game, but his skin flushed now. "Did you bring me here because MEGA-Man wants me?"

"Sure. You're important."

Chusho. They might be treating him like a guest, but he was undoubtedly a prisoner. He suspected the reasons MEGA-Man was so interested in him but asked anyway. "Important how?"

"Why you're a MEGA without being a MEGA!" Rodrigo laughed goodheartedly, though it made Jori's hair stand on end.

"So?"

"So. You're one of us."

Jori almost responded that he'd rather share a cage with a blackbeast than be one of them, but decided not to offend the person who'd finally told him what the hell was going on. "I don't want to be here. I want to go with Zaina to Marvdacht."

"That's silly." Rodrigo spoke with the same friendly yet grating grin. "You're among friends now."

Jori had no defense against the man's optimism. "Do you know what Vance's mission is?" he asked. "Or MEGA-Man's?"

"Naw." Rigo flicked his hand. "They don't tell me that stuff. I'm just a mouse, ya know."

"I think they're going to kill more people."

"Yeah. Sad." Rodrigo bobbed his head yet not a hint of sadness emanated from him. "But we gotta get the galaxy's attention somehow. How they treat us ain't right."

Jori pulled back. "Destroying a station isn't right either. Most of the people there were innocent—people like me and Zaina."

"I get it. I do. But we also got us *some MEGA-haters*." Rigo shot up his fist in triumph and whooped.

Jori side-eyed him and stepped away. Something was seriously wrong with everyone on this ship. Even this innocuous little mouse was off.

"You don't understand how much we've suffered," Rodrigo said as if he'd read Jori's mind, though that was doubtful. "So many of us have been abused, ya know?"

Jori understood to a point. The hate he'd sensed from those on the station was beyond reason. "What about you? Have people mistreated you?"

"Yup." Rigo bobbed his head. "Killed my ma. Almost killed me too. Someone serving MEGA-Man saved me. Gave me a job here."

Jori swallowed. Rigo's single-mindedness indicated he'd be no help against a ship full of fanatics.

*****

Jori ground his teeth. Talking Rodrigo into playing something else was as difficult as convincing him that kidnapping was wrong. It didn't matter how logical the argument was, Rigo talked around it. Jori bit down the urge to scream.

Doctor Humphrey approached the sidelines. "Vance would like to see you again, young man."

Jori's chest tightened. He didn't want to play another uneventful game of tenisi, but he'd rather do that than visit the chima. It was like making a choice between staying on an exploding ship or jumping out into space without a suit.

He clenched his fists. His last encounter with that madman had been weirdly intense, but he shouldn't be this afraid. It wasn't like he'd been hurt or outright threatened. Sure, Vance's body language had hinted at violence, but so what? In trying to pinpoint the root of his trepidation, all he came up with was the man's unpredictable nature.

Rigo clapped Jori on the back. "Hey! I think our boss likes you."

Jori's mouth twisted at Rodrigo's stupid grin. The mouse wasn't just single-minded, he was naïve.

Jori shook his head and reluctantly followed the doctor out. Thank goodness he hadn't passed Zaina on the way. As much as his insides whirled at the thought of facing the deranged captain alone, he feared for her safety more. Vance wanted him, not her.

The doctor led him into Vance's empty room and left with explicit instructions that Jori sit. He took the same chair as before and twiddled his thumbs as he waited for the psychopath to arrive. At first, he avoided looking at all the man's gaudy décor. After a few minutes of boredom, he gave in. A dull glowing lamp that emitted a rainbow of cycling light sat on a table nearby. A gold-plated statue of people in exotic costumes lay beside it. An abstract metal sculpture hung on the wall next to a round geometrically designed… Were those plates? Jori shook his head. The only useful things here were in the kitchen and…

The workstation in the corner gave him an idea. This was the perfect opportunity to snoop. Hacking the device should be easy enough, but just the thought of defying Vance's orders broke him into a sweat.

He rose and clenched his fists. *This is stupid.* He'd never done everything his father had told him to do, so why bother obeying now? Each step away from his chair made his heart thump harder, but he stubbornly kept going.

Vance's personal console blinked to life, displaying a blank blue screen. Jori tapped it, hoping for a password prompt or even an error message from the biometric sensor, but nothing appeared. He inspected the area for a bio-authenticator and found none.

A closer scrutiny revealed several ports. If Vance was a MEGA, perhaps he plugged in directly. Hacking via a port would be easier—if only Jori had the right tools. He groaned in frustration and glanced about for another option.

The door hissed open. Jori jumped back and snapped into his military stance. *Damn reflexes*. And damn Vance for not having a lifeforce strong enough to sense.

Vance walked in with a casual gait and settled into a chair. His expression was unreadable as he flicked his hand to where Jori was supposed to be. Jori evened out his breaths, attempting to quell his pattering heart, and eased onto the cushion.

The man sat erect, his hands palm-down on his thighs. "I told you to sit."

Jori's tongue felt like sandpaper.

"What were you doing up?" Vance asked with the same blank expression.

To tell the truth would surely incur the man's wrath but lying didn't come easy. Jori opted to remain silent instead.

Vance smiled. "You don't need to answer. I already know. You tried to access my console but couldn't. You growled in frustration. Sounded like a baby tiger."

Jori's mouth fell open and he scanned the room.

Vance's smile widened. "No cameras in here. I *see* things."

Jori's face froze as though struck by a blast of polar wind. Although Vance had a muted lifeforce, his words rang true. "How?"

"I'm better than you."

Jori's skin crawled more at his tone than the statement itself. He resisted squirming under the man's scrutiny as the minutes passed.

"Let's play a game," Vance finally said.

"I don't want to play games. I want to get off this ship and go with Zaina."

"Then you'll like this game."

Jori spoke through his teeth. "I don't want to play a game."

"Are you afraid to lose?"

"No," Jori replied, mimicking Vance's short and meaningless replies.

The staring contest ensued. More minutes ticked by. Saliva built in Jori's mouth, but he refused to swallow it, lest Vance see his unease.

"I won't hurt you—unless you cross me, of course," Vance said, moving nothing but his lips.

"Then what are you going to do with me?"

"That depends on MEGA-Man."

Jori's breath caught. A part of him hadn't quite believed Rigo. Hearing it confirmed by this madman made him feel like a rat in a trap. His pulse quickened. A wave of dizziness flooded over him. He forced himself to calm enough to speak. "I refuse to cooperate," he croaked.

"Your cooperation isn't necessary."

Jori almost choked.

"But it's preferred," Vance continued. "And there are ways to compel your compliance."

Jori scoffed. "They won't work." If his own father couldn't make him do something he didn't want to do, this chima wouldn't be able to either.

Vance nodded. "Your Jintal training. You think you can resist even if we use force."

Jori's hands trembled. No matter how hard he tried, he couldn't regulate his breathing. Each intake of air came in short. "How do you know about that?"

"MEGA-Man knows everything."

"Then he knows I won't give in."

Vance's smile took on a challenging curve. "And so the game begins."

Jori's entire body shook like an avalanche.

17
The Cyborium

A beep from a dome-shaped bot intoned with an irksome impatience. If Jori didn't know any better, he'd say this machine had emotions. More likely, it was a programmed response to being unable to move. Jori sighed and exited the conveyor. The bot followed him out with a whir, then rushed away.

Jori forced his drooping shoulders to straighten as he entered the medical facility. Dread from his encounter with Vance yesterday still weighed him down, but he'd be damned if he'd show it. Let them run their stupid tests. He'd endure without complaint until the time was right to resist. That time would come.

He willed away the anxiety and assessed his surroundings. Although he'd been here before, the vast open space cluttered with various medical, laboratory, and mechanical items brought on a new trepidation. If Vance did more than test him—say hook him up to an operating table and turn him into a machine—he'd fight like hell.

Zaina's lifeforce neared. Determination peppered her emotions. Jori's gut tightened. He was pretty sure she wasn't supposed to follow him here.

She appeared from around the corner and bestowed a guileful smile. "I don't remember Doctor Humphrey saying I couldn't be here, do you?"

Because you didn't ask. He would've complimented her cleverness if he didn't worry about what Vance would do if he found out. "That doesn't imply permission."

She winked and he shot her a worried frown in return. It was nice to see her coming through with her promise to be there for him, but she shouldn't pick this battle to fight.

At least she's fighting. It felt wrong to comply with Vance's wishes so soon after claiming to resist, but until he came up with a plan, it was better to play along.

Doctor Stephen Stenson arrived wearing a smile. "Welcome back."

Jori flashed a scowl. First Vance and his stupid games, then Zaina risking her safety for no good reason, and now… Well, this situation wasn't the doctor's fault, but his resentment spilled out anyway.

Zaina's anxiety lessened at Stephen's genuine greeting. "Thank you," she said. "I can't say I'm glad he's here, but I'm happy you're the one handling it."

Jori agreed, but still couldn't bring himself to reciprocate the friendliness.

"What will you be doing today?" Zaina asked.

"We're scanning and testing some of the young man's abilities." He cast an apologetic smile down at Jori.

Jori bit the inside of his cheek and kept a blank face.

Zaina scanned the room. "I thought this was just a hospital but it's more, isn't it?"

The doctor bounced on his heels, likely glad to have someone else to talk to besides a grumpy child. "Indeed. We call it *the cyborium.* It's where we maintain MEGAs, study their abilities, and sometimes implement new cybernetics."

Jori's heart jumped. "You create cyborgs here?"

His fear must've shown because the doctor replied, "Don't worry. No one will force you to become a MEGA. Everyone here who is altered or upgraded chooses to be so."

Jori sensed he spoke truthfully, but he still didn't believe him. "How do you know?"

"Because forcing the procedure can create problems. As I understand it, you're too valuable to damage."

Jori's relief at not having to endure modifications was short-lived. "You're taking my DNA so you can alter those who are willing?"

"That's right."

Jori shuddered. The thought of people like Vance having his abilities terrified him. "So you're creating monsters."

The doctor's emotions plummeted. Zaina's throat bobbed. She shared a worried look with Jori but said nothing.

If she learned of his visit with Vance yesterday, she might be more vocal. As it was, her mood seemed much better after her tour with Blakesley. The smile she wore when she returned had been almost as buoyant. The major's had too until he saw Jori and a sourness emanated from him.

Doctor Stenson wordlessly led him to a scanning bed. Jori got on and lay down without complaint. He gritted his teeth and bore the chill to his back. To be fair, the doctor wasn't trying to make him uncomfortable. And it wasn't like being cold caused any real suffering. It was more the humiliation of it that made this unbearable. Refusing Vance's orders would gain him nothing, so he kept his mouth shut while Stephen and his wife Celine prepped the diagnostic machine.

Zaina gripped his hand like a protective mother. Despite the danger of her being here, her comfort made the situation easier to endure.

His mind spun with questions as the scanning machine hummed and clicked through the calibration process. Vance had allowed them out of their prison so long as they obeyed his rules. But with no guards, how would he know if they violated them? Had he literally *seen* Jori access his console, or did he sense it and guess? And if he saw, how?

Vance had said there were no cameras, and he'd hinted at an ability. It must be a lie or some omission of the truth, though. Regardless, Vance was monitoring him. Until Jori worked out the specifics, his ability to plan was limited. Asking the Stensons might yield some answers, but he wasn't sure whether he could trust them. Stephen seemed nice enough but wasn't likely to do much with his wife at Vance's mercy.

Doctor Stephen Stenson placed his palm on Jori's chest where the necklace would've been had he not hid it under his mattress in his quarters. "We're ready now. It won't hurt, I promise."

Jori picked up on his sincerity but maintained his scowl as the giant circular scanner advanced over his feet like a python swallowing its prey. As it neared his torso, Zaina let go of his hand and bit her fingernails.

Doctor Celine Stenson reviewed the monitor with a relentless focus. Jori studied the strangeness of her lifeforce. It wasn't muted like some MEGAs. It was both intense and flat, as though she had only one aspect to her personality and it shone like a quasar. His thoughts shifted to his mother's simple-minded brother, Benjiro, which led to the reminder of what he'd lost. As much as he appreciated Zaina's support, he wished it was his mother standing here beside him. If only the Cooperative had sent him to her rather than to an orphanage on some faraway planet.

Celine's euphoria distracted his line of thought. Her emotions flared brighter with each incremental movement of the scanner. *What is she seeing?*

The blue scanning lights flashed over Jori's chest to his head, followed by red lights that reflected a grid pattern over his body. Celine pointed at the screen, emitting excitement. Stephen leaned over and examined it. His eyes twinkled, but in a way that seemed more preoccupied with her glee than the information.

The noise of the scanner made it impossible for Jori to hear their words. His curiosity didn't outweigh his worry that their findings would make MEGA-Man want him more.

He found it difficult to believe his abilities were so special. As the youngest of several now dead brothers, he'd often been overlooked. When his father *had* given him attention, it was to criticize him. It hadn't mattered that some of his skills exceeded his older brothers'. Nor that he had a touch of his mother's animi ability. Not even the fact that he was better at programming than their chief programmer had impressed Father.

When he came to the Cooperative, they'd scorned his abilities. He undoubtedly inherited them from ancestors who'd been genetically altered, but because those alterations had occurred before the MEGA Injunction, they'd called him a cheater. Within the Cooperative, only Commander Hapker had treated him with admiration.

The scan lights turned off and the scanner retreated to its original position at the foot of his bed. He sat up. Zaina returned to his side as Celine hurried away with exhilaration streaming off her like jet exhaust.

"What did you find?" Jori asked Stephen.

The doctor smiled, though it didn't hold any of Celine's enthusiasm. "Your bone density is amazing."

Jori nodded. "My people originate from a planet with a higher-than-average mass. I've never lived there, but we keep our ships at a comparative artificial setting so we won't have trouble visiting."

Doctor Stenson's forehead wrinkled up. "That's wise, but how is it you're so tall for your age? Generally, a greater gravitational force makes people shorter as well as stronger."

Jori shrugged. Because most Toradons were both strong and tall, the same topic had interested him. He'd never found the answer, though. It wasn't like his people had an abundance of scientists who had the time to study something that wasn't related to violence.

Rather than speculate, he changed the subject. "What's wrong with your wife?"

He beamed. "Oh, she gets delighted whenever she comes across interesting data."

"Not that. I mean… She's different."

The doctor's face fell. "They tried to alter her. She resisted and it caused some brain damage."

Zaina gasped. "I-I'm sorry. That's horrible."

Her dismay matched Jori's own. "I thought you said they wouldn't alter anyone by force."

"Yes, but that wasn't always the case." He sighed. "After what happened to her, we stopped forcing people to undergo alterations—well, people deemed too important, anyway."

Jori swallowed. "Will she be alright?"

"Oh yes, thank goodness. The procedure affected her amygdala, but I'm told by sentio-animis like you that her quality of life doesn't seem diminished. She may not enjoy the same things she used to, but her love of biology is the same." He wore a nostalgic smile. "She's a genius. I'm a damn good biologist, but she's always running circles around me."

"That's sweet," Zaina said. "But sad at the same time. She seems detached."

Stephen's expression turned down. "Yes. Very much so."

Zaina reached out and touched his arm. "Will she ever return to normal?"

"No. Probably not."

Jori detected the man's loss and warmed at his genuine love for her. An ache formed in the back of his throat. "Have you ever tried to escape?"

Stephen bobbed his head. "We did—once. It didn't go well." He locked eyes with Jori. "Don't cross Vance. He has a way of knowing things and he's highly intelligent."

Jori shivered. "What do you mean? Can he actually see what someone is doing without cameras?"

"I'm afraid so." The doctor glanced about, emitting nervousness. "He can see the future," he replied carefully.

"Impossible," Zaina said.

Jori almost choked. "See the future? Like premonitions?"

"Sort of. There's a theory that explains it, and we've tested it."

Chusho. "Does that mean the future is set?"

"No. Not exactly. The future is fluid. I believe he sees the *most likely*."

Jori wagged his head, trying to understand how this was possible and how in the hell he'd defeat someone who saw what he did before he did it. "How far into the future?"

Doctor Stenson cleared his throat. Fear wafted off him. "It's probably best we not talk about this."

Jori wanted to push but decided against it. If Vance was watching right now, the doctor might get in trouble. There must be another way to figure out his limits.

A scream echoed from the back of the room, startling the doctor into a panic. The man whirled about and took off into a sprint. Jori hopped down. No one stopped him as he followed, not even Zaina who matched his hurried pace.

A pulsing beep resounded, overriding all other sounds in the facility. Jori rounded a tall medical machine and halted. The room opened up to an organized cluster of over a dozen beds occupied by people who had tubes, wires, and IV lines stuck all over their bodies. He had sensed a few unconscious people back here, but not this many. More than half had no lifeforce at all, meaning they were either dead or living machines.

"Oh my God," Zaina said in a hushed tone.

The doctor and others in white coats bustled around a bedridden man with robotic arms and legs. Stephen Stenson reviewed the monitor by his bed, then hurried away.

Jori intercepted him. “What is this place?”

Doctor Stenson flicked his hand at the beds with a harried expression. “This is where we create and maintain MEGAs.”

Jori heated. “This is Vance’s idea of evolution? They’re machines!”

The doctor huffed out of his nose. “Agreed.” He sidestepped Jori and darted to what looked like a master computer.

Zaina covered her mouth and held her stomach. Jori tried to swallow but horror clutched his throat. Maybe these people had opted for this, but did they realize they’d lose their humanity in the process?

This is insane!

18
Benevolence

The cityscape ambled by in an endless maze of people and shops. The exotic architecture and the purple cloudless sky added an element of adventure to her excursion. Zaina Noman jogged on the treadmill, trying to distract herself with the virtual scene surrounding her. If not for the ache in her body reminding her of the stress she carried, it might've worked.

No, that wasn't true. Although the digital creation was realistic, right down to the city sounds and the synthesized odors from the passing restaurants, she couldn't forget where she was. The virtual people surrounding her didn't have any obvious augmentations, but she imagined them anyway. A simulated man she passed with his hands in his pockets could be hiding a mechanical hand like Rodrigo's. The woman wearing a hat might be covering computer ports.

Cybernetics rarely bothered her. Even on her homeworld where enhancements were highly frowned upon, some people in her neighborhood still had them. But a few of the ones here were so machine-like, she wondered whether they were alive at all. It made her skin crawl.

She plodded along on the treadmill, barely going faster than a walk. Her muscles worked, but only begrudgingly. Determined to do at least twenty minutes, she pressed on for the last three.

Time dragged as though she trudged uphill while towing a bus. When the timer finally went off, she nearly collapsed.

Her legs wobbled as she looked for Jori. He wasn't here with the cardio equipment. She didn't find him on any of the ball courts either. Nor was he in the weightlifting area. When she found him, her mouth fell open. The boy rammed his fist upward into a holographic soldier's jaw, then threw two more punches in quick succession. He followed up with a spin and an elbow jab to the back of the soldier's skull.

The holo-image faded. Jori turned, caught her staring, and his eyes popped. He scrambled to turn off the machine. His head hung as he approached. "I—I was just exercising."

Her shock wore off and she snapped her hands to her hips. "Is that what you call it?"

"I-I… Yes, ma'am." He glanced up at her with a furrowed brow. "It's not real."

"I thought we decided you should take a new path?"

Jori returned his chin to his chest. She waited for him to make an excuse, but none came. She chewed her lip and contemplated the best way to handle this. Making him ashamed of his heritage was the last thing she should do. He needed guidance.

She knelt before him and placed her hand on his shoulder. He refused to meet her eyes. She preferred her charges look at her when she spoke—it told her they were paying attention—but she didn't insist this time. "You are a remarkable young man and you have so much going for you. I understand that back home, you probably felt the need to fight. But that life is behind you. You don't need to fight any more."

The boy's gaze flicked up with a spark. "Are you sure? They've taken us prisoner."

She shook her head. "They haven't hurt us, or even threatened to hurt us. I agree they shouldn't hold us against our will, but fighting isn't the answer."

His brows tilted angrily. "Then what is? How do we get out of this mess?"

"We wait. And we pray the benevolence of these people will change their minds into letting us leave."

"Benevolence?" Jori spit. "You haven't met *Vance*."

She suppressed a shiver. There was definitely something off about that man. "You may be right about him, but you can't fight him. Somehow, we have to reason with him."

Jori scoffed. Zaina squeezed his shoulder. "Listen. I don't have all the answers. But there must be another way. Violence begets violence."

Jori swallowed. "I wasn't using the holo-program because I enjoy violence. It's only exercise."

She wanted to say that knocking a man out, even a virtual one, wasn't proper exercise, but that response wouldn't contribute to his understanding. "I get it. You've needed to defend yourself. And you're only doing what you've been taught. I'm not accusing you of being violent. I'm just saying there are other ways."

The boy's throat bobbed as he agreed. "I'm sorry."

Zaina embraced him. "Oh no, dear. You don't need to apologize. It's not your fault."

He pulled away. She wondered if that had sounded patronizing, but she didn't know how else to word it. He wasn't to blame. It was this crazy galaxy and the overwhelming doubt that humanity would ever overcome its flaws.

*****

A doleful cloud followed Zaina Noman all the way to her quarters. It was one of those heavy grey clouds that took up the entire sky and dribbled a chilly, bone-aching mist. She dropped onto the edge of her bed and massaged her forehead. Guilt wriggled through her. She wasn't sure whether it was because she had allowed Jori to remain at the gym by himself or because of their conversation. She'd believed him when he said he wouldn't commit violence, but she still feared for his future. How many children from abusive families had she seen repeat the cycle? Well, she wasn't that old, but a few too many.

Some might see it as irresponsible to leave him there just because she had other plans. But he had too much energy to spend. Besides, it wasn't like he was alone. Although the complicated jumps and flips he'd performed on the gymnastics mat had piqued her worry, plenty of others were around to get him help if he needed it.

She shouldn't be concerned. He was old enough and seemed mature enough to be trusted on his own for a while.

With that decided, she entered the sonic shower. It felt good but not like a proper one with hot running water. God, how she missed those.

By the time she changed into nice clothes, the door chimed and sent her heart fluttering. "Enter," she said, then put on her best smile.

A well-poised man returned the expression and bowed. "My Lady."

Major Abelard Blakesley wasn't the most handsome man in the galaxy—she wasn't a fan of beards—but his charm made up for it. He held out his hand and she automatically grasped it. With an easy gentleness, he lifted it to his lips and kissed the top.

Her cheeks burned. No one had ever treated her like this before. It was like out of a romance sim, only her reservations hindered her ability to enjoy it. However, he'd help pass the time and it'd keep her mind off the fact that she was stuck here. Plus, it wouldn't hurt to have a high-ranking friend on this ship.

"So what will we be doing today?" she asked, wondering what else there was to do on a ship full of people who could just plug in for entertainment.

"I've arranged a lovely meal in the upper lounge," he said.

She remembered the spot and wondered whether he had sensed how much she'd favored it during their tour. She didn't ask, though. They exchanged idle words along the way, with him taking such a keen interest that she suspected his genuineness.

When they arrived, she fell even more in love with the small lounge area. The flowering plants were the same, but this time the wall screen portrayed an ocean colored pink, purple, and orange by the setting star. A single table sat in the center. The beauty of the table settings almost surpassed the scene behind it. Two tall candles—real ones—illuminated the gorgeous bouquet of bright yellow and soft cream flowers set between them. The maroon plates were embossed with gold-leaf designs along the rims. Gleaming silverware rested beside them. A large silver platter held a meat-like substance surrounded by bright vegetables that were undoubtedly fresh rather than fabricated.

He pulled out her chair and invited her to sit. She was so stunned that it took a moment to snap into movement. She eased into the padded dining chair with a synthetic wood-carved back. "This is all so amazing."

He sat across from her and entwined his fingers. His eyes peered into hers and lit up with admiration. "Such a lovely lady as yourself deserves the best."

She shook her head and blushed. Suspicion rose again, but she couldn't imagine why he'd go through all this trouble just for her.

She'd never considered herself ugly, but neither was she beautiful enough to warrant such attentions.

Despite his obvious wooing, she didn't need a relationship right now—especially not while trapped here on this ship.

"Thank you," she said, hating how lame the words sounded compared to his generosity.

His smile appeared modest, but she swore it contained a hint of gloating, too. His smart blue uniform reminded her of a male peacock. So did the way he held himself upright and moved his hands when he talked, as though caressing silk.

He leaned in. For a moment, she thought it was because he wanted a kiss. The lift of his brows hinted at something else, so she bent forward as well.

"I left a message for your boss," he whispered. "I couldn't leave him a way to return it, but I'm sure he'll receive it."

She placed her hand over her chest. "Thank you." This time, her words came out with more appreciation. It occurred to her he might be lying, but he seemed so sincere.

The meal began well enough. Their conversation was mostly one-sided as he asked more about her life than she did his. Not that she didn't want to know, but he kept turning it back to her. She liked sharing, yet her anxiety increased. Although he probably held motives behind his charm, she wanted something from him too. If she asked for it and he agreed, she might feel obligated to give in to him. And if she didn't fall for his charms, she'd be the one taking advantage. The thought of either made her stomach sour.

But she'd promised herself she'd help Jori. The boy had seemed troubled after her tour with Blakesley the other day. Then his misery increased after they'd summoned him for more testing. Even though he appeared more energized in the gymnasium today, his eyes held a haunted dullness that caused her heart to clench.

She set down her fork and cleared her throat. "I'm worried about your boss."

Blakesley nodded. "He's a hard man sometimes."

She took a swig of the champagne and hoped the alcohol would kick in enough to give her some bravery. It didn't, but she pressed on through the jittering of her nerves. "He's more than that. I haven't been around him much, but everyone has warned me about him. What bothers me more is what he wants with Jori. Why is he forcing these tests on him?"

Blakesley's eyes sparked with annoyance. She couldn't be sure if it was directed at the topic or her. He set his fork aside and wiped his hands on his napkin. His expression turned thoughtful. "What do you know about this boy?"

She wanted to ask him the same thing but answered instead. "I know he's an exceptional young man, but I also know he's not a MEGA."

Blakesley seemed to put a lot of care into folding his napkin and placing it on his lap. "I agree. He's not a MEGA."

"So why? I get the harvesting of his genes—which is horribly unethical, by the way—but why the tests?"

Blakesley shrugged. And for some reason, he also darkened. "Vance is curious about his abilities. And when he wants to know more about something, he's relentless."

A shiver ripped down her spine. "How did he even find out about them? Those files are confidential."

Blakesley sighed. "I'm sorry. I can't tell you these things. This conversation already borders on the line of confidential."

She scowled. "So you're telling me that how you accessed his confidential information is confidential?"

He raised his hands in a defensive gesture. "I get it. I do. But there's not much I can do about it."

"Can't you talk to your boss? Or your boss' boss? Jori is just a child. We shouldn't be here and he shouldn't have to undergo these things. He's been through a lot already."

Blakesley bobbed his head, but he didn't meet her eyes. "I'll see what I can do."

She thanked him. Although the tough conversation was done, her guilt remained. The champagne was crisp and flavorful, the dinner was delicious, and desert was heavenly. Yet she didn't enjoy any of it. She'd used him and had no intention of letting him use her in return.

She played a pleasant guest while her insides ate at her, all while trying to tell herself it was his fault for keeping them against their will.

19
Reasoning

The air crackled with pent-up frustration. The conveyor opened to the command level. Major Abelard Blakesley blinked and uncrossed his arms. He'd been so lost in thought that he didn't remember getting into the car. His date with Zaina had gone well until she pressed him about that damned boy. Her emotions had dropped to where he had to grind his teeth to keep from snapping at her. *Damn her and her weepiness*. How could he possibly hope to earn the favor of someone so depressing?

Despite there not being much that was remarkable about her, she still tantalized him. Was it because she was the only real woman he'd had contact with in months? Or was it because she kept resisting him and he enjoyed the chase? Either way, it compelled him to follow through with her request. Not that it would do any good.

Ugh. Vance and his sick obsessions. He yanked on the hem of his uniform. An uneasiness built up in his gut as he headed to Vance's office. He chewed the inside of his cheek, hoping for inspiration on how to broach this subject. Providing alternatives to the man was like tiptoeing through a den of dozing lions. First, present it as Vance's idea without criticizing his current tactics. Second, convince Vance the advantages were in his favor. These methods didn't always work, though. Hell, they almost never worked.

Blakesley scratched at his palms. He had to try, but not for Zaina. Getting on her good side was still a worthy goal, but his own ambitions required he discredit this upstart boy.

Vance's door opened without prompting. Blakesley gritted his teeth. They both had sentio abilities, but Vance liked to flaunt his.

He entered. Vance sat at a grandiose desk made from genuine wood and put on a gloating smile that caused Blakesley's insides to writhe.

"You should be nervous," Vance said.

Blakesley froze. Despite his best efforts to block his thoughts and emotions, the man had somehow figured out why he was here.

Vance's eyes gleamed with a sick hunger. "I've been waiting for a challenge like this for a long time."

"What challenge?" Blakesley asked, his heart jumping into a gallop.

"This boy." Vance tapped the monitor on his desk.

"Um, I'm not sure I understand. He has a few good qualities but he's hardly a match for either of us. I'm beginning to think he's a waste of our efforts."

Vance shook his head. His smugness remained. "I get why you say that. You're weak. You'd rather eliminate a problem than face it."

Blakesley held back a retort. Antagonizing the man would get him nowhere but in the infirmary. *I need to reason with him.* "It's risky keeping him here. We have a mission to complete and if someone finds out we have him, it might create problems."

"No one knows he's here."

"How can you be so—"

"I'm sure!" Vance smacked the desktop.

Blakesley jumped, then closed his eyes to gather his thoughts. "The Cooperative will realize he's missing and will look for him." A creak from the man's white and gold throne-like chair caused him to snap his eyes open. Vance rose. The heat in his face frayed Blakesley's nerves but he kept his voice steady. "The boy's not worth the risk."

"He's worth *every* risk."

Blakesley took an involuntary step back as the man reached his full height. *Damn, he's so touchy.* "The DNA test shows he's no better than either of us."

Vance's eyes narrowed. "It seems we didn't read the same report."

Blakesley broke out into a cold sweat. Did Vance know he'd altered it? Maybe he hadn't before, but he certainly did now. Blakesley wanted to kick himself for his foolishness, but he kept his cool. He yanked at the front of his uniform again and cleared his throat. "Perhaps I just misunderstood it."

A grin spread across Vance's face. "Perhaps so." The man sat back down. "I'll let it slide, though. This thing you have for the woman has obviously muddled your brain."

Blakesley's dry throat itched but he dared not make another sound.

"Normally I'd say she's a waste of time," Vance said, "but go ahead, continue seeing her. And keep her away from the boy when he goes in for more tests."

"Of course. What reason should I give for no longer allowing her to accompany him?"

Vance's eyes hardened. "Don't give one. They need to understand *I* make the rules about who goes where and when."

Blakesley shivered. So that was it, then. Use her to coerce the boy into cooperating. He reconsidered his promise to Zaina and decided to break it. If Jori wanted Vance to stop, he could tell him himself. No sense risking his own neck.

"Dismissed," Vance snapped.

Blakesley pursed his lips and bowed.

"One more thing," Vance said just as he turned to leave. "If you mess with that boy's files again, I'll flay the skin off that pretty face of yours."

The man's matter-of-fact tone froze him in his tracks. "M-MEGA-Man won't let you maim me."

"That used to be true."

Every hair on Blakesley's body prickled. The room spun but he managed to remain steady as he bolted out.

Psychopathic asshole.

*****

The faster Major Abelard Blakesley walked, the more quickly his trepidation wore off and his anger spread. By the time he reached Doctor Stephen Stenson in the lab, his blood was at a boil.

The doctor looked away from the microscope and startled, his dark bushy brows almost lifting to the top of his forehead. "Major. Is everything alright?"

Blakesley clenched his fists behind his back and thrust out his chest. “No, it is *not*. Did it ever occur to you I had changed that report for a reason?”

“I-I,” the doctor stuttered. His eyes darted wildly as though looking for an escape route. “I-I didn’t want Vance to find out it’d been altered.”

Blakesley stomped forward.

The doctor pulled back. “H-he would assume it was me. I-I couldn’t risk that. He’ll hurt her.”

The man flicked his hand at no one, but Blakesley knew who he meant. Vance got a sick pleasure out of hurting people and enjoyed it more when their loved ones watched. And the good doctor would do anything to protect his addlebrained wife.

Blakesley ground his teeth. If he was like Vance, he’d threaten to harm her too. But alas, he wasn’t. Perhaps another tactic was in order. He jutted his chin. “Do you know what MEGA-Man intends to do with the boy? Surely you’d rather not cause *his* suffering.”

Stephen shook his head. “B-but if Vance thinks the boy is useless, he might kill him.”

Although Blakesley wouldn’t mind that outcome, he didn’t use it in his argument. He’d have to find another way.

What if he set something up that made Vance *want* to murder the boy? The thought tweaked his conscience. He didn’t need Jori to die to be rid of him. Zaina wanted to leave. Maybe he’d help her. She’d want to take the boy with her, so he’d make that happen too—and without Vance discovering his involvement. Of course, Vance would chase after them. However, if this imp was as intelligent as his genes suggested, he’d outsmart his pursuer and survive.

If not, oh well. It wouldn’t be Blakesley’s fault if Jori got himself killed.

20
Stamina

Mushin. No mind. The monotonous task of jogging on a treadmill with only a white wall to look at created a state similar to meditating. Two hours of running made Jori sweat, but nothing more. The mild burn in his legs provided a comfort. The air entering and exiting his lungs revitalized his body and brain. After weeks of sticking close to hard-nosed guardians, it was nice being able to use the gym every day. So long as he didn't think about where he was.

He barely noticed all the connecting wires now. Nor the sound of the treadmill spooling beneath him. Doctor Celine Stenson's excitement as she watched his stats added to the workout euphoria.

All this almost made him forget Zaina wasn't allowed to be here—almost. That split-second recollection of her stricken features as Blakesley had tried to comfort her caused his insides to burn and tumble.

The message was clear. Vance controlled everything.

Part of his anger was at Zaina. When she'd insisted on coming with him anyway, Blakesley bellowed at her idiocy. Rather than argue, Zaina had shrunk back in terror. In that moment, Jori had wished she had been a soldier like his other guardians. He'd shot her a dirty look and left her there without bothering to say goodbye.

Was fighting really so wrong? He couldn't reconcile the need to defend themselves and her claim that everything should be handled peacefully. He didn't expect her to fight, but she shouldn't have given in so easily.

Remembering her words when she'd caught him sparring inflamed his resentment. It wasn't like he'd resort to violence at the first sign of difficulty. She had no idea of the trials he'd faced.

Hell, violence had even found him on a supposedly peaceful Cooperative vessel.

Doctor Stephen Stenson came over and blew out a whistle when he checked the readout. "Impressive!"

"Almost as impressive as mine," Vance interjected.

Jori flinched, then silently berated himself. He kept jogging, face forward, and didn't bother acknowledging the man who'd snuck up behind him. A little voice inside his head said he was a coward for it, but he ignored it.

Stephen's emotions spiked into alarm. The same emotion tried to rise within Jori too, but he refused to let Vance intimidate him.

"Of c-course," the doctor stammered. "I believe you lasted twelve hours." He chuckled nervously. "And could have gone longer if not for that pesky need for sleep."

"Let's see if he can make it that long."

"H-him?" Stephen asked. "He's just a kid."

Celine's emotions brightened. "Oh, he can do it. I see nothing here that says he can't."

Jori winced at her innocent comment. The poor woman's simpleness would get him in trouble.

"He's old enough," Vance replied. "And he's like me. Run him."

Stephen cleared his throat. "O-oh. Alright. I guess we can do that." He touched Jori's shoulder. "I'll get you some water."

"No water," Vance said.

"No water?" Stephen's voice hitched up an octave. "He'll get dehydrated."

"No water. I want to see how long he'll last."

"B-but… But that's—"

Vance's voice dropped. "I want to see how long he'll last."

"I-I… Y-yes, Sir."

A swelling panic built in Jori's chest. He broke into jagged huffs. Running this treadmill like some lab rat was bad enough, but to keep going until he collapsed from dehydration? *Chima.* He peered over his shoulder and frowned. "Why? What is the purpose?"

"To prove you're like me."

Jori suppressed a shudder and stubbornly ran on. Vance watched a little while, then left. The hours passed. Doctor Stenson came by every thirty minutes or so, offering comfort only to leave again because Jori only responded with glowers.

Thirst hit him before fatigue did. Not being able to rehydrate eventually turned his tongue into a wad of cloth. Before long, a headache formed. It grew in intensity, stabbing through his skull like a screwdriver.

A wave of dizziness washed over him. He stumbled but regained his feet and concentrated on continuing despite the cramping of his muscles. His footsteps became heavier. His eyelids drooped. The room spun. The dry heat of his body made him feel like he stood amid the exhaust of a spaceship.

He considered quitting out of spite, but refused to run from a fight. He gritted his teeth and pressed on. Vance wanted to see how far he could go, so he went. It didn't matter if he beat his record, but he'd push regardless. His innate refusal to give up overruled logic.

This resembled an experience he'd had with a teacher back home. Hideji had been relentless in his training. One time, he'd deposited Jori at the foot of the Gaoshan mountains and told him he had one day to hike through the high-elevation pass. If he didn't make it in time, the transport ship would leave. He'd be stuck there, hoping the hungry mountain lions wouldn't mistake him for a meal.

Those dry mountains had caused him to run out of water. The fatigue cramping his body had nearly crushed him, but he refused to let this hated teacher see him fail. He made it, but just barely.

When he'd returned to the ship only half-conscious, Sensei Jeruko was furious. He'd taken Jori first to the infirmary, then to his mother's quarters where he spent a full day in recovery.

He missed his mother—her smile, her practical suggestions for dealing with his troubles, the way she softly hummed as she combed her fingers through his hair whenever he was upset.

A weight of sorrow fell over him, almost causing him to collapse. She couldn't have prevented Father from ordering Jori to undergo that excruciating test. Just like Zaina wouldn't be able protect him from Vance now. As much as he hated how useless Zaina was, he understood her helplessness. A clump of guilt for getting angry with her dropped into the pit of his stomach.

He still wasn't sure they'd be capable of handling this without a fight. He had no hope of defeating the man with his fists, but force would undoubtedly become necessary. The risk of Zaina's judgment weighed on him, but he didn't see another way.

An insistent beep sounded. Stephen darted to his side with frantic worry. Jori realized he must be in some sort of medical danger. The doctor chewed his fingernails. No doubt Vance's orders had made him reluctant to act.

Jori reeled, then tripped over his own feet. His chin struck the treadmill display, sending a sharp pain through his head that momentarily overpowered his headache. His body hit the tread with a smack and rolled him off. The cold floor shocked him. He tried to rise but was too weak.

Blackness whirled in his vision. He fought it, to no avail, as it engulfed him into a pit of nothingness.

21
Disillusioned

Disjointed images flittered inside Zaina Noman's head as she drifted in and out of slumber. Sometimes a thought poked through that caused her nerves to tremble and her mind to flee. Other impressions were so mundane, she didn't bother with them. One captured her attention, but its meaning lay beyond reach. She could've studied it harder, but letting it float away was easier.

The hydraulic hiss of the door roused her. She snapped awake, expecting to see Jori return, but the silhouette was too tall. She rose onto her elbow and rubbed the blurriness from her puffy eyes.

"My dearest!" Blakesley said as he rushed over. "I've been ringing for you, but you didn't answer. Are you alright?"

She pushed his hand off her shoulder. "I don't want to talk to you."

His brows curled as though concerned, but his eyes flashed with something else. "I'm so sorry for my earlier outburst. I was frightened."

She huffed.

"It's true. If I had let you go with the boy, we'd both be in serious trouble. You don't know what Vance is like."

"You said you'd speak to him." Her voice rumbled, partly out of anger and partly from her throat being sore from crying.

He pressed his lips together. "I swear I tried, but he can't be reasoned with."

She cradled her aching head in her palm. Disillusionment settled in her chest like a load of bricks. "He's never letting us go, is he?"

He glanced away without answering.

"What does he really want from Jori? Why test his abilities?"

"MEGA or not, he has skills MEGA-Man wants."

So this MEGA-Man the news has been speculating about is real. But why so much interest in a boy? If they wanted his DNA, couldn't they just take it? "Do you mean his ability to fight?" she asked, unintentionally letting her distaste for the violence he'd displayed show through her tone.

Blakesley cocked his head, then his eyes sparked as though realizing something. "Exactly. Much of Vance's interest in him is because they're a lot alike."

Her throat tightened. "What do you mean?"

Blakesley arched an eyebrow. "The information you have on him is only part of the story. There's a lot you don't know."

The hairs on her arms spiked at his sinister tone. "It said he's taken a life, but in self-defense."

"Oh, not just *one* life, many lives."

She gasped. "Many?" she asked with a squeak.

"You really have no idea?" His mouth quirked with incredulity and sent a chill down her spine. "Trust me. Your people are not equipped to handle him."

Zaina worked her dry tongue, but no words came out. It was too much to process.

Blakesley eased beside her and wrapped his arm around her. "Listen. I think I can help you."

She blinked. "How?"

"Vance isn't interested in you." His eyes tilted apologetically. "So I might convince him to allow you to leave, but only you."

"I-I can't leave him." She said despite her misgivings.

"You can't handle him, dear."

She shook her head. The prospect of taking a killer child to her homeworld was daunting, but he was better off there than with a bunch of people who wanted to use him. She wasn't a fool. Blakesley was a military man. Vance too. And they'd use Jori as one as well.

He loosened his embrace but didn't let go. "I want to help you." His eyes sharpened onto hers and he gripped her shoulders. "Until then, you *mustn't* defy Vance's orders. I get it. You want to be there for the boy, but you simply can't. Nor should you. He's perfectly capable of hurting you."

She swallowed down the lump in her throat. The tightness of his features and the firmness of his tone punctuated the danger she was in. Jori wouldn't hurt her, though. Would he? She wasn't sure about him, but she was fairly certain about that big scary man who ran this ship. "But I'm afraid of what Vance will do to him."

Blakesley's jaw twitched. "He won't kill him. You have my word."

She blinked several times. The promise sounded good if she didn't look too closely at the fact that he'd only promised Jori wouldn't be *killed*. "So what do I do?"

He rubbed her shoulders. "Trust in me and we can get through this."

Her distrust wouldn't allow her to reply. Blakesley must've taken her silence for agreement because he patted her hand and offered more reassurances. She heard him but wasn't really listening. Thoughts tried to formulate in her fogged brain to no avail.

"Zaina, dear? Are you alright?"

Before she could speak, the ache in her skull cracked like lightning. She moaned and let her head fall back on the pillow.

"Zaina!" Blakesley shook her.

"I'm fine. I'm fine," she mumbled. She attempted to wave him away but had little strength. "It's just a headache."

Concern etched his eyes as he studied her face. He pressed a hand to her cheek, then forehead. "Come. Let's get you to the infirmary. The doctor can give you another treatment and you'll be back in tip-top condition."

"But I can't be where Jori is," she murmured.

"He's not in that area. It will be alright."

Her chest tightened, but she forced in some air and exhaled noisily as Blakesley helped her rise. He hooked his arm in hers and half-carried her out. Her muscles protested but worked better by the time they reached the infirmary. Too bad the pounding in her skull remained.

Blakesley eased her onto a bed. She considered lying down, but stayed upright and scanned the room for Jori instead. He wasn't here, like Blakesley had said. She wasn't sure whether to be relieved or disappointed.

Doctor Claessen arrived. Her smile was soft yet off in a way that Zaina couldn't identify.

After a series of questions, the doctor retrieved a hypospray. "This will help for a while." She pressed the instrument to Zaina's neck. A hiss sounded, indicating injection.

Within moments, a freshness like cool water surged through Zaina's head. A sigh escaped her lips and she collapsed with relief. "Thank you so much."

Doctor Claessen patted her shoulder. "Of course. You know, I used to have the same issues you did. The stress was so intense, my body would fail. I'd be bedridden for days on end—one time for an entire month. I was such a mess."

Zaina held her breath, waiting for the doctor to divulge her secret. All thoughts about Jori fled.

"I learned about this procedure from a Doctor Garrett. He inserted a chip he calls motislaxo and it regulates my emotions so they no longer get out of control."

Zaina pulled back. "A chip?"

The doctor nodded. "It made my life so much easier."

Zaina turned to Blakesley and frowned.

Not a hint of surprise showed on his face as he dipped his head. "This has helped many people."

Zaina's thoughts warred. On the one hand, having a way to curb these hard emotions sounded like heaven. On the other, some here seemed more machine than human. "Would I still be the same?" she asked the doctor.

"You'll be yourself—just less stressed."

Zaina studied the woman. She had a chip yet she wasn't like many of these others. Her smile was natural. Her expression sincere.

It was almost enough for Zaina to say yes. Her nerves jumped like an excited dog against its leash. Something other than a leash held her back but she wasn't sure what it was. "I'll think about it."

Doctor Claessen smiled. "I'll send information to your tablet."

Zaina slid off the edge of the bed, eager to return to her quarters and see what this procedure offered. The prospect of getting out from under all her medical problems made her want to sing. She could get over this trauma, put in more hours at work, help more people, do more good. Her life would be hers again.

Since leaving him here was out of the question, she'd have the mental strength to help him. With more room for rationality, she'd be able to make a plan to get them both out of this situation without being crippled by her emotions.

I can finally be free.

22
Too Good

Eight hours and forty-seven minutes. Major Abelard Blakesley gnashed his teeth, which vibrated from the grating of the blaring medical alarm. He schooled his resentment as he glowered down at the half-conscious imp who'd beat his record by over an hour. Worse, he hadn't given up—just continued until he collapsed.

The impromptu conversation with Zaina earlier suddenly seemed like a bad idea. Not the part about the chip. If the doctors were careful, they'd curb her pathetic emotions without making her like Phoebe.

No, the part he should've put more thought into was what he'd said about Jori. His intention had been to drive a wedge between them so she'd be more open to his overtures. But what he really wanted was to retain his importance with MEGA-Man. Since discrediting Jori wasn't working, and since the imp was too damned good at everything, his best option was to get rid of him.

He'd prefer to do it by assisting in his escape, but dare he go against Vance? It was either take a calculated risk or be stuck in this life of mediocrity. Or worse, fall so far down in importance that he became expendable.

He side-eyed the psychopath standing beside him. The demented gleam in the man's eyes as he watched the boy suffer made Blakesley want to throw up. It also contributed to his ever-growing resentment.

Jori's eyes fluttered open. He tried to push himself up with no success. Doctor Stephen Stenson shifted from foot to foot as he darted glances at Vance. Despite Blakesley's distaste for this unnecessary mistreatment, a smile lurked behind his lips. Maybe he wouldn't have to help the boy escape after all. It would solve all his problems if he died.

Vance signaled the go-ahead with a dip of his head, dashing his hopes. Doctor Stephen Stenson rushed to remove the electrodes and other things attached to Jori's body. A med bot rolled up and the doctor scrambled for a few implements. The sweat on his brow betrayed his frantic worry. Perhaps Jori would suffer permanent damage. It would serve Vance right for pushing him so hard.

A diminished mental capacity wouldn't be enough to keep genetic material from being harvested, though. Blakesley clenched his fists as the doctor moved the boy to a bed and attached an IV to his arm. Within minutes of him getting liquid, the alarms ceased. Jori groaned and alertness crept back into his eyes.

Vance wore a stupid boasting smile. "Not bad," he said to the boy. "Not as good as me, but better than the major here."

An acidic taste surged into Blakesley's mouth.

"MEGA-Man will be pleased," Vance added.

The boy's face twisted in pure rancor. Blakesley suppressed the pleasure that welled up inside. It was obvious Jori didn't want to cooperate. This made Blakesley look good. It also meant the boy was likely to refuse implants, further highlighting Blakesley's value. *Maybe I could use this in another way.*

"What do you think, Major?" Vance said, his pleased smile still plastered to his face.

"He did well," Blakesley replied. "But having great stamina isn't much by itself."

Vance dipped his head. "Agreed." He turned to Mister Doctor Stenson. "Get him ready for the sentio test."

Stephen's mouth opened and closed. "I-I can do that, Sir. But if you want him at peak performance, he needs to rehydrate and get some rest."

No! Blakesley wanted to shout. *Let him test when he's at his worst!*

"How long?" Vance asked.

"T-twen—no, twelve hours. Perhaps a little more depending on how much sleep he needs."

"Have him sleep here and monitor the details of his recovery. I want to know the science behind his healing ability."

Blakesley's jaw hardened. *Damn it.*

The doctor bobbed his head. "Yes, Sir."

Jori's frown deepened.

Vance pivoted on his heel to go. Blakesley flashed Jori a smile as a phony offer of friendship, then turned to follow.

"Stay here," Vance said without bothering to look at him.

"Sir?"

Vance disappeared out the door. Blakesley frowned, wondering what the hell was expected of him. *Well, at least it's a good opportunity to feed this boy's discontent.* A wedge between Jori and his illustrious leader might work in his favor.

He returned to the boy. "I noted your emotions when Vance mentioned MEGA-Man," he said carefully in case Vance foresaw this moment. "You should be honored."

Instead of being offended, Jori emitted suspicion. "Why?"

"He's the most important man in the galaxy. If he's interested in you, it means he has great things planned for you."

"Is that why you don't like me?"

Blakeley flinched at the boy's accuracy. "I like you just fine," he blurted.

"Liar. You're in on it too, aren't you?"

Blakesley blinked. "In on what?"

"This test," Jori stated.

"These tests are Vance's idea, not mine."

"No, I mean this game he's playing. He wants to see if I'll ask you for help in escaping."

Fear seized Blakesley's throat. Of course this was why Vance had told him to stay here. Good thing he'd played it smart.

"I won't, though," Jori said with a glower. "I don't trust you."

Perfect. Blakesley withheld a smile. If this conversation led to Jori escaping on his own, then he wouldn't have to take any risks himself. "Sorry to hear that," he lied, knowing very well the boy would detect it.

Jori pressed his lips flat. Blakesley considered what else to do or say to prod him into taking Vance up on his challenge. No one had ever matched that psychopath before and lived, but he kept that to himself. Let the boy find out the hard way. If he escaped, good. If he didn't, even better.

For once, one of Vance's stupid games would benefit him. Now, if he could just let Zaina believe he was the one working on a plan, he'd win her too.

23
Sensations

Soft glowing patches of color developed amid the vast nothingness. Incoherent thoughts rippled by. Muted sounds became clearer—the whisper of movement, a voice, a periodic beep. Consciousness arrived peacefully at first, like a trickling stream. But as reality coalesced, discomfort swelled.

The more Jori woke, the more he noticed the lumpiness of his bed. It dug into his back, reminding him of the time he'd slept on a tree root during a survival excursion. If only he could do that again. He'd take extreme weather, meager nourishment, and wild animals over whatever Vance had in store for him next.

He filled his lungs and squinted against the bright lighting. Beige dominated this room with its patterned tiled walls, glossy countertop, and the faux-wooden cupboards. A burnt orange door wide enough to accommodate a recovery bed lay across from him. Two pictures of butterflies and flowers hung on the wall to his left. Despite the room's claustrophobic smallness, its quietude diluted his worries. It was a pleasant change from the sterility he'd seen elsewhere.

He fumbled for the bed controls and found them on the side. The bumpy patterns on the buttons probably signified which function was which, but he couldn't decipher them. Randomly pressing one made the area under his knees rise. The next button brought it back down. Another try didn't seem to do anything until he noticed a heat against his backside. He pressed the one after it and nothing happened. *Damn it.* Several more attempts finally put him into a reclined position.

The orange door swished open. The Stensons walked in, Stephen with a friendly smile and Celine with an odd intensity as she viewed something from the MM tablet wrapped around her wrist.

"You're awake," the man said. "And your vitals look great. How do you feel?"

"Like I've been through a planetary landing in a freelance cargo ship." The doctor cocked his head and frowned so Jori explained. "Most ships like that are older and tend to jostle."

"Ah. So you're not a hundred percent yet. Good."

Jori almost asked what he meant by *good*, but Stephen's worry reminded him of the impending test. Evaluating the extent of his sentio abilities didn't sound so bad, but Vance would probably add a few demented twists.

"How long have I been here—in the infirmary?"

Stephen pulled up his sleeve and glanced at his own MM tablet. "Twelve hours and twenty minutes."

Jori bolted upright, barely registering the protest of his muscles. "Is Zaina allowed to see me now?"

Stephen's drooping features answered his question. Jori bit down his annoyance and it turned into concern. He used his senses to search for her. Her familiar lifeforce enabled him to connect instantly. She felt exactly as imagined, though her worry was somewhat dulled from only being half awake. He wished he could be there to help her somehow—and tell her he was sorry for being angry with her.

Celine reached over to remove Jori's IV. Stephen placed his hand on her arm. "Not yet, dear."

She shot him a blank look. "But he needs to get ready for his sentio test."

Stephen patted her. "We'll wait a little longer."

"Now is better," she stated matter-of-factly. She didn't offer a reason, but her emotions reflected eagerness.

"Let the boy rest, dear."

"That's not necessary. He's ready now."

When she reached for the electrodes connected to Jori's head, Stephen grasped her arm and gently turned her away. "Why don't you review Divya's metabolic panel?"

She huffed. "That's boring."

"But we need to find out what's wrong with her."

"I already know."

"Did you treat her?"

"No. Too busy."

Frustration showed through the tightness of Stephen's face, but he kept his tone light. "She needs our help. Go take care of it. Then we can test Jori."

"I don't want to," she said without malice.

"You must, dear. You must. Remember, we talked about this? We have many duties to attend to and can't always pick the ones we'd rather do." He walked her to the door, a sad love emanating from him. "So, let's help Divya."

A small smile crept across Jori's face as he admired how Stephen still cared for her despite her inability to reciprocate. She consented but not with words or emotions. Her mind switched focus and she left with no hint of annoyance or resignation.

Stephen came back to Jori with downturned eyes. "I'm sorry, but I can't let you rest for long."

Jori understood. Vance didn't seem like a patient man. "What's this next test like?"

The doctor's mood lifted a tad. "It will be much easier, just a little more time-consuming." He licked his lips. "It's um…"

"What?" Jori asked.

Stephen looked at his shoes. "I hate doing these things to you. It's not right." He shook his head. "Not right at all."

The man emitted a guilt strong enough to make Jori's own stomach hurt. The sensation reminded him of how his father had pressured Bunmi, an old teacher back home, into causing him pain. "It's not your fault. I understand."

"I wish there was something I could do."

"Are you sure there's not?" Jori leaned in and whispered. "Doesn't he have a weakness?"

"If he does, I'm not certain what it is."

"His premonition ability must have limitations."

Stephen's eyes darted about the room. "Well, yes, but I can't tell you." He glanced behind him at the door Celine had gone through. "It won't do you any good anyway. You even try to outsmart him, and he'll…" He flicked his hand. "You know."

"Can you write it down?"

The doctor's head wagged. "He sees what you see, hears what you hear, smells what you smell."

Goosebumps rose on Jori's arms. "Can he feel what I feel? Or read my mind?"

Stephen pressed his lips together. His reluctance to say gave Jori the answer he needed. If Vance couldn't sense someone when predicting their future, then this might be a weakness to exploit.

Something else occurred to him too. If Vance foresaw this moment, had he done it through Jori, Stephen, or was he an outsider looking in? It was a good question, but the doctor's growing discomfort kept him from asking.

He plopped back onto the reclined bed and put on a pretend scowl in case someone was watching. Real resentment budded. Although Stephen was a prisoner too, Jori doubted he'd be much help. Zaina would be of little use as well. The responsibility was his, and his alone, to bear.

Loneliness swelled in his chest. He reminded himself that it wasn't the doctor's fault. Bullies had a way of getting what they wanted and Vance was the most dangerous bully he'd ever encountered—even more so than his father. At least Father had mostly ignored him, especially when he was younger.

The past few years had been tougher. As his skills progressed, his father's criticism worsened. Yet he still had more freedom than he did now. A sensation of being watched made him itch.

He maintained a false bravado and crossed his arms with a huff. "We might as well get these stupid tests over with."

*****

Jori ate the last bite of the flavorless nutri-cubes, appreciating the satisfying fullness of his stomach. The doctor's suggestion that he eat first had cleared the cobwebs from his head. He felt much better—physically, anyway.

Celine removed his IV but left the electrodes, then ushered him out and followed him with a mobile monitor. Stephen led him down one long hall, then another. Plasti-glass windows lined the way. Some rooms were dark, but others were brightly illuminated. They all looked normal enough until he passed an area where several MEGAs were submerged in cylindrical tanks. Wires were attached to their metal-plated heads and their eyes stared straight ahead as though they were dead. Jori didn't detect any lifeforces, but he swore one moved.

"What is this place?"

"Recharging station." Stephen's tone, coupled with his sour emotions, indicated he didn't want to explain.

Jori swallowed, his curiosity doused. Stephen stopped at a blue door and leaned toward a biometric eye scanner. The entrance hissed open. The room beyond seemed ordinary enough, almost like a sitting area. A vivid green couch sat against an azure wall. A small table on one side held a red vase containing fake variegated flowers. An orange padded chair took up the other end. He wondered if there was a purpose to the jarring colors, but only for a moment.

Stephen led him through another doorway. The lights flickered on automatically, revealing a plain white room. Jori suppressed a groan at the sight of the recovery bed. "Can't I just sit or stand for this test?"

Stephen twisted his lips as though in thought. "I don't see why not. As long as you're still hooked up to this monitor." He hurried off to find a chair.

Celine went to work, taking more wires that splayed out from her machine like a multi-armed sea creature and attaching them to his body. He practically wore a helmet, so many were stuck to his head. The ones placed on his chest itched the most.

Stephen returned with a chair, then handed him a tablet. He pointed at a small red box illuminated on the top right corner of the screen. "When this turns green, the test has begun. People will come into that room at random times over the next two hours." He barely blinked at the timeframe, but Jori tensed. Two more hours away from Zaina. "You are to notate their emotions. If there is more than one, estimate the percentages of each. Indicate whether they are male or female and guess their ages. See if you can figure out what they're thinking as well. You said you can't read minds but try anyway. It's important that you do your best."

Seems easy enough.

"If you don't," Stephen continued, "Vance will know, and he'll make you do it again."

Of course he will. Jori tightened his grip on the tablet and responded with a sharp nod.

"There'll be a few surprises as well." The man's emotions were flat, signifying they weren't anything bad. "If you notice something different, select *other* and type it in. Give as much detail as possible."

The doctors left, pressing a button and activating a thick metal door that clanged shut. It made sense. For the test to be accurate, he shouldn't see or hear the person on the other side.

Jori willed the green light to come on so he could get this stupid test over and done. Yes, he'd do his best, but he'd hate every moment.

The red square turned green. He closed his eyes and concentrated. Happiness shone through at first, then evened out into simple content. He marked it down, then noted how the emotion changed to one of boredom.

The sensation was from a man probably about the same age as Commander Hapker. Jori wasn't always certain when it came to ages and genders, but this one was clear. However, reading the man's thoughts proved beyond his ability.

Stephen emitted emotions that suggested another person had arrived, but he sensed nothing. Should he put this on the tablet? He decided against it. There was no point since he couldn't discern the age or gender either.

More people came and went. His own boredom threatened to interfere. He kept at it, certain of the emotions of those who had them, confident of their genders and ages, but never once sure about their thoughts.

He was trying but didn't have this aspect of his mother's ability. She not only read minds, but she also compelled information from them. Sometimes she even planted suggestions into them. She seldom used these abilities, though. The few times she had were either because his father had made her or she'd acted in self-defense.

His focus slipped as he remembered when she'd instinctively used it on his father to keep him from hurting her. Father had been pissed. He would've killed her for her audacity had Sensei Jeruko not suggested exile instead.

Jori squeezed his eyes shut as anguish welled up. She was too far away now—beyond his reach—and he'd never see her again.

The strength of his emotions increased, and he realized much of it came from someone without a clear gender. Before he had a chance to guess the cause, the distress drifted off. Jori marked it down and returned his attention to the test.

The next sensation took a few moments to discern. It differed from all the others in that it was more of a state of mind than an emotion. Its simpleness reminded him of an animal, probably a mammal. But what kind? He concentrated.

His nose twitched. For a moment, he thought he smelled food. A minuscule eagerness came in, making him think of a mouse. He almost saw it as it moved—no skittered—to the source. Its hunger grew and Jori's mouth watered as though he ate too. Something else entered his senses. This one had a flatter aura, but he still recognized it. Its primitive instinct to hunt reminded Jori of a reptile and he felt himself slither to the mouse.

An abrupt sensation followed by the pain of death struck through Jori's senses. Fortunately, the mouse's demise didn't hurt to the same extent as it did when people died.

The mammal's life ended. The reptile's hunting vibes switched to something flat again. It didn't have the same eagerness when feeding as the mouse since these types of animals acted more on instinct than on gratification.

Jori filled in the form and froze at the section on reading minds. He'd just sensed an animal to where he felt like he *was* the animal. In a way, he'd discerned its thoughts. That'd never happened before. It would've intrigued him had it not correlated with how Vance's premonitions allowed him to see, hear, and smell, but supposedly not sense.

The man obviously had the ability to detect emotions. Had Stephen's shrug meant it didn't work with his foretelling skill or had Jori misread it?

Dread rolled over him. He'd have to verify for himself and hope for the best.

He waited for several more minutes in a sensationless silence before the doctors returned. Celine entered with a broad smile, but it wasn't for Jori. She marveled at the information on her tablet. "This is amazing. You detected the lab animals. You even knew it was a snake and a mouse. This is beyond sentio-animi abilities."

Jori startled. "What do you mean?"

Her grin widened but she never looked at him when she spoke. "Most sentios only sense emotions, but you've provided more detail than I've ever seen. You also correctly guessed the subjects' sexes and you were within a reasonable range of their ages. Can you tell people apart?"

"Yes," he answered cautiously. "Are you saying other sentios can't do this? Vance can, right?"

"Well, yes," Stephen replied for her. "Yes to both questions."

"Most are not able, but a few are." Celine's eyes glittered with excitement. "However, I've never known any capable of identifying different animals—not even Vance."

"So what am I, then?"

"There's no term for it," Stephen said. "You're definitely not an extraho-animi. Not a single one of your guesses on their thoughts were correct. You surmised well enough that one person was bored with the test, and that another drank something delicious, but you couldn't tell what. However, you seem to have more insight with animals."

"Why do you think that is?"

Stephen shrugged. "Maybe because they're more primitive. I'm not sure. But like she said, this is a unique ability."

Jori was intrigued but also worried. Would Vance be jealous or would he relish the competition even more?

Almost as if on cue, Vance entered. The man's eyes gleamed. He wore a smile, but it wasn't smug as he planted himself in front of Jori. "Finally. A worthy opponent."

Icicles seemed to stab every part of Jori's face, prickling down his neck and spine. As much as he loved pushing the extent of his abilities, this was one challenge he'd rather do without.

24
Emotional Support

A hiss startled Zaina out of sleep. She didn't react in any other way, though. Fatigue had gripped her so tightly, she felt like a mouse in a snake's belly. The smothering. The oblivion. The resignation that it was all at an end.

Someone shook her shoulder. "Zaina," Jori said. "Please wake up."

She stirred. Anxiety crept through her gut as she recalled what Blakesley had told her. She still had a difficult time believing it, but why would he lie? *Jori deserves a chance.*

Ignoring her qualms, she rolled onto her back and gave Jori her attention. "Hmm?"

"I'm sorry I was gone for so long," he said. "Are you alright?"

"Just tired."

Jori shook his head. "It's more than that. I can tell."

The concern creased in his brows twinged her guilt. Blakesley must be wrong. If Jori were like Vance, he wouldn't care so much. "Don't worry about me. It's just a bout of depression. It happens from time to time." She noticed the reddish spots around his temple and forehead and startled. "Did they do something to you?"

He glanced away and bit his lip, tripping her concern. She would've bolted upright, but her body didn't obey. Sluggish would have to do. When she sat up, albeit hunched over, she prodded him with persistent questions until he told her about the stamina test. Her emotions bounced around from horror to worry to anxiety and back again. "Why are they doing this?"

It was a rhetorical question, but Jori answered. "Vance thinks I'm like him."

Blakesley's words echoed in her head. "*Part of Vance's interest in him is they're a lot alike.*" A twinge spread across her skull. "I've heard. Blakesley said..." She rubbed her brow. "He said you've killed more than once."

Jori pulled away and stared at the floor.

A pang erupted in her chest. "So it's true?"

Desperation warped his features. "I've only ever *intentionally* taken a life in self-defense!" He wagged his head. "I'm not like him. I'm not like Vance."

She pressed her palm to her heart, trying to quell the rising panic.

"Th-there was this one time..." He choked out the words. "It was my father. He let me fire our ship's weapons at a small outpost and..." His throat bobbed. "But I assumed it was full of soldiers. I didn't... I didn't think."

She struggled to compose herself. His face looked so earnest, and she knew very well that children could be coerced into doing terrible things by their abusive parents. She reminded herself that he'd never done anything to her. "I'm sorry. That wasn't fair." She reached out, hoping he'd take her hand but he didn't. "You must've been through so much."

"I-I didn't know how bad it was until I met the commander."

"The commander?"

"Commander Hapker. He's second-in-command of a Cooperative expedition vessel, and a good man. He cared about me despite who I am and saved me from my father." The anguish in Jori's expression would've melted steel. "He was going to adopt me, but the Cooperative sent me away so he couldn't."

"What? Why?"

"My father is a terrible person and they're afraid I'll be like him."

"Oh, Jori." A tear spilled down her cheek. She would have been upset at them for their judgment had she not done the same thing. "Maybe I can help you contact this commander. It's my job to find you a family, after all."

Jori perked up, but just for a moment. He hung his head and wiped his eyes. "No. I don't want him to lose his position. Besides, I doubt Vance will ever let me go."

Blakeley had said something similar. She frowned. "I don't understand their obsession with you. You *are* special, of course, but surely there are others they can recruit without having to resort to kidnapping."

Jori didn't reply, but the way his throat bobbed and his eyes averted hinted that he knew more. Fear nipped along the edges of her concern for him, and it interfered with her ability to think. If her insides could groan in despair, they would have.

She grasped for logic over the emotion. No matter what he'd done, it just proved he needed help. She'd provide that for him. There were people back home who'd work the psychological angle. And she'd contribute by comforting and guiding him.

Even with knowing the right thing to do, she was helpless. Her mind and body fought against one another. She willed herself to get over this and do better. She prayed, she cajoled, and she commanded. But the power didn't reside within her. Fatigue wound through her like bindings, crushing her until her brain was too tired to fight it.

The more she thought about it, the more appealing an emotion chip sounded. The information Doctor Claessen had sent her seemed promising. She'd read through it despite her foggy mind. Adverse effects had been documented, but the risks were low. She hated taking any risk at all, but she was no use to Jori like this. If she could only get a grip on herself, she'd be able to give him more of the emotional support he needed and perhaps even invigorate herself enough to figure out how to leave this place.

She decided to talk more with Doctor Claessen. However, her body didn't respond to her desire. She lay back down and closed her eyes.

I'll just get a little more rest first.

25
The Game

The Garborians tottered on the edge of annihilation. With their fate resting in the hands of a mere eleven-year-old boy, it was no wonder. Still, Jori did his damnedest to save them.

As much as the game of Galactic Dominions triggered the unpleasant memories of another murdering MEGA, he immersed himself in its complexity. Vance was a challenging opponent, more so than the admiral's aide had been. His moves were precise and ruthless. Jori had disabled the enemy's energy cannons, but it'd cost half his fleet. Only a quarter of his assets remained.

He had one trick up his sleeve. He'd hoped to use it in an all-out attack, but that opportunity never came. Now he had no choice but to put it into play.

Vance looked on with a gloating smile. Jori tried to ignore him as he considered his plan. What was it with these brain-augmented MEGAs and their stupid grins?

Pushing against his unease didn't make it leave, but he managed to focus a little better. There were only so many moves left, so he chose one that made the most of his secret defense. Earlier in the game, he had uncovered the enemy's transponder codes. He hoped when he attacked, the AI targeting systems of Vance's torpedoes would see him as an ally and bypass his fleet. He had to do this just right, though.

Jori programmed his move, making sure his ships wouldn't implement the transponder codes until the last moment. This way, it'd be too late for his opponent to reprogram their weaponry.

Vance's grin widened as he implemented a countermove. Jori's jaw dropped as his entire fleet blew apart in a rainstorm of firepower.

Losing had never bothered him. Not only was it an opportunity to learn, but it also made him look forward to the next challenge.

This move invigorated him. He forgot all about who this man was and marveled. "How did your torpedoes still hit me when I had your transponder codes?"

"I didn't use my AI targeting systems. I did it manually."

Jori blinked. Hardly anyone used manual targeting anymore. That Vance had utilized an old-fashioned method to beat him made him feel stupid.

"Disappointing. I thought you were smarter than this," Vance said.

The comment dampened Jori's mood. In his defense, how could he have guessed someone so advanced would use a technique so primitive? But he knew better than to make excuses. His father had always hated it when people blamed their failures on something other than themselves. Vance undoubtedly would too.

"Who made you?" Vance asked. His smile was gone but the gleam in his eyes remained.

"Huh? What do you mean?"

Vance jabbed his finger at his face. "Who. Made. You."

Jori blinked. "Uh, my mother and father."

Vance shook his head. "Your abilities," he replied, his tone firm. "Where do they come from?"

"I don't have any genetic or cybernetic augmentations."

Vance leaned in. A threat flared in his eyes. "You must."

Jori almost denied it but remembered how violently Vance had reacted the last time he'd contradicted him. His heart thumped and he swallowed down the lump in his throat. "My ancestors were genetically altered. Nearly all the lines in my family tree lead back to someone who had enhancements before the MEGA Injunction."

Vance didn't reply but seemed to accept the response. "Where did your sentio ability come from?"

"My mother, and she inherited it from her mother who inherited it from her father, and so on to a natural origin."

"Could she see animals?"

The way Vance's lips pressed together made Jori fidget. Although this man had said he wanted a challenge, perhaps he hated how someone had a skill he didn't.

"I don't know," Jori replied carefully. "My mother never mentioned it and I never met my grandmother."

"Hmm." Vance stared at nothing. Jori waited in tense silence until the man spoke. "Your ability to tolerate pain. Did that come from your Jintal master or did your ancestors have that talent as well?"

Jori gulped at where this conversation might be headed. "I suspect a little of both. Senshi warriors are expected to endure pain. Their lives could depend on it. So it's possible the skill has built over generations and the Jintal training enhanced it further."

"Hmm. Yes." Vance stared off once again.

Moments passed. Jori waited, not willing to break the tense silence.

Vance sprang to his feet with a suddenness that sent Jori jerking backward far enough to tip his chair. He grabbed the table and steadied himself.

"Let's conduct a test."

Jori's chest constricted. *Damn it.* He thought he'd gotten his fear of this man under control. What the hell was he afraid of, anyway? His Jintal teacher, Master Bunmi, had never made him feel this frightened and that man had once smashed his hand with a hammer. His father had always scared him too, but Jori had learned to suppress it with a stubborn anger. Not even when Father stabbed him in the heart had he been this nervous.

Vance headed to the rear bedroom. The sound of rummaging followed. Jori stayed glued to his chair, gripping the edges of his seat.

Vance returned and Jori turned ice cold at the lightning rod in his hand.

"Let's see who can handle the most."

Jori's pulse tripped into a patter. He was familiar with the device, having had to endure it from his father. But in Vance's hands, it looked like the serrated canine of a deep-sea monster. Not that it was sharp or pointy. It was exactly what its name implied—a rod that emitted an electric shock. Only this shock was a little different because it focused on pain receptors and didn't leave a mark.

If it had been Father holding that rod, Jori would've stood in an at ease stance and jutted his chin. And he would've gritted his teeth and endured.

He attempted to do that now. He rose from his chair and attempted to stand tall. His hands shook, even after clasping them behind his back. His chest caved in rather than pushed out and his eyes widened as Vance stuck it into his midsection.

Jori willed out a yell to cover his cry. It came out between his clenched teeth in a tone that bordered on hysteria. He unclasped his arms, intending to protect himself from the seizing pang, but forced them to stay at his back.

Vance pulled the rod away. Jori breathed through the residual pain. Then to his surprise, the man turned the device onto himself.

Vance's eyes hardened. His lips pressed. Jori sensed his hurt, but the man showed no other signs of it affecting him.

Crazy chima.

This went back and forth. Jori managed well enough, but not like he used to. His terror built up, making it more difficult to endure. After the fourth round, tears filled his eyes. He panted through his nose. Vance smiled and struck himself. Not a single thing about his demeanor changed.

Jori yelped in the fifth round. He tried to choke back the sob that followed, but it came unbidden. His entire body shook from both pain and fear. He wanted to curl up on the floor, just like he used to do from his father's abuse. This was far worse, though. Father's fury would dwindle. He'd storm out when his anger had been spent. But Vance didn't hurt him out of anger. The look on his face was one of boundless joy.

His father was mean. His condonement of torture and dismissal of life was cruel. But he never got any pleasure from those things.

Vance poked him with the rod again. White hot agony shot through his gut and radiated throughout his body, all the way to the tips of his fingers. It was constant—an endless ocean of suffering. He collapsed under the pressure. Despite his best effort, he curled into a fetal position and whimpered.

If Vance reacted, Jori didn't notice. He struggled to regain control of himself, but the pain searing throughout him didn't go away. His muscles convulsed.

Vance grabbed him by his collar. The hallway passed in a blur of tears and acute discomfort as his feet dragged along the floor. He managed to stand when Vance brought him into the conveyor, but he couldn't straighten.

The car stopped and opened. Despite his hijacked brain, Jori recognized the infirmary. His body still didn't work, so Vance tossed him out. Jori smacked the floor like a wet towel, the impact sharpening his lingering pain like a knife through flesh.

Someone gasped and rushed over. Alarm poured from Doctor Stephen Stenson. "What did you do?"

"I'm very disappointed in you," Vance said to Jori, his voice as cold as the polar caps on Zanzoria. "I expect better next time."

The doctor's emotions bloomed with disgust and anger. "Next time?"

Vance didn't reply. The conveyor shut.

"That fiend!" the doctor shouted as he hefted Jori up onto a gurney. "This is insufferable!"

Jori agreed but didn't respond. He synchronized his breaths with the ebb and flow of the throbbing, like Master Bunmi had taught him. "*Embrace the pain. It's neither good nor bad. It's just your body speaking to you. Listen to it. Listen. Listen*," the master had always said, his words like a soothing mantra.

He listened until the spasms resonated with every other bodily sensation, from the cool air on his skin to the warm blood coursing through his veins. No room for pity or anger and no time to plot his revenge. That would come later.

26
Meaning of Time

The warmth of the healing bed lights did nothing to ease Jori's suffering. He was no longer in physical pain, but the situation had swelled to hopelessness. Despite his best efforts, he had no ideas on how to fight or outsmart the psychopathic madman. Nor was there any reasoning, begging, or arguing—and so no options but to endure and do whatever he was told.

The bed beeped. Jori didn't bother opening the lid. What was the point? In here or out there, he was stuck in an oppressive situation.

His senses alerted him to someone entering the recovery room. Doctor Stephen Stenson's lifeforce was a welcome respite, even if he carried the same level of despondency.

The hood of his bed rose. Stephen smiled, pity etched his eyes. "Doing better?"

"Not really." Jori sat up with a groan.

The doctor put his hand on Jori's shoulder. "I know the man is horrible, but most days won't be like this."

"I must get away from here."

Anguish furrowed the doctor's brow. "I'm not sure that's possible. Besides, it's not always this bad. And you have friends here."

Jori's sinuses burned. Holding back his despair was getting more difficult with each passing day. "I'm grateful for you, but I'd rather die than live like this."

Doctor Stenson glanced down. Shame radiated off him like gamma rays.

Celine entered with a bright smile. "Time for more tests!"

Stephen's emotions plummeted further. His brows tipped apologetically. "Please forgive her. She no longer comprehends what this means."

Jori's breath hitched. "And what *does* it mean? What's the next test?"

"More pain," Stephen mumbled, his eyes remaining downcast.

The room seemed to shrink, suffocating him. "H-he already tested that!"

"He wants us to monitor you this time."

Stephen's tears prompted his own. He clenched his jaw and closed his eyes to keep the enormous swell of emotions from dragging him under. "W-who's inflicting this damned torture?"

"Vance," Stephen mumbled.

Jori's chin quivered. Why couldn't it be one of these cyber people? Hell, he'd even handle it better if Stephen did it.

What am I saying? Ultimately, it'd be Vance's doing no matter what. And why should this frighten him anyway? The pain wouldn't last forever.

He imagined Vance and his father together and let the image inflame his temper. *Fuck them!* He'd endure and he'd overcome, just like he always did. And he'd fight, too. He didn't care what Zaina thought of him. He'd stand up to this chima and refuse to cooperate. Sure, Vance would probably hurt him anyway. But he was no coward, and he wouldn't be cowed.

"I won't go."

Stephen's throat bobbed. "You must."

Jori leaned in and glowered. "No."

"B-but you have to. Vance expects you in fifteen minutes. That's not enough time."

Jori blinked. "Not enough time for what?"

The doctor bit his nails and glanced about. His hesitation wafted off him like smoke from a fire. "Promise me you'll go."

Jori pulled back. "What?"

Stephen grabbed his shoulder. "Swear you'll do what he says!"

"Why should I?" Jori yanked away. "You know what he's about to do to me."

"Yes." The doctor bobbed his head. "But he'll do it no matter what. And it'll be worse if you resist, so promise me!"

Jori scowled.

Stephen raised his palms into a prayer. "Please. Just promise—and *trust* me."

The word *trust* gave Jori pause. Doctor Stephen Stenson was a good man. It was in the core of his lifeforce. He also radiated distress, but something else was embedded within it too.

"Please." The man's brows twisted in desperation.

"Alright. I promise I'll do what he says—this time."

The doctor wiped his hand down his now sweaty face. "*This time*. But only because there's *not enough time*."

Jori frowned. Stephen had mentioned that already, but what did he mean? "Not enough for what?"

The doctor bit his fingernails again. "I must," he muttered to himself. "I can't let this go on." After a few incoherent mumbles, he faced Jori with a glint of determination. "The more time between a decision to act and the act itself, the harder it is to predict."

Jori straightened as the meaning clicked into place. He had suspected more time gave him longer to prepare but perhaps spacetime—for that is what he guessed Vance's ability somehow relied upon—would bend only so much. *I can use that*. "How long?"

The doctor opened his mouth to speak, but a beep from Celine's tablet made him yelp. Jori's heart did the same. The noise could've been a coincidence, but he imagined Vance might've caused it as a warning.

Stephen waved his palm in frantic paranoia. "No. That's enough. I won't say any more."

Jori didn't push it. The doctor had just taken a significant risk—one Vance might've foreseen. He dipped his head in thanks, hoping neither Stephen nor Celine would suffer the consequences.

He had two bits of information now. One, Vance's ability to sense emotions likely didn't work with his premonitions. Two, there could be a limit to how far into the future he could see. This second piece was still incomplete. After all, time always progressed forward so Vance would eventually see it. How did the time between the decision to act and the act itself tie into it?

He wouldn't resist just yet. But he would when it mattered—when he had a better chance of success. As soon as he recouped from this next bout of torture, he'd conduct his own experiments.

With his resolve solidified, he hopped off the bed. His fear remained but it cowered in the corner like a whipped dog.

Doctor Stephen Stenson led him out of the recovery area and through a maze of narrow hallways. Before long, they entered a room with an oversized metal chair in the center. The hairs on Jori's arms stood on end.

A skullcap hung above the chair. Robotic appendages splayed like spider legs from either side of the seatback. They terminated in three-fingered hands holding various menacing instruments. The needles sent a shiver down his spine. The knives turned him to ice. The saws triggered an overpowering desire to flee. When Master Bunmi had been forced to teach him how to endure pain, the jagged implements had been the worst.

Even though this was a less diabolical version of the torture chair his father had, both stubbornness and hopelessness kept him rooted to the floor.

Stephen prodded him. "You have to sit. Vance will expect me to make you, and…" He sighed. "Please don't make me."

Jori considered not doing it out of spite. After all, this man's reluctance to stand up for himself was one reason Vance got away with doing whatever he wanted.

No. That wasn't fair. Stephen was a victim too, and he wasn't just protecting himself. Being obstinate would only get them all in trouble.

Jori clenched his jaw and willed his feet to move.

"The original purpose of this was as a dentist's chair," Stephen said, not doing a good job of hiding his jittering reluctance. "A patient reclines while the dentist works on his teeth."

Despite the added modified repair bot and straps, Jori forced himself to see it that way. Removal of the padded cushions leaving just the metal skeleton didn't help. Jori's hands tremored. He managed a step. Then another. The shaking ran up his arms, then took over his entire body. He stumbled. Grasping the cold steel armrests saved him from crashing into the contraption. His gut twisted as though someone wrung it like a wet rag.

Jori turned and eased down—or tried to. His knees gave out and he plopped onto the hard seat with a clack and a creak. The doctor lifted his legs onto the rests and strapped them in. Jori's body tingled from within, like a million spikes running through his blood. Stephen emanated a reluctance strong enough to escape the gravitational pull of a star, but he continued on, tightening the straps over his wrists.

Jori attempted to calm himself by regulating his breathing. The pinch in his gut eased, but the clang of metal as the doctor manipulated the head-strap shot up his adrenaline.

The sensation spiked further when the entry hissed open.

"Is he ready?" Vance said.

Jori's bottom lip trembled. He glowered at the gleefulness on Vance's face and summoned his courage.

Stephen sniffled and dabbed his eyes with the back of his hand. "I-I just need to attach the electrodes."

"Good." Vance tapped on the console on the other side of the small room.

The doctor placed the electrodes under his shirt and on his chest. Then Stephen wiped the clear snot from under his nose and stepped away. "H-he's ready."

Vance peered down at Jori with an utter lack of compassion and dipped his head. While the doctor prepped the machine, Jori gathered his resolve and confronted his abuser. "Why are you doing this? And don't say because I'm like you, because I'm not."

Vance's lips spread but it wasn't quite a smile. "Maybe not yet. But you will be. A few cybernetic enhancements, and perhaps you'll finally present some real competition."

Terror clutched Jori's heart. "I will never agree to augmentations."

"Look at you. Your fear makes you weak. A simple chip can fix that."

"Never."

Vance's eyes blazed, but he didn't reply.

A whine from a moving robotic arm redirected Jori's trepidation and he let out a similar sound. An arm with a drill drew in from his right side. Jori's throat caught as it neared his face.

"N-no." Doctor Stephen Stenson wrung his hands. "You can't maim him."

"I can do whatever I want."

"B-but, Sir. If we damage something important, we'll have to replace it with cybernetics. And I thought MEGA-Man's plans for him would make this a bad idea."

Jori's gratitude for the doctor turned into a question. How much of MEGA-Man's plan did Stephen know?

"Good point," Vance replied without emotion.

Jori eased out a breath as the drill moved downward.

Vance positioned it over his upper arm. "This will bore down to the bone."

Stephen yipped.

"Problem, Doctor?" Vance asked. "Muscle and bone are easy to fix, right?"

The doctor grimaced but nodded.

Jori decided to be strong enough for both of them. Yes, this would hurt like hell, but he reminded himself it would end. He clenched his jaw in determination and hoped his bravery would give Stephen a bit of courage too.

*****

Time passed with no meaning. Jori was like a pebble falling into an abyss. Master Bumni teachings allowed him to separate himself from the pain. Instead of a victim, he was an outside observer, a spectator of a performance, a character in a story. Some part of him still felt it, but it was more of a dull thud than a pain—a distant echo. The only one who seemed to feel any anguish was Doctor Stenson, who blubbered through it all.

At some point, the glint in Vance's eyes shifted from glee to fervent anger. That he no longer enjoyed this sadistic game gave Jori a sense of being in control. He wasn't certain, but he believed he smiled before falling unconscious.

A ripping noise jolted him awake. Jori snapped his one good eye open. Mucus ran down Doctor Stenson's nose. He wiped it with his sleeve, then finished removing the strap from Jori's head.

The release of pressure broke Jori from his trance and aching waves rolled in.

"Is he done?" he asked through a thick tongue.

"Yes, but I'm afraid your suffering isn't."

Jori wanted to ask why not but didn't have the coherency to put more words together.

"He wants to test your healing ability next," Doctor Stenson said. "I'm so sorry. This was so unneces—" He pulled back and sobbed.

Jori had no strength to cry with him. Nor the desire. It wasn't as bad as the doctor thought. His father often extended his punishments by denying him treatment. He'd endure this. Most likely, he'd sleep through most of it.

Doctor Stenson reined in his emotions. Tears still fell, but he was able to remove Jori's wrist and ankle straps. "I'll put you in a nice, quiet recovery room and get you as comfortable as possible. He says you can keep hydrated this time, but he won't let you have an IV, so you'll have to wake up once in a while to drink and eat. I strongly suggest both."

Jori tried to nod but his body wouldn't obey. The doctor picked him up and carried him. Jori took the time to look inward and assess his injuries. They weren't as bad as expected. He'd heal in no time. The real question was would the speed of his recovery satisfy Vance or piss him off? And what did these tests add up to?

He had no opportunity to contemplate further as blackness closed in. He was still conscious enough to feel the softness of the bed as Stephen laid him down. The lightness of the downy pillow embraced his head. A warm blanket covered him. The doctor tucked it under his chin with the gentleness of a mother cat caring for her young.

"Zaina," Jori managed.

"I'll check in on her from time to time," Doctor Stenson replied.

"Don't tell…" He forced out the words. "Don't tell her what he did," he whispered.

"I won't. Now get some rest."

The lights in the room dimmed and he meditated himself into a sweet oblivion.

27
Highest to Lowest

The bitterness on Major Abelard Blakesley's tongue made him want to spit. He opened and closed his fists as he marched down the hall. He should've known Phoebe wouldn't satisfy him. All he could think about was Zaina—a woman with both a body and a soul. If only she were willing.

She'd called him on the comm earlier, saying they needed to talk. She wouldn't say what about, but it didn't take a genius to figure out it wasn't because she pined for him. It was that damned imp she missed. Thanks to Vance and his sick games, Jori had been kept away from her for too many days.

As he neared her quarters, the depth of her depression irritated him further. Between Vance's obsession and her weepiness, his nerves were a jumble of violent energy.

He rang her comm. Instead of telling him to come in, the door swished open. She met him with her hands planted on her hips. The furrow in her brow would've been adorable had it not been for the anger she spewed.

"Where. Is. Jori?"

Blakesley clenched his jaw and feigned a nonchalant attitude. "He's alright. Vance is just running a series of tests."

Her temper quickened. "More tests? Why? And why does it have to take days?"

"It doesn't, but they're getting along so well..." He could've kicked himself for saying that. Once again, his desire to drive her away from the boy and to himself caused him to speak without thinking.

Her eyes popped. "Getting along how?"

Blakesley inhaled slowly, using the moment to rethink his intent. He wanted Jori gone, but he also yearned for Zaina. The boy wouldn't escape without her... Or would he? He imagined Jori leaving by himself and Zaina being so upset that she threw herself into his arms. Pure fantasy garbage, of course, but still appealing.

Before he produced the right words, she jabbed her finger at his face. "I want him away from that man. He's *my* charge!" She pointed at herself. "No one should take care of him but *me*."

His chest burned. Why couldn't she just forget about that little imp? "I'm so sorry, dear—"

"Don't you *dear* me." Her fists returned to her hips. "You like me and I like you, but so long as you're the captor and we're the captives, I want nothing to do with you."

"It's not me!" he said, his pleading tone also conveying exasperation. "I can't stop Vance. No one can."

She darkened. "Do you get what that means? Because he is so dangerous is all the more reason to get that child away from him."

"I want to—"

"Then do it. Until then, goodbye!" She smacked the panel by her door. The last thing he saw were her blazing eyes.

He stood there fuming, fists clenched and air puffing out his nose. At first, he aimed his fury at her. But the more he thought about it, the more he realized all the blame led to just one person. Vance must be stopped.

With that madman out of the picture, Zaina wouldn't have any complaints about the boy's treatment. He dared not move against the man himself, though. That was suicide. So long as Jori was still here, Blakesley was dispensable. So only two options lay before him. Inspire Jori to end him or get MEGA-Man to intervene. He'd love it if the boy bested that psychopath, but Zaina would be inconsolable if he were killed. Not to mention the difficulty of maneuvering Jori with no one suspecting Blakesley's own involvement. Contacting MEGA-Man was easy enough, but if he got caught, Vance would inflict a brutal punishment. Obviously, this course of action was riskier. So what was it to be? The option with little chance of success or the one with more risk? Perhaps he'd work both angles—carefully, of course.

With his mind made up, he left her doorstep and headed to his office. Once there, he plopped down before his console and activated the bio-authenticator. His heart thumped as the screen flickered on. Surely Vance hadn't foreseen what he was about to do. If he had, he'd be here right now wearing a twisted smile.

The discomfort in his gut increased but he pressed on and entered the contact information. It didn't take long. He already had the words planned but hesitated. If Vance found out he went over his head… *To hell with him.*

To disguise the purpose of the communication, Blakesley treated it like a normal report. Amid the numerous updates, he included one line—*"Vance is testing the young prince's ability to endure pain"*—and hoped MEGA-Man would deduce the how of it.

It wasn't the first time Vance had operated outside of his purview. Once, MEGA-Man had ordered a squad of the more robotic crew members to intervene. At first, Vance resisted. He'd disabled a half-dozen cyborgs before someone finally injected him, knocking him out.

Blakesley had pulled him partway out of his medically induced coma several times over the course of the week to give him updates. He'd played it off like he was just doing his duty, but the truth was he wanted to gloat over the man's helpless position. Too bad he hadn't considered killing him at the time.

If he was lucky, he'd have another chance. Only he wasn't stupid enough to risk incurring MEGA-Man's wrath by committing the deed himself. He'd inform Jori and let him decide what to do.

The message icon appeared and Blakesley broke from his daydreaming. He clicked it, then blinked. "That's it?" he asked with a tone of consternation. "Noted? That's all you have to say?"

He drummed his fingers as vexation spurted into anger. He'd hoped for more, such as instructions for him to take charge. But *noted*? What in the hell was he supposed to do with that?

He pushed away from his desk with a huff. Since going higher up didn't work, he had the other angle to try. Jori didn't trust him, so he'd go through someone else—someone expendable with the lowest rank and lowest intellectual capacity. After all, Vance wouldn't be paying any attention to the doings of a mouse.

He exited his office, barely avoiding a cleaning bot, then used his sensing ability to verify Rodrigo's location.

The cafeteria. Of course. The young man visited there at the same time every single day. He entered the conveyor and considered his approach. Rigo had idolized the boy and his abilities before even meeting him. Manipulating him would be easy.

Blakesley turned into the cafeteria, not caring for how similarly sterile it was to the medical facilities. Most of their food came from the self-serve fabricors that the robots cleaned twice a day. The service bots also kept the white tables bright and sanitized the white dishware and flatware.

Rodrigo sat hunched over a table. He didn't use a fork as he picked up his bread and bit into it. Blakesley wrinkled his nose. Only animals ate with their hands.

After ordering a protein pie, he put aside his distaste and wore a smile instead. "Hello, Rigo. May I join you?"

The young man's mouth split into a delighted grin. "Sure, Major."

"Thank you." Blakesley set his plate on the small round table and pulled out the chair across from him. "How have you been?"

Rodrigo's head bounded up and down as he chewed a mouthful of the disgusting bread. Some sort of red and yellow sauce oozed from between the slices. Something more solid lay between them too. At least it was brown like a pseudo-meat.

"How about you, Sir?" Rigo asked with his mouth still half full of food. The sauces had mixed with the rest, making a vomit-inducing mash.

Blakesley attempted to appear sorrowful. "Well. Quite frankly, I'm worried."

"Yeah? 'Bout what?"

"Jori."

Rigo bobbed his head again. "He doesn't seem too keen on being here, ya know?"

"It's not only that." Blakesley picked at his meal, hating the texture of the pie. It seemed the fabricors needed tuning. "Vance is testing his ability to endure pain."

"Oh?"

Rodrigo's lack of concern told Blakesley he wasn't getting it. *Idiot.* "Do you understand what has to be done in order to tell how well someone can withstand pain?"

Rigo stopped chewing and cocked his head. Several agonizing seconds later, his eyes widened. "He's being hurt?"

"I'm afraid so."

"Aw, man. What do we do?"

"Since Vance won't be deterred, I'm at a complete loss. Sometimes I wish there was a way for the boy to leave this place."

"He can't leave!"

Blakesley shushed him and glanced about, hoping no one cared enough about the outburst to report it to Vance.

"He's important to our cause," Rodrigo added in a normal tone.

Blakesley bit down at the little man's fanaticism and wore an anguished expression. "But he's being tortured. What if Vance maims or kills him?"

"Naw," Rodrigo said, this time with no food in his mouth. "He wouldn't do that."

Ugh! Rigo worshiped Vance about as much as he did Jori. What would it take to convince him? "He might. And even if he doesn't, I fear the torture is turning the boy away from us."

Rodrigo's face scrunched up, then he shook his head. "The boss has hurt all of us at some point or another. It's all been for the good, ya know?"

Blakesley wanted to scream but he pressed on. "The difference is that Jori is a child. Not only is child abuse wrong, but children this age are stubborn. This boy included. He won't forgive this."

Rigo bobbed his head. "Yeah. Yeah. You might be right."

Finally. "I can't do anything to help him because Vance monitors me. But he trusts you. And Jori is your friend. *You* can do something for him."

"Hmm. I don't know."

"Just think about it. It's not like him leaving here now means he'll be gone forever. I have no doubt MEGA-Man will send others for him again. And perhaps that person will treat him better than Vance. It might even be someone the boy likes, like you."

Rodrigo sat upright for the first time since Blakesley had arrived. A beaming smile spread across his face. "Yeah. That'd be nice."

Blakesley inhaled. The satisfaction he'd been seeking finally suffused through him. By enlisting this man's help, he didn't have to risk involvement. The trick now was to somehow turn Jori's desire to leave into a desire to eliminate his tormentor.

Like his fabricated pie crust, the plan was flimsy.

28
Ally?

A crushing ache settled deep into the tissues of Jori's body. It sharpened now and then, keeping him suspended above the brink of unconsciousness. He dared not move, not even to open his eyes. Only his chest rose and fell, creating a rhythm that Master Bunmi had taught him to use as a meditative shield against the pain.

Whenever Father had withheld medical attention, he expected the prolonged suffering to inspire remorse. But all it did was bolster Jori's defiance.

This time was no different. He despised Vance as much as he did his father. His determination to stand up against him grew. He'd put on a guise of cooperation for Zaina's sake, but he'd never give in. Not ever.

Even now, he plotted.

A hydraulic hiss scattered his thoughts. Rodrigo's faint lifeforce invaded his private room. Jori wanted to groan but didn't want to reveal he was awake.

Rigo shuffled in. "It's true. It's true," he mumbled.

What's true? Did Vance maim him? The thought of being paralyzed and forever at that monster's mercy sent his heart racing. He willed his hand to move, then his foot. The tightness in his chest eased as his muscles responded.

Rodrigo's footsteps tapped on the floor as he paced. "This isn't right. No. Not at all. What to do? What to do?"

Jori imagined Rigo wringing his hands and bobbing his head as he rattled on. The temptation to open his eyes and ask what was wrong niggled at him. If he did, the steadiness of his pain would shatter, and he'd have to confront whatever horrible thing Vance had done to him.

"It's only for a while, though," Rodrigo muttered on. "He'll be fine. Better than fine. But he doesn't like it. I know he doesn't. How can I convince him it'll be okay?"

Every word the man spoke heightened Jori's confusion until he could stand it no more. He fluttered his eyes open, letting them adjust to the light. The hazy form of Rigo appeared, then slowly sharpened. The man bobbed back and forth just as he'd imagined but bit his nails instead of his usual handwringing.

Jori tried to get his attention, but the tightness in his throat prevented him from speaking. He swallowed. The resulting discomfort plunged through him like a demolition ship but broke out his voice in a pain-riddled moan.

Rodrigo halted and a grin spread across his face. "You're awake! Good. Good. Before you know it, you'll be up and about and enjoying yourself again."

Jori scowled. "Enjoy—" The dryness in his throat forced him to cough. He worked his mouth to build saliva. "Enjoy being a prisoner? Not likely."

Rigo wrung his hands. "But it won't be that way forever. You're special. They'll treat you like a king. You'll see."

The man's optimism grated on Jori's nerves. Arguing would do no good, so he deepened his frown instead.

Oblivious as usual, Rodrigo took it as a good sign. He bobbed his head and smiled. "You'll be the greatest MEGA ever. You'll see. You'll see."

"What were you talking about earlier?" Jori asked, his achy throat making his voice rough.

Rigo's eyes dulled in confusion.

Jori huffed. "You said it's not right. What isn't right? What did he do to me?"

"Who?"

"Vance?"

"Oh!" Rigo's brows shot up. "That. Well, you know already. I mean, you were there."

"No." Jori wanted to shake his head in exasperation, but his neck was too stiff and the throbbing in his skull told him it was a bad idea. "I meant, did he maim me? Will I be alright?"

"Oh, yeah. Better than alright. The best. You'll see."

"I don't want to see!" Jori clenched his fists, sending a pang up his arm that fed into his temper. "I want to get off this damn ship."

Rodrigo shrunk back. "But wouldn't you rather be great like Vance? Like MEGA-Man?"

"No," Jori barked, then winced as his pain sharpened.

"But—but you'll be a hero. Everyone will admire you. You'll have—"

"No," Jori said again, softly this time. He shouldn't take his anger out on this man. After all, Rigo wasn't a bad person. Just idiotically naïve.

Rigo cocked his head as though in thought, but Jori doubted his wheel spun in the right direction. His bobbing increased and his smile spread. "I know. I know what to do. It's a good idea. It is. You'll see. You'll *really* see."

"What damn it?"

"No. No. It's a surprise," Rigo said.

A surprise sounded good on the surface. He hoped Rodrigo would be an ally in helping him escape, but the disquiet wriggling through his gut told him otherwise.

The door swished open and saved him from further contemplation. The smile of someone far more intelligent lifted Jori's spirits, but only for a moment. Doctor Stephen Stenson's expression descended as he regarded Jori. Guilt spewed from him. "Would you please excuse us?" he asked Rodrigo.

"Sure. Sure." Rigo bowed a few times and left, still wearing that idiotic grin.

Stephen rested his hand on Jori's head. "I'm so sorry, young one."

"I'll be alright," Jori said. The doctor's eyes watered at the croaking of his throat. "It's not your fault."

"It is." Stephen patted him gingerly. "I should help you. I *want* to, but…" He sighed. "I'm too much of a coward."

"I understand. You're protecting your wife."

The doctor nodded. "Thank you. You're such a kind boy."

Jori wasn't so sure about that but warmed at the man's words anyway. Too bad Stephen couldn't be his ally.

"I-I... Uh," the doctor stuttered. "I have something for you. With permission from Vance. It's electrolytes." He attached a fluid-filled bag to a hook by his bed and pulled some items from a nearby drawer with shaky hands.

Jori sensed that he'd spoken truthfully, so what was he nervous about? "What are you doing?"

Doctor Stenson's smile was slight but genuine. "I need to stick a needle into you. Don't worry. I'm not doing anything to hurt you."

Again, the truth coupled with unease. Jori considered refusing the treatment but decided to trust him.

Despite the trembling of his fingers, Doctor Stenson slid the needle in without so much as a pinch. A tingling coolness diffused through Jori's arm. It was a refreshing respite from the bone-crunching ache.

The sensation spread. His pain eased. He shot the doctor a wide-eyed look. A subtle shake of the man's head stopped Jori from asking about it. Nor did he need to. Stephen had given him a pain reliever.

If his suspicions were right, Vance didn't feel what Jori felt in a premonition and so hadn't realized what the doctor had done. But couldn't he have foreseen the man's actions? Maybe he was incapable of watching more than two people at once.

"The answer is five days, by the way."

"Huh?"

The doctor's nervousness spiked. Instead of answering, he busied himself with checking over Jori's injuries. "Amazing. You're already in the proliferative stage of healing. You should be up and about in no time."

Jori pondered the meaning of his previous statement. Surely he hadn't been in this bed for that long. Stephen must've been referring to something else. Then it hit him. Vance only saw five days into the future. That wouldn't be much help if every day gave him another day. But Stephen's earlier words about the time between the decision to act and the act itself suggested a weakness.

The information lifted his spirits. When Stephen clasped his hand, Jori replied with a squeeze, sending him a silent thanks. The man had taken a tremendous risk. Rodrigo wasn't much of an ally, but perhaps the Stensons were.

29
Dangerous Experiment

Caught in a trap, the blackbeast paced, pining for its old life. When its cage opened, it tore out at the speed of a missile. Elation glistened in its eyes as it escaped the cruel confinement forced upon it by brutal masters. But its fervor extinguished and turned into ferocity the moment it realized its freedom had been a lie. The fighting arena was just another cage.

Liberated from the confines of his bed, Jori dressed without enthusiasm. Instead of his regular clothes, he slipped into a child-sized enviro-suit. The slither of the padded bright material made his insides squirm. Whatever Vance had in store for him would likely be as sadistic as his last so-called test. *Chima.*

As he fastened the front, he reminded himself that he had something to be grateful for—the Stensons. Not just Stephen for divulging a little more about Vance's abilities, but Celine as well. After her rigorous report on his healing rate, Vance had allowed Jori to finish his recovery using curative nanites. His body still carried a notable ache, but nothing like before. He could walk, or even run—which might come in handy soon when he did a test of his own.

The pitter-patter of his heart increased as he put on the suit's protective footgear. He feared the consequences of what he was about to do, but it had to be done.

He wished to visit Zaina first and ease her distress. However, Vance would foresee any decision he made, and he needed him to predict his next act.

With a deep inhale, he secured the last shoe strap and stood to his full height. The slow exhale that followed did little to temper his nerves. Nothing probably would. It was best to just get this over with.

He reinforced his mental wall to prevent Vance from reading his mind and forced his feet to move. Out the door, through the main medical center—or cyborium as the Stensons called it—then into the wide corridor. So far, no Vance.

His eardrums pounded. Adrenaline coursed through him but hurt rather than numbed. He pressed on.

Every step around the angular curve of the hall intensified the pulsing in his chest. It sped like his thoughts, bringing him closer to an unpredictable monster.

He halted at the conveyor. *This is stupid.* How many risks would he take before he had enough information to outsmart Vance? Why not just take one risk and escape now?

The car door slid open. He grudgingly entered. The more he learned about Vance's limitations, the better chance he had of success later.

"Communications."

The computer didn't deny him. At first, he was thankful Vance hadn't restricted this location. Then he realized the man might've allowed it on purpose. *Damn it.*

The door hissed open. A blast of cool air struck him, prickling his face. He wavered. Fear of the consequences warred with the logic of following through.

A chime sounded, indicating the conveyor door would close. Jori pushed out at the last moment. Vance had likely set a trap, but this didn't deter him from his true purpose.

He came upon the communication room, but it didn't open for him. Maybe this wasn't a setup after all. Despite the anxiety trembling through him, he popped the cover off the panel to the bio-reader. Its inner workings were familiar, allowing him to disable it with ease.

His senses didn't pick up anyone inside, but that meant nothing on a ship full of soulless cyborgs. He squared his shoulders and entered.

A smug face confronted him, making his insides twist.

Vance leaned against a console with his arms and ankles crossed. His smile spread. Jori swallowed. Vance clicked his tongue. "So obvious. I thought you were smarter than this."

Jori blinked. The man's words should have chilled him, but the statement had revealed an important piece of information. He forced all emotion from his face and clasped his hands behind his back.

He'd known before starting that he had no chance of calling Hapker or his mother since he didn't have their contact details. But this wasn't about reaching out to them. This test proved Vance hadn't foreseen his thoughts or emotions, only his actions.

"You know what this means, don't you?" Vance rose with menacing slowness.

Jori swallowed involuntarily as the man towered over him, but he remained firm. "Do your worst. I can take it."

Vance's eyes gleamed. "What about Zaina? You care about her?"

Jori's blood froze in his veins.

"She's inconsequential," Vance continued as though talking about dirt. "Her life has no significance—except to you, apparently."

Jori's chin quivered. His breaths came out in ragged chunks. "If you hurt her," he managed to say, "I'll fight you—even if it means my death."

Vance emitted a closed-mouth chuckle that chilled Jori's spine. His heart thudded as the man approached, but he stood his ground. Despite his best effort to hide his trepidation, his body shook. When Vance dropped his heavy hand on his shoulder, he almost yelped.

"I'll tell you what," Vance said in a chillingly calm tone. "I'll let it slide this time. But if I ever catch you here again…" He put on a wicked grin.

Jori couldn't breathe. He didn't like this game. Not one bit.

*****

A chime tore through the silence, making Zaina Noman's heart leap and her tea spill. Her mind raced as she scrambled to find something to clean the mess. The buzz sounded again, and she abandoned the task. The door didn't react to her approach, and it took the third ring to make her realize she had deactivated the motion detector. After two tries, she pressed the open button.

A swish and a whisper of air revealed the last person she wanted to see. Major Blakesley stood before her with a ridiculous bouquet in his hand. At least his smile suggested Jori was probably alright. But he wasn't here—where he should be.

She cocked her head and folded her arms. "What do you want?"

"I want to apologize and explain."

He held out the flowers but she ignored them. "Where's Jori?"

"What? Oh. He's alright. Vance has him undergoing another test."

"Another one! How many damn tests does that man have to run? And why does it require Jori to be gone for so long? Is he okay? Did Vance hurt him?" Her heart skipped into a sprint at the thought.

"He's alright. I promise. Listen. I'm sorry Vance is keeping him away. I tried. I really did." His stricken eyes pleaded. "But please understand, I'm as much of a victim as the Stensons. Unless we want to be punished—or even killed—we must obey. We have no choice."

She pressed her hand to her chest. Maybe she'd judged him too harshly. She'd assumed that as the major, he'd have more influence. But perhaps it had just been wishful thinking. "Jori's alright?"

"Yes." His shoulders dropped. For a moment, she thought his reaction was because of annoyance. But when he smiled, she realized he was merely relieved she'd finally decided to listen.

"You promise?" she asked.

"I promise. And I swear I'll help you out of this."

He looked so earnest that she let herself smile. Then she took the flowers and sniffed them. "They're beautiful. Where'd you get them?"

"From one of the biology labs. They're…"

A ding and a swish of the conveyor from down the hall diverted her attention. If he kept talking, she didn't notice. When a small figure emerged, she dropped the bouquet and brushed past Blakesley. "Jori!"

Jori's eyes tilted in anguish as he rushed to her. They met in a full embrace. He held on to her as tightly as she clutched him. It was a gesture she'd never expected, and it wrenched her soul.

30
Skilled Labor

The remote lounge area with its somber furniture and stark décor suited Major Abelard Blakesley's mood perfectly. The giant viewscreen displaying a lovely sunrise over the tundra of Baldesh *did not.* He accessed the controls and selected a live scene from outside the ship. External lighting stifled the shine of the distant stars and galaxies, but he wasn't here for stargazing anyway. He planted himself before the scene and crossed his arms. Silent curses ran through his head as he tapped his upper arm with his index finger.

That damned imp was out there, showing him up once again, doing the job of a skilled technician. The boy's white enviro-suit reflected a brightness that hurt his eyes, but he tortured himself by watching anyway.

It helped that Jori wore a defeated expression, but only a little. If it hadn't been for Vance's threat toward Zaina, Blakesley might've been wearing a smile. It didn't surprise him that the psychopath had changed the rules of the game, but he hated the timing. If Zaina knew Jori was being forced into compliance because of her, she'd likely put some of the blame at Blakesley's feet.

Her rebuff wasn't the only consequence of Vance's obsession. Blakesley's already clenched jaw tightened further. Earlier, on the way to visit Zaina, he'd caught the tail-end of Vance's threat. With her life hanging in the balance, he wasn't sure if he could maneuver the boy into killing Vance. Either Jori would want to do it because of the threat, or he'd simply let himself be used like Doctor Stenson did.

It would've been much easier if Blakesley's attempt to create dissent had succeeded. But that damned woman—that lovely and elusive woman—persisted in advocating for the boy.

When she'd finally answered the door, he'd almost convinced her to forgive him. But Vance must've decided to underline Jori's weakness by allowing him to visit her before this test. The little imp had shown up and ruined everything. Zaina practically shoved Blakesley aside to get to him. The love pouring from her as she embraced the child had ignited an anger so deep that Blakesley had bitten his lip in a struggle to contain it.

If the boy were to figure out how to escape, Zaina would go with him before Blakesley had a chance to satisfy his longing. The only way to earn Zaina's affections was to take action himself.

Damn it. Why was this boy so much trouble?

He shoved aside his musings and returned to the moment. From what he'd been told, Jori's EVA repair task was a simple one. Anyone could do it—any but him, of course. Not only did the vastness of space unnerve him, but he also had no training. He'd always eschewed such jobs as beneath him.

I hope he gets a hole in his suit. Blakesley huffed. Impossible since the ship shielded against particles, but it was a nice daydream.

Vance stepped beside him. Blakesley flinched and hoped his mental shield had hidden his thoughts. Considering the admiring smile Vance directed toward the boy, probably so.

Unnerving silence ensued until Vance spoke. "You went behind my back."

Blakesley's heart convulsed. "What?" he asked, ruining his feigned innocence with a high-pitched tone.

The conflagration roaring in Vance's eyes belied his flat expression. "You went behind my back," he said again, his voice stretched thinner than an elastic band.

Blakesley tried to speak but it was as though a fisher's hook had lodged in his throat. He'd gotten caught and now he was being reeled in. Soon, he'd be bludgeoned to death.

Vance pivoted to face him. Blakesley crumpled to his knees and put his hand up as if in prayer. "You were hurting the boy! I was afraid you'd kill him. He's too important. I knew you wouldn't listen to me, so I told *him*."

"Liar!" Vance bolted forward and swept Blakesley up by the throat, pinning him against the wall. "You did it out of jealousy!"

Blakesley couldn't refute it, even if he wanted to. Vance's grip cut off both his air and his blood circulation. He kicked but his brain was too starved to make a concentrated effort.

This was it. His end. His soul screamed for survival, but his thoughts became resigned. He should've known better. Vance was too powerful.

His body collapsed to the floor, though he didn't understand why. When his autonomic reflexes prompted him to suck in air, he realized Vance had released him.

Before he digested this information, Vance hauled him back to his feet. The man's hot breath burned his ear. "If you ever go against me again, I will rip out your throat with my bare hands. Do I make myself clear?"

Blakesley tried to respond but it was as though his neck was still garroted.

Vance grabbed his face and slammed his skull against the wall. "Do. I. Make myself clear?"

"Yes. Yes!" Blakesley's words spilled out as he bent low and cradled the back of his head. "Yes. I understand. I'm sorry. It was a mistake."

Vance withdrew without a word, but his eyes retained a murderous glint. The tension in Blakesley's gut kept him from straightening but he managed to unwrap himself from his cowering position. "It won't happen again. I promise."

Vance backhanded him, sending a flash of white through his vision. "Damn right." He spit on Blakesley's face. "Useless craven."

Blakesley remained rooted to the floor. Spit oozed down his cheek as his mind struggled to process what'd just happened. Going behind Vance's back had been a risky undertaking. He should be lying on this floor in a puddle of piss and blood.

But here he was, still breathing. Why? Was it another one of Vance's sick games? Letting him live so he could torment him again later? Or perhaps MEGA-Man had spoken on his behalf. It was possible, but Vance wouldn't let him off so easily.

Unless he doesn't see me as a threat. He wiped the spittle from his cheek. Vance was right. He was a craven. His initial plea had been a lie, but he'd earnestly given the promise not to do it again. How pathetic.

Vance returned his attention to Jori. Blakesley swallowed and eyed the corridor with a primitive instinct telling him to run and hide. Everything would be better if Vance was dead and Jori was gone, but he didn't have the courage to make it happen. Not with the prospect of having his throat ripped out by a psychopath.

"Stay put," Vance said, probably for no other reason than to exert his dominance.

Blakesley suppressed a groan and obeyed. His only choice was to live under the constant threat of Vance's wrath. All the while, his value diminished under Jori's burgeoning importance.

There might still be some hope if the boy acted on his own.

He hung his head. So that was it then. He'd take the coward's way out and depend on a child to save him from despair. If he were alone, he'd laugh at the absurdity.

Vance grunted, bringing Blakesley's attention back to the events outside. Flashes of reflecting light indicated something small had come loose and was spinning out into space. Jori lurched for it. His tether went taut. Blakesley held his breath, hoping it would snap even though that was unlikely.

The boy grasped the object at the last moment. His tether remained secure and he pulled himself back into place.

Vance smiled. Blakesley gritted his teeth. *Figures*. The boy had failed by losing something, but he'd retrieved it in time and rendered his failure moot.

"Makes me wonder why I bother keeping you around," Vance said.

Blakesley's face heated. No doubt the man thought the statement would grind him further under his boot, but it made him realize something else instead. Putting his future into the hands of a child was foolish. If Jori killed Vance, there was no guarantee it would horrify Zaina enough to turn her away from him. The way things were going, she'd likely see the imp as a hero.

Blakesley clenched his fists. To get Zaina to succumb at least once, *he* had to be her hero. Of course, she wasn't worth dying for. But Vance's threats had backed him into a corner. Should he take a risk for the sake of his future, or spend his miserable existence under Vance's thumb and eventually slip up and get killed anyway?

Fear clutched him like the phantom sensation of Vance's hand wrapped around his throat, but it also spurred his anger. He despised this man, and he hated that boy. It wasn't fair.

To hell with them both. He must keep plotting. Surely he could grow a little bit of a spine and come up with an infallible plan.

To rely on Jori to do what he wanted was foolish. He had to take matters into his own hands. It wasn't enough for the boy to escape this ship either. MEGA-Man was both infinitely persistent and vastly patient. With his ability to manipulate and forecast future events, he'd capture Jori again. That meant Blakesley had to eliminate both oppositions.

A flash of insight zipped through him. Vance side-eyed him but said nothing, implying Blakesley had adequately shielded his thoughts.

Five days. According to Doctor Stephen Stenson, there was a five-day weakness in Vance's foretelling ability. Apparently, there was a link between settling on a course of action and engaging in the action. If he implemented a plan now, one that wouldn't play out until after five days had passed, Vance *might not* foresee it. It made little sense, but it was all he had.

The upcoming battle was too soon, but not the visit to the asteroid. That locale was perfect. It required visiting via a shuttle, and if Vance took Jori rather than himself, perhaps a little accident could be arranged. Blakesley's lips curved, attempting a smile, but he corrected it before Vance noticed.

In the meantime, he'd arrange to transport Zaina another way. It'd be easy to hide her in one of the giant crates full of materials they intended to trade. Of course, he'd never actually send her. A few little lies would convince her he'd tried to save the boy. She'd be weepy for a while, but it'd be in his arms.

Now, to warm Vance up to the idea that Jori should accompany him.

"He's good," he said. "Perhaps we can give him more responsibilities here."

Vance glanced at him sideways, eyes narrowed. "You have an angle."

Blakesley shifted his feet, then tugged at the hem of his jacket. His nerves wound so tight that subtlety had eluded him. He cleared his throat and sought an acceptable truth. "I want him to fail."

Vance faced him with a hard look bordering on violence. "Of course you do. The only pathetic little chance you have of winning the game is by not playing." He harrumphed. "It won't work. The boy is too good. But I'll indulge your cowardice."

Blakesley blinked. It seemed Vance believed he'd been cowed. He hadn't meant to beg earlier, but it worked in his favor. Goodness knew he shouldn't be stupid enough to try anything again, but damn it to hell if this man didn't inspire a loathing too deep to uproot.

You're dead, you sadistic bastard. And you too, you little imp.

31
Nightmare

Sleep was as elusive as a pay raise. Despite the fatigue weighing on Zaina Noman's body, disconnected thoughts flitted from one subject to another, keeping her mind running like a never-ending day at work. Getting comfortable was impossible. Resting on her left side made her arm fall asleep. On the right, her hip ached. And if she slept on her back or front, her headache hammered into a nauseating crescendo.

Rest should've come easier after Jori had returned, but her worries only escalated. He'd told her he was late because Vance's tests had been rigorous yet wouldn't say how. All he said was he was fine and not to worry. His expressions gave nothing away, but she swore she saw a flicker of fear in his eyes. If he'd just tell her what'd happened, the worries would have a name and she could focus on a solution. Not knowing burned in her gut.

One thing she was certain about. That son-of-a-demon had hurt the boy again. She clenched her teeth as sadness, fury, frustration, worry, and a myriad of other emotions whirled inside her. But she might as well be shaking her fists at a storm for all the good it did.

Jori lay sleeping now, though in a deeper restlessness than her own. His blankets were crumpled and twisted, and his head skewed off the pillow. He mumbled every so often, but she let him be. Even fitful sleep was better than none.

She sat up and crossed her legs. With wrists resting on her knees, she took in a deep inhale, held it, then slowly exhaled. Thoughts intruded. She shifted back into focus and tried again. Concentrating on the air filling her lungs to their fullest sounded easy, but her brain insisted on paying more attention to the meaningless stuff.

She gave up with a huff. Everything she'd ever heard or read said meditation would help her with her anxiety, but she just couldn't do it. Her mind rebelled. It wanted her to stay this way, to suffer and wallow in this tedious pit of distress.

If only an emotion chip had been an opportunity a long time ago. That attack wouldn't have had such a profound effect on her and she'd be better at supporting Jori. Other aspects of her life would've been improved too.

Jori bolted upright with a gasp and all her self-pitying fled.

*****

The nightmare besieged Jori like a malevolent cloak of shadows. He fought to escape, but no matter how hard he tried, the scene kept rewinding, forcing him to relive the moment again and again. Father towering over him. The knife in his hand. The madness in his eyes.

At some point, his father's face turned into Vance's. It was difficult to say which was worse—Father's snarling rage or Vance's steely coldness. The blade reached his chest, and the nightmare began anew.

This wasn't the first time his subconscious had forced him to relive this moment, but it was the first time he recognized it as a nightmare. Yet he couldn't wake.

Vance came at him again. His gloating smile trapped Jori like prey in a blackbeast's jaws. When the tip of the knife touched his skin, everything changed. He watched the scene instead of being a part of it. Vance's eyes gleamed as the blade plunged down onto someone else.

Jori busted free, the nightmare shattering into a million painful pieces. One part insisted on remaining—the expression of horror on Zaina's face as Vance stabbed her.

His chest heaved as he attempted to thrust the image away.

"Jori?" Zaina whispered through the dark.

"I'm alright," Jori croaked, giving away his distress.

The rustling of blankets, then footsteps. "Lights," Zaina ordered the computer.

The room illuminated. Jori squeezed his eyes shut despite the dim setting.

Zaina settled next to him, her soft fingertips brushing his wet hair from his forehead. "You don't look alright. Do you want to talk about it?"

The urge to unload this horrible burden pressed on him, but he didn't want to relive it—certainly not the part about what Vance had done to her. He choked back a sob.

Zaina wrapped her arms around him. "Shh. Shh. It's alright. It's over."

No, it wasn't. The threat to her was real.

"I understand if you're reluctant to tell me," she said, "but it helps." When Jori didn't speak, she continued. "I suspect this nightmare has to do with your past. Our tendency is to bury those traumas. We put them away and go about our day, doing whatever we can to keep our minds off them. But that only works for so long. The more you try to suppress those memories, the more they want to get out. It helps to talk about them because you're giving them permission to come out *on your terms*."

Jori considered. Commander Hapker had said something similar, and it resonated. How many times had he attempted to repress a memory only to have it haunt his sleep?

Telling her wouldn't be easy, but easier now since he trusted her. He'd keep the part about Vance to himself, though.

"My father," he started, then took a deep breath. "My father wants me to be like him, but I *hate* him." A gush of heat swelled inside him. With the gate open, his words pushed out. "I don't want to be like him. When he wanted me to hurt someone that I considered a friend, I refused." That day when Father had strung Commander Hapker up and tortured him with the lightning rod had been heart wrenching. "He kept berating me, threatening me. Then he punished me, assuming I'd eventually give in. But I didn't. I went behind his back and helped that person get away. My father found out and…" A sob broke out. He tapped his chest. "And stabbed me."

"Oh my dear God!" Zaina slapped her hand over her face. "No wonder you have nightmares." She embraced him. "You poor boy. You poor dear boy. I'm so sorry."

Jori didn't like being pitied, but he folded into her arms and wept.

"How could he do something so terrible to his own child?" she murmured.

It probably wasn't a question she expected him to answer, but he pulled back, wiped his tears, and replied anyway. "He did it because I betrayed him. Loyalty is very important in our culture, and I did the most dishonorable thing anyone could do."

She wagged her head. "That still doesn't excuse his actions."

"I know."

She rubbed his upper arm. "He never should've pushed you so hard to begin with. Using the term *loyalty* to get you to do something that is immoral…" She tsked. "Sometimes people put emphasis on the wrong virtues to justify their behavior. It's like a bully insisting snitching is bad to guilt their victims into keeping quiet. What's right or wrong has so many nuances. It's up to us to weigh them and do what's in our hearts."

Jori agreed. He'd used a similar argument to enlist Sensei Jeruko's help.

"It sounds like you did the right thing," she continued. "I'm sorry it came at such a great cost."

"I have no regrets," he said with a scowl.

"Good for you." She turned about as though looking for something, then reached over to the small table by her bed and grabbed a tissue. After dabbing his cheeks, she tossed it aside for recycling later and retrieved another. "How did you survive?"

Jori blew his nose. "The person I saved was Commander Hapker. In his escape, he brought me to his ship where they stabilized me and grew me a new heart."

"That's a good man right there. I definitely need to find a way to reach him when we get out of this."

"No. Don't. He can't adopt me. The Cooperative won't let him unless he gives up his position, and I don't want him to do that."

"Why would they do that? Cooperative officers adopt children all the time."

They do? He didn't know that. It heartened him, but also reminded him of something else.

He hesitated. "I'm Tredon, or Toradon Nohibito. My file doesn't say that, but the Cooperative allowed a more general entry to protect me."

She didn't react the way most people did when they found out. "Well, that explains a lot about the things they *did* put in your file. But it's not right to condemn the commander if he adopts you. It shouldn't matter where we come from, only what we do. And I'd say risking your life to save someone else has got to be the best testament to the person you are."

Jori's face burned. He wanted to agree but knew better. He'd still done a lot of bad things. And although he was supposed to be on a new path, he wouldn't hesitate to stab Vance through his withering, black heart if the opportunity presented itself.

She pointed to the side of his neck. "What's this?"

He pulled away and snapped his hand over the chain of his mother's necklace. It must've found its way out during his tossing and turning.

"I'm sorry," she said. "I wasn't going to take it. I was merely curious."

Jori relaxed. He didn't think she'd steal it. It was just a stupid reaction. "It's my mother's."

"Ah. It's lovely. What happened to her?"

Jori filled his lungs and answered. "Father sent her away—far away. To a place I can't reach, even if I knew how to get there."

"Your mother is out there somewhere? If you have a good parent to care for you, that's where you should be."

"It's in Toradon territory."

"That shouldn't matter."

Jori remembered thinking this same thing when the Cooperative told him it was impossible to take him to her. He'd ultimately realized it was all for the best. "Father knows where she is and if he finds me there, he'll realize I'm alive and it will put her in danger."

"Oh, that's awful. There must be some way."

Jori shook his head. "I won't risk it. A new path, remember?"

She pressed her hand to her heart. "I'm so sorry." She grasped his hand and squeezed. "I'll do whatever I can to make things right for you. You deserve the opportunity for a good life."

He took comfort in her words but didn't put faith in them. So long as they were under Vance's thumb, hope was as impossibly distant as the nearest galaxy.

32
Lifeforce

A hushed glow created a gauze of shadow that did nothing to conceal the starkness of the room. Zaina Noman drifted in and out of sleep, wishing it could be darker so she could fall into oblivion. But she'd left the light on for Jori's sake—perhaps her own as well.

The remnants of their conversation lingered in her thoughts and disturbed her soul. The galaxy was a cruel place. The things adults did to each other was bad enough, but to a child? Jori's history was one of the worst she'd seen. The agency she worked for was full of children with troubled pasts. The abuses enacted on these innocent little beings sickened her, and she gave everything she had to help them.

Jori was no different, though she didn't have much left to give. Her damned emotions were overtaxing her to where she was a useless mess.

Once again, the idea of an emotion chip beckoned. She desperately needed one, but her will fled every time she saw a cyborg. These people were obviously biased. She wanted to trust Doctor Claessen and her faith was bolstered by how normal she seemed. But unlike the Stensons, she supported Vance.

She forced her heavy lids to open and peeked at the boy. He looked so serene as he read the tablet, but her heart ached at the turmoil he carried within. He needed her, and he needed her to be strong.

She pushed herself up. Wallowing like this helped neither of them. A stabbing pain exploded in her skull. She squeezed her eyes shut, but the piercing sensation remained. She pressed her palms to her temples and moaned.

"Miss Zaina! Are you alright?"

The vibration of his voice intensified her agony. Nausea swished in her gut, urging her to vomit. She swallowed it back and stayed still, hoping it'd pass.

"I need medics here, now," Jori called through the comm.

"N-no," she managed. "It's alright." She pulled in some breaths. The pounding subsided but refused to leave. "This is no different from the last time. It's just a headache."

"Let them come. They can give you something for the pain."

"I'll be alright." She met Jori's worry-filled eyes and forced a smile. "I really will. This is my brain's way of telling me to get my butt out of bed."

The wrinkles in Jori's brow eased. "My mother would get like this sometimes."

"Yeah?" She intended to ask more, but a ding sounded, making her wince.

"Enter!" Jori called, the loudness adding to her discomfort.

Emotionless medics came inside. After a quick scan, they ushered her to the gurney. The piercing sensations through her skull impelled her to comply. She eased onto the bed, every movement shooting a blast of white-hot agony. When flat on her back, she squeezed her eyes shut. They escorted her out, along with Jori who held her hand.

She tightened her grip. "I'm sorry you have to deal with my problems."

"I don't mind," he said, then glanced down.

A pang of guilt twisted in her middle. "But?"

"I'm worried." He eyed the medics. "I'll tell you later."

Left hanging, her anxiety kicked up a notch.

The medics brought her into the dreaded facility they called the cyborium. Despite her pounding skull, she forced her body to move into a sitting position. Concern etched Jori's features, so she patted his hand. "Laying down doesn't help, so I'd rather sit up and hear what you have to say."

With the medics now out of earshot, the boy leaned in. "I want to escape, but if I try and Vance catches me, he will hurt you."

Her shoulders slumped and she cradled her forehead in her palm. This news didn't surprise her, but the additional burden he carried must be affecting him as much as it was her—just in a different way that he kept well hidden.

She filled her lungs and gathered herself. “Don’t stay here on my account. If we can’t get out of here, he’s bound to hurt me regardless.”

Jori’s throat bobbed. His mouth opened as if to say more but Doctor Claessen swept in. “Another headache?”

“Yes.”

“It’s understandable considering the constant stress you’ve endured. Don’t worry. I brought you something to help.” The doctor pressed a hypospray to Zaina’s neck.

Zaina gasped as the sharpness in her skull abated. A dull ache remained, but she could function.

Jori frowned at the doctor. “Isn’t there anything you can do to keep this from happening again?”

Doctor Claessen replied to Zaina. “Have you given any more thought to my advice?”

Zaina hesitated. “It seems so drastic.”

“It’s a simple procedure. You read Doctor Garrett’s case files, right?”

“Yes, but that’s not what I meant by drastic.” She wasn’t sure what she’d meant.

“What’s she talking about?” Jori asked.

Doctor Claessen’s smile brightened. “It’s a procedure to help her manage her emotions.”

Jori’s eyes widened. “How does it do that?”

“We insert a chip—”

Jori hissed. “You can’t! Don’t you know what that does?”

Doctor Claessen cocked her head. “Of course. I’ve had the procedure done myself and it’s made my life much easier.”

“It dulled your lifeforce.”

Her mouth quirked in amusement. “Lifeforce? You mean my spirit?”

“I’m not sure what it is, but every living thing has it.”

Zaina’s spine tingled as her suspicions about trusting the people on this ship resurfaced. Her emotions warred. On the one hand, having a way to curb these hard feelings sounded like heaven. On the other, what if Jori was right? “Doctor Garrett didn’t address this. How can I be sure I’ll be the same person afterward?”

Doctor Claessen’s eyebrows drew together. “Of course you’d be the same. Just not as stressed.”

"No!" Jori threw up his hands. "If you don't have a lifeforce, then you're not truly alive. You're a machine!"

Doctor Claessen emitted a high-pitched, snooty huff. "Having cybernetic implants doesn't make us less human."

Zaina nodded. The woman had a point.

"But what if it does?" Jori said. "How do you know you're still you? How do you know it didn't change you in such a profound way that you lost your soul?"

The boy might be on to something. Zaina's viewpoint shifted. "Yes, that."

The doctor planted her hands on her hips. "So you think I'm less than human?"

Guilt budded in Zaina's gut while Jori darkened. "I don't know what you are," he said.

"I'll tell you what I am." The doctor's face tightened. "I'm a person with thoughts and feelings. Just because I've improved myself doesn't mean I'm inferior. If anything, I'm better."

Jori growled in frustration. "It's not that I think you should be treated like you're less than human. It's that something is off. I've always sensed a lifeforce from every living thing… That is, until I met MEGAs. Not all MEGAs, just some—the ones with brain augmentations."

Zaina recalled what Jori had said about plants. If it was true, then flora was more alive than some cyborgs.

Doctor Claessen resumed her calm, almost as though she'd flipped a switch. "I assure you, I'm still me."

Jori's brows folded into a plea. "But what is it that makes you who you are? Your brain, right? If you mess with it, you might be altering things that weren't meant to be altered."

Zaina glanced back and forth between the two of them. Both arguments had merit. But even though the doctor seemed normal to her, Jori's sensing ability allowed him to see something different. Could he actually detect the soul?

She regarded those around her. The medical facility was as busy as usual. A few people sat or stood at workstations. Some worked in the lab. And others simply passed through. It came across as typical until she realized everyone operated both independently and coherently at the same time—like parts in machines. Suddenly, the name cyborium didn't sound so odd.

Her head spun with the implications. "If I put something in that downplays my emotions, what about my compassion? I care about people. I enjoy caring *for* them. Would I care less?"

The doctor held out her hand. When Zaina took it, the woman squeezed gently. "I still care about people, but I no longer agonize over them. There's a difference. Wanting to help people doesn't mean I carry their weight for them."

Oh God. That makes sense too.

The thunder in Jori's eyes reflected his disagreement. His fists clenched at his sides. "This is what Vance wants done to me. He said I needed a chip inserted to *curb my fears*." His face twisted in disgust.

"Is that true?" Zaina asked the doctor.

"Of course," she replied. "But only when the young man says he's ready."

Zaina pulled back. Stephen had mentioned that a person should be willing, but she doubted Vance would let Jori have a choice. And if Vance threatened her life to get him to obey, then he might agree.

"If he consents right now, you'd do it?" The thought of him getting a brain implant horrified her. For herself, her hope of being better had outweighed her sense. But applying the consequences to someone else… This was madness.

"Yes. This is one of our missions," the doctor replied.

A fire burst inside her. "Are you crazy? Even if he agrees, he's a child! Doing such a thing at his age is unethical."

The doctor straightened as though finally getting it. "Yes, I see. It would be unethical—"

"Damn right it is."

"—but MEGA-Man has his reasons."

"I don't give a *crap* about his reasons. There is no excuse."

"It's for the best." Doctor Claessen rested her hand on Zaina's shoulder like a friend.

Zaina jerked back. "I understand Jori now. No way in hell will I get that procedure done."

The doctor's jaw twitched. "The boy is wrong. I'm quite human and perfectly capable of making logical decisions."

"That's just it. Logical is not the same thing as ethical. Something has warped your values. Not only you. This Vance guy.

And whoever the heck this MEGA-Man is. It's immoral to alter children. Period."

Doctor Classen clicked her tongue. "You're not seeing the bigger picture."

Zaina's jaw dropped. This was unbelievable. How could she respond to such an unwavering line of reasoning? "Jori's right. You people have no soul."

The doctor's face turned as red as her hair. "How dare—"

"I agree," a booming voice interrupted. Doctor Stephen Stenson glowered as he approached. Somehow, his kindness still showed through. "Humanity is truly lost when you rationalize hurting and augmenting children."

"Yes, Doctor," Doctor Claessen said with attitude. "We are all aware of your unwillingness to evolve."

"Call it what you will," Doctor Stenson replied. "I've seen what your *evolution* has done to my wife."

Doctor Claessen jutted her chin. "It's her own fault for resisting."

Stephen's face turned purple. "She *resisted* because she knew the procedure wasn't perfected. It's still not, yet you insist on clinging to this farce of an evolution."

Zaina shivered.

Doctor Claessen huffed. "It's not a farce. *I'm* living proof of evolution."

Stephen didn't respond. She lifted her nose as though she'd won the argument and sauntered out.

Doctor Stenson scowled at her back. "That woman has no idea how cold she's become," he mumbled. He faced Zaina and filled his lungs. "Sorry about that."

Zaina swallowed. "I almost agreed to an emotion chip."

His eyes grew in dismay, but Blakesley sweeping in interrupted any response he had lined up. "My dear!" he said, concern laced through his tone.

Jori scowled at him. Zaina related with his annoyance. Although she couldn't read emotions the way he could, she'd picked up on Blakesley's impatience. The more she resisted his charms, the more fake his endearing words seemed. She suspected her continuous medical problems had a little to do with it too.

People who didn't understand how debilitating depression and anxiety could be often had no patience for it.

Rodrigo trailed in after, bowing and smiling along the way. It was good to see the young man but the sour twist to Blakesley's mouth told her something else was afoot.

She dropped her head in her palm. *God, please don't let it be more drama. I can't take much more of this.*

*****

Major Abelard Blakesley suppressed his exasperation and wore concern instead. Ignoring the dirty look from Jori, he grasped Zaina's hand and brought it to his lips. "You poor thing. I'm so sorry you're not feeling well again."

She pulled her hand away and made a smile that held no warmth. "Not *again*. I'm stressed for the same reasons as before—I'm a prisoner and I'm helpless to do anything to stop your boss from harassing my young friend here."

Jori inched closer to her and folded his arms. Blakesley ignored him and put on a hurt expression. "I understand. I do. Which is why…" He leaned in so Rigo wouldn't hear. "… I'll help you."

Her eyes narrowed. "How?"

He glanced sideways at Rodrigo. "I'll tell you later. For now, I think Rigo has a surprise for you." He tried to appear positive but hadn't yet been told what this *surprise* was.

"For Jori. For Jori." Rigo bounced up and down on his toes. "But you may like it too."

"What is it?" Zaina asked, her mouth open in eager anticipation.

"I'm getting enhancements!"

"What?" Blakesley cried out at the same time as Jori and Zaina.

"It's true. It's true." The idiot bobbed and a stupid grin split his face. "I want to show you how awesome it is to be a MEGA."

"No," Zaina whispered. She shot a glare at Blakesley. "No!"

Blakesley's jaw dropped. "I didn't know what it was. I thought he wanted to help you."

His words fell on deaf ears as Jori and Zaina pleaded with Rigo to not go through with it. But being the fool that he was, Rodrigo insisted they'd be pleased.

"I have another surprise," the mouse said. Blakesley and the others glowered. Rigo's giddiness remained, though. "I'm using your DNA."

The outrage on Jori's face was priceless. His brows furrowed over darkening wide eyes and he bared his teeth.

"A tribute, ya know," Rodrigo continued, oblivious.

Although Jori's swelling horror meant he might agree to stop Vance, Blakesley realized he was losing Zaina's trust. He grasped Rigo's upper arm and pulled him over to him. "Are you mad? They're right. You can't do this."

"I must. I must. Surely you understand. You're one of us."

"I only have a communication chip. No other."

"But you don't need others. You're a genius."

Blakesley smacked his hand over his face. There was no getting through to this man. He shook his head and caught Zaina's eye. The approval in them gave him hope. If he kept taking her side, maybe she'd finally let him have a taste. That's all he needed. Just one night of adventure under the sheets and her pleading for more. Any more than that and her pathetic emotions would drive him to insanity.

The former thought heated his core and spread throughout his body. He took her arm in his and whispered in her ear. "I'll see what I can do to stop this."

She rested her hand over his. It was cold, but her touch electrified him.

If only I actually had the power to stop it.

33
Exams

An exhilarating surge of euphoria surged through Jori as the complexity of the problem unraveled in his mind. He leaned toward the screen. His eyes dried, reminding him to blink. As far as tests went, this was fun. He loved solving puzzles.

Only, he had a difficult time concentrating. One moment, he'd get immersed in working out a solution. The next, his thoughts shifted to Doctor Claessen or Rodrigo. He replayed both conversations over and over. His cheeks flushed with shame regarding his words to Claessen. He was right to warn her about diminished lifeforces, but regretted how he'd implied she was less than human. His heart told him something was off in those who chose certain brain augmentations, but who was he to decide?

From there, his thoughts drifted to Rodrigo. No matter how bad he felt about hurting Doctor Claessen's feelings, his temper flared at how Rigo would use *his* DNA to augment himself. The man was a complete idiot. He needed a boost to his brainpower, but who would he be when it was done? Would he still be Rodrigo, or would he be some freak Rigo-Jori hybrid?

He shook his head, trying to dispel the thought, then forced himself to focus on the examination. Even though all the options for this multiple-choice question had merit, only one adequately solved the problem. He embraced the euphoria that came with knowing the answer and typed it into the console.

Next was a short-answer coding question requiring a mathematical computation. Math was easy for him as well, but sometimes converting a formula into a format the computer understood took a little finagling. He figured out the hardest part first. The rest came together almost instantly. An unbidden grin spread across his face.

The next problem seemed complicated, but Jori broke it down with ease. He tapped the console with an eager energy. The questions kept coming and he continued answering.

The programming test lasted another hour. His dry eyes and achy muscles forced him to stop and stretch. Vance entered the study room, catching him in the awkward position of touching his toes. He snapped upright and faced the man with a stiff military stance. Vance leaned against the wall and crossed his arms. The glee in his eyes made Jori squirm.

"Had enough?" Vance said.

"Just taking a break."

"Hmm. You're good at coding."

"Yes," Jori replied, unsure if he should offer more. Tiptoeing around Vance had become second nature. He still hadn't figured out what would set him off.

"Can you program bots?"

"Yes." One of the lower-caste workers had taught him. Sometimes when he was supposed to be training with Hideji, he'd sneak off and learn more about repairing machines. One time, he'd given a bot instructions to set off the fire suppression system in Hideji's dojo. To keep from being implicated, Jori had timed it to occur just before his arrival to class. Hideji had stormed from the room, spewing a string of curses.

Unfortunately, Jori's attempt to avoid being blamed had caused several of the workers to be punished. Hideji was a vindictive chima, but Jori didn't hate him nearly as much as he hated Vance.

"Good. I have a job for you."

"Job?"

"My people are busy. I need someone to keep up with service and maintenance bot repairs."

Jori hid his eagerness. Not only would it alleviate the boredom of this ship, but it'd also present some opportunities. Setting off the fire suppression system in Vance's quarters would be a glorious prank. But if he was going to punish this chima, he'd do something far more drastic—something that would keep the man from hurting anyone ever again.

What if this was another setup, though?

"Oh, yes. I'll be watching you," Vance said. "There's nothing you can do that I won't see."

Jori bit the inside of his cheek. *Damn it.* Although Vance's expression seemed open to the challenge, Jori worried about the risks of playing this game. He shoved down his fear and vowed to find a way to outsmart the psychopath.

*****

Major Abelard Blakesley's heart skipped as he held Zaina's hand. She'd decided to give him another chance. He caressed the top of her hand with his thumb and fell into the loveliness of her brown eyes.

They sat at a small round table in the same lounge he'd been in the day before. The furniture didn't seem so drab now. Neutral colors dominated the fabric of the couch and chairs, but the intricacy of the swirled patterns was actually rather striking. Even the items in the display cabinet seemed to have more life in them than they did before. He appreciated the grey stone carving depicting a lively scene of ancient Earth people dancing. Beside it, a marble statue of a bird had its wings outstretched and its beak open as though in song. The detail of its feathers was amazing. And the woman in the ivory carved relief had Zaina's smile.

He was giddy that she'd agreed to see him. But her terms came with a stipulation—his actions must put truth to his words before she'd be convinced. This was the other reason for the erratic trembling of his heart.

He had a plan and part of it was in motion at this very moment. Although he worried Vance might foresee it, he kept reminding himself the man was too busy watching Jori to care what he was up to. Plus Vance believed he'd been cowed. The five-day limit tying the decision to the act also worked in his favor. Then again, a myriad of other confusing factors played into those premonition skills. Doubt crept in as his thoughts spiraled.

To hell with it. He had to take a chance. So long as he remained under Vance's thumb, his life would be miserable. He needed him gone and he needed this beautiful woman in his bed. Never mind that she teased him with her manipulative coyness. He'd earn her affections, then leave her wanting more.

"We'll be visiting an asteroid soon," he said, taking in her fragrant scent as he leaned in. "There's a base there run by an unaffiliated agency. By unaffiliated, I mean it's not MEGA or anti-MEGA. Nor is it associated with any specific nationality."

Her eyes lit up and her mouth parted in a way that made him want to kiss her, but he refrained. The expression was one of hope, not longing. Although she had warmed up to him, he wanted her hot.

"This could be an opportunity," he said.

"You think they'll take us in?"

"I'm not sure yet, but I'll convince them. Vance is the one who'll conduct business, and they'll see him for what he is."

She made a face that marred her features. "I certainly get that. The man gives me the creeps. But will it be enough? Doesn't this ship have weaponry? Won't Vance want to fight them to get Jori back?"

"I've got a plan to disable them," he lied. No way would a fervently neutral base take in some random woman and child. But she didn't need to know that. "Besides, the station has defenses of its own. Sophisticated ones at that. After all, being neutral means they don't have the protection of a planet."

Her eyes beheld him with gratitude. "How will we get there?"

He tightened his grip on her hand and put on a pained expression. "You're not going to like this, but Vance will want Jori to accompany him to the station."

Zaina pulled back but fortunately didn't take her hand away. "You're right. I don't like it."

"It can't be helped, I'm afraid. But this will actually make your escape easier."

"*My* escape or *our* escape?" she asked.

"Both. Think about it. Vance doesn't believe Jori would leave without you and he'll never expect you to figure out how to get away on your own."

"How will I do it?"

"Our reason for visiting the base is to trade goods. You'll hide in one of the crates that we'll send out."

"And how will Jori break free? Doesn't Vance have a way to foresee him making the attempt?"

He explained what the boy would need to do and repeated the five-day rule. "Vance will never see it coming." He wanted to gloat over the cleverness of the plan. So why was she still hesitant?

"I'm not sure," she said. "I don't like him going off alone."

He squeezed her hand. "You must be strong, dear. For the boy's sake. This is your best chance. I don't expect another opportunity for quite a while."

She chewed the nails on her other hand. He pulled her close and leaned in, making an expression that conveyed the urgency of the situation. "The sooner you two get away, the better. There's no telling what other things Vance has in store for that boy."

She met his eyes with her brows curled inward. "You're right. So what's next?"

"Give Jori the plan. In the meantime, I'll set up a way to deactivate the weapons, figure out how to get you into a crate, and contact the base to arrange for them to take you two in."

She heaved a sigh. Her eyes welled with tears. "Thank you. Thank you so much."

He brought her hand to his lips and kissed it. "For you, anything."

Her smile brightened, then turned sad. "What about the Stenson doctors?"

"Who?"

"Doctor Stephen and Celine Stenson?"

It registered, but not because she'd said their first names. He knew who they were, but it took him a moment to understand why she'd asked. "I'm not sure if I can risk getting four people out. It will be difficult enough helping you and Jori away."

Her features turned down. "But they don't want to be here either."

He clenched his teeth. Pretending to help the Stensons would increase his chances of getting caught. Besides, he only wanted Vance and Jori to die. A glorious image of their shuttle exploding while on the way to the asteroid bloomed in his mind and stifled his frustration. "I understand, but it will be challenging enough to convince the base to take two people." Her hand jerked like she wanted to pull away, so he held tight. "I'll tell you what. I promise I'll help them after I help you."

"How?" Her brows curled in a challenge.

"I'm not sure yet, but *please* trust me." *For goodness' sake, woman! Trust me.*

"I don't know if I can leave them behind knowing they've already been kept here against their will for so many years."

Blakesley wanted to snap at her, but he gritted his teeth to hold back his harsh words. "They are not in as much danger as you or Jori. They will be fine for a little while longer."

Her obstinacy wavered at the mention of the boy, so he enhanced his plea with raised eyebrows. "Please. You must trust me."

"What about Rodrigo?"

"He doesn't want to leave."

"No, I mean about his enhancements. He has such a kind soul. I'd hate for him to lose it."

Blakesley huffed and almost spit out a curse. *Actions*. He needed to prove himself with actions, but how? Damn this woman. He felt like a student undergoing a finals exam.

Zaina must've seen his hesitation because her anxiety ticked up. "You can't let Rigo do this."

He was all for self-improvement—especially for a fool like Rigo—but Jori had made a good point when he'd tried to talk the mouse out of it. People with too many brain implants lost something of themselves. It was one reason Blakesley had never considered anything more than an internal communication chip. Although he agreed about the soul, he didn't care a whit about Rodrigo. But for Zaina, he had to try.

"I'll see what I can do."

Her grateful smile was stunning, but he hated the reason for it.

Ugh. How in the hell do I convince an idiot not to be an idiot?

34
Qualms

An eerie hush pervaded the gymnasium. About a dozen people worked out here today, but none did anything more strenuous than lift weights or jog on the treadmill. All the sounds Jori would hear in the communal gym back home were absent. No clacking of hand-to-hand combat weapons. No grunts, smacks, or fighting yells. And no words of camaraderie or dispute. This place should've been peaceful, but even with Zaina beside him, he felt isolated.

The two of them strode around the track encircling the gym. Jori preferred to run and let the strain of it clear his mind, but Zaina wanted him to join her so they could talk. Jori's curiosity was piqued but it wasn't enough to bring him out of his funk. Although the job Vance offered presented some possibilities, it implied a permanency that he wasn't at all comfortable with.

"It'll be fine," Zaina said in an annoyingly upbeat tone. She was in a great mood.

"Maybe. But I can't help but wonder if this is another test, though."

"As far as his tests go, getting to do something you enjoy doesn't sound so bad."

"Not that kind of test. He might be setting me up."

"Setting you up for what?"

"To see if I'll try to escape."

She giggled. "I don't think we have to worry about that anymore."

He shot her a questioning look.

"Abelard has a plan," she whispered. A smile stretched across her face, turning her cheeks pink.

Jori soured at her use of Blakesley's given name. "Careful. If Vance is watching us, he'll hear you."

"Abelard said the chances are slim since there's a five-day blind-spot between our thoughts and actions—or something to that effect. I'm not sure I understand it, but he said—"

"Stephen mentioned the same thing." Hearing this from two different sources gave Jori hope, but he remained wary. It wouldn't hurt to hear her out, though. "So what does he have in mind?"

She outlined the details as they strolled, passing a metal-armed cyborg testing her strength on the bench press, a well-built man Jori recognized as one of the cyber soldiers practicing on a speed bag, and a woman with no apparent cybernetics and also no lifeforce working on the rowing machine.

The plan seemed promising but he couldn't shake the feeling that Vance had foreseen this very moment. Surely it wasn't as easy as exploiting a five-day limitation—especially since it made little sense for a man who could read thoughts to be blind to an event just because someone had thought of it longer than five days ago. Too bad he couldn't risk asking Stephen for more details.

"How will I get away from Vance?" he asked anyway. No one ever won a battle without taking risks.

"Check the toolbox in your workroom later," she said with a wink.

He imagined a weapon of some kind. He hoped for a phaser powerful enough to send Vance to hell, but it was probably something less obvious. Despite his misgivings, he itched to find out. "How does Blakesley know Vance will want me to go with him?"

Her brows drew together. "Not sure, but he'd know better than anyone."

"I don't like it. What if one of us gets away but the other doesn't?"

She sighed. "I don't like it either, but now long until we get another opportunity?"

True, but… "I don't trust him."

She halted. "Who? Abelard?"

"Yes," Jori replied with a pointed look.

"Why ever not?"

"He doesn't like me, and I don't trust people who dislike me for no reason."

"Oh, I'm sure he likes you just fine."

Jori wagged his head. "I can sense emotions, remember?"

Her expression warred as though trying to reconcile the difference between how he treated her and how he viewed Jori. "Well, I trust your instincts," she said, still emitting uncertainty. "But why would he try to help you if he didn't like you?"

Jori frowned. "Because he wants me gone." Considering the importance MEGA-Man attached to him, it came as no surprise that the major had a lifeforce tainted with envy. Though jealousy might serve as a plausible explanation for the desire to aid in his escape, the possibility of a darker motive lurked beneath the surface.

"Well, that still doesn't sound so bad." Zaina's emotions spiked, indicating her trust was almost blind. Whether she believed in Blakesley because she was desperate or developing a strong attachment toward him, Jori couldn't tell. He didn't want to dash her cheerful mood, so said nothing.

Something else occurred to him. Had Blakesley only spoken to Zaina about this plan because he knew Jori could detect deception? Asking the major outright might dispel the doubt that niggled in the back of his mind.

"Just look at it this way," Zaina said. "We can escape without having to fight."

Her words stung. Did she think he was incapable of coming up with a plan that didn't include violence?

He tried to disregard the hurt but between her and Blakesley, his stomach ached. The urge to do strenuous exercise took over. Racing around this track would be a poor substitute for the holo-fighting machine but was better than nothing, especially since he needed to get his head in order before taking on the new job for Vance.

35
Blind Mouse

Major Abelard Blakesley swooped into the cyborium with the urgency of a hungry hawk. His haste fueled his muscles and kicked his pulse into overdrive. The medics and assistants jerked to a halt. He swept by, ignoring them. They weren't the prey he was after. His target was a mouse.

He finally glimpsed his quarry through a prep-room window. Rodrigo lay on a hospital bed, eyes closed.

Damn. He hoped he wasn't too late. He smacked the button to the door, then slid inside and shoved aside a slow-moving med bot. "Stop!" he said to Doctor Stephen Stenson as he neared Rigo's face with an oxygen mask.

Stephen jerked to a halt. His emotions reflected more relief than surprise. Apparently, Zaina wasn't the only one who didn't want that brainless pest to go through with this.

"Hey, Major," Rodrigo said with his usual idiotic expression.

The doctor's brows drew upward. "Is everything alright?"

"No, it's not," Blakesley snapped. "You can't possibly be ready to do this procedure already. If I remember right, it took you months to isolate my genes before you imposed them onto someone else."

Stephen lowered his chin. "You are correct, Major. I'm not ready. But…" His chest heaved. "… You know… Orders." He waved his hand toward the exit even though Vance was likely on the bridge a few decks up and behind him.

Orders. Of course. No one did anything on their own around here without permission from the madman. "Did he specifically say you had to proceed with Rigo?"

"No. But…" The man sighed. "I don't have anyone more willing."

Because nobody is stupid enough. "Rodrigo. You can't do this."

Rigo lifted his head. His thick brows furrowed and his ridiculous grin quirked. "Why not?"

"Didn't you hear? The doctor said it's not ready."

"It'll be fine. I trust the doc here." Rodrigo shot Stephen a confident smile.

Blakesley ground his teeth. "Jori is right." He worked the sourness from his tongue. "This procedure will make you as good as dead. It's life without a soul."

"Naw." Rodrigo flicked his hand. "I don't believe in stuff like that."

"Even if you don't," Doctor Stephen Stenson interjected, "this will alter your brain in such a way that you won't be the same person."

"Well, that's the point, ain't it, doc?"

Blakesley puffed. He should've known the mouse wouldn't budge. "At least take it slow, like you've been doing. Upgrade your eye. Didn't you say the other day that you wanted full spectrum vision? Or what about another cybernetic hand?"

"I don't want those things. It's the gene stuff that I need. I wanna be as smart and as athletic as Jori."

"So just start with a few mechanical enhancements. You can get bionic legs or enhance your endurance."

"They don't do enough. I'm tired of being useless," Rigo said.

You're useless because you're an idiot.

"I want to be like Jori," Rodrigo continued.

Blakesley growled and shot a glare at the doctor. "Isn't there anything we can do or say to convince him?"

Stephen cleared his throat. "You know, Jori doesn't want you to do this."

Ugh. He hated how everything seemed to revolve around that damned imp, but the argument was sound. "That's right. He has the same sentio ability as I do, so he knows what this procedure does to people's brains."

"He calls it a lifeforce," Doctor Stenson added.

Rodrigo only smiled. "He'll change his mind once he sees how much his genes will improve me."

Blakesley suppressed the urge to slap the man. "Or he'll be so horrified, he'll turn away from our cause." Which was what he wanted, but it wouldn't matter in a few days anyway since the boy would be dead.

"Naw, it'll be alright. You'll see."

Blakesley tightened his fists. It was like having a conversation with a fabricor. Only Rigo was dumber.

Enough was enough. "That's it. I won't let you be experimented on like some sort of lab rat." *Or lab mouse, in this case.* "Since you won't listen to reason, I'm giving you a direct order. Get the hell off that bed and go to your quarters."

A stricken expression twisted Rodrigo's face. "But—"

"No buts! I gave you an order." To Stephen, he said, "Cancel the procedure."

The doctor brightened. His gaze targeted something over Blakesley's shoulder, and his features fell. Blakesley turned around and stiffened.

"Proceed," Vance boomed.

"B-but, Sir!" Blakesley blurted, remembering too late that he had to be careful when challenging Vance's orders. He yanked at the hem of his jacket and composed himself. "What about the boy? He already disdains our objectives. Once he sees how dramatically this procedure—"

Vance stomped into their midst. "Proceed. I'll see that Jori becomes a champion to our cause."

The man's hot breath sent a shiver down Blakesley's spine. Unable to back away, he forced himself to remain calm. He doubted Vance would ever convince the boy of anything other than that he was a homicidal psychopath, but he dared not say so.

"And you," Vance said as he jabbed his finger at Blakesley's chest, making it smart. "You ought to be ashamed of yourself. Letting a woman blind you to our purpose." Vance shot a blob of spit off to the side and planted his hands on his hips. "We are MEGAs. Trying to talk people out of becoming like us is offensive. No wonder MEGA-Man is seeking a mere child to replace you."

A fire spread from Blakesley's cheeks and sizzled through his entire body. Had it been anyone else who dared insult him, he would've lashed out and beat them to a bloody pulp.

“Proceed,” Vance said once more, then left.

Blakesley shook with fury. He remained rooted in place as he struggled to put out the flames of his outrage. This was all Jori’s fault. Rodrigo’s idiotic decision was for his sake, no one else’s. Zaina wouldn’t see it that way, though. She’d blame him and deny her affections.

Damn it all to hell! If only he could fast-forward to that asteroid and get rid of the imp.

His temper didn’t cool, but he forced his features to loosen as he faced Doctor Stenson. “If you get a chance, please tell Zaina that I tried my damnedest to stop this madness.”

The doctor barely met his eyes but dipped his head.

“It’ll be alright,” Rigo said. “You’ll see.”

Blakesley snarled. “Shut the fuck up, you imbecile.” He stormed out of the room with his fury raging like a tempest.

36
Battle

A rancid oil smell had settled within the layers of grime that had coalesced into the carpet on the maintenance room floor. Everything from simple cleaning bots to sophisticated mechanic bots cluttered the corners, shelves, and rear wall. Some had been there so long enough to collect dust.

Jori frowned. Considering the efficiency of the rest of the ship, it surprised him that no one kept up with this place. A 20CAPAI med bot was covered with greasy residue. Same with the obsolete cleaning bot that might've lasted several more years had anyone bothered to fix its loose wheel. And the foodstuff on the fabricor had long since rotted and dried.

Jori leaned over the workbench and reviewed a tool bot's coding. He scrolled through the stack trace of the most recent memory dump, trying to understand what had gone wrong. After cross checking against the code, he found an expression that looked unusual. He stepped through it and decided this was what had broken the program. A few simple tweaks should fix the bug.

The repair was too easy to trigger the excitement that often arose whenever he solved a puzzle. With the changes made, he reran the diagnostics.

> No Errors Found

Good. He tested the bot's applications to make sure. The smaller of the two mechanical arms adjusted its digits into a mini screwdriver. The larger arm detached its multimeter and put it in its proper slot, then inserted its drill. A whir sounded as it activated.

Everything seemed in order. He leaned back in his chair and eyed the other machines. A small toolbox caught his eye. Its red handle indicated this was the one Blakesley had referred to. Something inside would supposedly help in his escape, but he didn't trust the major enough to retrieve it yet. Nor did he like the idea of leaving the Stensons behind.

That Vance might still be watching him also fed into his reluctance. How reliable was the five-day rule? He'd gotten the impression the man could foresee him at any time, even when nothing significant happened.

Despite the slow burn of trepidation, he decided on another experiment. After accessing the bot's functional parameters, he inputted a set of instructions. If it worked, the bot would go to a maintenance tunnel and disrupt the circuitry so that the fabricors in the cafeteria went offline. Although Vance might still foresee it and not care, Jori hoped no intervention meant he wouldn't expect it.

The door swished open. Jori's breath jolted to a halt as though he'd been struck in the chest. Vance blocked the doorway, feet planted at shoulder width, hands clasped behind his back and a smile plastered onto his face.

Jori forced himself to rise and take the same stance. If he had been standing before his father, he would have jutted his chin. Instead, he stood on shaky ground, waiting for violence to strike. Maybe it wouldn't come. Or... *Chusho!* What if he went after Zaina?

Tendrils of fear coiled around his heart as Vance glanced about. The man wore his usual smile, but Jori couldn't tell if it was triumphant, amused, or just there.

"I see you've found your calling," Vance said.

He doesn't know? "It's easy," he replied, wondering if his tone had given away the jumpiness of his nerves.

"I expected as much. I have another task for you."

Jori swallowed, suspecting the man had something sinister lined up for him. He studied Vance's expression, wishing it wasn't so bland.

"Get this mess cleaned up and join me on the bridge."

Before Jori could ask why, Vance turned on his heel and left with the indifferent decisiveness of a machine. Jori's mouth hung open as he tried to decipher the situation. Had Vance come because of a premonition or had his appearance just been a coincidence?

Although uncertainty niggled at him, he sent the tool bot on its way. Leaning out of the doorway, he monitored its progress down the empty corridor. When it retreated beyond his line of sight, he put the workshop into some sort of cohesive order, then headed to the bridge. A myriad of questions flitted about as he traversed the corridors. Not just about Vance's abilities either. All of it—Blakesley, Zaina, Rodrigo, escape, his future. His thoughts raced with every turn, yet answers remained tantalizingly out of reach. Not even the smooth ride of the conveyor settled his mind enough to come up with anything definitive.

He exited the car onto the command deck and nearly collided with a someone in a royal blue uniform.

Major Blakesley's already narrow eyes thinned further. "What are you doing here?" He hid his emotions, but his tone carried distaste.

"Vance ordered me here."

The major squinted at the conveyor. His downturned lips curved up into a forced smile. "I see. Well, come along then."

Jori stuck to his side as they marched around the hall of the command deck. The layout was much the same as many larger vessels. Having the single entrance on one end of the circular corridor and the primary operating center on the other made sense from a defensive perspective.

"I don't know what help you can be here," Blakesley said tartly, "but I'm sure Vance has his reasons."

The major's attitude reignited Jori's suspicions. "Zaina told me about something, but I don't understand. Why are you helping me?"

"I'm not helping you," Blakesley replied in a clipped tone. "I'm helping *her*."

Jori flinched inwardly at such a blatant truth. He'd been expecting the man to pretend niceness—lie even. He should've known better with the way the man's emotions swelled with a craving every time he looked at her.

"But you gave me something," Jori said, not wanting to talk about what had been left in the toolbox out loud.

"Because she wanted me to."

Jori's senses detected the truth of those words as well, but they were also evasive.

Before he could prod further, they reached their destination. Jori entered the bridge and noted the layout. It was smaller than what he was used to—more cramped. The central chair was just as ostentatious as the one his father had, but it seemed larger with the workstations crowded around it. Even someone as small as him was hard-pressed to find a place to stand that wasn't stifling.

Goosebumps prickled his skin as he took in the cybernetic crew. Not one had a fully human face. They were a mismatch of augmented eyes, cochlear implants, and metal plated heads with ports. Some were dull-eyed as they sat before their stations, yet their monitors flickered through information.

Uneasiness settled in. Jori directed his attention to the front. The giant screen displayed a small space station in real time. He didn't recognize this outpost. Like many others, it had a gravity wheel and a spoke that housed the mechanisms that kept the station turning. Some of the larger stations Jori had seen were bigger around, and generally the spokes were as tall as the wheel's diameter. However, this one was about half the size. The wheel was fat but not wide, and it resembled a ringed planet more than an elongated spaceport.

Blakesley planted himself on Vance's other side. His stance held a military air, but his pinched expression revealed a simmering resentment. That it was partly directed toward Vance gave Jori hope. Maybe he was an ally after all.

"Ramir," Vance said to someone at a workstation. "Tell us where we are."

A short, roundish man with two mechanical arms answered. "The Panchu station, in the Thames district."

"Never mind all that. Tell me what this space station is for," Vance said.

"The Panchu station is home to the Hanesian branch of the MEGA Inspections Office."

Jori's blood turned cold. They weren't stopping here for a visit. They were here to destroy it.

He had no love for those MEGA Inspectors—or MEGA hunters as some called them. They had poked and prodded him more times than he cared to count. And when they hadn't found what they wanted, they got angry—like it was his fault he wasn't a MEGA. The doctor he'd encountered on the Cooperative's PG-

Force vessel had been the worst, but the ones on the Cooperative homeworld were barely any better. Apparently, it took a certain type of person to want to be a MEGA Inspection Officer. Or perhaps those were the only types of people who made the cut.

Vance's likely intentions still didn't sit well with him. Even MEGA Inspectors had families. And he was willing to bet that since they worked at a remote outpost, they resided here too. Some eleven-year-old like him was with his mother right now, a mother who might be the unwitting wife of a heartless MEGA hunter.

This felt wrong, but he was in no position to stop it.

"Why are you upset?" Vance asked. "These are your enemies as much as they are ours."

Jori didn't waste his time explaining.

Blakesley snorted. "A warrior who doesn't have the stomach to kill. Pathetic."

Vance shot the man a glare, but Blakesley pretended not to see it.

Although Jori distrusted the major, he was right. The thought of killing anyone made his gut writhe. He wanted nothing more than for Vance to die, but premeditating the act reminded him of his ruthless father. If Blakesley came through, he wouldn't have to do anything. He could leave here and start the new path Zaina had offered.

"We're within firing range," Ramir said.

Vance slid the tray-sized console attached to his chair to Jori. "Let's see how good of a shot you are."

Jori glimpsed the tactical display. His insides plummeted and he was sure his face turned a deathly grey. He took a step back as the horror of what was expected of him pressed against his soul. "No."

Vance's eyes snapped with a dangerous glint. "What did you say?"

Jori shivered as though he were caught in a blizzard. He regarded the space station once more. Although he couldn't tell which section belonged to the MEGA offices and which were the living quarters, he imagined children like him traipsing the corridors or playing in the common areas while their mothers watched over them. The necklace he kept hidden under his shirt seared his chest.

Gruesome memories of the time he'd attacked another outpost pushed through as well. If his father hadn't taken him to the station afterward, he might not have felt bad about the shattered bodies of the mother and infant. Nor for the mutilated worker whose limbs had contorted at unnatural angles. The worst was of a girl near to his own age. Her eyes, frozen from the exposure of space, still haunted him.

"I won't do it," he said, his words shaking. "I won't commit murder for you."

Vance's face turned steely. Jori's heart thudded, but he hardened his own expression. "Threaten me or Zaina all you want." The heat building inside him added more force to his tone. "There are probably a hundred or more people just like her on that station and I refuse to kill many to save one."

Vance's lip curled. His knuckles whitened as he gripped the armrests of his chair. Jori's blood pounded in his ears, but he held his glower.

Blakesley's face brightened into a smug expression. "See. I told you he's not worthy."

Jori took the insult as a compliment since he didn't belong with these unscrupulous freaks.

"He's not one of us," Blakesley continued. "He may be good at a few things, but he doesn't have what it takes."

Vance backhanded the major with a lightning strike. "If anyone is unworthy, it's you." The low menace in his tone complemented the slow rise to his feet. His nostrils flared and his eyes flickered like a storm.

Blakesley waved his hands in front of him and backed away. "I was merely pointing out his weakness."

"His *one* weakness is nothing compared to all of yours," Vance said, his voice rumbling with barely contained violence. "Keep your jealousy in check, Major. I tolerate you for my amusement, but I'll kill you as soon as your entertainment value has diminished."

Jori blinked. He'd detected Blakesley's resentment but hadn't believed his abilities were that superior—until now.

Blakesley retreated with ungraceful haste.

Vance eased back into his seat and made a noise that reverberated between a chuckle and a growl. His attention snapped onto Jori. "It looks like you're my second-in-command today."

Jori eyed the console. His heart quivered in the abyss of trepidation, but he mustered up his resolve and met Vance's penetrating stare with a defiant jut of his chin. The man's fingers coiled like steel cables. Jori's mouth dried but he remained firm.

Vance leaned in. It took everything Jori had not to pull back. If only he had a knife. He'd plunge it into this monster's eye—to hell with the new damned path Zaina wanted him to take.

"You called my bluff," Vance said, his voice carrying an undertone of suppressed anger. "I won't kill her. I'll abuse her so badly that your sentio ability will go insane with her suffering."

Jori's knees buckled. He grabbed the edge of the console and remained standing. His thoughts whirred like a heating system attempting to combat the crystalizing chill of space. "Don't you dare," he managed with a quiver in his voice.

"You think I won't?" Vance's eyes carried a sickening gleam.

Jori considered. Zaina, the woman nearly as broken as him, suffering under Vance's thumb. His chin trembled. His eyes watered. What were a few anonymous people compared to the reality of her kindness? She wasn't his mother. Not by a longshot. But she tried. And her feelings toward him were genuine.

He wanted to give in, just like he had with his father. But then the dead, frozen girl slammed into the forefront of his mind. Her mouth hung open. Her brows drawn up in terror. She'd died because of his selfishness. He'd cut her life short, all because he thought it was fun to eradicate a space station.

"I won't do it," he finally said through a throat almost too dry to speak.

Vance rose with the swiftness of a blackbeast. Before Jori registered the threat, the man clutched the front of his shirt and slammed him against the side of the chair. His eyes bored into Jori's like a drill. The gold flecks in them sparked with a menacing gleam. The stare held. Jori couldn't shy away, even if he wanted to. But despite the terror coursing through him, his defiance remained firm.

"Fine." Vance flung Jori to the floor, his eyes sparking dangerously. "I'll take care of this—this time." He sat and pulled the console back to himself. "But if you don't change your attitude soon, it won't matter what MEGA-Man wants."

Jori released a quivering breath. An icy meteor shower raced along his spine, leaving trails of apprehension in its wake.

*****

The pain of death seared through Jori's core as the station suffered a series of missile strikes. One moment, he stood in helpless anguish. The next, the bombardment of a thousand suffering souls dropped him to his knees. The intensity of it blinded him. Vance grabbed his hair and yanked his head back. The sharp twinge was nothing compared to the agony of all those deaths.

The man yelled something. Jori wasn't sure what, but the phrase *pathetically weak* ricocheted through his thoughts. His father had said similar words many times.

He wasn't ashamed of how much the pain of death crippled him. The insult bothered him because he was weak in another way. Had he been older, stronger, and smarter, he would've been able to prevent Vance from murdering all these innocent people.

Logic told him he wasn't to blame, but he couldn't help but carry the burden. His mind reeled, trying to make sense of the slaughter. Although he had the ability to distinguish individuals, his brain detected all of them at once. A room full of people engulfed in a fire strong enough to sear flesh from bones. Men and women raising their arms against an overwhelming inferno. Children screaming as their parents turned into a pile of embers only to have their voices extinguished by the firestorm.

His body remained on the bridge, but his mind suffered every death. If Vance punished him, he didn't feel it. Nothing could compare to this senseless well of agony.

37
Holo Fight

Jori's temples throbbed in a relentless rhythm while his brow furrowed in desperate concentration. As soon as he read the bot's code, the meaning slipped away and his vision blurred. He tried again but his stubbornness only aggravated the ache in his skull.

He hadn't wanted to repair bots today but here he was, hoping that doing something other than lying in bed would keep his mind off things. With an exasperated sigh, he pushed back from the worktable. It was no use. All he could think about was how helpless he'd been when Vance destroyed the space station.

His stomach convulsed. Tears hovered on the edge of his eyelids. He blinked them away, then darted a glance at the red-handled toolbox. He didn't trust the major any more than he had before, but damn it, he had to do something. With a swiftness that sent his chair skidding back and his head whirling, he bounded to his feet and marched over. The lid of the box creaked open. Inside were a bunch of regular bot maintenance tools—mini screwdrivers, small clamps, a soldering iron, logic probe, and more. He dug around until he found a round device that fit into the palm of his hand. Like a globe, it had a top and bottom hemisphere plus two caps at the poles. Using the thumb and index finger to press those caps down would activate it and send out a pulse of blinding light.

He jammed the flash bomb into his pocket, hating that he had to depend on someone who despised him in order to escape. His decision was made, though. For Zaina's sake, and with limited choices, he had to see it through.

The door swished open, causing Jori to nearly jump out of his skin. His shoulders relaxed just a tad when only Doctor Humphrey appeared.

"Vance wants you in the gym now," the man said, his green eyes bright but still somehow dull. His lab coat was as immaculately white as ever and his black hair slicked back in the same style as always. He probably waited in a recharging station until called upon.

Jori shuddered and obeyed. The flash bomb in his pocket practically burned against his thigh. If Vance found it, he'd be in serious trouble. Unless, of course, Zaina was punished instead. He repressed an even more violent tremble.

He trailed behind the doctor and eyed the corridor for a place to hide his weapon. Except for the occasional toolbox or emergency kit, the halls were bare. Both were good spots, but he couldn't very well open one with Doctor Humphrey around. Stuffing it in a door recess wasn't an option since a cleaning bot would pick it up. All the rooms they passed were closed, so dodging inside one wouldn't work either. *Chusho.*

They reached a conveyor. The doctor pressed the button in much the same way a mindless robot would. When the door swished open, he went in first. His eyes never veered from straight on. Hell, the man didn't even blink. He used to have a little personality.

Goosebumps prickled Jori's skin. He didn't need to ask why he'd changed. *Damn cybernetic upgrades.*

"Deck twelve," Doctor Humphrey said.

"Wait," Jori replied. "Vance wants me in the gym."

"You must change."

Oh. Thank goodness. An opportunity to hide the flash bomb.

As the car traveled, he wondered what other sort of torment Vance had in store for him. It seemed unlikely he'd repeat the endurance test again, but one never knew with that madman.

The conveyor halted and opened. The doctor led the way without a word. Jori entered his quarters while the man waited outside like a stone sentry. A blast of coolish air struck him. The lights were on, revealing the drab and sparse furnishings.

Zaina lounged on her bed, an MM tablet in her hand. Her head snapped up and a smile creased her face.

"I thought you were going to lunch with Blakesley," Jori said.

Her emotions dipped. "The fabricor wasn't working."

Jori almost jumped with glee. His actions had gone unnoticed—or at least overlooked. He would have smiled had Zaina's despondency not swamped his senses. "What's wrong?"

She set the tablet aside and rose with the slowness of a planetary star breaching the horizon. Her shoulders hung like the dying petals of a flower. "Rigo's going through with his procedure."

A shock like Vance's lightning rod jolted through his body. "What! Why? I thought Blakesley was supposed to stop it."

"He tried." She rubbed a knuckle under her eyes. "He said Rigo was determined. No amount of arguing would convince him."

"Chusho," Jori cursed. Although he didn't trust Blakesley, his explanation was plausible. Rodrigo was unerringly shortsighted and stubborn. He considered asking Doctor Stephen Stenson to intervene, but Rigo probably wouldn't listen to him either. "Maybe it'll only affect him a little."

"I hope so," she said. "I understand it's his choice and all, but I can't help but feel worried about him. If he's not the same…" A sob broke from her throat, but she recollected herself. "If he's not the same, does that mean I should mourn his death?"

Jori almost told her yes, but he didn't know what the chips really did. Perhaps it merely stifled the brainwaves—or whatever it was that he detected.

The door comm beeped, interrupting his reply.

"Yes," Zaina said.

"Vance is waiting," Doctor Humphrey transmitted.

Jori responded to her quizzical look. "He's running another test on me."

She pressed her palm to her chest. "Oh no. Not this again."

He avoided her eyes as he grabbed his gym clothes, then entered the bathroom to change. His headache pushed against the inside of his skull, making him want to tell Vance to go to hell. If it were just him here and not Zaina too, he probably would. With her at stake, he dutifully removed his clothes and stuffed them into the laundry bin.

Wait! He fished the flash bomb out of his pocket, then stuck it in the tiny cabinet where they kept their toothbrushes.

Once ready, he composed himself and returned to the main room where Zaina perched on the edge of her bed with worry creasing her brow. "It'll be alright," he said, unsure whether he'd lied.

"Be careful!" she called out as he exited.

Normally, a chance to visit the gymnasium brought on a euphoric buzz. This time, his nerves droned. Why wouldn't that stupid chima just leave him alone? He'd be glad to escape him, but to keep him from coming after him again, he needed to eliminate him. After all, the galaxy didn't need this demented madman.

As soon as he entered the gym, Vance met him with the hard stance of a soldier. Jori reflected it, though his wasn't as steady.

"Don't worry," Vance said. "You'll like this test."

The pattering of Jori's heart told him differently. At least the man hadn't said anything about the flash bomb. That was a good sign. *Wasn't it?*

Vance led him to a holo-fighting program. Jori's emotions rose a little, but he worried there was a catch that would put him in the recovery room again.

"I hear you're a level nine," Vance said as he entered the settings.

"Yes—" Jori replied, barely stopping himself from saying *sir*.

"Good. I'll start you out at level five."

Jori swallowed. Then he attempted breathing exercises, hoping to gain battle-focus. Zaina wouldn't like this, but he had an excuse now. Too bad he wouldn't enjoy it. Leave it to this chima to ruin something fun.

The holo-man appeared. Jori clenched his teeth and stepped onto the platform. Getting into the fighting stance and facing his virtual opponent helped settle him. The holo-man punched. Jori bobbed and countered with a strike to the kidney. The holo-man blocked it and flowed into a counterattack. Jori dipped behind his opponent. The holo-man turned, swinging his arm into a backhand. Jori dodged.

They traded blows, Jori getting in a few decent hits but not having the strength to disable the opposition. In a real fight, the best strategy against a bigger rival was to avoid blows and wear his opponent out. But simulated beings didn't get tired. The only way to win was to keep hitting while avoiding strikes.

Level six came. He caught glimpses of Vance watching him, but he managed to ignore him well enough. Sweat beaded his brow. He ducked and swept out his foot at the same time. His virtual opponent fell and disappeared before he smashed his fist into its face. A level seven holo-man appeared next. Jori fell into defense as it attacked with swift fury.

Dodge. Parry. Swing. Repeat. The process intoxicated him. Why did Zaina see this as wrong? He knew the difference between a holo-man and a person. He'd never hurt anyone unless they tried to hurt him first. Someone like Vance, for example. Not that he'd fight the man. He wasn't stupid enough to confront a monster head-on. But if he could defeat Vance, wouldn't that be a good thing, especially considering what'd been done to that space station?

Level eight forced him to banish his thoughts and concentrate. Jori usually switched up his opponents' sizes, some being as small as him. Sensei Jeruko had said that even though he probably wouldn't ever fight a child-sized person, practicing doing so now would make it easier for him to defend himself from someone his own size when he grew up. But Vance had him competing against adults. It was fine. He'd still win, but he wouldn't use his full potential in this way. While his head was within reach of his opponent, he couldn't easily get to theirs. Most of his strikes and kicks targeted the kidney, solar plexus, and legs. Except for his speed and agility, he was at a severe disadvantage.

The level nine holo-man appeared… And took Jori out in three quick punches. A red X shimmered in the air above him and imposed over Vance.

Jori liked the irony of X-ing out that man until Vance crossed his arms and scowled. "I thought you could beat level nine."

"I can, more than fifty percent of the time," Jori replied.

"That's not good enough. Do it again."

Great. Jori wiped his clammy hands down his thighs and attempted to shake off his unease.

The holo-man reappeared. He fought it. The fight lasted two minutes with Jori mostly on the defense before he finally lost.

The Vance's eyes hardened. He said nothing, but a touch of irritation poked through his muted emotions. Jori dared not make excuses regarding his headache or how fighting an adult was harder. Sensei Jeruko, who could be a strict but benevolent teacher, would never accept an excuse—even a valid one. He doubted Vance would either.

He gritted his teeth and fought once more, keeping a fierce eye on his virtual opponent and shutting Vance out as much as his anxiety allowed. The thrill of the contest helped. He ducked and blocked as often as the holo-man did, and landed as many blows. They were tied. Jori's focus tightened. This simulation had a pattern. It liked double-punch combos. Jori anticipated the next one, sidestepped, and struck it in the kidney.

The holo-man disappeared. He won, but just barely.

The flintiness in Vance's eyes didn't dwindle. "Good. Until you succeed more consistently, you'll keep going."

This was what Jori would've done on his own anyway—he loved challenges—but Vance's insistence rattled his nerves.

"Let's make this more interesting." A feral smile spread over Vance's face. "You have questions, but I haven't given you any answers. Nor have you given me any. So here's what I'll do. You beat that level, you may ask me a question. I'll answer it, but only on the condition that you answer mine in return."

"Why? What do you get out of it?"

"A worthy opponent."

Jori understood. It was never about winning. It was about digging deep and aspiring to win despite the power of the opposition. "How do I know you won't lie?"

"The same reason I know you won't lie—I'm no coward."

The truth banished much of his doubt. But while as he wanted answers, the idea of having to reciprocate knotted his stomach. Refusing would put Zaina at risk. He had no choice but to play this game but… "Fine. So long as you don't ask anything stupid like *who made me*."

Vance's lip curled, but he nodded.

Jori solidified his resolve. As soon as the holo-man appeared, he let himself get immersed in the contest.

Block. Punch. Duck. Jab-jab. His battle-focus tightened. Mushin—no mind. All he saw was his opponent. All he felt was the exhilaration of the fight. No thoughts. Just actions. Fudoshin—immoveable mind. Not a drop of doubt niggled through his brain as he strived to win.

He rammed his fist into his opponent's chin. The holo-man blinked out. A silver champion's cup appeared in the air.

Jori's awareness spread beyond the game and fixed on Vance. The man's flat expression gave nothing away. Was he happy? Was he upset? Jori didn't care for how his sensing ability failed against this chima.

Vance crossed his arms. "Ask."

Jori considered all the things he needed to know. Confirming the five-day limit might be a good idea, but doing so would involve Doctor Stenson. Or he could verify whether Vance sensed emotions during premonitions. Since others had already risked themselves giving him this information, he asked something else. "How do you get your visions? Do you ask for them or do they just come?"

Vance smiled. "I prompt them."

"Do you select what you can see, or is it random?"

"That's another question."

Jori jutted his chin. "It's part of the same question." He remained firm as Vance stared at him. Whether contemplating or getting ready to explode, he couldn't tell.

"Very well," the man finally said. "Telling you only increases the challenge. It's both. If I don't direct my ability, it's random. I can also select specific people. You, for example. In both cases, I see the futures that will affect me the most. If nothing of interest is happening, I still get a glimpse."

Jori's spirits lifted. This was a better answer than expected. Vance could've lied, but unlikely. Lying didn't fit the man's personality. And his response made sense considering there'd been no mention of the reprogrammed bot or the flash bomb. His first action wouldn't affect Vance if he ate from the fabricors in his own quarters. And, if he'd understood Doctor Stenson correctly, Vance might not have foreseen him with the mini bomb because it didn't have any effect on him within five days. However, there was still a risk if Vance selected to watch him even when nothing interesting happened.

"My turn." Vance's eyes turned flinty. "Why do you resist us?"

"I'm not like you."

The man smirked. "Although you're not legally considered a MEGA, everyone knows your abilities have been unnaturally acquired—like ours."

"No. I mean I'm not..." He almost said *an uncaring psychopath* but thought better of it. "I don't go around hurting people just because I want something."

"They are not worthy."

"Yes, they are. Some might not be as smart or as talented, but it doesn't mean they deserve to be murdered."

"Those people hate you because you're superior." Vance's bearing remained the same, but the octave of his tone increased with each word. "Even this mediocre and weak woman looks down on you because of your abilities."

Jori scowled. The argument sounded much like the one Gottfried had given. "No she doesn't."

"She does. How many times has she judged you for your ability to fight?"

The discomfort that the man knew what she'd said was overshadowed by the fact that he was partly right. Although she hadn't outright criticized him, she kept saying he needed to be on a new path.

Vance harrumphed. "She *wants* you to be mediocre like her."

Jori disagreed on that point but didn't say so out loud. She might disapprove of his fighting ability, but it wasn't the same thing as wanting him to be mediocre. It hurt that she made assumptions about him because of his heritage, but it didn't mean she or others deserved to die.

Even though he hadn't spoken his thoughts, Vance's temper exploded. "You still resist!"

Jori's fright skyrocketed and he stumbled back.

"Face it," Vance said, his voice rumbling like an aftershock. "You're like me."

Arguing only pissed the man off more, so he kept his mouth shut and wrestled to untangle his terror.

Vance held his glare. To keep from flinching at the sparks in the man's eyes, Jori stared into his pupils instead. Unfortunately, they were as dark as black holes and just as dangerous.

Like a switch, Vance reverted to a flat demeanor. "Next round."

Jori's legs wobbled as he returned to the holo-platform. The contest began right away, and he found himself unprepared. He lost in less than a minute.

It took two more rounds before he won again. Winning didn't give him the same satisfaction it used to. He stepped off the platform and went into a shaky military stance. His mind was so unsettled that all the questions he had about Vance's ability fled.

"Why is it so important that I be like you?" he spurted.

Vance didn't reply. Nor did he move. Not even the severity of his eyes changed. Jori refrained from fidgeting. Was the man frozen in much the same way Gottfried had locked up whenever confronted with a complicated question or was he simply trying to figure out the reasons behind his obsession?

"Because you are my match," the man eventually replied. "Or you will be when you stop holding back."

"And why does that matter?"

"Because no one has ever been a challenge to me before."

He'd said something similar before, but Jori wasn't satisfied with the answer. "What does this have to do with MEGA-Man?" Although he suspected the reason, confirmation would give him an idea of how big of a problem he faced. "Obviously he wants my DNA, but there's more to it than that. Why does MEGA-Man want my cooperation?"

"That's another question."

"Again, it's part of the same question since you're not the only one who wants me to be like you."

Vance grunted as though impressed with Jori's ability to out-think him. "Because we are destined to change the galaxy together. MEGA-Man has foreseen it."

Jori's insides twitched. That wasn't the answer he'd expected. "How?"

"That's another question," Vance said through his teeth.

Jori didn't push it this time.

"My turn." Vance's smile twisted wickedly, making Jori cringe. "Why do you need mediocre people like this Zaina woman?"

Jori blinked. He felt the reason in his heart, but he wasn't sure how to explain it. Zaina was a single star in a sea of darkness. She was caring like his mother and accepting and amiable like Commander Hapker. Even though her new path suggestion stung, she never intentionally hurt him or anyone else.

He wouldn't say this to Vance. It was bad enough the man used his feelings for her against him. "People's value shouldn't be based on our abilities. Zaina contributes to the world with her generous nature."

Vance's lips curled. "That's stupid. Of course it should. Otherwise, we're a drain on society—a waste."

The man might as well have stabbed him in the chest. Believing people like Zaina had value wasn't stupid. And she wasn't a waste. A spark ignited a fire inside him.

"You disagree," Vance said. "But you'll see soon enough."

Jori's emotions tumbled back down. If Vance decided to prove it by hurting her, he doubted he'd be able to prevent it. He changed the subject, lest the man think about this too much. "Should I try this again?" He swept his hand at the holo-machine.

"You still haven't answered my question," Vance said. "Why *do you* need her?"

Jori stiffened. *Because I don't want to be alone. Because everyone else who's ever given a damn about me is either far away or dead.* Did he dare say this out loud, though? Vance might see her as the reason he remained defiant.

Vance leaned in. "Well?"

Jori chewed the inside of his cheek. He had to answer. Lying didn't sit well with him, but he should do it anyway—for her sake. If only he could think of a lie Vance would accept.

"We had a deal," Vance said in a dangerous tone.

Panic rose to Jori's throat as the man advanced. Like a flamethrower, Jori spewed out a response. "Because she doesn't want to hurt me! She's nice to me! She doesn't treat me like some stupid lab rat!" Jori paused, expecting to be struck, but the man's expression didn't change. "I hate you," he said without yelling. "You're a madman and I want nothing to do with you."

Vance's mouth quirked. "I knew it. You need her because you're weak."

"*Emotion is weakness, boy,*" Jori's father had always said. This was true now more than ever, but he couldn't help how he felt. He bit his tongue and looked away. "I don't expect you to understand."

"Oh, I understand alright. You're lucky you're still young. If you were an adult, I'd never believe you'd amount to anything worthwhile."

The words were undoubtedly meant to hurt, but Jori used them to fan the flames of his hate for this monster. He fixed his gaze on Vance and contorted his face into what he was sure was a look of pure malice.

If I were an adult, I'd kill you.

38
Apex Predator

The clomp of footsteps echoed in the corridor. Clap, clap, clap, like a slow ticking time bomb. Jori wrestled with the anticipation sizzling through his nerves as he and Zaina trudged to their destination.

Neither of them hurried because neither wanted to see what had become of the man who called himself a mouse. They didn't speak either, not even in the conveyor where Zaina grasped his hand. She probably intended to reassure him, but her nervousness paralleled his.

After passing several laboratories, they reached the designated facility. The door matched most others on this ship—a basic flat-white frame, a single sliding panel, and a wide window.

Doctor Claessen approached from the other side. The woman's smile enhanced the sparkle in her deep-set eyes as she activated the opening mechanism. "I'm glad you came." She stepped aside and waved them into a featureless anteroom with only a few thin padded chairs. "Rodrigo is looking forward to showing you his upgrades."

"That was fast." Zaina brightened, likely thinking the same thing Jori was—that Rigo had listened and decided to take it slow.

"Oh, he's not done yet," Doctor Claessen replied, dashing Jori's hopes. "The bionites we've implanted have only just begun to do their work."

"Bionites?" Zaina asked.

Jori was familiar with them, though he'd known them as simply nanites. It seemed a lifetime ago when his father had allowed cyborgs to implant them into him and his brother before their first solo mission to Depnaugh space station. That assignment had set off a series of perilous events, eventually bringing him here.

"They're protein-based machines that will alter Rodrigo's physiology," Doctor Claessen said.

Permanently. Jori soured. The ones he'd received had been designed to self-terminate after a specific time. They'd been useful in helping him escape the Cooperative ship, but he was glad they were gone.

The question on Zaina's face prompted the doctor to continue. "We inject a few thousand bionites to start. They travel to their prospective areas and replicate as needed. Most perform the genome editing process. Some will enhance his physical features such as his lungs for stamina, muscles for strength, and neural pathways for muscle memory." She beamed down at Jori. "All this, thanks to your DNA."

Jori scowled, but she seemed not to notice as she swept her hand toward the hall. "Shall we?"

She led them down a corridor that was just as bare and had as many offshoot rooms as those crisscrossing the rest of the ship. She tapped the panel beside the last door on the left. The hiss of it opening sent a feeling like bugs crawling down Jori's spine.

They entered, Zaina with caution and Jori with impatience. The room was larger than he'd expected, but still unassuming. A variety of machines cluttered the area around the head of the bed, some familiar and others looking more like the equipment used by mechanics.

Doctor Stephen Stenson's eyes widened at their appearance. Guilt oozed from him like paste from a food tube.

The man on the bed turned to them with a vacant expression. If not for the reddish-brown hair, Jori never would've guessed this was Rodrigo. The openness of his always smiling face was gone. The crinkles of his good humor were now flat, giving him an almost plastic veneer. He sat up straight, as though someone had crammed a metal rod through his spine.

"Jori," Rigo said, his voice monotone and devoid of his usual friendliness. "What do you think?"

Zaina gasped and held her arm over her gut. "Oh my God!" Tears filled her eyes. "What have you done?"

Doctor Stenson hung his head. Since he didn't reply, Doctor Claessen answered instead, and with an ear-grating brightness. "We made him better." She eyed Rodrigo as though he was a speedster she'd built herself. "Just look at him. He's magnificent. No more hunched back or groveling nature. The sniveling mouse we all knew before is gone and replaced by an apex predator."

Jori's entire body shuddered like a dying ship staggering into port. *Apex predator?* That's what they thought of his DNA? He'd never preyed on anyone, but he was born from a killer and still wanted to fight like one. Zaina's subtle criticisms echoed in his head, making cheeks burn.

"You've killed him," Zaina said with a sob. "He was such a nice man and now he's… I don't know what he is."

"He's better," Doctor Claessen snapped.

Zaina clenched her fists and screamed, "He's dead!"

Rodrigo stared blankly through all this. Not a flicker of emotion crossed his features or peppered his aura. Jori's throat tightened. *He really is dead.*

Doctor Claessen tsked.

"I've been reborn," Rigo said.

Tears streamed down Zaina's face. Jori wiped his hand across his own cheek and realized he was crying too.

Doctor Claessen swept out of the room with an air of someone offended. Doctor Stenson frowned at her back. When the door swished shut behind the woman, he glanced at Jori with downturned eyes.

Jori pressed his lips into a thin line, rejecting the man's self-condemnation.

"I didn't have a choice," Stephen said.

Jori's mouth curled. "How many lives have you ruined with your science? How many more will it continue to ruin?"

The doctor's chin dropped to his chest.

"It's not his fault," Zaina replied.

Jori's temper fizzled out. She was right. Although MEGA-Man had promoted this situation, he couldn't help but feel sorry for his part in it. His DNA had done this, after all. For a moment, he wished he wasn't leaving tomorrow. He didn't want to stay, but neither did he wish to leave the Stensons behind to continue their work. And he certainly didn't want any trace of his DNA here. Who knew how many more Rodrigo's they'd destroy in their quest for so-called evolution?

But the date was set. To change his mind now might affect the five-day rule. Besides, he had no way to stop any of this. The best thing he could do was leave… And get Zaina to safety.

If only I really was *an apex predator*.

39
The Asteroid

The day of freedom had finally arrived. If he were a blackbeast, this would be the day he'd escape from his cage. He looked forward to getting the hell away from here but also wished to slay his captor along the way. Leaving Vance to commit other atrocities made his gut writhe.

His angst was nothing compared to Zaina's. She bit her nails and paced as much as their small room allowed. Unlike Jori, she hadn't donned an enviro-suit yet. Vance had told him to wear his, but if he saw her with one too, he'd be suspicious. Blakesley would get hers soon enough.

"What if Vance knows what we're up to?" Zaina asked as she turned about and marched toward the opposite wall.

Jori remained seated. He had the same concerns but sat up straight and attempted a confident poise. "We must take the chance. The longer we're here, the more opportunities they'll have to hurt us." *To hurt you.*

"What if there's no room in the crate?" She pulled her hand away from her mouth and made a grand sweeping gesture. "Or there's a problem with my suit. Or we don't reach our destination?"

"Blakesley won't let anything happen to you." *Most likely, anyway.* Although the man had seemed frustrated with her earlier, his sincerity when he'd given his assurances hadn't wavered.

"What if you can't get away from Vance? What if you're not there when I get there?"

He almost liked that idea. If she was safe, he couldn't use her against him. Thus allowing him to put up more resistance. Perhaps he'd also end Vance and prevent others like Rodrigo from being turned into mindless soldiers. "Then go on without me," he replied.

Her brows furrowed into a stricken expression. "I can't leave you!"

"You'd have no choice. Think of it this way… If you get away and I don't, at least you can alert the authorities."

Her countenance portrayed several emotions—worry and hope, reluctance and determination, vulnerability and strength.

Jori rose. "It'll be alright."

She stopped. An appreciative smile spread across her face. "Look at you. Such a brave young man." She reached out to him. "I should be the one consoling you."

Jori wasn't sure about the brave part, but he let her pull him into an embrace. He rarely felt comfortable with this hands-on affection, but she was like a warm blanket on a cold day. The way her arms folded around him triggered thoughts of his mother. Even her scent shared similarities. The necklace hiding under his suit warmed against his skin. Although he'd only known Zaina for a short time, he'd come to care about her. He only hoped he wouldn't lose her too.

He released her and eased back. She did the same, albeit with more reluctance.

"I have to go now." He patted the pocket at his waist. The flash bomb resided there, hidden within the folds of his bulky enviro-suit. "Vance is expecting me."

"Wait. What about your helmet and gloves?" She touched his hair like a doting mother. "If something happens, you'll need protection."

He pressed an inverted button on his left wrist and a totimorphic material extended outward and encased his hand. Another couple seconds after that, it had created a thin but strong layer over each of his fingers. "This suit has a retractable helmet as well."

Zaina nodded as though she'd known that all along. "Okay. Good." She wiped her eyes with a knuckle and sniffled. "You take care, now. And I'll be seeing you soon."

After deactivating the glove, he clasped his hands behind his back and bowed. It was a respectful gesture that stemmed from the formalities of home but seemed fitting in this moment as well. Before tears formed in his own eyes, he pivoted and left.

Every step away from Zaina toward the shuttle bay frayed his jangling nerves. He attempted meditative breathing to control them lest Vance get suspicious, but it was tough. He shared all Zaina's concerns. So much could go wrong. Vance might find out. Something could happen to Zaina. The people on the station might not be as willing to help him as Blakesley had said. Then his mind took him back to the self-reproach for not finding a way to stop Vance—and the guilt for leaving Doctor Stephen and Celine Stenson behind to fend for themselves.

Like he'd told Zaina, they had to get away as soon as possible. Besides, their freedom meant they could call the authorities and give them information to track down Vance's ship.

He reached the entrance to the shuttle bay and stopped short. A moment more to collect himself wouldn't hurt. He took a deep breath, pulled back his shoulders, and entered.

Despite this being his first time in this part of the ship, he noticed only the ominous aura that seemed to hang about the domineering man before him. *Chusho. He knows.*

"Come along," Vance said with a sinister glint in his eyes.

Jori realized he'd been rooted in place. He mentally kicked himself and moved his feet. *He doesn't know. You're just being paranoid.* He dipped his head, hoping to convey subservience.

He walked in a daze as they headed to the shuttle. It was one of three, located on the far right. Its boxy shape made it look like a frog without legs. He would have admired its simple design had he not been preoccupied with misgivings.

The man's silence set Jori's teeth on edge as they entered the shuttle's side opening. The narrow entry and cramped space didn't help either. His attempt at bravery faltered as the shuttle hatch closed and trapped him inside. If Vance knew, surely this would be the moment to gloat and inflict punishment.

The man led the way to the cockpit without so much as a knowing smile. "Take the copilot's seat, but I want you flying this thing."

Jori's apprehension retreated to the back of his awareness. The prospect of getting to put all the simulation training he'd received at home to the test sparked his enthusiasm. His eagerness died when he plopped into the seat and buckled in. Flying spacecrafts had been his older brother's specialty. Thanks to Jori's attempt to stop his father from creating a planet-killing weapon, his brother was dead.

His grief must've shown through his mental wall because Vance shot him a disapproving frown. Jori tightened his focus and initiated the departure sequence.

The shuttle turned toward the aperture. The turntable clicked every few degrees but the process was otherwise smooth. Jori verified Vance's ship matched the asteroid's velocity and synchronous orbit, then calculated the shuttle's trajectory. The computer had already run the numbers, but Jori liked to verify the math in his head, just to see if he could do it. Having a madman sitting next to him made concentration difficult, though.

As the tracks inched the shuttle forward, air pumped out of the bay and depressurized it. The volume of the clicks decreased until the vacuum eliminated all sound from outside the spacecraft. The only noises came from the inside, and mostly from within his own body as his heartbeat pounded.

Vance remained uncommunicative. Jori didn't sense his emotions, but noted the intensity of his eyes, the fine line of his tightly pressed lips, the firmness of his twitching jaw, and the extreme rigidness of his posture. Suspicion that the man knew of his escape plan sprouted once more, but he clung to the hope that it was just his runaway imagination.

The energy field protecting the docking hatch deactivated, removing the bluish haze and revealing the black maw of infinite space. Traveling through a void had always made him a little nervous. With Vance by his side, it had swelled to where he barely felt anything else.

Vance reviewed his work. Neither approval nor dissatisfaction emanated from the man, though his severe body language remained.

When Vance returned to staring straight ahead, Jori took it as a sign that all was well. He flipped a switch. A jolt indicated the release of the docking clamps. The shuttle, already at the edge of the aperture, drifted out. The thrusters engaged, sending the little vessel out. Leaving the gravity of the ship behind triggered a queasiness in Jori's gut and caused his body to drift against his restraints.

The trip began slowly as the shuttle veered safely away from the ship. Seeing the vessel from the outside for the first time filled Jori with trepidation. He'd suspected it would have a unique design, but the contrast was greater than he'd imagined. The hull was amazingly smooth. He didn't see a single seam. It was as though it'd been constructed of one enormous piece of metal. Even the thrusters, vents, exhaust, and what he assumed were weapon turrets appeared to have grown organically from the monster ship.

"The Cooperative doesn't stand a chance," Vance said, making Jori flinch. "Neither do you," he added.

Jori's heart kicked into overdrive, but he forced himself to reply. "A chance for what?"

Vance turned to him with a wicked smile. "I know something you don't."

"I'm sure you know a lot of things I don't." The retort slipped out. However, he put on a scowl, intending to appear rebellious despite his growing uncertainty.

Vance chuckled without humor. He said nothing more as the shuttle neared the distant dot of the asteroid. Jori's insides twisted and turned, much like the tumbling chunk of rock. One moment, he was sure Vance had caught on to his plan. The next, he told himself his anticipation caused him to imagine things.

Until the chima says something, I'll proceed as planned.

He forced himself to sit back and wait. Eventually, the asteroid came into visible range. The false lighting filter and zoom features of the camera provided him with a better view. It was roundish with a knob at one end that made it look like an oblong fruit, only this was more pitted. The giant crater at the bulbous end almost resembled a bruise, except it was the same color as the rest of the asteroid.

Although the rock was relatively close now, they had over an hour before arrival. Too much acceleration followed by abrupt braking at this short of a distance was a waste of fuel. Plus, he still had to match the shuttle to its rotation.

Time dragged in the thunderous quiet of his companion. He quelled most of his anxiety, but it ticked up again when the base came into view. He'd expected to see mining operations, but the sophistication and interconnectedness of the domed buildings reminded him of the colonization structures on uninhabitable moons and planets.

Nervousness jittered on his insides. The base was the same rose-grey tint as the asteroid itself, making them nearly invisible. The only reason to do this was to hide. He imagined them as a radical community wanting to protect their twisted way of life. Or perhaps a research facility operating in secret to avoid planetary laws. Maybe a military or pirate hideout.

Since no habitable planets or moons were anywhere nearby, it confirmed the information Zaina had passed along about it being an independent operation. This might be a problem when it came time for escape. Hell, it'd be problematic even if this place did have ties elsewhere, especially if those ties were with MEGA-Man.

A dome opened. Vance grinned like a ferocious blackbeast about to pounce on its prey, sending a burning chill down Jori's spine.

"What are we here for?" he asked, hoping to finally learn the purpose of this stop.

"You'll see." Vance's smile tilted into something more challenging. "Or maybe you won't."

The coldness coursing through Jori's body sharped into pain. Was that a threat or a hint that he was onto him?

Jori gritted his teeth against a growing disquiet.

Chusho.

40
Crated

Like a deer that'd just heard the snap of a twig, Zaina Noman proceeded cautiously down the corridor. Not a soul—or soulless robot—was in sight but she couldn't shake the feeling that something stalked her.

She'd experienced this sensation a few times in her life. She didn't live in the gang-riddled East quarter, but her neighborhood still had a few rough edges. Daytime wasn't so bad, but after dark was another matter. Petty thieves, young adults carousing and looking for trouble, and ribald drunkards badgering passing women. These were the obvious dangers, but there were worse things lurking in the shadows.

She swiveled her head, feeling the same intense anticipation she had those nights she'd worked too late to catch a transport. Only this time there were no murky alleyways or shadowy corners. The hallway was bright and—except for the pounding in her eardrums—quiet.

Zaina hurried to the conveyor where she hoped to escape the crawling sensation of spying eyes. *You're being ridiculous*. Vance had departed and would be gone for hours. Abelard was in charge now, so she had nothing to worry about.

Get a hold of yourself.

The car doors shut her in. Hesitation stuck in her throat. Once she stated her destination, there was no turning back. She wanted to escape, but what if Vance hadn't left? What if he knew and had cyber soldiers waiting to arrest her?

Jori was already gone, though. She clenched her fists and filled her lungs, determined to follow through so he wouldn't be on his own. "Cargo bay five."

The car eased into motion. Nausea rolled through her insides. *Please let this work. Please let this work.*

The conveyor opened. She squeezed her eyes shut and held her breath.

"Darling!"

She snapped her eyes open. Abelard stood at the threshold with a grin. She blew out air and grasped his offered hand.

Despite his presence, she exited with care and glanced about. Before her sat a pristine white transport vessel that took up most of the cargo bay space. The size of it awed her, though it was only a little bigger than the maglev train car she'd take to work.

No windows adorned it, which she'd learned was because those features weakened the integrity of the vessel. Not even the front had one, but she spotted external cameras and sensors.

The small cargo bay housed only a single cargo ship. Its titanium walls were blemished with conduits and lockers. She imagined the cabinets held parts and tools, and perhaps a few maintenance bots. Dotted here and there were red buttons the size of her palm. Above them were exhaust-stained words written in a language she didn't know.

Blakesley led her to the rear of the ship where the hatch lay open. A bulky bot operated a forklift, and on it was a massive container. Like an idiot, she'd expected a wooden crate. Of course the ones here were made with some sort of composite material instead. *No trees in space.*

The lip of the crate reached her chin, causing her to stand on her tiptoes to peer inside. The nook Blakesley had cleared for her triggered her anxiety with its smallness.

"I'm sorry, dear," Blakesley said. "It must be a tight fit so that if the ship is jostled, you're not tossed about. I'll add foam insulation as well, but don't worry. You'll be able to break out easily once someone unlocks the crate."

What if no one unlocks it?

He grasped her shoulders and turned her to him. "It will be alright, my dearest."

He pressed toward her. If not for her apprehension rooting her in place, she would've stepped back. He lowered his head. She blinked at the realization that he wished to kiss her. She wasn't sure she wanted him to, but maybe she should allow it. After all, he was risking his life to help her right now.

She tilted up to meet him. His hot breath carried an edge of desperation. When their lips met, he bore down on her with a passion she didn't share. His tongue swept between her teeth. She almost bit it but allowed the frenzied assault.

When he pulled back, his eyes were wild—and triumphant. She coughed, breathlessness making it hard for her to take in air. Her heart thudded, but not with his excitement. She wasn't sure what she felt. Dread perhaps.

He frowned. She lowered her head, knowing full well he'd sensed her emotions. She tried to block them, using the method Jori had said he used, but her nerves were too rattled.

He traced his thumb down her jaw, then sighed. "Come. Let's get you suited up. You'll have plenty of oxygen for the trip." He glanced at the MM tablet wrapped around his wrist several times as he led her to a dimly lit closet where a suit waited on a shelf.

"Is everything alright?" she asked, worried about Jori.

He didn't answer right away, then snapped his attention to hers as though finally registering what she'd said. "Oh, yes. Of course. I'm just monitoring bridge activities."

A crease of confusion still etched his brow, but she took him at his word. Surely, if it was something important, he'd tell her.

"Here you go." He waved her inside. "Take your time. You want to make sure it's on correctly. I can help you with the helmet."

She entered and he stepped back, letting the door shut her in for privacy. Her anxiety had become a steady buzz. It was just enough to cause her hands to tremble as she grasped the dull white suit. It was bulky but appeared in good repair, though not as pristine as Jori's. And the helmet and gloves were separate pieces. She slipped her leg beyond the body, surprised at how snug it was. Her foot pinched despite the largeness of the shoe.

When she slid her arms in, her chest tightened. *You can do this. You must do this. Freedom is just on the other side of that door.*

With effort, she managed to get the enviro-suit on sans the helmet. Tucking it under her arm, she waddled out.

Blakesley chuckled. "You look positively adorable!"

The burn in her cheeks wasn't entirely from self-consciousness. "It's hot in this thing."

"Ah!" He rushed to her. She flinched, thinking he'd take her into his arms again. But he grasped her gloved hand. "See this?" He tapped a display embedded in the suit's forearm. It lit up, displaying three large buttons spaced far enough apart that her fat protected fingers wouldn't hit the wrong one. "There are nibs on the tips of your gloves. Just use them to tap through to the temperature options and adjust."

She tried it. The suit cooled almost immediately.

"Go ahead and see what other features it has," Blakesley said. "It's a good idea to know how it operates."

He glanced at his MM again. His brows drew in and deepened as he tapped the screen.

The sense that something was wrong grew stronger. "Has Jori made it to the space station yet?"

"Not yet," he replied without looking up. His jaw twitched as though he were grinding his teeth.

"How much longer?" She pressed.

He pinched his lip, but he didn't seem to be thinking about her question. "Fifteen minutes." He huffed. "Excuse me a moment."

"Sure." She brought her hand up and touched her mouth, then realized the gloves wouldn't allow her to bite her nails and settled for folding her arms instead. That didn't work so well either. The suit was too damned bulky.

Abelard stepped away and turned his back to her. He tapped the comm behind his ear. "Ramir, am I seeing this right?" he asked. "Vance's shuttle just initiated the docking procedure?"

Zaina didn't hear the reply, but Abelard's noisy exhale told her he was irritated. For the life of her, she couldn't figure out why.

He returned to her with a smile. She cocked her head. "Are you sure everything is alright?"

"Of course," he replied.

Her insides wriggled. He could be lying, but why would he do that? Did something happen and he was protecting her? That didn't explain his irritation, though.

Abelard's demeanor switched to a forced cheerfulness. "Now let's see about getting the helmet on and secured."

She agreed, letting him place it over her head. A cool, stale air circulated and chilled the perspiration on her forehead. He directed her to the crate. She climbed inside despite her unease.

Oh, please God. Let everything be alright.

41
Sucker-Punch

The shuttle's ramp eased down with an ear-splitting whine. Jori wiped his palms down his thigh. That took care of his hands, but a clamminess remained over the rest of his body. He brushed his fingertips over the object in his pocket, feeling somewhat reassured.

Air from the asteroid base whisked in. He filled his lungs to calm his nerves. A musty scent clung to nasal cavities. A hint of cleaning chemicals combined with the deeper metallic one of machinery was only a small part of it. The rest reminded him of hot sand on a cool day.

The ramp touched down. Vance's steps jounced, signifying a low artificial gravitational setting. Jori followed and realized outrunning this man wouldn't work. Vance would capture him in one mighty bound. The element of surprise combined with agility were Jori's only advantages.

He assessed his surroundings, noting the multiple docks separated by energy fields. Cargo vessels, transport ships, escort fighters, or a combination thereof occupied the six docking platforms. Luggage carts, mobile maintenance vehicles, and other machinery such as forklifts, stackers, and pallet jacks dotted the floor.

It was perfect. All he needed now was a destination.

He licked his lips and reached for the flash bomb. Vance gripped his shoulder, making his heart jump. He peered up, expecting the worst but all Vance's attention focused on the three approaching individuals.

The bald woman with a broad face wore a white coat-like outfit, marking her as either a doctor or scientist. Her large, round eyes were glued to a tablet. The pale man with mechanical arms reminded Jori of an engineer. He had on an azure jumpsuit that looked similar to those worn by the nearby mechanics, but stains didn't blotch his. His brows curved in apparent anger but Jori only sensed boredom. The leader was a dark-complexioned man wearing a buttoned-up maroon jacket that made him look like an ambitious spacecraft salesman.

None spared Jori a single glance. Their motions didn't hint at any interest in him either.

Sweat beaded on Jori's upper lip. Although he'd assumed they'd be cautious about tipping Vance off, he hadn't expected them to utterly disregard him.

The man in the jacket put on a grandiose smile and bowed to Vance. "Welcome, Sir. I'm sure you'll be pleased with your new acquisition."

"Where is it?" Vance asked in a clipped tone.

"It will be along shortly. I trust you have our payment?"

Vance waved his hand at the medium-sized crate just inside the shuttle. "Here."

Jori's eyebrows snapped up. *Here? I thought Blakesley was sending it.* Two shuttles, he'd said. The second one would leave as soon as they'd struck a deal. He'd even seen it on the schedule.

An invisible weight laden with uncertainty descended upon him. Had Vance created a fake entry? It would be just like him to string Jori along and give him false hope. But if that was the case, how had Blakesley not known?

He considered the others in the bay. If these three weren't in on his escape, perhaps someone else was. But not a single person paid him any mind.

Another trio of people arrived, leading a roll cart carrying some sort of device. Jori's fingers twitched over the flash bomb as he waited for a sign. However, these new arrivals also showed no interest in him. He caught the eye of a grey-haired man, but it was no more than a cursory glance.

Jori's pulse quickened. Something wasn't right. He recalled Vance's demeanor on the shuttle and suspected a connection.

The man in the maroon jacket made a grand sweeping gesture toward the machine. "And here it is. Just as you ordered." His grin spread, showing his straight white teeth. His eyes twinkled as though showcasing a masterpiece.

A rectangular box nearly as tall as Jori encased the contraption. The showman opened it up, displaying components recognized as an oscillator, transistor amplifier, heat sink, and electronic circuitry.

"This is one of the most powerful signal jammers ever made," the man said. Jori didn't detect a lie, but the boast was evident.

The man closed it back up and patted the top of the machine as though it were his favorite child. "Just attach your antenna and plug it to an adequate power source and this baby will give you a hole plenty wide enough for your vessel to pass through."

A chill sizzled down Jori's spine. As the man explained the controls, Jori looked about wildly. He wanted to make a break for it, but where were his rescuers? A closer inspection of the other people in his line of sight revealed cybernetics. The mechanic working on a ship on a nearby platform used tools that were a part of his cybernetic arm. Another technician had a cord running from the back of his head to the diagnostic panel. And when the big-eyed woman lifted her eyes to answer one of Vance's questions, a glint of mechanisms appeared in her pupil.

These people weren't on his side. They were MEGAs. Jori wouldn't be surprised if they also worked for MEGA-Man.

Chusho. He should run for it anyway—hide, find a communications room and make a call, stowaway on another ship stopping for a visit. He must do something.

A clap and a pinch to his shoulder jolted him. Vance peered down at him with a dangerous glint. "You're not going anywhere."

Jori locked up. Did he know? Had Blakesley ratted on him or had Vance figured it out somehow?

"What do you think of my new device?" Vance asked as he flicked his hand at the contraption.

Jori swallowed, the dryness scraping his throat. "What's it for?"

As the showman ordered workers to retrieve his payment and put the machine in its place, Vance's creepy smile made Jori's bones quiver. "It will disable a shield."

If not for his trepidation, Jori would've rolled his eyes. "What shield?"

Vance's grin widened. "I'm going to destroy Halden, the Tanirian Protectorate's home city on Vanir."

Jori almost choked. The Tanirian Protectorate was one of the Cooperative's most influential members. It comprised two star systems with two habitable planets and seven moon bases. To attack their government headquarters would be a detrimental blow to both their egos and their economy.

A wicked gleam sparked in Vance's eyes. "Now that I've told you my secret, you will tell me yours."

Irritation poked through his dread. He almost said, *not this again*, but the man's grip on his shoulder tightened painfully.

"What's..." The calm of Vance's voice hinted at a menacing monster coiled beneath. "...In. Your. Pocket?"

Jori's gut lurched as though he'd been sucker-punched. He should say something, but his tongue stayed locked inside his mouth.

"No need to tell me," Vance replied. "I already know. Hand it to me now or I'll take it from you. And truest me—" His eyes flashed. "—you won't like that."

Jori's spine stiffened, but it was too for willful action. He'd been caught. His insides tremored, but he retrieved the flash bomb from his pocket and placed it in Vance's hand without revealing his trepidation.

*****

Breathless and with a cold tingling sensation spreading over his body, Major Abelard Blakesley darted onto the bridge. Something was wrong. The shuttle should've exploded.

"What's happening?" he demanded.

"Vance received the device and will leave the base in fifteen minutes," the woman at the operations station replied in a monotone voice.

"Jori too?"

"Yes, Sir."

Damn it! That the imp hadn't escaped was the least of his concerns. Did the bomb Blakesley had planted get discovered and disabled? Or was there a glitch that would cause it to go off on the return trip? Both would be bad, but the latter might still be salvageable.

He rushed to his office. The terminal wouldn't turn on quickly enough and his heart battered like an industrial jackhammer. It finally blinked on. He tapped away. Surveillance, bot repairs, maintenance logs. He checked it all. If Vance had found it, there'd be some evidence. And he would've confronted him already, too. Perhaps the wiring in the bomb had come loose or the timer malfunctioned.

Blakesley dropped into his chair and ran his hand down his sweaty face. That must be it. It malfunctioned. Maybe it wouldn't go off at all. This would set back his plans, but only a little. There'd be other opportunities.

Everything will be fine. He repeated the thought despite the niggling disquietude. There was nothing he could do but wait and see. And if Vance returned without incident, he'd meet him with a smile, then discreetly let Jori know to get Zaina from the crate.

The boy would realize there'd been no rescue from the base, and he'd tell Zaina. How would Blakesley handle that? Alienating them created unnecessary complication, but it'd be worse if Vance knew.

The sensation of a thousand phantom spiders crawled through his insides. *He probably knows and he's playing with me.* He bounded to his feet. The need to keep up with his racing thoughts prompted him into the hall where he broke into a fast walk. Where he headed, he had no idea.

He held no hope of being pardoned a second time. His only recourse was to fight back. For that, he needed a weapon powerful enough to penetrate Vance's armor.

A cold realization stopped him in his tracks. His initial plan had fallen apart, which meant Vance would foresee such a decision. *Damn it.*

I can run. Vance likely wouldn't see it coming since all his focus was on Jori. The idea had its appeal for another reason. Blakesley filled his lungs with purpose and headed to the cargo bay where Zaina waited.

The little vessel wasn't as fast as the *Black Thresher*, but it had a cloaking device. All he had to do was disable the transponder. It'd be easy.

A nearby conveyor opened. Three cyber soldiers emerged, withering his conviction. They turned a sharp ninety degrees and faced him with the same alert dullness held by most of their enhanced soldiers.

Blakesley's comm chimed, making him yelp. He swallowed, then answered. "Yes, Sir."

"Meet me in the shuttle bay," Vance said.

Blakesley's thoughts spun and splattered in a million directions. Before he made up his mind to flee or fight, the soldiers converged at his sides, their body language declaring that he had no choice but to comply.

This means nothing. Perhaps Jori had tried getting away and Vance only suspected Blakesley had something to do with it. Or he just wanted him to see the device. The man couldn't be aware of his attempt to blow up the shuttle. He'd taken precautions and had been extra careful. All this was merely a coincidence. It had to be.

I'm not ready to die.

42
Obsolete

Jori plodded along like a prisoner headed to his execution. The shock of getting caught had worn off. Heavy resignation replaced it. Mind dazed, body numb, and eyes downcast, he entered the shuttle. It occurred to him he should put on a guise of courageous defiance, but what was the point? Vance would see through the lie to the pathetic and defeated person underneath.

He eased into the copilot seat and buckled in. He did those things, but it seemed like someone else did them and he merely watched. The same disconnect took over his brain as well. He had so many questions, but they remained hidden as though trapped beneath a thick layer of ice.

Vance double-checked the straps securing the device, then approached the cockpit. He didn't speak, nor had he spoken since Jori had handed him the flash bomb. Despite the silence, he cringed inwardly as the weight of the man's fury pressed around him.

This was worse than his father's blustering rage. At least with Father, the consequences had been swift. This hollow anticipation of punishment felt like drifting through the abyss on a low tank of air.

Vance secured himself in the pilot's seat. Jori studied the hard set of his jaw and the flare of his nostrils. The man operated the controls, jabbing a button here, yanking a lever there, and ignoring him with blatant loathing.

A heat grew over his face, partly due to shame for getting caught. Although he'd accepted the consequences of his failure, he might not be the only one to suffer. Anger also fueled him. Vance had no right to be upset. Of course he'd tried to escape. That's what people did when held against their will. *Stupid chima.*

His internal temperature spiked with indignation. "How did you know?"

Vance's jaw muscles knotted. "You still haven't learned, have you?"

Jori clenched his teeth. Couldn't the man give a straight answer for once? "Learned what, exactly?"

"To see! You're so intent on a single aspect that you failed to recognize the most obvious one of all. You're blind… And you're stupid."

Jori scowled. That last comment sounded much like one his father would say, and it had the same effect. He didn't deny it out loud, knowing it would do no good, but resentment curled his lip and made him wish he had the strength to strike this chima down.

"Think!" Vance bellowed, making Jori jump. "How did I know?"

"You had a premonition, but how?"

"That's your problem, right there," Vance said, his tone deep and accusatory. "You assume the only way I see is with my premonitions, but I have *two fucking eyes*." He jabbed his fingers at his face. "And I have surveillance all over the damn ship. No place is safe. Not the corridors, the gym, the cafeteria, and not your quarters."

All the heat in Jori's body evacuated in one fell swoop, leaving him chilled to the bone. How could he be so stupid? First, the AI targeting system versus the manually guided torpedoes in their game of Galactic Dominions, and now this.

Surveillance. It was so obvious. He wanted to kick himself for being such an idiot.

"See?" Vance said through his teeth. "Stupid."

This time, Jori agreed.

No one spoke for the rest of the trip. Vance's stormy silence drowned out the hum of the shuttle's engines, the occasional tap on the instrument panel, and the whisper of air coming through the vent. Jori's inner turmoil waxed and waned. One moment, he resigned himself to his fate, believing he deserved any punishment Vance had in store. The next, he swore to fight this hateful man every step of the way.

He also worried about Zaina. As they neared the *Sublime Liberty*, or officially the *Black Thresher*, Zaina's lifeforce became more evident. That meant Blakesley was in on this too. But how had he evaded Jori's ability to detect lies?

Poor Zaina. He expected her to be frightened but uneasiness peppered her anticipation. He suspected she was still in the crate on the ship, and undoubtedly wondering when she'd be able to come out. What would she do, what would she feel, when she realized she'd never left?

Part of the answer came to him as they entered the bay. Her emotions switched to surprise, then consternation. Someone must've let her out. He wondered if it was Blakesley but couldn't tell.

Her distress increased as he sensed her heading this way. Vance eased the shuttle inside. After settling, the docking bay clamps jolted the ship into permanent repose. The engine shut off and Jori's heart ticked into overdrive. Although he detected nothing from Vance, something about the man's rigid posture and tight expression told him consequences would be worse than a Perovian lightning storm.

Jori unbuckled and rose from the chair. Vance grabbed his upper arm and walked—no, hauled—him out of the cockpit. It was all he could do to keep up. Vance didn't let go as he waited for the hatch to lower into a gangplank. If anything, his grip tightened, right along with his face.

As the door lowered, Blakesley appeared. He wore a white-lipped smile. His eyes darted about. His feet shifted. The mental wall he'd had up wavered, then crumbled. Fear exuded from him.

Three hulking cyber soldiers loomed behind him. Two more arrived, carrying a petrified Zaina between them. Blakesley's mouth opened and closed but no words came out.

The hatch hit the floor with a reverberating click. Vance stormed out, pulling Jori along with him. "I'm surrounded by incompetents!"

Blakesley flinched. Jori's heartbeat took off like a revving engine. He tried to wrench free from Vance's grip but the man's iron hold remained.

"S-sir," the major stammered. "I-is everything okay?"

"You are no longer any use to me. You are obsolete!"

Vance flung Jori onto the floor, causing his knees to strike it with a crack. Then he stormed over to Blakesley.

The major raised his palms and retreated. "It was a mistake. I realize that now. But you left me no choice."

Jori found his feet but wasn't sure what to do as the tension crackled between the two men. Blakesley glanced behind him and turned to avoid an inactive tool bot. Excuses poured out of him as Vance closed in. Space was running out. Blakesley must've realized it too because he halted. His wide eyes darkened and he bared his teeth.

Vance attacked. The major darted out of the way and threw a fist. He landed an ineffective blow on Vance's shoulder. Motivated by the action, Jori bolted toward them. He didn't give a damn about Blakesley, but the two of them together had a better chance of ending this madness.

A cyber soldier sidestepped into his path. As he zipped around him, another soldier caught him by the arm and jolted him to a stop. Jori twisted and kicked, but the first one grabbed his other arm, leaving him suspended between immovable pillars.

Vance and Blakesley circled each other. The major wore a worthy scowl, but it was nothing compared to the rage seared on Vance's face.

"*You* are the one who is obsolete!" Blakesley yelled. "You think you're better than everyone but you're only a mindless ape. You were supposed to win the boy over, but you've failed! Now you have two enemies who hate your fucking guts!"

Blakesley rushed in, poised to strike. Vance flipped his arm to block. The major avoided it at the last moment and jabbed his other fist into Vance's side.

Jori struggled against his captors. Despite the futility, his hope surged as Blakesley's swiftness and agility played against his opponent's beefy slowness.

The major delivered another blow to Vance's midsection, but at a great cost. A thunderous uppercut popped Blakesley's jaw and sent him flying. He landed with a thud. Vance stomped over. Blakesley didn't have the sense to do anything other than moan. Vance hauled him to his feet, making his head bob. Jori thought Vance would strike him again, but he grabbed his throat instead. His knuckles turned white as he squeezed. A deafening crunch followed. Blakesley's eyes bulged. A rush of crimson flooded his face. He flailed his arms, but even if Vance let go, it was too late.

Jori doubled over as the pain of death stabbed through his brain. He barely heard Zaina scream. He didn't know whether she was horrified or had been hurt. Either way, he couldn't help her. The external agony overtook him like an unrelenting lava flow.

The soldiers released him. He dropped to his knees and held his arms over his head. Before the pain subsided, someone yanked him to his feet. He blinked and attempted to regain his composure. Blakesley lay on the floor, kicking and grasping his crushed throat. No sound escaped him. Nausea rolled. Jori bent over and heaved. Vance forced him up again, causing the vomit to splatter. He ignored it and concentrated on remaining standing despite the chaos in his skull.

Zaina bawled. Her body and feet hung limply as the cyber soldiers pinched her arms and kept her upright. "Why?" she cried.

Vance wore a gleeful smile as he regarded the dying major. "He betrayed you," he said to her. "He had no intention of letting you go." He chuckled and turned to Jori with a wild spark in his eyes. "And he didn't just betray her. He also betrayed you. Did you know he intended to blow up our ship before we reached the base?"

Jori glanced at the major's body in the last throes of death. The pain of Blakesley's impending demise remained but seemed more resigned now. Despite the betrayal, Jori pitied him.

"You're such an idiot," Vance said. "You are *not* worthy."

Jori swallowed as the man bared his teeth and seethed. His bravery crumbled and he took a stumbling step backward.

"But…" Vance spit off to the side. "MEGA-Man has plans for you. Therefore, I won't punish you."

The words should've comforted him. But when the man's gaze turned to Zaina, he forgot all about Blakesley's agony. His own emotions erupted forth.

"No!" He charged and rammed his head into Vance's hip.

The man grabbed Jori by the hair and tossed him. He skidded across the bay as Vance neared the now hysterical Zaina.

"No!" Jori leapt to his feet.

Zaina blubbered as she tried to back away. The cyber soldiers defeated her efforts. Her toes scraped the floor, trying to find purchase.

Jori sprinted forward. He jammed himself between them. Vance attempted to snatch him instead, but he weaved out of the way. "You won't hurt her!"

Vance's face scrunched up like a snarling beast. "What did I tell you would happen?" He grabbed for Jori.

Jori ducked and slammed his fist into the man's kidney. He pivoted and punched again. None of his strikes did any good but anything was better than letting the chima harm Zaina.

Vance growled as he spun this way and that, trying to catch him. Jori was relentless. He hit, kicked, jabbed, and chopped at every opportunity. Vance's rage grew. Spittle flew from his mouth as he snarled and cursed.

"Don't hurt him!" Zaina screamed.

Her reaction disrupted Jori's concentration and he barely avoided the man's mighty fist. In dodging it, he lost his footing. Vance pounced after him. Jori scrambled back. Vance lunged. Jori rolled away, getting a whisper of Vance's knuckles by his ear. He found his feet and skittered out of reach of Vance's frenzied swings. Fear crawled through him, but it was a mere tickle compared to his defiant rage.

He'd redirected Vance's attention from Zaina, but now what? He'd said he wasn't stupid enough to fight Vance one-on-one, yet here he was.

He backed into a wall. Vance dove toward him. Jori bobbed under his arm. Vance's fist struck the wall with a crack. Before Jori could get out of reach again, Vance twisted and swung in a backhand and smacked Jori in the temple. The blow frazzled his vision, but he remained standing. Huge arms wrapped around him. His face smashed into the hard armor of Vance's uniform. He struggled to twist away, but only put the man at his back.

Jori kicked and would've punched too but his arms were pinned.

"You defied me!" The boom of Vance's voice stabbed Jori's eardrums. "And now you will pay!"

Jori thrust his heel backward, striking the side of Vance's knee and almost making him buckle.

"Stop fighting it, boy! Or you'll end up like the major!"

Jori grunted against the man's tightening hold. "I don't care!" He jerked his body, trying to break free. The realization that he was about to lose this game for good gave him an idea. "If you kill me, you'll lose your game with MEGA-Man."

Vance roared. His backbreaking embrace crackled Jori's vertebrae. Jori tried to yell some more, but the air had been squeezed out of his lungs. He kept kicking, knowing full well he couldn't escape but determined to fight to the end.

*****

Tears streamed down Zaina Noman's face as Jori and Vance fought. It wasn't much of a fight, though. Jori whipped around with a skill that would've amazed her under other circumstances, but he was so small that all his efforts only enraged the giant beast of a man.

She tried to wrench free, but the grip of the cyber soldiers neutralized her struggles. She jerked her arm back. Again forward. Nothing worked. She kicked but only hurt her foot.

Her tenacity surprised her. Ever since the assault, she'd freeze in the face of the mildest confrontation. Perhaps her subconscious was tired of letting others fight for her. Or maybe her mind reacted differently because of how close she and Jori had become.

Vance's features contorted into a snarl. He yelled something too filled with fury to be understood.

"Don't hurt him!" She wailed and struggled some more. Nothing worked. "Please don't hurt him," she said through her raw throat.

Jori fell. Even with the raging monster coming for him, his expression remained fierce. His eyes had an intensity that matched Vance's except with more focus. While Vance seethed with a rash madness, Jori darted about with calculated determination. Despite her terror, she couldn't help but admire his tenacity.

Her heart constricted when Vance grabbed hold of him. Jori shouted. His words were laced with relentless temerity, but she hardly heard him through her unbidden bawling.

Vance roared. Zaina's throat caught as Jori's cries cut off. *Oh no! He's going to kill him too.*

Just when she thought the boy would get crushed, Vance let go. Jori dropped to the floor. His look of bewilderment probably matched hers.

"You're right," Vance said with seething coldness. "I almost forgot our deal."

His baleful eyes fell on her, making her squawk.

"No!" Jori bellowed, his voice full of both rage and desperation. "Leave her alone!"

Vance turned back to the boy with a gleeful smile. Jori struggled to his hands and knees. His face twisted into a fierceness that said he wouldn't give up. "Don't you dare touch her!"

"You don't have what it takes to stop me."

"I will fight you."

Vance laughed. "And lose."

The boy rose to his feet. Hate and malice contorted his features to where he no longer looked like a child. It didn't bother her since that madman deserved every bit of his disdain.

"So be it," Jori replied. "To the death. Failing that, I'll take my own life. After all, if you kill her, I have nothing left to live for."

"You're bluffing."

"I don't lie."

Zaina swallowed. *No. What's he saying?*

"I've learned a little something from your stupid games," Jori said. Vance smirked. Jori pressed on. "Sometimes winning requires a sacrifice, so I sacrifice myself. I may be dead, but you'll end up that way too when MEGA-Man finds out what you've done."

"No," Zaina whispered. She must not have heard him correctly. The stress was playing tricks on her.

Vance's stony features resembled a volcano about to explode.

"I mean it." The boy's hands balled at his sides. "If you hurt her, the game is over."

The man's eyes widened, then narrowed. Time stopped, as did Zaina's heart, as he and Jori glared like two lions sizing one another up.

"Fine," Vance finally said. "Have it your way. But if I let her be, *you* had better start living up to expectations."

Jori didn't reply. Vance jabbed his finger as though to press the issue, but then stormed out with an enraged roar instead.

Her mouth hung open. *What just happened?* Everything that had zoomed by her during the intense situation came rushing in with a crisp clarity that almost seemed unreal. Blakesley's death.

His body flailing and twitching on the floor. Vance storming toward her with violence etched on his face. Jori intervening. Jori fighting. Jori threatening to kill himself to save her.

She fought for breath as her tears fell. Jori's chest heaved as he remained locked in a battle pose. The stiffness of the soldiers persisted, as did their grips on her upper arms.

Her sobbing ebbed. The raggedness of Jori's breaths smoothed and lengthened. The hardness in his eyes abated. When they snapped and focused on her, his brow furrowed and he rushed to her side.

"Let her go!" he said.

The soldiers obeyed. The unexpected freedom made her stumble. She didn't fight it as her legs buckled.

Jori sank with her. "Are you alright?"

"Yeah," She pressed her palm to her chest, willing her racing heart to slow. "You? I saw him hit you."

Jori felt his temple but didn't wince. "It'll bruise. Nothing more."

She touched his cheek. "Thank you. Thank you for saving me."

Tears filled Jori's eyes as he nodded.

She pushed up onto her knees and rubbed his shoulders. "I know I said we should never resort to fighting, that there are better ways to handle things. But... I was wrong. That man is a crazy son-of-a-bitch, and I just don't see any other way you could've handled this. You fought because you had to, and if you hadn't..." She broke down. "I'd be dead like him." She indicated Blakesley's body and emitted a hushed wail. It was all too much. Her feelings about the man were mixed, but he certainly didn't deserve this.

Neither did Jori. Reflecting on all that he'd said wrenched her stomach. She couldn't believe he'd kill himself for her, but the firmness of his tone had lent truth to his claim—"*I don't lie*." She nearly choked on her shame.

Jori dropped his head on her shoulder. "I don't want to lose you."

Her tears spilled anew, but for a different reason. "Oh, Jori. I'm so sorry." She pulled him close. "I should be the one sacrificing myself for you."

"You can't stop him."

He was right, but she couldn't keep letting her fear control her. "But I'll give it one hell of a try." Gone was the overwhelming terror and in was a profound relief coupled with an endearment so strong that it almost hurt. "We're done playing his games. We're getting out of this." She pulled back and gripped his shoulders. "You understand me? And if anyone is to sacrifice anything, it'll be me. You don't need to protect me anymore." *At least I hope you won't need to*. "We'll figure out how to stop him."

Jori wiped his eyes. "It won't be easy. And if we fail again, he'll kill you."

"Don't worry about me." A powerful resolve took hold of her. She felt like she'd finally kicked her anxiety to the curb once and for all. Hopefully, that feeling would stick. "No matter what happens to me, you keep fighting. You'd said you'd have nothing left to live for if I die, but that's not true. There are at least two people out there who care a great deal about you. Promise me that no matter what, you'll find a way to reach them."

Jori's eyes hardened again, but this time with more resolve than anger. "When he threatened to hurt you, I vowed to fight to the very end, and I meant it."

She grasped his hand. It wasn't the response she'd wanted but she'd make sure he didn't have to keep that vow. "It won't come to that. We'll get out of this. You and I. Together."

43
Cracked

The air in the cyborium carried an irksome chill. Now and then, the artificial fragrance of soap wafted through the acrid antiseptic odor. The typical sounds of doctors and medics going about their business buzzed in the background, along with the high-pitched beeps of monitors and rumbling diagnostic machines. More than half the staff bore obvious cybernetic implants, but Jori hardly noticed anymore. This place had become too familiar, and he hated it.

He sat on the edge of a hospital bed, likely the same one Zaina had lain on when she'd been here for her anxiety. As the only patient in this sizable room, he felt like the center of everyone's attention—something else he had an aversion to.

In a way, he *was* the primary focus. He crossed his arms and frowned as Doctor Stephen Stenson ran the thera-pen over his temple. The man's breath carried a sour tint, yet Jori remained still as the pen healed the giant bruise Vance had left. The wound didn't hurt unless he moved his brows. Even then, the pain was minimal. Normally, he'd just let it mend on its own, but allowing the doctor to care for him made Zaina feel better.

She hugged his side, more so than ever before, and wrapped her arm around his shoulder. She no doubt intended to be both comforting and protective, though he doubted she'd be capable of safeguarding him against a madman like Vance.

Stephen cleared his throat. "I'm reluctant to ask, but how did this happen?"

Zaina's emotions plummeted right along with Jori's. They both hesitated to speak, Zaina with a glance sideways and a twisted brow. The outcome was too troubling to put to words. But after a heavy sigh, she recounted the horrific incident.

Doctor Stenson halted his work. Concern mingled with dismay exuded from him like exhaust from a dilapidated ship. "H-he killed the major? Then he tried to hurt you?" His voice came out in a troubled whine. "And you protected her?" he asked Jori.

Jori shrugged off the doctor's admiration. "I hate how he uses her to get me to obey."

Stephen nodded. His cheeks turned pink as shame emanated from him. He glanced toward the other side of the facility, undoubtedly at where his wife had been moments before.

"That madman has really cracked this time," Zaina said matter-of-factly. "I've knew he was dangerous…" She pressed her palm to her chest as though to curb a racing heart. "But the extent of his fury was like…" She inhaled, her breath shaking. "Like a vicious dog."

Jori almost huffed. *She hasn't met my father*.

"He's always been unpredictable, but ever since you arrived…" Stephen shot Jori an apologetic glance. "No offense, but the extreme nature of his behavior has multiplied. I've never seen it so bad. I wonder what sort of pressure MEGA-Man is putting on him."

"I don't think MEGA-Man is just after my DNA," Jori said. "He also wants me to ally with the MEGAs."

The doctor shook his head but not in disagreement. "That makes some sense, but not entirely. I mean, why do you have to ally with them? I thought all he wanted was to use you for your genetics, and he doesn't need your cooperation to do that."

Jori didn't reply, though he knew the answer. MEGA-Man undoubtedly had a lot of uses for the last heir of the Toradon empire. Vance might be the current scourge of the galaxy, but he was a lone wolf. As the next in line to the throne, Jori would command a horde of Dragon Warriors who were far more ferocious. Never mind that he'd never return home. His father believed him dead, and he wanted to keep it that way.

Zaina rubbed Jori's upper arm and pulled him into a half hug. "The man is obsessed."

"There is that," Stephen replied. "He's always been intently focused on his objectives."

"And what are his objectives, exactly?" Zaina asked. "Because his actions are all over the place. You say he wants you—" She tapped Jori's shoulder. "—to ally with him but he treats you like a lab experiment."

The doctor cupped his elbow with one hand and rubbed his chin with the other. "I suspect his motivations are conflicted. He must comply with MEGA-Man's demands, yet he has an inherent need to dominate, and this young man here presents a notable challenge."

"Him and his stupid games," Jori muttered.

The trio fell silent while their troubled emotions spun about like a tornado. They must escape this madman.

He took in his two companions and despaired. While he might have the advantage of knowing how to fight, he was too small to take on a monster like Vance. Their most recent engagement proved that. Zaina had neither the physical nor the mental strength. And the doctor was much too concerned about the safety of his wife to risk anything.

The situation was hopeless. Jori wasn't smart enough to consider all the angles and match wits with this psychopath.

Doctor Stenson puffed and returned to his work of healing Jori's temple. His resignation suffocated Jori's own emotions, which were just as dispirited. At least threatening to sacrifice himself had worked in keeping Vance from hurting Zaina, but how long would that last? Zaina was right. The man had cracked.

"How's Rodrigo?" she asked, dampening the mood further.

The doctor's throat bobbed. "He's gone."

Zaina gasped. "He's dead?"

Stephen halted his work on Jori's temple once more. "He might as well be. His body lives, but all the things that made Rodrigo Rodrigo are no longer there."

Zaina's eyes watered. Jori tried to force his emotions down so he wouldn't follow suit. He and Rigo weren't close, but it still hurt to see his quirky personality destroyed.

Jori's sinuses burned as he recalled the reason the mouse of a man had done it. MEGA-Man and Vance put him on such a high pedestal that Rigo wanted to be like him. Guilt crept through him.

No. I didn't do this. He clenched his fists. Rodrigo had made his own choice. Even so, the bulk of the blame rested with the culture on this ship that said the only people with value were the ones with enhancements.

He glanced at Zaina, who shared a sad smile, then at the doctor. These were real people. They had their faults, but their kindness was more than enough to redeem them.

His gratitude didn't last as the reality of their situation pressed around him. No amount of kindness would get them out of this mess.

Perhaps it was time for him to stop playing nice. No more pussyfooting it with Vance. He must make a plan and take action—to hell with the consequences.

If only he could come up with an idea on how to do that.

44
Weaknesses

Jori jerked awake. He blinked through the darkness, wondering what had brought him out of his respite. The severe lack of light kept him from seeing anything, so he concentrated on listening. The only sound was the whisper of air blowing from the vent and Zaina's soft breathing. It was the first time in days that she'd slept so deep, and he hoped he wouldn't have to break her away from it.

Blakesley's betrayal and subsequent death had taken its toll on her. She'd put on a brave face, but he'd sensed her uninterrupted turmoil.

He focused his other senses. The room smelled the same. His sentio ability didn't detect anything out of the ordinary. And there was nothing unusual about his placement in bed. His head rested on the pillow as usual. The blankets sufficiently covered him without tangling his limbs. Everything seemed normal.

A pulsation from the counter made him flinch. He swung his feet to the floor and rushed over. The vibration stopped, but he didn't need his eyes or ears to find the tablet. The room wasn't that big. Two steps brought him close enough to probe for his device.

The act of picking it up caused the screen to brighten. He blinked until the light became bearable. A message icon flashed in the corner. Angst flicked through him. No one had ever contacted him here before.

He tapped it open. His lips parted at the sight of Doctor Stephen Stenson's name. The man had never engaged in an electronic conversation before. With the confession that Rodrigo was gone, what else was there to talk about?

The muscles in Jori's upper body stiffened. Vance's mention of surveillance prompted him to press the tablet to his chest. Stephen must have something important to say.

He whisked back to bed and pulled the covers over him. If Vance was watching right now, all he had to do was hack into his tablet and bypass the spyware detection Jori had placed on it. But if the scene was merely being recorded, Vance would learn later—too late—that he'd received a message.

Half expecting the madman to barge through the door at any moment, his heart hammered. His finger froze over the open button. Six tense and watchful days had passed since Blakesley's death and the doctor's treatment, so it was possible Vance wouldn't foresee any of this. Or perhaps Jori was overthinking it. Maybe Stephen just wanted to ask how he was doing.

Jori gritted his teeth and tapped the tablet. His pulse quickened as he read Stephen's message.

> <S. Stephen> This past incident has me fretting. I can no longer stomach the endless atrocities being committed by that deranged sociopath. It's time to put a stop to this insanity. This note is the first step. Read it thoroughly, then let's talk in a few days. I'll do whatever it takes.

Jori skimmed the words, his anticipation too great to take it slow. Stephen verified that Vance couldn't read thoughts or emotions during a premonition. Something about the distance between the decision to act and the effect of the act itself might trigger his premonitions but he wouldn't detect the motivations behind it.

> <S. Stephen> He can only foresee the most probable future, but this is tricky because of the counting principle and other mathematical factors that I haven't figured out yet. I suspect if you make a decision that affects him, and it's within five days, he'll see it. But if it's beyond five days, there's a chance he won't foresee it.

This reiterated Vance's blind spot where he had difficulty perceiving an event that had been decided upon more than five days prior. So even if the act was only three days away, that Jori or whoever had decided to commit that act more than five days ago prevented Vance from seeing it. Stephen's detailed explanation on how it worked made Jori's head spin, but he trusted the information.

The doctor went on to explain how Vance had to tie his premonitions to specific people, but it didn't work on everyone. Those with too many implants, for example. The doctor suspected Vance couldn't use anyone with no lifeforce for his foretelling ability.

Interesting. Jori read on. Vance saw the future from one individual, but he was incapable of seeing through more than one person in the same timeframe, even with a separate vision. *Also interesting.* Jori pinched his lip. Perhaps Zaina could do one thing while he did another. Vance would watch him, not her.

Stephen also confirmed what Vance had told him. The man saw things that affected him the most and he needed to make a conscious effort to foresee through a specific person even if they weren't up to anything. Even if it was something decided over five days ago—meaning the beyond five-day rule didn't always hold true.

Damn. That complicated matters, but it was still good to know. Jori's nerves sizzled with the possibilities. Only this time, he accounted for the other tools Vance might use to his advantage—such as surveillance.

> <S. Stephen> P.S. I hope this note finds you in your sleep cycle. This is Vance's rest time too and I doubt he has the means to spy on you every moment.

Jori reread the message, taking more care and committing it to memory. Then he deleted it, being sure to wipe it from the system. He switched off the device and plopped his head onto the pillow. Staring through the pitch black of nothingness helped him digest the information and add mental notes. That Vance had discovered Blakesley's ruse using real-time monitoring meant there were cameras Jori never noticed. Perhaps bots and cyborgs were spying on him. What about Doctor Stenson himself? This could be a setup orchestrated by Vance to test Jori's loyalty. *Or make the game more challenging*. Jori soured.

Another possibility was that Stephen might rat him out to protect Celine. He'd need to talk to the man in person later and gauge his emotions.

The cooling vent turned on again, spewing chilled air. Jori pulled his covers around his shoulder and curled to the side. Despite the comfort of a blanket tucked under his chin, sleep still evaded him. He had to think beyond Vance's skills and delve into his limitations. The man's foretelling ability didn't extend beyond five days. Nor could he visualize from more than one perspective at a time, determine the motivations behind acts, or see through people with no lifeforce.

But even knowing Vance's weaknesses wasn't enough. Jori needed to counter them with his own strengths. He certainly wasn't smarter. Nor was he a better fighter. But he was fast and agile. His smallness might be of some use.

What about his programming ability? Chances were Vance had seen him program that bot to disrupt the fabricors in the cafeteria. But it was possible he thought nothing of it because he didn't understand coding well enough to realize what'd been done—another advantage. Vance's obsession with him and not Zaina or the doctors would also be helpful.

What else?

Jori turned onto his other side and fluffed his pillow. If he could flip about his disadvantage of being small, what about his weakness of caring about others? His father had always said that his sentiment made him weak, and Vance almost proved him right by threatening Zaina. But Commander Hapker had once stated otherwise. Doctor Stenson was a prime example. Stephen had finally agreed to help him because of emotions.

How else could he use his propensity to care about people against a madman? Well, wasn't he already doing that? Vance undoubtedly believed his threat against Zaina would keep him in line. It did, but only to a point. His desire to protect those he cared about went beyond mere obedience.

What about his gift with animals? The ship's extermination bots got rid of mice and other stowaways, but two labs on the ship kept small animals.

Jori doubted mice and snakes would be of much use, but perhaps implementing a plan for every scenario would overwhelm Vance's ability.

He tossed and turned some more. Thoughts swirled. Some plans fell away while others solidified.

For the first time in a while, the possibilities bloomed like flora after a storm. This all led to one conclusion… He'd do whatever it took to defeat this monster.

45
Second in Command

Not long ago, a summons to the command center had filled Jori with consternation. He carried a bit of dread this time as well, but it was a drop compared to the embers burning inside him. The more he agonized over the intolerable situation Vance imprisoned him in, the harder his determination became.

He entered the bridge with his shoulders pulled back and his rancor hidden beneath a deadpan expression. Vance wore a look just as unreadable as he sat upright in the central chair. He waved his hand, directing Jori to the empty spot on the floor beside him. Jori marched over without an ounce of the disquiet that usually accompanied him whenever he'd dealt with this man. He planted his feet in a stiff at-ease stance and clasped his hands behind him.

The main viewscreen loomed ahead. A few bland views of space and various monitoring stats quilted it. Fortunately, they were much too far from anything worthy of Vance's homicidal attention. *So I'm not here to witness another massacre.*

With his mental wall in place, he turned to Vance with his brows tilted into a question. Rather than get a reply, the man merely looked at him with unblinking eyes. Jori stared back, refusing to be cowed by more of this man's stupid games. His hate boiled beneath the surface, and he used it to fuel his determination to outsmart this chima once and for all.

He still wasn't sure how to do that, but it didn't matter. He'd find a way.

"You got a message last night," Vance finally said.

"Yes," Jori replied simply while also quelling a rise of panic. The Stensons being in danger didn't deter his resolve, so he jutted his chin.

Vance's jaw twitched. "From who?"

Jori's worries fled. The doctor's trick had worked. "You didn't see it?" he said, attempting to sound innocent.

Vance jerked toward Jori with a curled lip. "Don't get smart with me."

Jori's heart skipped a beat, but nothing more. He returned the man's glower and held it.

Vance gripped the arms of his chair like talons. "Who was it from, and what did they say?"

Jori should've made up a lie, but any attempt to come up with one muddled his thoughts. He opted to keep silent instead.

As Vance drew closer, the dark dance in his eyes intensified. Jori pressed his lips and remained obstinate. Even with the threat to Zaina, he wouldn't give in by trading one life for another.

Vance's thick fingers curled into a white ball capable of cracking a skull. Jori waited in anticipation of a strike. He almost welcomed it. For so long as he was the target, his friends would be safe.

Just when he was sure the man would explode, the man's eyes tilted in amusement. "Go ahead. Keep your secret. It won't matter in the end. Besides, that's not why I brought you here."

Vance paused, possibly expecting Jori to prompt him for more information. He didn't bother. If Vance wanted to play a game, let him play it by himself.

"With Major Blakesley gone…" Vance finally said through his teeth, "I need a second officer. MEGA-Man appoints you."

This time, Jori replied—but only with a frown. His confidence wavered. Damn the man for conscripting him into another game anyway.

"That's right," Vance continued. "MEGA-Man wants you to take Major Blakesley's place."

"Why?" Jori asked.

Vance's lips curled as though he'd eaten something bitter. "He says you're ready for it," he said, his tone cutting like a knife over flesh. "He believes that allowing you to do more of the things you want will give you a taste of the power you can wield by serving him."

Jori almost rolled his eyes. Serving MEGA-Man would make him a puppet. But he kept a straight face. The skin between Vance's brows tightened as though he hated this idea. MEGA-

Man's clout must be strong. Not that he cared. This arrangement might benefit him.

"Don't get too excited," Vance said. "Despite my orders, I don't trust you. I'll be watching and informing him of all your actions."

The chima could watch all he wanted. Jori would find a way.

"Well?" Vance asked. "Are you ready to serve MEGA-Man?"

Jori almost huffed. He wasn't about to swear fealty. But he couldn't lie and say yes either. It would be easy to do if the duplicitous words would just leave his mouth. "What does being your second entail?"

Vance smiled. "Smart question. We'll start slow by prioritizing and assigning maintenance requests."

Hmm. This could be a good opportunity. "Can I keep repairing the bots?"

"Yes. And since you've shown quite the aptitude for programming, I'll also have you assist Doctor Humphrey."

This just keeps getting better and better. It might be another trap, but he'd make it work. "Do I get to give orders?"

Vance's mouth quirked as though he'd taken a bite of bitter fruit. "Yes."

Despite the man's reluctance, Jori didn't believe it. "Yes?"

"Yes!" Vance's eyes flashed and his jaw tightened. "But I will know every command you give. And you won't give any order that contradicts mine or works against our cause."

Right. Or he'll report to MEGA-Man. He wondered if he could use MEGA-Man's influence over this monster but discarded the idea. No way would he ally with someone who'd already shown he'd murder innocent people just to push his agenda.

He dipped his head, but in acknowledgement rather than agreement. "Will I have access to the entire ship?"

Vance bared his teeth, intending to smile. "Why? You have plans or something?"

"I don't," Jori replied truthfully. *Not yet.* "But I'm curious." Also the truth. "It's not like any other vessel I've ever seen."

Vance grunted, but whether in doubt or acceptance, Jori wasn't sure. "Fine. Now do you want the damn job or not?"

"Yes."

"Good. Then I want you to help plan our next attack."

Jori perked up. If he was in on it, he'd have a better chance of stopping it.

"That interest you, does it?" Vance's grin appeared pleased. "It's about time you take your place at my side."

Jori put on a smile himself. This might be another setup, but he didn't think so. If MEGA-Man was even half as omnipresent as everyone implied, he'd realize a man like Vance had no chance of gaining willing followers. He also suspected Vance's understanding of human nature was so off that he assumed murdering Blakesley and threatening to harm Zaina had finally elicited compliance. Or maybe Vance thought he liked the prospect of battle so much that he'd do anything to help.

Either way, he wasn't about to contradict him.

46
Exploration

A flame of fascination danced in Jori's chest. The layout of the *Sublime Liberty*—no, the *Black Thresher*—differed from every other ship he'd studied. A quick review of the schematics showed it had all the same amenities but in different places. Most larger vessels had a top-down approach where the bridge resided somewhere on the upper decks. Work areas followed by living quarters generally took up the middle. Manufacturing, engineering, and recycling almost always occupied the lower sections.

However, this ship had more of a fore-aft and inner-outer design. The fore contained the fabricors and water and sewage centers while the main propulsion units were at the aft. The very center of the vessel housed the bridge, which made sense from a strategic standpoint. Much of the surrounding areas were dedicated to scientific endeavors. Living quarters came next, with some being called recharging stations instead. And the engineering sections and workrooms containing communications, weaponry, and shielding devices were within the outermost hull. Only the docking bays were in the standard places along the sides of the ship.

Jori tapped his foot as he waited for the conveyor. When it opened, he darted in with an enthusiasm he hadn't felt in a while. "Engineering," he ordered the computer. An almost imperceptible jolt commenced an effortless ride. He arrived within moments and exited to a nondescript corridor. No signs directed the way, but his memory of the schematics sent him to the right. A narrow hall led him to a set of double doors that automatically admitted him with his new access.

The vast room on the other side stopped him short. This place was much larger than the ones on other ships that housed the arc drive. He entered and stretched his neck, amazed by how this thing that surely wasn't a traditional arc engine took up four decks. The tall cylindrical reactor was quieter too. It emitted a low hum that also vibrated the floor and contributed to Jori's awed energy.

At first, he thought the blue squares high above were monitors. But the way the lighting flashed made him realize they were observation windows. What was this and how did it work differently from an arc drive? And why in the hell would someone want to view it through a window? Windows in anything weakened a structure, so having one on something powerful enough to propel a starship didn't make sense.

He'd take the time to learn more about this later. In the meantime, he had more to explore. He wandered about, both in the engine room and beyond until he found what he was sure was the ship's transponder.

Vance had recently corrected him regarding the name of this vessel. *Sublime Liberty* was just a front. Even the appearance of it was a façade. To someone observing it via signals, it looked like an ordinary cruise ship. Advanced camouflaging technology hid this vessel's unusual features and weaponry. It also held up against a close-up observation.

Jori inspected the numerical readouts on the display to make sure this was indeed the transponder. A few taps to the monitor revealed its fake name, flight path, and designation. At least the trajectory and designations seemed true since it listed Halden, Vanir, Tanirian Protectorate.

The workstation also provided access to the camouflage generators. He doubted it would give him permission, but bypassing security was easy enough. Simply set up a fake repair and let a maintenance bot go to work. The only question was, would Vance see it coming?

Probably.

The feeling that this newfound freedom was a trap reared its ugly head once again. To ignore it would be foolish. At least he had several days to plan.

He left the transponder and continued his exploration. Taking his time to investigate every little thing might avoid triggering Vance's suspicion. Plus, he found it all intriguing. It made him wish his new life would be on another ship. Not that he didn't enjoy being on planets. Nature also fascinated him. He needed a good mix of both. Living on a vessel that traveled from place to place would provide that.

After a while, he located the shield deactivation device Vance had purchased. Three cyborgs worked on it. Jori asked a few innocuous questions while considering how he'd disable it. Since he couldn't do two things at once, he had to enlist Zaina's help. Getting her either to the transponder or this device would be easy enough. But her nervous tendencies might hamper her from doing anything too complicated. Not everyone had the ability to face monsters, not even imaginary ones.

He sighed. So much had to be done and doing it all alone was impossible. He needed her. The doctors too. Putting them at risk didn't sit well, but Vance's inability to watch more than one person in a single moment presented him with a significant advantage.

Jori continued his tour. After passing about twenty laboratories that looked so much alike, he thought he'd been going in circles. It was refreshing to reach the one with the animals. Well, not quite refreshing. The smell was a deluge of sweet, fusty, and pungent, and the air held a sticky humidity.

None of this bothered him. Having lived on a spaceship his entire life, interacting with something other than people excited him, especially on this ship where most were cybernetic. It helped that all these creatures felt content.

He studied the reptilian scales of a fat snake—possibly the same one he'd sensed in Vance's test. The mottled brown and tan pattern captivated him. The study of space was complex enough. Add in the intricacies of life, and the unfathomable possibilities overwhelmed him.

Moving on down the cages revealed turtles, frogs, fish, strange and colorful marine organisms, and even insects. At first, he questioned why a spaceship specializing in making cyborgs would need all these animals. Then he remembered how genetic modifications didn't come only from human DNA. His gut clenched at the thought of people with animal genes. Not that this type of experimentation hadn't been done before, but he'd assumed society had learned its lesson.

The following cages contained an assortment of birds, including a small bird of prey with beautiful rust and slate-blue feathers. A variety of small mammals from fluffy little mice to some sort of weasel-like creatures came next.

The lifeforces of the birds and mammals were more colorful than their reptilian and invertebrate friends. Their emotions ranged wider, yet they still weren't as complicated as people. Some animals were marked with dye or had feathers or fur removed, but none emanated stress over their situations. He focused on the weasel, noting how its lifeforce seemed to be missing something. The lack had nothing to do with a chip implant, though. Perhaps it was domesticated. Not having to hunt or fear predators likely had an effect.

The rear half of the room contained plants. Their exoticness indicated they hadn't been grown for eating. Succulents, flowering bushes, ferns, and more rested in raised beds or inside incubators. He considered exploring them too, but the animals were far more interesting.

An idea occurred to him. In thinking beyond the obvious, he could use these creatures as sentries. Since he couldn't sense Vance or many others on this ship, these animals, set loose, would emit a startled sensation whenever they saw someone. It'd require strict concentration on Jori's part, but he could do it.

He didn't settle on the idea right away. There were other aspects of this plan to consider—mainly, how to achieve all his objectives without getting him or his friends killed. Ending Vance would be the most direct way to stop this madness, but he doubted he had the ability to outplay the man to the point of death. Still, it had its appeal.

The next part of his tour brought him to a smallish infirmary where Doctor Humphrey examined an unconscious Rodrigo. Generally, he passed by the places where cyborgs were being worked on, but curiosity drew him inside.

"Is there something wrong with him?" he asked.

Doctor Humphrey's green eyes flashed. His frown accentuated the dimple in his chin. "You don't start your training until tomorrow."

"Rodrigo was my friend. I want to know what happened." He peered at the unconscious man, noting the IV, electrodes, and wires.

One such wire plugged into the side of Rigo's head and led to the monitor Doctor Humphrey observed. "I'm just refining his programming."

Jori leaned in, inspecting the coding. The language was familiar, but he'd need to do more studying to understand it better. "Programming for what?"

"Military."

Jori suppressed an eye roll. "What aspect of the military?"

Doctor Humphrey didn't look up from his work as he spoke. "Security."

"You mean he's a security guard?"

"Precisely."

"Who will he guard?"

"You."

"Me?" Jori's heart jumped. "As my bodyguard or my warden?"

"Bodyguard."

Jori twisted his mouth. "Why do I need one? Is there someone here who wants to hurt me?" *Besides Vance?*

The doctor didn't react. "I don't know. I'm just following orders."

"Whose orders? Vance's or MEGA-Man's?"

"Both."

Jori scoffed. Despite what the doctor had said, Rodrigo would more likely act as his warden—and spy. But he didn't bother revealing his suspicions. Although having a robotic babysitter would make his tasks more difficult, maybe he could tweak some of his programming in his favor. "Can I help you with him?"

"I don't need help."

Jori gritted his teeth at the man's abstractedness and rephrased his question. "Will you *allow* me to help you fix Rodrigo's programming?"

"You don't start your training until tomorrow," the doctor repeated.

Jori bit down harder, making his jaw hurt. Time to put his newfound power to the test. "I know, but I want to begin now. Show me."

Doctor Humphrey paused. His eyes seemed to glaze over in a way that reminded Jori of how Gottfried would freeze. Sometimes it was because the man had been thinking through a problem that required his internal processors. He suspected the doctor's reason was due to him having a conversation using a comm implant, which meant his authority wasn't as definitive as he'd hoped. Then again, perhaps the doctor was rearranging his schedule to accommodate him.

"Of course," Doctor Humphrey finally said.

The man sidestepped, giving Jori room in front of the screen. Instruction began and lasted for well over an hour. One good thing about learning from someone who was more machine than human was Doctor Humphrey never got irritated with all Jori's questions and he gave succinct and clear answers.

At the end of the lesson, he stepped away with the certainty that the Rigo he'd known was gone. Everything he did was a pre-programmed response. All independent thought had been eradicated.

Sorrow had built throughout the doctor's instruction, but so had a few ideas. Not only did he understand how Rigo's programming worked, but he also knew how to alter it. Later, when Rodrigo took over his new job, Jori would plug him in and enter a few additional lines of code.

He doubted the mouse would be able to defend against Vance, but the extra protection would undoubtedly come in handy.

47
Coordination

Zaina Noman ambled to her bed. The deep ache in her legs made the short distance feel like trudging through thick mud. The weight she carried symbolically buried her in the stuff. Even her room held a musty scent that reminded her of dirt.

She plopped onto the mattress but didn't lie down despite her fatigue. To be in a good physical and mental state for Jori's sake, she'd gone to the gym and pushed herself. Thirty minutes of on-off cardio wasn't bad unless she considered it was more off than on. At least she hadn't given up. And her mood had somewhat lifted. It was just enough confidence to help her stay awake until bedtime.

Her eyelids were already drooping, though. The ache behind her eyes screamed for rest. She wouldn't give in. It was a trap. One step into the sand, and she'd sink into a fitful sleep that'd leave her feeling worse than she did now.

Fight it, damn you. She rubbed her brow. Some caffeinated tea might do her some good, but it was easier to sit here than it was to get up.

If only Jori were here. He'd help her stay awake. Vance kept him busy, though. When the boy first told her he'd been given Blakesley's old job, she nearly had a panic attack. Just thinking about what orders Vance would give made her insides writhe. Plus, that madman had murdered his last second officer.

Oh, God. She covered her face with her palm and held back a sob as the memory of Abelard's death replayed in her mind.

No. I can't think about this. Focus. She swallowed down the ache in her throat.

Jori had promised this promotion would help. He'd been given access to the entire ship. He'd hinted at something else, too. *More ammunition*, he'd said, and she suspected he didn't mean weaponry. The glint in his eyes suggested a plan. This troubled her too. Though she wanted desperately to get away from here, she imagined the worst.

It made her stomach ache. She attempted to set aside her worries and grasped the tablet from the table next to her. A message popped up. Bold text told her to act like she was sick and hide under the covers before reading more. If not for her curiosity zapping her awake, she would've eschewed the idea of getting into bed.

She threw her arm over her head and groaned, pretending to have another migraine. Clutching the tablet, she crawled under the blankets and tapped the screen. A much longer message appeared. "*I need you,*" it started, and her heart jumped into a patter.

It didn't show who'd sent it, but she guessed easily enough. The language was to the point, just like Jori. Other than stating he needed her, there were no emotional undertones. It had a few typos, though. Perhaps he'd typed it without looking in case Vance foresaw his actions.

She bit her nails as she read, then read it again to make sure she understood. Vance kept a very close eye on him, but probably not her. The word *probably* struck her like a bad chord of music. Jori reassured her by explaining some of Vance's limitations. If she committed to disabling the transponder now, he wouldn't foresee it. Plus, the man would likely be too busy to watch her in real-time.

Jori also promised she'd have access to that part of the ship. It was doubtful anyone would stop her since he'd create a distraction. He didn't elaborate on how.

"Trust me," he'd written, and she did. She wasn't sure she trusted herself, though. Going to a restricted area would be scary enough. She imagined cyber soldiers gripping her arms and hauling her away, much like they'd done after Abelard's murder.

Don't be a coward. Hiding in her room and doing nothing was no longer an option. It was her turn to make a sacrifice. Besides, she had more to worry about with the transponder. She didn't even know what one looked like. Both Jori's directions and instructions seemed simple enough, but would she remember everything in her anxiety?

Afterward, she'd need to get to the shuttle bay where he'd fly her and the doctors out of there. Vance wouldn't stop them, he'd written, because he planned on having him trapped somewhere. He didn't provide details on how he hoped to achieve such a feat. Anxiousness about her task coupled with concern over him. At least he explained how he'd used her tablet to input the message. Her device wasn't connected to the network, so sending each other messages during sleep hours was a genius idea.

Her eyes lingered over the last line.

> <Jori> I know it's risky, but this must be done. I need you.

She clasped her hands and prayed for strength. *I can do this. I* will *do this*. She reminded herself that even though she was taking a chance that might lead to her death, she couldn't keep living like this.

Jori was right, it must be done. She tucked the tablet under her shirt and eased out of bed. Clutching her side to both hold the device in place and maintain the appearance of looking ill, she trudged across the room. She didn't need to pretend the limp caused by her aching muscles.

The fatigue pressing down on her kept her hunched over as she left. Doctor Stephen Stenson should be in the infirmary today. He'd be tending to a patient Doctor Claessen didn't have the expertise to handle. Zaina hoped it was true, but not just because she didn't care for that woman.

She pressed her elbow against the tablet, hoping the ruse held. Jori had a message for the doctor too. Though she didn't know what it was, it made sense to coordinate a plan with him. After all, he and his wife also needed to escape.

Zaina's nervousness amplified as she entered the conveyor and told it her destination. She managed to press it down and keep her goal firmly in her mind.

Don't worry, Jori. I won't let you down.

*****

A nervous energy vibrated through Jori's body as he headed to the infirmary. His sensing ability combined with his emotional connection to Zaina told him she'd read his note and complied. Doctor Stenson's emotions had indicated he'd seen his portion of the message as well. Both emitted a restlessness that threatened to fold if he didn't reassure them.

A man with no lifeforce dipped his head as Jori passed. Lots of people here had been doing that as of late. Whether that meant they complied with MEGA-Man's wish or this was part of some grand scheme, he wasn't sure. He'd conducted a few tests earlier. The first time, he ordered a woman in the cafeteria to get his lunch. The second, when he'd been working in the shop and wanted someone to bring him a drink. And yet again when he told a man to jump the rest of his way to his destination. He'd try something more daring in a moment.

Rodrigo's footsteps echoing beside him represented both a concern and an opportunity that played tug-of-war with his insides. Whoever this man was now, he had his uses, and Jori intended to exploit them.

They entered the infirmary where Doctor Stephen Stenson pretended to tend to Zaina. They weren't speaking, but somehow his entrance still made the room go quiet. Skittish glances darted about.

Jori put on a smile. The ease he'd hoped to instill didn't come. The two remained nervous with Zaina fiddling with her fingers and Doctor Stenson shifting his feet.

"It'll be alright." His friends didn't look convinced. "Let me show you something," he said, and turned to Rodrigo. "Hop on one foot." Rigo obeyed. "Stop. Make a sound like a mouse." Without opening his mouth, he played a noise that undoubtedly came from an actual mouse. "Now, go stand over there. Face the corner, and don't listen in."

The cyber man did as he was told. Zaina's jaw dropped. Stephen looked back and forth between Jori and Rigo. As Jori had hoped, a tad of hopefulness penetrated their worries.

"How did you do that?" Zaina asked.

"Vance gave me command, remember?"

"So he'll do anything you say?"

Jori shrugged. "Yes. It's in his programming."

Doctor Stenson's brows drew together. "You need to be careful. If you abuse your position, Vance may take it away."

Jori doubted the man had that authority, but he didn't know all MEGA-Man's intentions. At least all these frivolous orders might disguise his real ones. "Do you trust me?"

They nodded. He sensed their truth. He wanted to provide more assurances—tell them that as a team, they could do it. But too many words would give too much away to any listeners.

"Can I trust you?"

They dipped their heads once more. Zaina slid off the bed, then came over and wrapped her arm around his shoulder. "You can count on me," she said with a wink. "I'm under your command."

"Same," Stephen replied.

"Good. I'd like a tour of this facility, Doctor. I want a better understanding of why I'm here. It might make living here easier."

"Of course."

"Let's start with how my DNA is enhancing others." Jori smiled, hoping they'd see it as confidence and Vance would assume he'd decided to be compliant.

"You should come too," he said to Zaina. His plan wasn't just to instill the horribleness of what these people were doing, but also to find out whether him leaving here would be enough to keep MEGA-Man from using him to create more monsters.

Her trepidation roared once more. He eased out from under her arm and grasped her hand. Firming his countenance, he stared at her, then Stephen, until he had their full attention. "I realize it's scary. I'm scared too. But this is important. Are you sure about all this?"

Stephen's head bobbed, as did Zaina's throat. She firmed her jaw and gave a sharp nod.

"So, shall we?" Jori asked. To an outsider, it might sound like he meant the tour. But his real purpose was to confirm their dedication.

Doctor Stenson huffed. "Yes. We shall." He smiled, telling Jori that he would do his part, which was to destroy his files, notes, and samples to make sure no trace of Jori's DNA remained.

"Good," Jori said. "So long as we work together, everything will be fine."

Their nervousness abated. The muscles in Jori's shoulders relaxed. As Doctor Stenson began the tour, he followed with steps as light as air.

This will work. I just know it.

*****

Jori was both awed and horrified. The precision and complexity of genome editing was far greater than he'd imagined. So much could go wrong. In fact, Doctor Stenson had said the success rate was only twenty percent. That didn't mean eight out of ten died. More than half of those survived but didn't function as intended. With the hit and miss of inserting the right genetics, it was no wonder.

MEGA-Man had both the time and the expertise to overcome these obstacles, though. According to Doctor Stenson, Jori's DNA profile had already been mapped. It wouldn't just be a matter of leaving and asking the doctor to destroy his blood and tissue samples. Although live samples ensured accuracy, MEGA-MAN undoubtedly had everything he needed and there was no way to retrieve it.

"Are you the only one creating cyber soldiers?" Zaina asked, beating Jori to the same question that'd been tumbling around in his mind.

Stephen looked down as he shook his head. "There are other facilities. I'm not sure how many, but at least three."

Jori swallowed. "Are they already using my DNA?"

"Yes," the doctor answered.

The answer felt off. Jori furrowed his brow.

"Even your ability to detect truth and lies," Stephen added, smiling wider this time.

Is he trying to tell me something?

The doctor cleared his throat. "MEGA-Man has a perfect replication of your DNA—so perfect, in fact, that he has the means to grow a whole new you."

Zaina gasped. Her horror showed both on her face and in her emotions. Jori experienced a different sensation. His jaw dropped at the forcefulness of the doctor's lie. So MEGA-Man didn't have an accurate map of his genes. Did that mean Doctor Stenson had modified it somehow? He dared not ask to confirm. Not yet anyway. Perhaps after they'd gotten away from his horrible place.

"Thank you, Doctor." Jori bowed lower than the protocols at home would've required of him. This man deserved his respect. All this time, he'd seen him as a coward, but he'd been rebelling in his own way.

"You're most welcome."

Zaina frowned as she glanced back and forth between the doctor's widened smile and Jori's sincere deference. She might not have caught the lie but suspected something had passed between them and didn't remark about it.

"You know," Doctor Stenson said to Jori, "You seem remarkably mature for your age. How is that? I haven't pinpointed anything in your DNA that accounts for it."

"I've been wondering the same thing myself," Zaina said with a twinkle in her eye. "Some adults aren't half as mature."

Jori's cheeks flushed. "I don't know. Maybe because children in the Toradon Empire must wise up fast."

Stephen cupped his chin. "Hmm. Yes, environmental factors. Having to learn how to survive through tremendous hardships would accumulate over many generations. Are you aware that dogs act like juveniles a lot longer than wolf pups? In fact, wild animals, wolves included, have a larger brain volume per comparative body weight than their domestic counterparts. They need more brainpower to find food and shelter, avoid predators, and combat rivals."

Jori had noted the differences in lifeforce between domestic and wild animals but never heard about their brain capacity. It made sense.

"Are you saying he's like a wild animal?" Zaina asked, not quite serious but not joking either.

The doctor chuckled. "I'm saying, my dear, that he really *can* do this."

Jori wasn't sure he could defeat Vance, but they needed his confidence. And their confidence boosted his own. It also helped that Stephen had already taken care of one aspect.

He expanded his lungs and bowed to the doctor once more.

Now to encourage Zaina to uphold her part.

48
Innocuous

Sweat trickled down Jori's forehead and pooled over his brows. He wiped an escaped stream running down the side of his face. It was unusually hot here today. Or suppressing his nervousness had overtaxed him.

He reminded himself to relax. Vance couldn't watch him every moment of the day. He had too much to do to get ready for his attack.

He'd been fixing bots here in the workshop for several hours. A combination of being in an enclosed space for so long combined with the effort of taking apart a few machines and setting them up to do things Vance wouldn't like had taken its toll.

Sneaking in unsolicited repairs had been a part of his routine for a few days. That wasn't the only way he found opportunities, though. Maintenance requests were submitted daily, but some weren't legitimate. He'd added a few fake ones in while doing Blakesley's old job. Having this retrieval bot sent here was one.

He knelt before the waist-high machine once painted pale green. It now had a pattern that resembled a speckled fish he'd seen in the lab the other day. Two articulated arms ending in clamps protruded from the bot's body and a flatbed with a bit of edging extended from the back. Its job was to convey items from storage or the fabricor and transport them to the person who'd ordered them.

A quick tug and its access panel popped open. Jori plugged in his diagnostic equipment and waited a few moments for his screen to flicker to life. Its work orders came up first. A few taps and he'd added an innocuous task labeled as a test.

Now for the next bit. He pulled up its operating system, scrolled down, and found the test job. He leaned closer to the monitor and squinted as though something was wrong, then made a few minor changes that would have a significant effect. With any luck, his body blocked the readout from the surveillance cameras. If Vance had seen this using his ability—a real possibility—perhaps he wouldn't understand the coding well enough to realize what'd been done.

Jori wiped his face with the crook of his arm. So far as he could tell, all the other bots he'd reprogrammed had retained their instructions. One sent to work in maintenance tunnels had left several of the screws keeping the access covers loose, which would allow Jori an easy escape, if necessary. Another bot's task was disrupting internal communications. Setting that up had been tricky since he needed it to perform upon a remote trigger, something it wasn't designed to do.

He synced other bots with the remote as well, including ones that would retrieve Zaina and the doctors and lead them to one of the off-limit shuttle bays. If all went as planned, he'd sneak away from the bridge where Vance would likely want him to be, then set off a series of cataclysmic events. A transmission would send designated cyborgs to their recharging stations. Parts of the ship would go into lockdown. Other areas would be impassable because a few bots would trigger fire suppression systems.

The comm hooked behind his ear beeped. His new command meant constant interruptions, but he suppressed his irritation and answered anyway. "Jori here."

"Major Tran," Doctor Claessen said, using his false surname. "I just saw a mouse in the cyborium."

"Noted," Jori replied, then cut the communication. It was the best response since he had no intention of reactivating the pest control bots. Earlier, he'd programmed other bots to retrieve mice and other small mammals from the labs and release them throughout the ship. When everything went down, Vance would soon notice Jori missing. Even with internal communications out, he'd send people after him. Jori couldn't detect many of the crew members, but if an animal saw them, they might be frightened enough to alert his sensing ability.

He also hoped that with comms out, Vance would come after him himself. Since Jori couldn't sense him either, he needed the animals to tell him when he left the bridge. The man would have access to one conveyor that would halt halfway to its destination and hopefully keep him confined long enough for everyone to escape.

With the attack still several days away, Vance's ability shouldn't pick up on anything—unless he forced premonitions. Even then, he might *feel* Jori press the remotes but wouldn't recognize what they were. And he will probably *see* him go through the ship, but not know why.

Jori unplugged the diagnostic equipment. This bot had a more important task. Six days from now, it'd retrieve a bomb from a weapons locker. The remote would then send it to Vance's shield deactivation device where it would trigger the explosion.

He'd considered retrieving more bombs or even some phasers from the locker, but the more he took, the greater his risk of getting caught—hence the reason he needed Zaina to disable the transponder.

He smiled. As far as he could tell, no one had questioned any of his work. Considering how many bots had been here when he'd started repairs, everyone must've been too busy to mess with them. And if anyone had reviewed his work in the beginning, they'd probably stopped since he'd fixed everything properly.

The only one who'd be checking on him was Doctor Humphrey, and that was only with what he was about to do with Rodrigo.

"Rigo, come here," he said to the cyborg standing like a statue in the corner.

Rodrigo came, his non-cybernetic eye staring straight ahead and without a hint of emotion. Jori rose, his head barely reaching the man's upper torso now that he stood upright.

"Turn around," he ordered.

Rigo turned, revealing a thin rectangular box adhered to his back just below his shoulder blades. Jori grabbed the electric screwdriver and yelped. *Chusho!* Instead of repairing bots, he should fix the short in this damn thing. He kept forgetting to order a new cord from the fabricor. Doing that now was a good idea, but he was in the middle of something.

He set the defective equipment aside rather than put it back. Part of his plan included leaving random tools and such behind all over the ship as though forgotten. Some here. A few in the engineering areas. Several left in maintenance tunnels. And at least one on the bridge.

Vance had caught him once, but his words suggested he believed Jori was just sloppy. No decent worker would leave his tools lying around. But he'd be foolish not to set up some contingencies in case Vance waited until the last moment to reveal that he knew what Jori was up to all along.

The thought made him shiver. All this could be for naught.

Since he had no way to know, he pushed his worries aside and grabbed another screwdriver. Removing the tight screws from the box took a little effort. Rigo endured it without complaint. The inside looked much like the innards of most computers—a hard drive, CPU, motherboard, cooling fan, and so on.

Using the equipment Doctor Humphrey had given him, he plugged its cord into Rodrigo's back and pulled up the operating system. Fortunately, the doctor agreed to allow Jori to work in his workshop. The man would review it later, but hopefully only the assigned section. Surely he was too busy to check every line. Even if he did, he might not question the subtle changes.

Jori spent a good half hour on his appointed task. Next, he examined the protocol that instructed Rodrigo to protect him. They'd implemented an exception for Vance, so he deleted it, hoping no one would pick up on what he'd done. He also removed instructions that required Rigo to keep him from leaving the ship.

He re-reviewed his work. The subtle changes were perfect. He set about erasing his tracks and closed Rodrigo back up.

"You're done," he said. "Return to the corner."

Rodrigo obeyed. Jori crossed his arms and studied the man's blank stare. His heart ached at how Rigo had wanted nothing more than to be like him. Well, that certainly hadn't happened.

"Maybe you're not like me," he said out loud, "but at least you can help me."

Rigo remained as still as stone. His one non-cybernetic eye held a deep vacancy too chilling to contemplate. And the face that had once worn an easy smile was now more placid than an ice-covered pond.

Jori quelled his sadness with a sigh, then returned to work.

49
Calm Before the Storm

Breathe in. Hold. Breathe out.

Jori breathed easy. He faced Zaina, who sat in the same cross-legged position. While he'd reached a state of calm, her emotions fluctuated, indicating a busy mind—or monkey-mind, as Sensei Jeruko had always called it.

A rustling sound suggested she shifted, probably to get more comfortable. Soon after, her emotions evened out.

She's improving, the thought flickered. He let it pass by, like a ship drifting off into space.

They'd been practicing together every day. He'd let his routine slip somewhere along the chain of cascading events and getting back into it had eased some of his mental anguish. Hard moods such as anger or anxiety, and even loneliness, still visited him from time to time, but they didn't get stuck in his head. It'd made implementing his plans for escape much easier.

A beep sounded, making Zaina yelp. He slowly opened his eyes. She pressed her hand to her chest and stared at the door behind him as though expecting a monster to break through. Yes, she was getting better, but not quite to where she should've been relaxed enough to not get startled over such a simple thing.

"It's for me," he said.

Her eyebrows tilted into something more serious. "I don't like you working for that man."

Jori glowered at her, hoping his sternness would remind her of the surveillance. "To cooperate is in our best interest."

She met his eyes and frowned. "Doesn't mean I have to like it."

True. He didn't like it either, but a semblance of cooperation was necessary if he wanted to fool that psychopath into letting down his guard.

Zaina rested her hand on his knee. "Be careful."

He dipped his head in promise, then answered the door where Doctor Humphrey waited. Without a word, the man turned and walked away. Jori kept the same silence and followed.

To his surprise, the doctor led him to the bot maintenance room rather than to Vance. "Retrieve your diagnostic tools," the man said as he stood by like a sentry.

Jori withheld his questions and entered with the same formality. His case lay open on the table, its corresponding equipment haphazardly misplaced. He snatched up a few and tossed them inside.

The trek resumed as before—wordless and austere. As the doctor led him to the command deck, unbidden concerns about why Vance had summoned him churned in his head. Had the man finally caught him? Would he force him to witness another murder? Had he decided to resume his sadistic tests?

The bridge door opened with a hydraulic hiss that triggered a hitch in Jori's breath. He entered reluctantly while bracing himself for the worst. For a moment, he worried they'd arrived at the planet already. But Vance's stiff dispassion coupled with the viewscreen's unremarkable display released his tension.

He halted before the man and fell into a formal at-ease stance with his feet planted at shoulder width, chest out, and hands and case held behind him. As with Doctor Humphrey, he kept silent.

One side of Vance's mouth twitched. "I need you to look at this." He flicked his hand at the workstation. "Every time I ask it for this computation, it freezes."

Jori let some of his worry fall away. "Did you reboot it?" he asked, not caring if the question was insulting.

The darkening of Vance's face was enough of a reply, so Jori reviewed the man's command. It seemed straight-forward and contained no glaring formatting issues that would cause the error. It required a closer study to understand what had gone wrong. He plugged in his diagnostic equipment and opened the operating system. His familiarity with fundamental structures made it possible for him to pick up the purpose of any new program.

The realization struck him as an opportunity. This workstation had a direct connection to the shield disruption device Vance had set up. If Jori made a few adjustments, perhaps he could keep the man from using it against the Tanirian Protectorate's homeworld.

He studied the algorithm and marveled. Nothing, not even a shield generator with a fluctuating frequency, was truly random. This AI program had an ingenious way of anticipating their defenses. It would likely disable a shielded defense within a few minutes. But the code was delicate—a simple tweak in the right place would render it useless.

But did he dare? No. Their destination was less than five days away. If he sabotaged it now, Vance would know. He decided on another test to verify whether the man understood coding.

He deleted a section. Several agonizing seconds passed. Although Vance peered over his shoulder, he said nothing. Jori scrolled up. Still, the man didn't question his actions. Did that mean he had no understanding of what'd been done? Or was he letting Jori play his little game?

He exhaled, hoping for the latter. Back to work, he re-pasted the line of code, then studied the rest. He didn't notice any bugs, so he pulled up Vance's command.

"Why did you use this syntax?" he asked.

"It's what they told me to use."

"Let me see."

Vance showed him the instruction manual displayed on the microcomputer embedded into his forearm. Sure enough, it said to utilize this syntax for this function. However, the program required a different format.

"Here's the problem," he said. "This is either a typo or they changed it and forgot to update the manual. Try this." He typed it in.

The program executed the command and didn't lock up this time. He faced Vance with a tilt of his chin.

The man glared in return. "Why are you so helpful all of a sudden?"

"It's not sudden," Jori replied.

A side of Vance's mouth quirked. "You didn't answer my question."

Jori's insides squirmed. His cooperation was a façade, but he couldn't say that. He searched for a truth the man would accept but came up with nothing. He pressed his lips together in defiance instead.

Vance's eyes darkened. "Don't want to answer? Fine. Let's play another game."

Jori silently cursed the man as he wore a mask of practiced coolness.

"You know this one," Vance continued. "An exchange of questions for honest answers."

Jori suppressed a huff. Although Vance had never exhibited any deceitful qualities, he had no real sense of honor. Nothing would prevent him from being dishonest. Jori's aversion to lying put him at a severe advantage. Dancing around the truth presented another challenge.

"You go first," Vance said. "Ask me a question."

Jori considered refusing. Doing so, however, might raise suspicion and cause the man to take a closer look at everything he'd done. Besides, even if Vance didn't play fair, this was an opportunity to learn something useful. He allowed his placid expression to give way and furrowed his brow in true contemplation.

I know. He crossed his arms as though daring the man to answer with the truth. "You didn't like MEGA-Man's command that I take Blakesley's place, yet you obeyed. Why? You're a mighty warrior. Why bow to someone else?"

Vance's nostrils flared, but his smile hinted that he applauded Jori's shrewdness. "MEGA-Man made me who I am. And he has the power to unmake me."

Jori soured. That this great being had the means to force a man like Vance to obey didn't bode well for his own future.

"My turn." Vance's tone cut through Jori's contemplation. "Why are you so cooperative now?"

Jori spoke without thinking through his response. "You said MEGA-Man believes allowing me to do more on this ship will encourage me to side with his cause. He's right, but only to a point. If you hadn't subjected me to painful tests, bullied me, or threatened Zaina, I'd be more inclined to cooperate. I don't like bullies, and you are a bully. But perhaps MEGA-Man is not." All true, yet he had still sidestepped the question.

"So you're cooperating for MEGA-Man, not me," Vance stated.

Feeling willful, Jori stuck out his chin. "That's another question." The man growled, but he held his ground.

Vance's eyes flashed. "Fine. Your turn."

Jori considered asking him whether the earlier trials had been his idea or MEGA-Man's, but he suspected the answer and didn't want to waste his opportunity. "If MEGA-Man can unmake you, why did you go against his orders and make me undergo those horrible tests?"

Vance's hands twitched. Jori got a sneaking suspicion that violence was about to ensue, but the man eventually spoke. "Clever, but the answer won't help you."

"Tell me anyway."

Vance bared his teeth into what he probably intended to be a smile. "You're like me. The tests prove it." A fever seemed to take hold in his eyes. "But you're obviously no match for me. Why MEGA-Man keeps insisting otherwise is foolishness."

He's jealous—like Blakesley.

"Now," Vance continued, "answer my question. What are you scheming? Tell me the details of your little plan, and we won't play the game where I let you think you're fooling me and wait until the last moment to catch you in the act."

Jori narrowed his eyes. That was what Vance had done in the past, but he didn't believe for a second that the man would give him this opportunity to come clean... *Unless he doesn't know the details.* That gave him hope, but he still had to answer.

He straightened as a flash of insight cut through him. "I'm trying to figure out why MEGA-Man bothers keeping you around when you keep going against his wishes," he said truthfully, dodging the real question once more.

"My obedience is solid."

"I'm sure you follow orders, but that's not what I said. You go against *his wishes*."

"Such as?"

"I doubt he wanted you to torture me. Or kill the major."

Vance's face turned to stone, confirming the accusation.

"Now it's my turn again," Jori said. "How many of MEGA-Man's *other* interests are you ignoring?"

His muscles tensed at the fury dancing in Vance's eyes. Provoking the man was dangerous, but his reaction suggested that he might be onto something.

Vance rolled his neck, making it crack. "I'm not answering that question, but I'll tell you this." He jabbed Jori's chest with his huge finger. "If you betray me again, I will kill you and no one, not even MEGA-Man, can stop me."

The menace of his voice sliced through Jori's core. His arms remained folded but in a protective way rather than a rebellious one, yet his defiance didn't waver.

"This game is over," Vance said. "No. Not over. You win this round, but the bigger game is still on. When it ends, only one of us will stand victorious."

The iciness zipping within Jori's veins ignited a spark. A scowl formed unbidden as his hatred for this despicable madman skyrocketed.

It'll be me, you monstrous chima.

50
Arrival

Jori's hands shook as the expanse of uncertainty loomed before him. The *Black Thresher* had entered the star system hours ago. Vanir was still a mere dot on the bridge's viewscreen, but it wouldn't be long before the planet's vast oceans and rich landscapes became discernible.

According to the countdown clock on the bottom right corner of the screen, Vance's attack would commence in fifty-three minutes. However, the planetary defenses would detect this ship in a mere sixteen minutes. Jori would initiate his plan shortly thereafter.

The pattering in his chest intensified. The bridge was the last place he wanted to be, but here he was, standing at the madman's side, waiting for the right moment to trigger his remotes.

As usual, passionless cyborgs manned the stations. Only two of the people here had a lifeforce, and weak ones at that. The closest anyone came to displaying emotion was the quirk of a smile on Vance's face.

Jori swallowed. A glance at his personal guard triggered a tumble in his gut. Rodrigo stood off to the side, staring straight ahead, oblivious to the imminent events. He'd accompany Jori as the plan unfolded but would have to stay behind once it was time to leave the ship. Zaina had suggested he come with them. She'd hoped someone could help him. It was too late for that, though. All they'd do was take him apart and study him.

The tingling on Jori's arms spread over the rest of his body, so he redirected his thoughts. The plan ran through his head over and over, like a spinning wheel going nowhere. Alert Zaina and the doctor. Activate the bot that would destroy the shield deactivation device. Sneak out. Let the caged mice he'd hidden in a vent loose in the hall and in the conveyor, then hope they'd tell him if Vance came after him. Sabotage the conveyor when the man got inside. Send the cyborgs to their recharging stations. Set off the other disruptions, including ship comms, that would hopefully prevent others from coming after him and his friends. Go to the shuttle bay and get the hell away from this damned place.

These final steps worried him the most. Although he'd made these decisions days ago, Vance could've foreseen them via a conscious effort to spy on him. Why would he do that, though? Because he was a stupid chima who wanted to be in ultimate control. Then again, maybe Jori's cooperation had relaxed his vigilance. After all, it must be a hassle to constantly watch someone.

Please let this work. Jori shook his hands, attempting to ward off the painful tingling that'd sprung up.

Minutes passed. More details of Vanir became clear, revealing features common to most habitable planets. Its ocean was small, covering perhaps only a sixth of its surface. He noticed other bodies of water, though. A couple had to be at least two hundred thousand square kilometers—one that looked like the splatter of a giant tear and the other cup-shaped.

He couldn't tell from this distance, but from what he'd read, this land was crisscrossed with hundreds of wide, raging rivers. It reflected this with its brightly-colored vegetation visible from space. Brown splotched it here and there, signifying mountain ranges and a few deserts.

"There it is," Vance said.

The view displayed on the front screen flickered to an even closer perspective that focused on the night side of the planet. Halden, the capital city, shone like a star cluster with most of its brightness concentrated in the center and smaller lights radiating out. The Tanirian Protectorate headquarters occupied several square kilometers of that city, making them easy to target.

"*Sublime Liberty*, this is Vanir security," a female voice broadcasted. "Please restate your transponder code and your purpose."

The cybernetic comms officer responded, but Jori barely heard him through the throbbing in his ears. *Almost time.*

Vance rose from his chair and approached the scene. His rock-like hands clasped behind his back as he planted his feet at shoulder-width. Jori couldn't see his face, but imagined he wore a gloating smile.

A ping sounded, making Jori's heart jump. The communications officer tapped his monitor and the autoresponder from the planet's security system appeared on the bottom left of the viewscreen. *Sublime Liberty*'s identity and purpose had been confirmed and it had permission to proceed.

Vance glanced over his shoulder, revealing a sickening spark in his eyes that made Jori want to crawl into a corner. Instead, he waited until the man turned back around, then slipped his hand in his pocket and pressed the two buttons that would initiate the first stage of his plan.

The thumping in his chest felt like the pulsing of an overworked engine. It was time to get moving, but his feet were heavy. *Go, damn it!*

He took a step, only to halt when Vance turned about. A hiss of the door opening behind him followed by the tromp of footsteps set his hair on end. Vance's smile spread. The gleam of triumph was gone and replaced with an infuriated fire that sent a shockwave of trepidation through Jori's body.

"Going somewhere?" Vance said.

Jori peeked over his shoulder. Three cyber soldiers blocked his escape. *Chusho*. He turned back to Vance and jutted his chin. On the outside, he hoped he appeared unabashed and unafraid. On the inside, every fiber of his being quaked.

"You know…" Vance's lip curled. "I might not have bothered to foresee this moment had it not been for the bot you sent to hide mice in the ventilation system. Did you forget about surveillance?"

Jori hadn't forgotten. He'd just hoped no one would think anything of it. After all, bots traipsed about this ship all the time. He didn't voice his excuse, merely braced himself for punishment.

"I must admit," Vance continued, "using your ability to read animals to tell you when I enter the trap is clever. But you're a stupid boy." Vance's face darkened from red to purple.

Jori's body locked up as though held in a mighty grip. Damn his cowardice. Why did this man frighten him so? *Run, you idiot!*

What was the point? Since Vance had found out about the mice, then he'd probably also discovered his other tricks. Plus, he likely used his ability to foresee this very moment and every move Jori would make here onward.

"Go ahead. Try to escape," Vance said with a menacing smile. "It won't do any good. I see your end."

Jori gritted his teeth against the chill that ran down his spine. If he could stand up to a man like his father, he could face this chima.

Clenching his fists and forcing his feet into a fighting stance, he prepared for violence.

51
Willpower

A disturbing clackety-clack echoed from around the curve of the hall. Zaina Noman halted, as did her heart. Leaving her room had been easy. The desire to help put an end to all this madness had spurred her out the door and to her destination. But now that the moment of sabotage was near, her anxiety threatened to send her running and screaming back to the security of her quarters.

She pressed her hand to her chest and forced herself to breathe. Jori had said everyone would probably ignore her, but she couldn't help but fear the worst.

Run! Her flight response kept egging her to get away, but she remained rooted to the spot.

Deep breath in. Pulling in air was like eating more food after a seven-course meal—only more painful.

The thudding of her heart coincided with the approaching clacks. An articulated appendage appeared. Then another. And another. She almost choked. It was undoubtedly that man who'd gotten multiple legs as his cybernetic enhancement, but her imagination screamed robot-spider.

The man clicked by, not once looking at her. When he disappeared around the curve and his resounding steps faded, she finally pulled in a breath.

Get a hold of yourself! A wave of dizziness made her brace herself against the wall. Breathing the way Jori had taught her became easier. There was something to this meditation thing after all. She still had hard emotions, but every day of practice brought her a millimeter closer to dealing with them.

With one last big intake of air, she straightened and moved once more. Her legs wobbled for the first few steps, then steadied.

You can do this. You must *do this.* As she repeated the mantra, her willpower grew and her steps quickened. She held her breath while another person passed, but she didn't stop.

The directions Jori had sent her were a bit convoluted, but he insisted she follow them exactly. "*Do not stray*," he'd stated. Although his warning was text-based, she inferred the seriousness of the tone. It was imperative that Vance not foresee them together.

The entrance to Machine Room B came into view. She entered, taking in the hot musty air and the confusing tangle of odd-shaped machinery and their interconnecting conduits. The unfamiliar motley sapped her courage. This was a mistake. No way would she be able to locate the right device in this mess.

Even if she did, what then? All she could think about was Abelard's death. Vance had known all along yet waited until after-the-fact to punish him for it. What if it was the same here? What if she did what Jori asked only to exit the facility and run into that madman?

Her throat caught at the thought of Vance's hands squeezing her throat. She wrapped her arms around her middle and tried to quell her terror. Nausea rolled. She couldn't do this.

Don't be stupid. You must *do this. Jori is counting on you.*

What was it he had said in his message? "*Take a chance now or live in fear forever.*" At the time she'd read this, the words had resonated. She was tired of being afraid. But standing here with a fright that quaked through her bones, she yearned to give in and go back to the way things had been.

Vance is a psychotic killer, you idiot. We can't stay here.

"What are you doing here?" someone said.

Zaina yelped, nearly falling over her own feet. "I-I…" She choked out the words. "I have orders from Jori."

"Orders? Do you have proof?"

"He told me in person," she replied, hoping the uptake in her voice reflected incredulity rather than nervousness. "How the hell am I supposed to provide proof?"

The question on the man's brows disappeared. He dipped his head and moved on with an abruptness that left her stunned. The boy really had clout.

She gathered her wits and took in her surroundings. What were Jori's instructions? Left. Second right at the upright cylindrical tank painted with a red and yellow warning sign. Down to the end. Left again. She couldn't miss it.

Despite being fairly certain she was going the right way, she crept along, planting her palms on the wall to keep her legs from giving out beneath her. The distance was further than his instructions had implied. Sweat tricked down her back and pooled at her waistline, creating a chafing dampness. She plodded down a long, narrow aisle lined with a series of rectangular machines dotted with displays, knobs, and indicator lights.

"Hey!" a voice yelled.

Zaina nearly jumped out of her skin. She tripped, falling against one of the machines. She grasped it in time to keep her from hitting the floor.

Someone yanked on her upper arm and whirled her about. "You need to leave," Doctor Claessen said with an edge to her tone.

Zaina eased out of her grip and wrung her hands against the numbness that'd cropped up. "J-Jori told me… Wait. What are you doing here?"

"I've been instructed to keep an eye on you. You have no business here, so get out. Now."

Oh no. She filled her lungs and collected herself. This wasn't entirely unexpected. Jori had hoped Vance wouldn't be watching her but had planned for it anyway. She wagged her head. "I-I c-can't. Jori told me to come here."

The doctor planted her hands on her hips. "Why?"

Zaina swallowed the dryness from her throat as she struggled to remember what he'd told her to say. "Y-you need to ask him."

"Fine. Let's go ask him, then." Doctor Claessen grabbed Zaina's arm once more, pinching it hard enough to make a mark.

Panic surged up Zaina's spine. She couldn't leave. She had a job to do. Jori needed her to do this. She wouldn't let him down.

She yanked her arm, but it didn't break free from the woman's iron grip. Pulling back and bracing herself didn't work either. Doctor Claessen jerked her forward with surprising strength. Zaina had no choice but to follow.

Before a full-blown panic had time to take hold, an explosion rocked the ship. Zaina's ears popped with both sound and pressure.

Her vision rattled as a violent quake swept her feet out from under her.

What the... Before a thought solidified, she caught sight of Doctor Claessen pushing herself up. Zaina was free from her grasp, but she had to get her ass up off the floor right now and do something.

A swell of energy burst inside her. And in a sudden flash of motivation, she both saw and grabbed the handle of an object partially obscured beneath the oil-blackened machinery. Its weight surprised her, but the double-headed hammer balanced well in her grip. She wielded it with desperation. "Stay back. I-I don't want to hurt you."

The doctor rose. "Then don't. Put that down and come with me."

"I can't. I have orders from Jori. Aren't we all supposed to obey him now?" Zaina stepped back.

Doctor Claessen advanced with a tight smile. "Not if he goes against Vance's orders."

"I don't know anything about that," she half-lied, desperation heightening her tone. "Vance hasn't given me any orders, but Jori has. So let me be."

The doctor's eyes flashed, then she charged. Zaina reacted and struck her shoulder. The woman dropped with a grunt. Zaina yelped. She hadn't meant to do that. Instinct zapped her into a sprint. The hammer remained clutched in her hand. She intended to release it, but footsteps resounded behind her. In her panic, she almost forgot which direction to go. Fortunately, she'd reached the tail end of Jori's instructions and turned left.

The machine loomed before her, just as Jori had drawn it. She dropped the tool and activated the operations panel with a smack of her palm. The screen blinked to life. The fluttering of a million bees in her head inhibited her ability to think. She couldn't remember his instructions.

"Stop!" Doctor Claessen stomped forward. Her face was as cold as an iceberg. Her shoulder sagged and her arm hung, but her demeanor held a strength that sent alarm bells ringing through Zaina's skull.

Zaina lunged for the tool once more and wielded it in front of her. "Stay back."

The doctor rolled her eyes. "Come now. Get a hold of your emotions and think about what you're doing. We're friends, remember?"

Friends? The woman's frown flipped about, conveying a sweetness that made Zaina's skin crawl. The doctor was right about one thing, though. Her emotions were out of control. The pounding in her chest was a relentless toll of dissonance. Her effort to hold on to the hammer was like struggling with the leash of a frenzied dog.

"We're not friends." Her words almost sounded like a question. The doctor had done nothing to hurt her or Jori, but her lack of a moral compass made her dangerous.

"Of course we are. All I've ever wanted to do was help you."

"By taking away my humanity."

The doctor's eyes sparked. "Your emotions cripple you. How can you not see it? You're a mess, Zaina."

Every single one of the woman's words resonated, but she was still wrong. The human psyche was too complex to thrive on logic alone. People needed compassion too. Jori's situation exemplified this. Sure he required structure and guidance—but he also needed love.

"Listen," she said. "I *need* to do this. It's the only way to save him."

Doctor Claessen tilted her head. "Save who?"

Zaina would've groaned had her resolve not strangled her exasperation. "Jori."

The doctor laughed. "He's already saved. He's with us."

A flame ignited in Zaina's skull. "He's not! Can't you see how much you're hurting him? How much pain Vance is causing him? He's not safe here."

An uncharacteristic growl erupted from the doctor's throat. "You don't know what you're talking about."

"I know exactly what I'm talking about!" The loudness of her own voice scared her, but she pressed on. "You're the one who doesn't get it. You've numbed your emotions so much that you no longer see the pain and suffering you're inflicting."

"I have liberated myself!" the doctor screamed back. "Look at you. You're pathetic. And your whimpering sympathy is keeping that boy from his destiny."

"Destiny?" she asked with incredulity. "This isn't a damned fairy tale. He's still a child, and I won't let you hurt—"

"Enough!" Doctor Claessen leapt.

Anger and desperation fueled Zaina's reaction. Her hammer connected with the doctor's temple, followed by a sickening squelch. Zaina squeaked, then turned away.

What have I done? What have I done?

Bile rose in her throat. She swallowed, then pressed onward. Jori needed her. This was his only chance to get away from these soulless people.

She stumbled to the device and tapped the interface. Heart hammering like a thousand drums, she fought to breathe away her stress and selected through to the right option. With a jab, she shut off the ship ID transponder.

A red box surrounding the word *disabled* flashed on the monitor. She stared at it dumbly. Had she finally overcome her anxiety and done something useful?

She stepped back, pointedly ignoring Doctor Claessen. *Did it work?*

Alarms sounded—or she'd only just noticed them. With her heart in her throat, she bolted down the corridor, away from the consequences of what she'd done to the doctor and to the freedom that both she and Jori deserved.

52
Advantages and Disadvantages

A chilling yet baleful quiet pervaded the bridge. Jori locked eyes with Vance, his trepidation spinning like a battered turbine. He was trapped like a caged animal, and not a giant blackbeast either. More of a scrawny whelp with tiny teeth.

The cyber soldiers loomed behind him, ready to apprehend him if he tried to flee, curtailing his options. Using his peripheral vision, he searched for the sharp-nosed pliers he'd purposely left lying about the last time he was here. He spotted it under a console on the far side of the bridge, too far to reach. Rodrigo was his only defense, but he was no match for the hulking cyber soldiers.

Fight and likely die or submit and live to fight another day? His brain screamed at him to give up, to just take his punishment like he'd always done with his father. But his heart wouldn't abandon Zaina and the doctors. She was making her way to the transponder at this very moment. Stephen and his wife were eliminating all physical traces of Jori's DNA. If he surrendered, they'd certainly lose. Zaina would pay with her life and the Stensons would undoubtedly be even more miserable than they were now.

The chances of success were minuscule, but they weren't zero. His jaw hardened. His muscles twitched.

Vance bared his teeth. "You do it, you die."

"Fuck you, chima." Jori dove backward and somersaulted.

The soldiers came for him. He darted between their legs. Their immovable limbs made it a tight fit. One of them grabbed his leg, sending a trill of panic through him. He twisted out of the hold, wrenching his knee. Another soldier snatched his arm. Jori struggled to break free but the man's hands were like the claws of demolition equipment. He kicked the soldier in the kneecap instead. It did no good.

Adrenaline shot through him. His senses heightened, emphasizing the coldness of the soldier's grip, the sharp smell of oil and metal wafting off his armor, the magnified sounds of their struggle, and the vividness of the surrounding scene.

Events unfolded in slow motion. Rodrigo appeared behind Jori's captor. Another soldier reached for Jori's other arm. Rigo raised his fist. The pliers Jori had left protruded from it. In a movement too fast for the eye to see, the man stabbed it into the soldier's shoulder.

The grip on Jori's arm released. He ducked away from the other soldier. Before the cyborg reacted, Rodrigo tackled him. The soldier, too big to bring down, merely stepped back. But it was enough. Jori slipped by.

To his surprise, the bridge door opened. If Vance knew he'd try to escape, why hadn't he locked it? He shot a glance over his shoulder as he leapt past the threshold. All three cyber soldiers converged on Rigo. One punched him in the face. Another twisted his cybernetic arm, making it squeal with a metallic whine. And the third shoved him in the back and forced him down.

Vance stood in the middle of the bridge wearing the confident grin of a madman. "Go ahead. Run!" he called after Jori. "I know where you're going." A chilling exhilaration tinted his thunderous laugh.

Chusho! That chima *wanted* to chase him.

He bounded into a sprint. Vance's laugh echoed behind him, spurring him on despite the hopelessness of the situation. Staying put or running, either way the man would foresee it. His every move would be predicted, regardless of how unpredictable he tried to make it. Contemplating the time puzzle made his head spin.

He darted for the conveyor. No one followed him but the timbre of Vance's voice. "See you soon, you ungrateful—"

The doors hissed shut, cutting off the rest of his words. Jori choked in air. If Vance was going to catch him anyway, he might as well follow through with his plan. Although the man had noticed the mice, he'd also referred to a trap. Did that mean he knew about the conveyor? Likely so, but perhaps he didn't know about the other things he'd set up.

Jori's optimism crumbled under the reminder that his luck hadn't held up so far. "Deck eight," he yelled at the controls.

A tremble beneath his feet signified he'd despaired too soon. The rumbling vibration could only mean one thing—his bomb had gone off. Whether it had destroyed the shield deactivation device was another matter. But at least this meant Vance hadn't discovered all his setups.

The conveyor opened, revealing two hulking cyber soldiers.

Damn it! He scanned the floor, hoping this was the car he'd left the wire cutters on. It wasn't. The soldiers revealed no weaknesses either. He refused to move, forcing them to come inside to retrieve him. When they stepped beside him and turned around, he lunged, jabbed the close button, and darted out.

The soldiers must've caught the door in time and pushed their way out because tromping footsteps reverberated behind him. His short legs went only so fast, but the weight of their armor might hinder them. He doubted they'd tire, though. Luckily, he had a plan.

Despite the likelihood of Vance knowing about the conveyor trap, he slipped his hand into his pocket and pressed the corresponding trigger. He sprinted around the curve of the hall. Lab 8G. 8F. 8E. There it was. The vent he'd left unscrewed. Falling to his knees, he slid it up and over. The opening was big enough for him but not for bulky cyber soldiers.

Digging in with his elbows and wriggling his legs, he squirmed inside. Something touched his foot. He kicked before the soldier took hold and slithered further in. A grunt followed by the pounding of metal on metal suggested a super-soldier with a cybernetic hand reached in. The tension in Jori's body eased. He'd gotten far enough back to escape the hulking beast. The disadvantage of being small had become an advantage.

This reprieve wouldn't last long. If Vance had foreseen this, he'd see where Jori would go before he knew himself. The door locks and the fire suppression systems he'd planned on triggering would do him little good now.

He came upon a vertical shaft and halted. The duct also continued straight but he needed to stop and figure this out. Since Vance knew where he'd be, he couldn't go to the shuttle bay and reveal Zaina and the doctors had been in on it too. But if he didn't go there, there'd be no one to fly them away.

He rubbed the sweat from his forehead. Despair snaked its way through him much like he'd slid through the confines of the ventilation duct. No matter which choice he made, his friends were doomed. He imagined the glee in Vance's eyes as he strangled Zaina. The image sickened him. That chima didn't deserve to live.

Wait. He blinked. Running wasn't the only option. He needed a weapon. Vance would undoubtedly predict this next move, but there was another reason to go for a weapons locker. The more the man gave chase, the more it diverted his attention from Zaina and the doctors. Besides, maybe Jori would get lucky. It was a vain hope, but he clutched it nonetheless.

With his mind made up, he shimmied down the shaft. The space was small enough to keep him from sliding out of control. Still, his heart fluttered and jumped. All he thought about was facing a crazed psychopath. The most frightening part wasn't getting a beating. It wasn't even death. It was surviving and being used as a permanent target for the man's sadistic whims.

But hadn't Vance said this would be his end? Somehow, dying didn't seem as terrifying.

He found the next horizontal shaft and edged in, feet first. He knew the way, thanks to all the work he'd done on this ship plus the schematics his new rank had allowed him to access.

Pausing at his destination, he used his sensing ability to determine whether anyone was there. He sensed no people, but a hamster he'd let loose was nearby and emitted a spark of fear. Jori concentrated. Though he couldn't see what it saw, he somehow determined two predators roamed the hall.

The little creature huddled somewhere, probably a doorjamb, and shook. His trepidation heightened. Jori shivered, feeling it too. Then the sensation waned. Footsteps tromped just on the other side of the vent. Their booted feet were visible for a split second. The steps faded. Jori counted down until he guessed them far enough away to be beyond the curved corridor.

He braced himself against the slick metal walls and kicked the duct cover. The first contact did nothing more than make a noise that sent the creature scampering off. He kicked again and felt a little give.

Four more times and he finally created a decent gap. He pushed until it bent far enough for him to wiggle through. The soldiers must've heard because the tromp of their boots neared. He found his feet and jetted.

A few turns brought him to a weapons locker. Before popping open the control panel, he tried the bio-reader. His rank should allow him access unless Vance had predicted this and revoked it.

He leaned in, letting the scanner read his eye. The door slid open, the hiss setting the hairs on his neck on end. It was empty.

"You damned chima," he said under his breath. Not only had Vance foreseen this, he let it happen.

Chusho. What next? He crossed his arms. A deep-rooted dread gnawed through his core as a final, desperate plan took shape.

Vance wanted a showdown. Knowing him, he'd also want the advantage while still giving Jori a fighting chance. The psychopath liked to win but he also liked a challenge. Jori would give him that challenge.

Yes, he'd likely die. Zaina probably would too. But at least MEGA-Man could no longer use him to murder more innocent and naïve people like Rodrigo. He abhorred the idea of sacrificing her life too, but Vance hadn't given him much choice.

So much for finding a different path.

53
Shadow of Death

Rodents, stoats, lagomorphs, shrews, and even a few birds hunkered down or skittered about. Some traipsed in the less populated areas such as storage. Others had taken to the vents. Several had found offices or labs to hide in. And a few still roamed the corridors.

Their lifeforces reflected only a trickle of information, but they gave Jori an idea of what went on around them. Prey tended to be jumpy so every noise caused their apprehension to splatter like raindrops. Nothing stood out strongly enough to locate Vance, but they helped him avoid several cyborgs.

On the way to Vance's quarters, a bird had alerted him to two super-soldiers guarding his door. A mouse in the room showed no sign anyone was waiting inside, so he moved on. When he'd extended his senses to his own quarters, the rat that'd holed up in the vent also emitted a calm that signified vacancy. After that, a trio of mice helped him avoid soldiers arriving via a conveyor.

With this corridor clear, he stopped and focused. He tried the cafeteria. Nothing. The gymnasium. Not there either.

His heart hammered. Where could Vance be? Would he have stayed on the bridge after all? The animals didn't show him.

He kept trying. When he concentrated on the mice who'd taken up residence under a shelf in his workshop, he caught nervous energy issuing from their little brains. It was the same sensation they'd given off whenever he'd been there.

So that's where you are, you chima.

Although he'd just decided to go there, had Vance already seen him do it? If he changed his mind and went elsewhere, would Vance foresee that too? The doctor's explanations had suggested Vance could predict events even if his actions immediately followed his decision to act. So it didn't matter how often Jori changed his mind, Vance probably knew the way he'd ultimately choose. The conundrum of cause and effect niggled in the back of his mind, but he ignored it as he hopped onto a conveyor.

His imagination played out the possibilities of this confrontation. There were heavy tools available to use as weapons. The space was small, but plenty big enough for someone his size to dart and dodge. Despite these advantages, all the hypothetical scenarios ended with Vance's hands around his throat.

The conveyor opened. He shoved down the terror that'd been trying to take hold of him and marched to his destination. After all, he was a warrior and true warriors didn't back down from a fight.

This would be his final battle. He was certain of it.

The workshop door slid open. He clenched his fists and let his racing heart galvanize his body. Vance stood inside with a gloating smile. The two faced off, neither moving nor speaking. The air seemed to crackle between them.

Jori used his peripherals to locate something to use as a weapon. A wrench would make a good club. Screwdrivers could stab like dull knives.

"You disobeyed," Vance said, his voice carrying a dangerous undertone.

Jori jutted his chin. "You crossed too many lines."

Vance's lip curled but he didn't defend the statement. "I don't know how you've avoided my soldiers, but you'll still lose."

Jori ignored his remark as well. "Is MEGA-Man aware that you mean to kill me?" The darkening of Vance's face gave him the answer. "What will he do to you when he finds out you've betrayed him?"

The cords in Vance's neck bulged and his expression turned darker than a black hole. "You'll pay for what you've done to me."

Jori frowned. It didn't sound like the man meant the betrayal since he'd been wanting, if not expecting, the game to come to this point. "What are you talking about?"

"I can't see beyond your death."

That's interesting. "Maybe MEGA-Man kills you for killing me."

Vance barked a laugh. "He wouldn't do that. I'm too valuable."

Jori spread a smug grin that matched the one the man had earlier. "Maybe *I* will kill you."

The intensity of rage filling the man's face made him look ready to explode, but he maintained his smile. "That's the stupidest thing you've ever said," he replied, though something about his eyes indicated he didn't believe his own words.

Vance lunged at the same time courage detonated through Jori's core and obliterated all traces of his fear. The prospect of failure no longer crippled him. At least he'd take this chima with him.

He ducked low and dove inside the room, grasping the handle of a ratchet. Vance spun about and charged. Jori leapt up, using the table beside him to get more height. His agility came in handy as he flipped and smacked the man on the back of the head at the same time.

The man's responding roar rattled the tools and machinery. Jori jetted toward the exit, tossing objects behind him as he went. Like a stone skipping on water, they bounced off Vance's armored physique. Even flinging the palm-sized motor of a wheeled bot didn't faze him.

Jori stepped past the threshold only to get yanked by the collar. "*Never turn your back on the enemy*," Sensei Jeruko's words flashed through his head.

He rolled away just as a meaty fist grabbed for his arm. He sprang to the balls of his feet. Using the tables as leverage, he leapt up and out of the way of the man's crazed attempts to maul him. Vance cornered him, but Jori used his agility to tumble to another area.

Sweat poured from his forehead down to his brows. He dared not take a moment to wipe it away, or even blink. *Keep your eye on the enemy.*

Vance's rage spewed like a volcano. His moves became more erratic. Jori remained coolheaded, reveling in his battle focus. His heightened concentration caught every twitch in his opponent's body. The anticipation of each move allowed him to react without thought.

The dangerous dance continued. Vance's bulk made him clumsy while Jori's smallness enabled him to dart about like a flying beetle trying to escape a cargo hold. Yet he couldn't get past the man and out of this room.

Foam formed at the corners of the man's mouth. Still, Jori evaded him. Low to high. Left to Right. He even landed a few more blows. The wound he'd inflicted by Vance's eye had revealed a metallic shine through the aggregation of crimson ooze.

Jori bounded from one table to another. A snap tore through the sound of Vance's enraged bellows. The table folded. Jori wheeled his arms as everything beneath him crumbled. He crashed onto the hard floor with a clunk loud enough to pop his eardrums. Air escaped his lungs, leaving him breathless.

Despite the shock, his fighting instincts compelled him to move. He twisted around and scrambled to his hands and knees. Before his feet found purchase, a monstrous hand seized his shoulders and tossed him onto the flat of his back. Jori's breath shattered once more. His vision flickered with black and white sparks. He tried to choke in air only to realize Vance pinched his throat.

"Now you die!" The man's voice rumbled with a sinister glee.

No!

Jori clawed uselessly at Vance's big fingers. Excruciating agony wracked his entire body as his looming death took hold. His mind reeled with disjointed flashes of memories. His mother's soft touch as she caressed his hair and hummed. Commander Hapker's easy smile. His father's stormy tantrums. Major Blakesley's murder. Sensei Jeruko's sober but kind demeanor. He and his brother sparring. Lieutenant Gottfried. Captain Arden. Washi and Michio… Zaina.

So much heartache and turmoil but peppered with just enough good people to make life worth living.

I don't want to die.

54
The End?

Jori groped blindly for anything that could help him. The toppled shelf beside him was too heavy. All its contents had spilled beyond his reach. White blurry objects capered through his darkening vision.

The mice.

He reached out and grabbed something both prickly and soft. *They made a nest.*

It wasn't much, but he flung it in Vance's face. The man flinched and let loose just enough for Jori to get in a momentary burst of air.

With their hiding spot exposed, the mice scrambled about, looking for escape. Jori snatched one and tossed the poor creature into Vance's eye. The man roared. The mouse squeaked as it bounced onto a lower shelf. As it scampered off, its tiny feet kicked off a hex key. It wasn't much, but it was something.

As Vance's grip re-tightened, threatening to crush his esophagus, he grasped the key and stabbed it into the man's hand. Vance growled, loosening his hold once more. Jori scrambled back only to have blackness close in on him anyway. His throat was too constricted. He still couldn't breathe.

The darkness took over. He didn't even have time to contemplate the end.

*****

A smattering of light.

A forceful throb.

Another, more insistent.

Jori gasped. Air tore through his windpipe and filled his aching lungs. His body tingled as oxygenated blood rushed to his head and extremities. He opened his eyes, seeing only spots of color. He tried to rise, but something pinned him down.

Renewed panic surged through him. He struck out with his fists and kicked his legs, hitting a solid and metallic object. At first, he thought of Vance without his skin, but his fright lessened when he realized it was a bot.

A thump followed by the clamor of tools crashing onto the floor triggered a flood of adrenaline. He shoved the bot aside and turned to where Vance and Rodrigo fought. Vance snatched the cybernetic man by the neck and thrust him against the wall. Rigo's arms punched with remarkable precision, but Vance took it with his teeth bared like a blackbeast.

Jori rolled onto his side, intending to find his feet and fight, but struggled to temper the tremors of his body and regain his faculties. The battle raged on. He imagined Vance winning, then standing over him with a gloating smile. He had to get up and help Rodrigo, but not even the hormones surging through his blood made his muscles cooperate.

Damn it. When he'd been ready to die so MEGA-Man couldn't use him, he'd almost gotten his wish. Then he wanted to live. And so now he was alive, trapped in a nightmare with a monster who'd never let him escape.

Despite the bleakness of his future, he forced himself up on an elbow and blinked. His vision sharped, not quite back to normal but good enough. The workshop lay in the same state as before. Broken bots sat or stood in silent accusation. The shelves remained somewhat organized. Screwdrivers, pliers, and wrenches were strewn about.

He grabbed the one closest to him and yelped. The shorted electric screwdriver dropped from his hand. He picked it up more carefully this time, then limped into the fray.

Vance had Rodrigo pinned against a broken table now. A vein nearly as purple as Rigo's face pulsed on his forehead. He held Rigo in place with one knee and knelt on the other. Rodrigo struck the side of his head, creating a bloodied mush. Vance didn't relent.

Jori gripped the screwdriver. He aimed for the monster's eye and stabbed. "Die, chima!"

The point plunged in with a sickening squelch, but only by two or three centimeters. If Jori had been stronger, he might've penetrated the brain. But all he'd managed to do was enrage the beast.

Vance bellowed as he rose with a cinematic slowness. Jori stumbled back. Vance grasped the handle protruding from his eye. Sparks flew. Vance's yell cut short. His body twitched. His arms flailed like branches caught in a tempest. The pain of death surged from him despite his emotions being muted by implants. Then it stopped.

Vance crashed onto to his knees, then toppled forward.

Jori's chest heaved as he eyed the inanimate heap. The pain of death lingered in his memory, but the combination of both horror and relief drowned it out. A shock from the shorted screwdriver shouldn't have been enough to kill anyone, but Vance likely had metal parts in his head. The electrical surge had probably shot through his brain. The more metal he had, the more damage it would've done.

Chusho.

Jori's trembling legs threatened to give out. He leaned against a shelf and regarded Rodrigo. The man now stood like an alert soldier as though nothing had happened. Blood rolled down his right temple. The bottom half of his face was a gory mess of flesh. "Are you alright?" he asked in a whisper. His larynx smarted, no doubt damaged by Vance's deadly assault.

Rigo dipped his head. "Yes."

Jori swallowed. *It worked.* Not his initial plan, but the contingencies he'd set up. He wasn't sure which stunned him more—the animals, the shorted electric screwdriver, or Rodrigo's programming.

He was finally free.

That he'd been responsible for Vance's death didn't bother him. Not even Zaina's wish that he be on a different path brought him any guilt. He was a warrior. Born and bred. Considering the evilness of some people in this world, it was a good thing. He was alive. His friends were too.

The thought reminded him that they still waited for him in the shuttle bay. Zaina was probably biting her nails. Stephen likely paced. Celine undoubtedly wore the same placid expression as always. Or she fidgeted because she wasn't doing any work. Either way, he needed to get to them.

But first, the bridge. He'd destroyed the shield disruptor and the transponder. The Tanirians had likely realized they'd been duped and were mounting an attack.

"Rigo," he said through a scratchy throat. "Clean up. Fast. Then go tell Zaina and the doctors that I'll be there shortly."

The cyber man retreated. Jori followed him out, then headed in the opposite direction. While setting a hurried pace, he considered his next move. Vance had made him second-in-command. If he really was in charge now, he must either order a surrender or flee. Surrendering held serious consequences for many of the crew members. People like Rodrigo might be eliminated—or worse, dissected. And even though the Stensons had been unwilling participants, Jori doubted the authorities would be quick to forgive.

As much as he liked the doctors, this ship shouldn't be allowed to continue under MEGA-Man's control. No doubt others like it had been sent out into the galaxy to wreak havoc. Turning this vessel over might help the Cooperative find them and prevent other attacks.

His thoughts warred as he rode the conveyor. Neither option presented a happy ending, but one would end more disastrously than the other.

He entered the bridge. The acid swirling in his gut intensified as he beheld in the viewscreen. Tanirian fighters, marked as red blips, attacked but had yet to inflict any damage. The *Black Thresher* fired a rapid series of energy blasts at the city of Vanir. The defenses held, but it wouldn't be long before either the ship ran out of firepower or the shield gave. Considering all the other advanced technologies of this vessel, Jori suspected the latter.

"Cease fire!" He rasped loudly as he marched to Vance's chair and sat. They did. A combination of surprise and relief almost derailed Jori's thoughts. He cleared his throat, hoping to alleviate the cracking in his voice. "Have the Tanirians contacted us?"

"Yes, Sir," a man with a cybernetic earpiece said.

"Open the channel. Request visual."

A window popped up on the bottom center of the viewscreen. An older man with silver-streaked black hair and hard eyes appeared. His brows twitched as though confused while his scowl remained. "What in the hell are you playing at, boy?"

"My apologies, Sir," he said as clearly as possible despite the fluctuating whisper of his voice. "My name is Jori Tran."

"I don't give a damn what your name is. Get your ass out of that chair. I want to talk to whoever the heck is in charge."

A corner of Jori's mouth tugged, but he kept a straight face. "That man is dead. I'm in command now."

The man scoffed. "So what? I'm dealing with a child who thinks this is some sort of game?"

"I didn't order the attack, Sir. I contacted you to stop it. As you can see, we're no longer firing."

"This is a trick."

"I assure you, it is not. Hear me out."

The man didn't speak so he continued, "My name is Jori Tran. I'm with Zaina Noman. We were on the Avalon space station and tricked onto this ship. We've been prisoners, but the man that was in charge has just been neutralized. Now we're prepared to surrender."

"You're cutting out. Did you say—"

The ship jolted and the man's face disappeared. Jori pushed out of the chair and bounded to his feet. "What happened?"

The woman at the helm spoke with her back still to him. "We're not permitted to surrender, Sir."

Jori clenched his fists at his sides. "So what did you do?" he asked at the same time as he reviewed the readouts. It appeared they'd left the star system, but that couldn't be right.

"We're retreating," she replied.

"How did we get so far away so fast? Did you initiate the arc drive?" The thought made the blood drain from his head. It was against all sense to trigger that engine within a gravity well. This ship should've been ripped apart. They should be dead.

"We initiated the jump drive."

Chusho. He'd noted the difference in systems but had no idea any vessel had such a capability. This changed everything. The authorities had to know about this. "Go back. Surrender."

"We must not deviate from MEGA-Man's primary command."

Jori growled, hurting his throat even more in the process but not caring. "Which is?"

"Return to Anoteros."

"Where?"

She paused as though considering his question. “You call it Cybernation.”

No. The room spun. Jori grasped the side of his chair. After all he’d been through… This couldn’t be happening.

He forced himself to calm and take stock of the situation. So the crew wouldn’t surrender. But he was still in charge, wasn’t he? He should broadcast a signal. Maybe find a way to reach Commander Hapker.

A familiar fluttering of emotions trickled into his senses. *Zaina!* She and the doctor waited in the shuttle bay. Their worry had grown so strong, he almost tasted it.

He abandoned the bridge and rushed to the conveyor. There was still a chance to get out of this. Eagerness contributed to impatience as he willed the car to hurry. When it stopped, he sprinted out. The corridors zipped by in a blur.

Before he knew it, he was in the bay. Zaina’s shoulders fell to where he thought she’d collapse. She pressed her hand to her chest and called out to Stephen.

The doctor poked his head out from the open shuttle. A smile spread across his face. “You did it!”

“Thank God!” Zaina cried. She dashed forth and grasped him in a hug. “I was so worried.”

“So what happened?” Stephen asked. “Can we go now?”

Jori ignored his first question. It was probably rhetorical anyway. Besides, he wasn’t sure whether he wanted to tell them just yet. “Yeah, let’s get out of here.”

The doctor returned to the shuttle. Zaina grasped Jori’s hand and followed. Rodrigo stepped in front of them. He’d cleaned up, but a split lip revealed missing teeth. Jori attempted to go around, but the man put himself between him again.

“What are you doing?” Jori asked, his heart in his throat.

“You can’t leave.”

“What!” Zaina cried out.

Jori wanted to scream in frustration. “Why the hell not?”

“MEGA-Man has plans for you.”

“I don’t give a damn about his plans. You promised to help me, remember? I *programmed* you to obey my orders.”

“I still do, but MEGA-Man has ultimate command.”

A chill ran down Jori's spine, partly for the cyber soldiers entering the bay and partly from Rigo's words. "When did you talk to MEGA-Man?"

"I'm always in contact with him."

Jori and Zaina shared a look. "How do you do that?"

"Through the Great Commune."

The chill turned into ice pricks and spread from Jori's arms to his neck. "What's the Great Commune?"

"It's a real-time communication system that allows a selected few of us to connect."

"Impossible," Zaina replied.

Jori swallowed. Though a communication hub allowed for instantaneous conversations, it required giant stations at intervals throughout space. Somehow, MEGA-Man had figured out how to input that technology into people. "Did Vance have this? Or Blakesley?"

"No."

"Why not?" he asked, despite the other pressing matters. None of this made any sense.

"Only those with the most extensive components can handle it."

In other words, those who'd become machines. As much as the science of it both frightened and intrigued him, he had an idea. "Can you speak to MEGA-Man now?"

"Of course."

Jori planted his feet at shoulder width and put on his most stubborn expression. He'd rather be with his mother or Commander Hapker, but the last thing he wanted was for them to be kidnapped and taken to a MEGA planet. He glanced at his advocate and swallowed the lump in his throat. "Tell him that if he wants my cooperation, he must let my friends go."

Zaina grasped his arm. "What? No! I'm not leaving you here."

Jori didn't respond. Not yet. Everything depended on MEGA-Man's response. Rigo stared straight ahead. Seconds ticked by. An ache spread through Jori's body as he waited.

After what was probably only a minute, Rigo spoke. "Agreed."

"No!" Zaina roared like a mother bear. She pulled him closer to her. "I won't go. I won't leave him here with a bunch of monsters!"

Jori firmed his jaw and held back the wave of sorrow that threatened to overwhelm him. The cyber soldiers neared. He could try to evade them again, but there were still cyborgs operating the ship. His earlier plan had been to get away while they focused on defending against the Tanirians. That wouldn't work now.

"You *must* go," he said to Zaina.

She covered her mouth and wagged her head. Her anxiety shot up like a rocket. Tears brimmed in her eyes. "No, no, no. This isn't right. I can't leave you."

Jori faced her and grasped her hands. "Listen."

"No." She tried to pull away.

He held tight and waited until she looked at him. "I don't like it either, but it's the only way."

"Only way to what? Let them torture you? I can't let this happen. I'm supposed to protect you." The last word came out in a sob.

Tears slid down Jori's cheeks. He hated this, but it didn't mean it was the end. "If you don't leave, then no one will know I'm here." Except the Tanirians, but it could be weeks or even months before that information reached the right person.

Anguish poured from her.

Jori gripped her tighter. "Contact Commander Hapker. Tell him what's happened. Tell him MEGA-Man is taking me to Cybernation."

*****

Loneliness enveloped him like the fingers of a chilly mist. Jori brooded in Vance's chair on the bridge. He rested his elbow on the arm, his cheek propped against his fist. His other hand fiddled with his mother's necklace. Rodrigo and three cyber soldiers hovered somewhere behind him. They'd never touched him, never tried to hurt him or lock him away. But the message was clear. Jori was in charge so long as he didn't deviate from their destination or escape. He'd considered fighting it, but he'd made a deal. Besides, attempting to defeat a ship full of machines under direct control of a being with omnipresent abilities was well beyond his capabilities.

At least they had permitted his friends to leave.

Watching Zaina go had nearly broken him. She'd eventually agreed, but only after Rodrigo contacted MEGA-Man again and received a promise that Jori wouldn't be harmed.

The doctor had interrupted the conversation to ask about Vance, his worry palatable. Jori hadn't wanted to tell them, but they needed assurances that the man wouldn't barge into the bay and slaughter them all.

Zaina had taken the news of his death well. Considering all the times she'd told him that violence wasn't the answer, he expected her to be disappointed in him. But she'd nodded, then explained how she had to defend herself against Doctor Claessen. In that moment, she'd done what was necessary for her survival—and his. Then she'd continued vehemently. "*Some people don't deserve to live.*"

He still ached at the fury on her face. More than that, he remembered her unwavering kindness, the way she tried so hard to protect him, and how she would offer comfort no matter how bad she was feeling.

But those memories would eventually fade. They'd disappear into the never-ending blackness, just like his mother. Just like him.

He filled his lungs and rose from the chair. Feet planted and hands clasped behind his back, he faced the viewscreen. "Reduce speed by half."

They obeyed. Apparently, MEGA-Man wasn't worried about *when* he'd arrive.

The thought of being on this ship for another few months made him want to crawl into bed and never leave. Since he couldn't fight these beings, maybe someone else would come to his rescue.

He'd discovered that the cyborgs had garbled his message to the Tanirian, so that man had never heard his or Zaina's name. He only hoped Zaina would be able to reach the commander. One couldn't simply contact a high-ranking officer without the right authority or the right connections, but he believed in her tenacity. She wouldn't give up on him.

Hapker, I hope to see you soon.

Did you enjoy this novel? Leave a review. Authors love reviews!

Next:
Find out whether Jori will finally be reunited with his family and friends in Fated Warriors: Book Six, coming in 2025.

Sign up for my newsletter by visiting my website, DawnRossAuthor.com, and get great deals!

The first thing you'll receive is an exclusive Prequel to Book One. You'll also get access to the first few chapters of the current books plus upcoming books. There may also be more free short stories related to the main story.

Connect with Dawn Ross online:
DawnRossAuthor.com
Twitter.com/DawnRossAuthor
Goodreads.com/author/Dawn_Ross

Glossary

20CAPAI med bot – A med bot model.

Abelard – Major Abelard Blakesley serves as second-in-command of the *Sublime Liberty*, aka *Black Thresher*, which is captained by a man who calls himself Vance. Vance, in turn, serves MEGA-Man.

Adela – One of the children that Zaina Noman takes care of on Marvdacht.

Angolan – A proper adjective used to describe something or someone from Angola. In this case, it's a café serving a food inspired by the food from Angola, a continent on one of the Cooperative planets.

Anteros – The formal name of the planet Cybernation. It's ruled by MEGA-Man.

Arc drive or Arc reactor – This is one of the largest components of a spaceship. It is the engine that allows a ship to travel many light years away without violating the speed of light by bending space-time.

Arden – Captain Silas Arden is the captain of the *Odyssey* and Commander J.D. Hapker's commanding officer.

Arnielis plant – A plant that grows only on an island on the planet Falmouth. It has fantastic healing properties and may be the reason why the inhabitants of a particular island on Falmouth are so happy.

Avalon space station – A space station within the Prontaean Cooperative territory.

Baldesh – A place mentioned by Blakesley as having a tundra.

Benjiro – Jori's simple-minded uncle.

Biometric authentication – A security measure that uses retina scans, fingerprint identification, voice recognition or other unique biological characteristics to keep anyone but the authorized persons from entering certain areas or using certain devices.

Bionites – Nanites that are made from biological components.

Bio-reader – A device used to read biometrics. Some bio-readers are used in the medical field and some are used for security purposes.

Bio-sensor – A device used to read biometrics. Some bio-sensors are used in the medical field and some are used for security purposes.

Blackbeast – An animal that Jori often refers to. It is never described but it is hinted that it might be dog or wolf-like.

Black Thresher – Also known (falsely) as the *Sublime Liberty*. It's a spaceship captained by Vance and commanded by Major Abelard Blakesley, and serves MEGA-Man.

Blakesley – Major Abelard Blakesley serves as second-in-command of the *Sublime Liberty*, aka *Black Thresher*, which is captained by a man who calls himself Vance. Vance, in turn, serves MEGA-Man.

Bunmi – Master Bunmi was Jori's Jintal teacher.

Celine – Doctor Celine Stenson is a doctor serving on the *Sublime Liberty/Black Thresher* with Vance and Blakesley.

CFC – The Children First Center is a childcare place for children without parents.

Children First Center – The CFC is a childcare place for children without parents.

Chima – Means *vile one* or *hated enemy* in Jori's language.

Chusho – Means *shit* in Jori's language.

Claessen – Doctor Claessen is a doctor serving on the *Sublime Liberty/Black Thresher* with Vance and Blakesley.

Comm – A communication device.

Communication hub – A form of communication that uses quantum entanglement technology for an instantaneous exchange.

Conveyor – An elevator-like car on a spaceship that moves vertically and horizontally.

Cooperative – Jori's people consider the Prontaean Cooperative their enemies. The agency that governs the space within a portion of the galaxy. It has numerous treaties with various worlds that provide its charter to keep space safe, ensure peace, regulate fair trade, and colonize new worlds. Its powers are granted by several planets, and the number of planets that are part of the Cooperative continues to grow. The Prontaean Cooperative has two aspects to it. The first is the Prontaean Colonial Cooperative (PCC). This sub-organization handles intergalactic relations, conducts space exploration, performs space-based scientific endeavors, assists travelers, and sometimes provides transportation. The second aspect is the Prontaean Galactic Force (PG-Force). This sub-organization polices space.

Cybernation – Unlike most places in the galaxy, this planet is ruled by MEGA-Man and encourages mechanical enhancements and/or genetic alterations. Its formal name is Anteros.

Cyborium – The facility on the *Sublime Liberty/Black Thresher* that serves as a hospital, laboratory, and cybernetic enhancement center.

Depnaugh space station – A space station outside of Cooperative territory. It was the station Jori had visited just before meeting Commander J.D. Hapker in Prontaean Cooperative territory.

Divya – A cyborg mentioned by Doctor Stenson.

Dragon Emperor - Emperor Mizuki, Jori's father, is the ruthless ruler of the Toradon Nohibito/Dragon People, aka Tredons. He is often referred to as the Dragon Emperor.

Dragon Warrior – The elite warriors serving the Dragon Emperor.

Elias - One of the children that Zaina Noman takes care of on Marvdacht.

Enviro-suit – A form-fitting spacesuit that uses nanites to regulate body temperature and protect the wearer from just about any environment, including the void of space.

Expedition-class – The largest of the Prontaean Colonial Cooperative (PCC) spaceships. Though the officers who run this ship are formal personnel of the Cooperative, they are sometimes considered civilians because they are mostly doctors, engineers, and technicians. This ship has a small presence of Prontaean Galactic Force (PG-Force) officers for security. Expedition-class starships have the broadest scope of responsibilities. They are the ships most often used for exploration and scientific endeavors, but they also provide transport, medical and mechanical assistance, and are used for diplomatic missions.

Extraho-animi – A mind reader who can pull thoughts from others. It is the second level of a reader. The Cooperative requires any of their personnel with this ability to register themselves.

Fab-meat – Meat grown in a laboratory.

Fabricor – A replicating machine. There are various types such as a food fabricor, a clothing fabricor, and a parts fabricor. Fabricors work much like our digital printers of today but the types of things that can be made has expanded greatly.

Falmouth – A planet within the Prontaean Cooperative.

Fudoshin – Means *immoveable mind* in Jori's language. *Immoveable mind* means don't let doubt creep in and strive to achieve.

Galactic Dominions – A highly complicated strategic game that utilizes a holo-table and a myriad of pieces that follow one of many storylines.

Gaoshan mountains – A mountain range on Meixing, which is a planet within Toradon territory.

Garrett – Doctor Garrett perfected an emotion regulation chip that can be inserted into the brain. The chip is called motislaxo.

Gottfried – Lieutenant Gottfried Krause was secretly a MEGA who served as Admiral Belmont's personal aide.

Gravity wheel – The device that gives the ship artificial gravity.

Great Commune – The wireless network connection composed of cyborgs who fall under MEGA-Man's rule.

Gresher – Second Lieutenant Rik Gresher is one of two lieutenants serving under Captain Arden and Commander J.D. Hapker on the *Odyssey*. He also accompanied Jori during the conflict involving Gottfried.

Guiding Principles – The written principles that the Prontaean Cooperative claims to follow.

Guita - One of the children that Zaina Noman takes care of on Marvdacht.

H-2000 bot – A maintenance bot.

Halden – A city on the planet Vanir. It's where the Tanirian Protectorate's home base is.

Hamilin – A wide-spread religious group known for wearing red robes and for often smoking their ceremonial cigars outside of religious functions.

Hanesian – A proper adjective used to describe something or someone from Hanese. In this case, it's a branch of the MEGA Inspections Office set up by the Hanesian government.

Hapker – Vice Executive Commander J.D. Hapker is second-in-command of the *Odyssey* under Captain Arden. He has supported Jori throughout his ordeals.

Hideji – Hideji was one of Jori's teachers.

Holo-man – A projected image of a person. This projection uses haptic technology that allows it to be touched and felt. It is used for various functions including as a visual instructor for dancing, exercise, and martial arts. It isn't always a man. It can be programmed to look like just about anything, including animals and objects. There is a more technical term for this device, but most call it a holo-machine.

Humphrey – Doctor Humphrey is a doctor serving on the *Sublime Liberty/Black Thresher* with Vance and Blakesley.

Hypospray – Used by medics to inject medicine or nanites.

J.D. – Vice Executive Commander J.D. Hapker is second-in-command of the *Odyssey* under Captain Arden. He has supported Jori throughout his ordeals.

Jeruko – Sensei Jeruko, aka Colonel Jeruko, was Jori's mentor and primary martial instructor.

Jintal – A Jintal master is an instructor that teaches people how to endure pain.

Jori – Prince Jori Mizuki, now Jori Tran, is the youngest son of the Dragon Emperor. He is an eleven-year-old warrior from a race of people the Cooperative calls Tredons. Jori refers to his people as Toradon or Toradon Nohibito/Dragon People.

Krause – Lieutenant Gottfried Krause was secretly a MEGA who served as Admiral Belmont's personal aide.

Lightning rod – A torture device that triggers nerves to feel pain.

Lockhart – One of Jori's temporary guardians assigned by the Prontaean Cooperative to escort him to the planet Marvdacht. Lockhart is a military man.

Maesterdons – People from the Cooperative planet Maestero are known for wearing fancy suits with white lace frills.

Marvdacht – The planet that Jori is supposed to go to. They have strict laws about MEGAs.

MDS – This is a read-only device used to access the Main Data Stream, which is a digital public library. Media can only be accessed via a direct-connection port and must be uploaded onto it.

MEGA – Stands for mechanically enhanced genetically altered.

MEGA hunter – A slang word for a MEGA Inspection Officer.

MEGA Injunction – Some decades ago, it was popular for rich people to get genetic and biometric enhancements. Common people felt such enhancements were unfair, especially since these enhanced people considered themselves superior and tended to seek positions of power. Protests became violent. As such, governments all over the galaxy stepped up. People with unnatural abilities were ejected from positions of power and strict laws were made to protect future generations.

MEGA Inspection Officer – Aka MEGA Inspector or MEGA hunter. This officer works for an organization that roots out MEGAs and makes sure they get filed in the intergalactic database. Many officers are fanatic about their work as they strongly believe that alterations to the human body is immoral.

MEGA Inspections Office – The formal name of the organization that roots out MEGAs.

MEGA-Man – A cybernetic man who has made himself into the most advanced man-machine in the galaxy. He is the leader of a race of cyborgs.

MM – Stands for Mini Machine. It is a computer that is most often worn around the wrist like a brace but can be flattened and held like a tablet.

Motislaxo – An emotion regulation chip that is inserted in the brain.

Mushin – Means *no mind* in Jori's language. *No mind* means to do your task so well that you don't need to think about it.

Nadeem – A shopkeeper on the Avalon space station. He fixes bots and he has a cybernetic hand, albeit one that doesn't violate the MEGA Injunction because it has no functionalities beyond a normal hand.

Nanites – Microscopic machines with various capabilities. The Cooperative uses them in their healing beds, enviro-suits, and more. The nanites that were in Jori's body could replicate into various properties. Some specialized in helping him heal while others created electronic functions that record, emit signals, or send out pulses. His nanites had a short shelf-life and so he no longer has them. The Cooperative highly regulates the use of nanites since they can be used as weapons and can be dangerous if there is a flaw in their programming.

Nohibito – Means *people* in Jori's language. It is often used together with Toradon Nohibito, as in Dragon People, though they are not literally dragons.

Noman – Zaina Noman is a social worker, aka advocate, from the planet Marvdacht and was assigned to retrieve Jori from the Avalon space station.

Nutri-cube – A common food-form for space travelers. It's easy to produce and contains valuable nutrients.

Panchu station – A small space station run by a branch of the MEGA Inspections Office.

Perovian – A proper adjective used to describe something or someone from Perov. In this case, it's a lightning storm.

PG-Force – The Prontaean Galactic Force is the sub-organization that polices Cooperative space.

Phoebe – A cyborg mentioned by Blakesley.

Plasti-glass – See-through panes that are stronger and more flexible than glass.

Prontaean – It is a word that describes the known galaxy. It is believed the word is derived from an ancient Earth Indo-European language where the prefix pro- means advanced or forward and the suffix -anean means relating to.

Prontaean Colonial Cooperative – The PCC is the sub-organization that handles intergalactic relations, conducts space exploration, performs space-based scientific endeavors, assists travelers, and sometimes provides transportation.

Prontaean Cooperative – Jori's people consider the Prontaean Cooperative their enemies. The agency that governs the space within a portion of the galaxy. It has numerous treaties with various worlds that provide its charter to keep space safe, ensure peace, regulate fair trade, and colonize new worlds. Its powers are granted by several planets, and the number of planets that are part of the Cooperative continues to grow. The

Prontaean Cooperative has two aspects to it. The first is the Prontaean Colonial Cooperative (PCC). This sub-organization handles intergalactic relations, conducts space exploration, performs space-based scientific endeavors, assists travelers, and sometimes provides transportation. The second aspect is the Prontaean Galactic Force (PG-Force). This sub-organization polices space.

Prontaean Cooperative Council – The Prontaean Cooperative is ruled by an elected council.

Prontaean Galactic Force – The PG-Force is the sub-organization that polices Cooperative space.

Quintina – A cyborg mentioned by Rodrigo.

Ramir – A cyborg who works on the bridge of the *Sublime Liberty/Black Thresher*.

Rodrigo – Also known as Rigo or Mouse. He is a MEGA who serves Vance, Blakesley, and MEGA-Man.

Romance sim – A virtual reality experience simulating a romance novel.

RR-5 rifle – A phaser rifle with multiple settings and functionalities.

Sailor's Warf – A tavern located on the Avalon space station.

Sareena - One of the children that Zaina Noman takes care of on Marvdacht.

Senshi – Means *warrior* in Jori's language.

Sentio-animi – The lowest level of a mind reader. They can sense emotions only. Their ability does not force anything out or in and so people with this ability are not required to register with the Cooperative.

Shokukin – Means *worker* in Jori's language. In the caste-based society, shokukins are barely considered better than slaves.

Stenson – The surname of two doctors serving on the *Sublime Liberty/Black Thresher* with Vance and Blakesley.

Stephen – Doctor Stephen Stenson is a doctor serving on the *Sublime Liberty/Black Thresher* with Vance and Blakesley.

Sublime Liberty – Also known as the *Black Thresher.* It's a spaceship captained by Vance and commanded by Major Abelard Blakesley, and serves MEGA-Man.

Tablet – A small hand-held computer device much like the tablets of the 21st century, but with more functionality. Some tablets can be folded around the wrist, and are then called an MM.

Tanirian Protectorate – A ruling body comprising of two star systems with two habitable planets. Their home base is in the city Halden located on the planet Vanir.

Tenisi – A game like tennis played by two people hitting a ball over a low net.

Thames district – An area of space consisting of space comprising a star cluster.

Thera-pen – A medical device used to heal minor wounds.

Toradon – Means *dragon* in Jori's language. It is often spoken as Toradon Nohibito, which means Dragon People, though they are not literally dragons.

Tran – The new surname given to Jori after he became a Cooperative citizen.

Tredon – This is what everyone outside Toradon calls this race of people. It sounds like the words *tread on*, which is what the Toradons are known to do to people.

Vance – He is the captain of the *Sublime Liberty*, aka *Black Thresher*, though he doesn't like to be addressed as captain. He is a super-soldier who serves MEGA-Man.

Vanir – A planet within the Cooperative.

Viewport – A large screen that shows the view from outside. Ships don't have windows, but a viewport simulates a window.

Viewscreen – A large computer screen.

VR-Ex center – Virtual reality experience center. It's a room utilizing virtual reality technology to create fake environments that visitors can interact with.

Wristlet – A watch with a lot of functionalities beyond telling time.

Zaina – Zaina Noman is a social worker, aka advocate, from the planet Marvdacht and was assigned to retrieve Jori from the Avalon space station.

Zanzoria – A place mentioned by Jori as having polar caps.

Books by Dawn Ross:

The Dragon Spawn Chronicles

StarFire Dragons
Dragon Emperor
Dragon's Fall
Isle of Hogs (a novella)
Warrior Outcast
Orphaned Warrior

Connect with Dawn Ross online:
DawnRossAuthor.com
Twitter.com/DawnRossAuthor
Goodreads.com/author/Dawn_Ross

About the Author

Dawn Ross currently resides in the wonderful state of Kansas where sunflowers abound. She has also lived in the beautiful Willamette Valley of Oregon and the scenic Hill Country of Texas. Dawn completed her bachelor's degree in 2017. Although the degree is in finance, most of her electives were in fine art and creative writing. Dawn is married to a wonderful man and adopted two children in 2017. Her current occupation is part time at the Meals on Wheels division of a senior service nonprofit organization. She is also a mom, homemaker, volunteer, wildlife artist, and a sci-fi/fantasy writer. Her first novel was written in 2001 and she's published several others since. She participates in the NaNoWriMo event every year and is a part of her local writers' group.

Made in the USA
Monee, IL
02 December 2024

70406915R00184